T0369287

THE TAJ MAHAL OF TRUNDLE

MARGARET SUTHERLAND

REVIEWS OF PREVIOUS BOOKS

USA

Sutherland's language is spare, but her voice is consistently strong, unusual and gifted.

Publishers' Weekly

These stories, skillfully worked and subtly surprising, reveal a deadly accurate perception of the dark regions of the ordinary.

Library Journal

GREAT BRITAIN

A high degree of originality and a keen freshness of style.

Catholic Herald

The abyss between the values of hippydom and those of the solid citizen has rarely been so subtly charted as in this highly impressive first novel

The Irish Times

AUSTRALIA

Sensitive, perceptive, skilful – they sound like the traditional words of praise trotted out for every new novelist. But in Margaret Sutherland's case they are true and very much worth saying again.

Marion Halligan

These are quiet stories, but don't rush by: there are treasures to be mined

The Age

NEW ZEALAND

This collection demonstrates Margaret Sutherland's outstanding versatility as a story writer. She can portray great tenderness and devotion in many human situations.

Evening Post

This country should be proud to claim her for this is an excellent collection of short stories.

Christchurch Press

...a skilfully sumptuous collection of adult tales, stories filled with light and hope. I am overjoyed to have discovered her.

Daily Telegraph

Also by Margaret Sutherland

The Fledgling

The Love Contract

Getting Through (stories)

Dark Places, Deep Regions (stories)

The Fringe of Heaven

The City Far from Home (stories)

Is That Love? (stories)

The Sea Between

Leaving Gaza

Windsong

Hello I'm Karen (for children)

Acknowledgments

Thanks to Dr Judy Galvin and Jean Kent for their constructive comments on earlier drafts; to the Auckland Subud group; and to Gill Ward for *Victorian Gilt*. And special thanks to a special sister.

A useful reference and source of quotes was *Taj Mahal: The Illumined Tomb,* by W.E.Begley and Z.A. Desai.

Author's Note

Trundle is entirely fictional and bears no relationship to any real town of the same name. Likewise, the characters are fictional and drawn from my imagination.

THE TRUNDLE TIMES
Editorial, 16th June 1980

THOREAU COMES TO TRUNDLE?

Those of us conditioned by the decade of the '60's might have wondered when we heard the news that, two decades on, a commune is thriving on Trundle's outskirts. Memories of *Woodstock* and *Hair* suggested latter-day hippies and dropouts strumming peace songs on our pragmatic doorstep. The alternative lifestylers said their brief was to acquire land and develop a peaceful and cooperative lifestyle close to nature.

Three years on, a number of people hold communal title to a large tract of previously useless bushland. A casual visit to the centre confirms thought, energy and creative vision have brought a dream into reality. Gardens grow in what was a wilderness. Wooden chalets provide attractive accommodation for both permanent residents and visitors who seek rest and reflection. A craft centre is in the early stages of development.

Asked what quality most appealed to those who appear to have turned their backs on material society, Honor Stedman, a spokeswoman for the group, explained. 'It's a place of beauty and of peace, where you can get away from the hustle and bustle of the world. While we do our work of building and growing, the mind is free to receive insights into our natures and our choices in life. In a sense we are seeking a spiritual growth, though we are not in any way a cult or a religion.'

A tour of the Pelican community will allay the mockery that such a concept perhaps stirs up. Hippies and dropouts the residents are not. On the contrary there is evidence of productive work in an appealing bush landscape. Thoreau took himself off to live in the woods for a time. Perhaps we could all benefit from an interlude at Pelican, away from the hurly-burly of life.

Mac Booth

PART 1

COMING HOME

PART 1

1

The sisters left the city on a bright, hot day and drove north, hardly talking. The freeway slithered forward to an unknown future. Every two hours they spelled each other with the driving; pleased to stretch or buy tea and sandwiches at a service station. It was late afternoon when they passed the faded billboard that announced their arrival in Trundle. The slow brown river eddied round the bridge pylons as it always had. The long drab main street looked much the same. Marie dozed in the passenger seat.

'Wakey wakey.' Ronnie squinted as sunlight blurred the dusty windscreen and cast hard light on the lines on her gamin face. 'We're home.' Marie yawned and struggled upright. She carried more weight than suited her, these days.

Ronnie swung right into the grid of side streets. Within minutes she pulled up outside a white weatherboard house where unmown grass grew lushly right up to the verandah's edge. Ringlets of mauve wisteria dangled from the pergola. A rich, almost sickly scent of jasmine filled the air. The pair sat staring at their childhood home. Marie's expression was nostalgic. All Ronnie could see was months of solid work ahead as she pushed back her cap of short reddish hair and began to unload the luggage. It felt strange, uncertain—coming home.

The trouble started with the arrival of the letter from the council, advising of an application to build a residential dwelling on the vacant land next door.

That first year back in Trundle had worked out well. Job prospects in the country were uncertain for middle-aged women, but they'd both found employment. Few nurses as well qualified as Ronnie applied at the Trundle District Hospital; already she was a supervisor. And it was a change from her previous job at the rehabilitation unit, where injured sportsmen were so like Max—the partner she'd loved and coddled until he abandoned her. Ronnie hid her sense of loss. Marie, who was suffering her own grief at her husband's death from leukaemia, had sunk into voluble mourning; trailing off to psychics and going over and over the details of life with her beloved Hugh.

It had been Ronnie who stepped in and insisted they make a new start together in the house they'd inherited, back in Trundle. The decision had been wise. Marie's depression lifted as she renewed her friendships from the past. Kitty Playfair, her best friend from schooldays, offered her work in a little gift and teashop in town. Doing up the house took up the sisters' spare time. They never talked about their past lives as women who'd known intimacy and loved deeply. Work schedules, the garden and discussions on colour, texture and design held at bay the forlorn neatness of separate rooms and single beds.

Marie read the council letter and forgot about it. Ronnie wrote an efficient reply, objecting to a modern house in the midst of heritage architecture. They heard no more. In September, the disruption began. It wasn't so bad for Marie, who was away during the daytime. Ronnie worked shifts and bore the full brunt of the noise. All through spring she endured grinding, clanking, revving, roaring. Delivery trucks potholed the road and churned up grass verges. All through summer and autumn she put up with hammering, shouting, talkback radio. Hills of metal and mounds of wet cement spilled onto the footpath. Concrete blocks, bricks and tiles defaced the old street's charm. Finally the new house, in all its looming ostentation, was built. There it was, and nothing could take it away. A high front wall broken by an ironwork gate was erected. For a full day, men unloaded a removal van. The new neighbours, their vehicles and animals moved in. The nightmare at least was at an end.

So Ronnie had thought. But there was the laryngeal rooster and the tethered dog. Barking and anguished howls kept her awake after night duty. The rooster started up at dawn.

2

'Very soon I'll go mad,' said Ronnie.

Marie was dashing off to work. She just smiled, that vague, infuriating smile of inaction. 'We could go over and see them,' she suggested. 'I'm sure they don't realise you work shifts. I'm late, must fly. Leave my dishes, I'll do them later.'

With a wave and a slam of the door she was gone. Ronnie followed the progress of her old car as it took off, jerking and backfiring, in a haze of smoke. She went to get a sleeping pill from the medicine cabinet, whose silvered mirror reflected a haggard face with a complexion like screwed-up brown paper. Her head was throbbing. She opted for paracetamol and, pressing a cool washer to her forehead, went back to the untidy kitchen. She dumped Marie's dishes in the sink, put the kettle on to boil and stood staring out at the long back yard with its sprawling lawn and old established trees—the magnolia and the huge camphor laurel down by the back fence.

The garden had been let go for years. Ronnie had worked furiously there in her spare time, uncovering archways and rockeries where ferns ran riot. Marie's style of gardening was just another of their differences. She dabbled with herbs and cottage plants, was mad on old roses. She'd drift among her plants, a mangled sun hat pulled over her faded curls, looking as absorbed as the blonde child she'd once been, arranging a dolls' tea party on the childhood lawn. She hummed her little tune, sniffed here and fiddled there, gathered petals to make *pot pourri*. Marie, the elf, the innocent; subject for a painter's eye. *Woman in a Rose Garden.*

Who'd want to paint me? Ronnie wondered. I'm just the jealous Ugly Sister.

Funny, she did most of the work yet it was Marie who earned the compliments. Nobody admired Ronnie's asters or dahlias. No, they exclaimed over Marie's lavender, her hanging baskets, her heat-struck roses that unfurled and collapsed like time-lapse photographs. Her flowers just seeded, popped up anywhere. Ronnie's had a regimented look.

The side gate clicked and a man walked past the window. Ronnie recognised the Indian from the house next door. She'd made no attempt to meet the new people.

If there was going to be trouble, and Ronnie was ready to go to the council about that pest of a dog, she didn't want the complaint softened by spurious gestures of friendship. But the last thing she needed now was a confrontation. The headache was building. She yanked at the belt of her yellow chenille dressing gown as he knocked. The light struck like a dagger. She gave an involuntary frown and shielded her eyes as the visitor introduced himself.

'Good morning. I am Mr Lal.' He smiled. 'Your neighbour,' he added, as Ronnie was silent. 'We recently moved in. My wife and family and myself.'

'And your dog. And your rooster.'

'Ah, Bimbo! Yes. That is one reason I have come to see you. That is about the fence. Also to speak about the tree down there.' Mr Lal waved towards the boundary with his free hand. In the other he carried a glass jar of sweets which he thrust towards Ronnie as though offering a bone to an aggressive puppy. 'These are *jelabis*. My wife has made them for you.'

'I don't eat sweets. My sister will like them. What do you mean... the fence and the tree?'

'We are keeping poor Bimbo tethered because that side fence is full of holes. But he is barking.'

'I've noticed.'

'Yes. The noise is irritating. A good high Colorbond fence along there will fix the problem. Of course as neighbours we pay half each—agreed? And then there is the tree.'

'What tree?'

'It overhangs and it is making quite a mess. My poor wife, who is not well, is sweeping, sweeping. The gutters will be full of leaves, the drains will block. In this case, I am willing to pay for the removal of the branches. Of course there may be tip fees. We can negotiate on that?'

'You have the nerve to tell me you want to cut my tree down?'

The small and dapper man brushed back a lock of silvering hair.

'That is correct. It is creating a problem.'

'Mr Lal, you are the problem. I am a shift worker. I've had to put up with your noise for nearly a year now. I thought it was over when you moved in. It's now ten times worse than before, thanks to Bimbo who I have frequently felt like shooting. I think your rooster should be strangled. I don't like Colorbond. I don't intend to pay for an eyesore.

And if you attempt to cut off even a twig of that wonderful tree I will go straight to Council and report you for defacing heritage property. I have a terrible headache and I'm going to bed. Good morning.'

She firmly closed the door. The Indian pursed his lips, then walked thoughtfully away. He was a landlord, well used to awkward exchanges. The matter at least had been raised. The dog heard him returning and began an ecstatic crescendo of barks.

'Good boy, Bimbo.' Mr Lal patted him. 'Keep up the noise. We'll soon have a nice strong fence, and then you can run free.'

Perhaps she should have handled the Indian's visit differently.

It wasn't strictly true to claim the house was heritage-listed; much less the camphor laurel, which had probably started life as a seed in a pigeon dropping and would have been more at home in a large country paddock than a suburban yard. As for the fence, it was falling down. A little diplomacy on her part might have solved the real problem of the dog. Now she was off on the wrong foot with her neighbour.

That upsetting exchange, the headache and Bimbo's volleys of noise put paid to her hopes of rest. At least the stint of night duty was finished. She should go for a walk. The house was depressing, with reminders of the past in the embossed wallpaper, floral carpet and venetian blinds with their drooping cords. The place reeked of thrift and making-do. Her father, a roof tiler, the survivor of the marriage, had lived on alone for years, becoming taciturn and miserly. She had a flashback to her last visit home, not long after her registry office wedding to Max. Her father had been abrupt; probably displeased that his daughter had fallen for a young good-looking sportsman with poor earning prospects. He'd not even let his daughter prepare the meal, and made no effort at all to talk to Max. When, three years later, he died in his sleep, no one knew for days.

What had he seen in Max that she'd been oblivious to? She'd met him in hospital, when he was having knee surgery. He'd already broken local sprint records, had his sights set on the Olympics. In his words, it didn't sound so unlikely. At first she thought he was kidding when he asked her out on a date. He kept at her until she gave in. He didn't want to talk about world events or current affairs. She was drawn in to his single-minded ambition. He was a warm-hearted lover. Quite soon she was head over heels in love with him.

Yet the marriage had lasted less than two years. Marie was luckier. She and Hugh were lovebirds all their married life. Her blazing grief when he died had been overwhelming. At least the move to Trundle had shaken her back to the present. She was even playing her piano again; the dignified old Lipp with its chipped ivories. Her music could transform the room. She'd shown such promise, always done well in exams and competitions. Now she played alone. Coming in from the garden or back from work, Ronnie would sometimes hear that rippling beauty, abruptly silenced, perhaps because of nerves or self-consciousness.

Marie was childlike. All those dolls and teddy bears perched on her bed like a surrogate family. Worth a mint of money. Stiff-lashed stares and moulting plush could pay for the renovations, but Marie was horrified if Ronnie pointed out auction sale prices. *Sell my precious babies? Never!*

Marie always did claim she wanted a family. It hadn't happened. Ronnie wasn't the motherly type—or was she? She'd built up quite a collection of dependents. Geriatrics, paraplegics. Max. He'd always had his clean socks, wet-weather gear, hi-protein shakes; cosy, but not fuel for lasting passion. Shattering to lose your protégé to a young aerobics instructor with a sexy body. The year he deserted her, she lived like a hermit, trying to hide his casual destruction of her self-worth. Marriage wasn't just between two people. Along with Max departed the joint routines and social props they'd built. On her birthday she stayed indoors. All she wanted were the books and CDs she'd brought to the marriage; rubbed jerseys and old adornments reminded her she'd had a life before Max, she'd manage to live again.

She'd made a pretty good recovery. She had no specific goals. There was no risk in superannuation and a retirement village down the track. Did Marie feel the same? They didn't really talk. The house, the garden, shopping lists… Sisterly concerns. With any luck, they'd settle on colour schemes and get stuck in to the painting over the weekend. Marie's enthusiasm was waning. Always some excuse. If the grass needed cutting, she claimed a weak back. While Ronnie lugged the lawn mower, Marie would be wandering like a Victorian lady, her wicker basket filled with flowers. While Ronnie broke her nails scrubbing brickwork, Marie would drift to a shady seat under the magnolia, calling *Ronnie, let's have tea?*

A noticeable silence recalled her to the present. Bimbo presumably napped. Ronnie stole back to bed, wary as a mother who has finally rocked the baby off to sleep.

Locals recommended the coffee at Kitty Playfair's shop on Main Road. Devonshire teas, which somehow went with travelling, were also a speciality of *The Trendy Trinket,* and when tourists paid they could select a map or souvenir tea towel of Trundle. Marie had to set aside her memories of her job at the city antique shop. She was lucky to have work at all. She had Kitty to thank for that.

She and Kitty went back a long way. They'd been little girls playing under the gum trees in the schoolyard, then giggly teenagers eyeing off the boys outside the cinema. When Kitty married Sam Playfair, the freckle-faced, sandy-haired son of the local butcher, Marie was bridesmaid in orchid pink satin.

For a while they went different ways. Kitty was the model housewife. Marie heard of Pelican, the new commune on the coast, and went out to see for herself. The founders were a cosmopolitan group. Their talk of the environment, pollution, and shared lifestyles offered ideas very new to her. Older members like Honor Stedman could recount firsthand stories about Gurdjieff Institute in England. Theories of free love were bandied about among the younger ones. Drawn by the unknown, Marie joined.

She was washing dishes as Kitty came through the beaded curtain divider, carrying a stock catalogue.

'There're some new lines available. *Scented tulips that last forever.* Do you think they'd sell?'

'Why ask me?' said Marie, who hated artificial flowers.

'These are cute.' Kitty pointed to strange accretions of shells, pipe cleaners and leather ears, described as *Curious Critters.* 'You don't think so? I suppose they're outside our range. People do buy strange things.'

She picked up a tea towel showing a faded view of Trundle's historic hotel and began to dry the cups. The same age as Marie, her face was free from lines and her fair hair showed no grey, as though care and worry had somehow passed her by. Yet in her pleated skirt and synthetic blouse tied with a neck bow, her hair waved in an old-fashioned way, she allowed Marie a glimpse of the elderly woman Kitty would one day be.

'Any plans for the weekend?'

Marie shrugged. 'Ronnie's keen to start painting the front room. The never-ending renovating.'

'Can't you take a break?'

'You know Ronnie! Actually, I'm trying to drum up courage to visit Pelican.'

She had left the commune under a cloud of scandal when she fell in love with Hugh, a gentle bearded man in his thirties who lived at Pelican with his unstable wife and five-year-old daughter. In that atmosphere, it seemed permissible; even right. They kept their affair secret for a while. In time, Hugh's guilt and his angry wife drove them out of Trundle. Kitty had stood by her; just hugged her friend, her pretty, worried face conveying the doubts she didn't voice. Now, it was almost as though the intervening years had never been.

'I'm surprised you've left it so long,' Kitty said, having nothing in her own past that she didn't want to face. 'Honor and Laurie Stedman are still there. They come in to shop in Trundle. What's holding you back?'

'The old business.' In that brief phrase she summed up the bitterness that had resulted. Hugh's wife had punished him by denying access to his daughter, Rowena. She, in turn, had grown up blaming Marie for stealing her father and breaking up her home.

'How did it end up?'

'The mother took little Rowena away up North. She was extreme in everything; went quite mad in the end. Rowena moved back to Pelican. She wrote to Hugh, just before he died. Suggested meeting. She has a child of her own now. Hugh's grandchild!'

'You ought to give her a chance. By now she might understand. You really loved Hugh, didn't you?'

'Still do.'

As always, when she heard Hugh's name, tears filled Marie's eyes and she turned her wedding ring. She'd half-expected Trundle people to say, *Serve her right, she's being punished.* Instead she'd been welcomed back. Perhaps time did heal memories.

Kitty touched her arm. 'At least you had all those years of happiness together.'

She sounded somehow disappointed with her life. Yet she had a husband and children, a home, a business, a place in civic and church activities.

'How are things at home?' Marie asked.

'Oh, fine.'

'Sam's business going well?' He was the local land agent. Perhaps house sales were in the doldrums.

'I suppose so.'

'How's Holly?' Surely Kitty must miss her eldest daughter, who was doing volunteer work in India.

'Apparently all right.'

'Must be quite a change for her.'

Are you happy? Marie wanted to say. It didn't seem like the time or place as the shop bell sounded and Kitty bustled out to serve.

Later, closing up shop, the pair walked along Main Road. Outside Sam's office they parted. Marie wandered on, in no hurry to go home. Ronnie was so moody lately. She eyed shop displays, visualising goods rearranged with a touch of flair. Trundle stores dealt in everyday needs. Surely everyone had room for imagination?

She paused at an untenanted shop. In her mind's eye she dressed the shabby window with rich red velvet curtains, lace cloths, peacock feathers. A beaded dress, antique dolls and button-eyed teddy bears created an era of opulence and fantasy. The plate glass sparkled, a cascade of Chopin drifted in the air. *Victorian Gilt*, in gold lettering, adorned the shop window.

The vision accompanied Marie to her car and all the way home. She had some money left to her by Hugh. There were contacts back in the city and her own treasures, half of them still packed up in boxes in the shed. And she had an eagle eye for a bargain buried in the usual dross of garage sales. She wondered how much the rent would be and whether Kitty would be offended or see Marie as a competitor. She'd soon find out. Sam was the agent for the shop. Elated, she parked, rammed on the handbrake and went into the house to share her brilliant idea with Ronnie.

2

Mr Lal was an accountant. He and his wife had lived in many dwellings since their migration to Australia, where he quickly found his qualifications cut no ice. In the early days he had to make do with any casual work that he could find, while the young couple at first stayed with distant relatives, then moved on to shabby rooms and rundown flats. After the babies came they discussed their concerns—the rough elements, racial prejudice, the exorbitant cost of city housing—and decided to move to the country. They came to Trundle, where Mr Lal was able to put a deposit on a tidy fibro cottage for his family, and invest his small savings in a dilapidated rental house in Railway Street. By relocating, he had reversed his position from tenant to landlord.

He had business cards printed and placed a running advertisement for accounting services in *The Trundle Times*. Slowly word spread about that the Indian fellow's fees were half of McCready and McCready's and his tax and investment advice was shrewd. He worked from home in a converted bedroom. Shanti became expert at whisking the children out of the way whenever a client knocked on the door. In any spare moment, he studied the economy, the movements of the stock market, rises and falls in interest rates, bonds and futures. Wealth was the only possible tool with which he could hope to educate his children and demonstrate his worth. This was a materialistic culture. Of course money mattered in India, but so did its rich past, rulers, kingdoms, monuments, religions and spiritual icons. Indians accepted endless rebirth with its cycles of patient learning. Here, you had one lifetime and you grabbed everything you could get. Here, poverty meant you had failed.

When Shanti asked for a little more to spend on food, Mr Lal told her to economise. When the children shivered in July he told them to go outside and run around. He would not let them have a puppy; that would be another mouth to feed. He dug a good vegetable plot in the fertile soil and bought a few hens to provide eggs. The children cried when they saw him wring the roosters' necks but he made Shanti prepare the curry.

'What do you think villagers do in India? Make pets of goats and chickens?'

Vijay ate the food in silence but Vimla stamped her foot and sobbed and cried until he took her on his knee and allowed her to have rice instead. No doubt about it, she could wheedle her way around her father.

The numerous economies became small savings, then quite large investments. The children started high school. Shanti wasn't invited to contribute to canteen or fundraising efforts and had no friends. She served her family but somehow her heart was in the past. She wore plain *saris,* cooked Indian food, did *puja* every day at the little altar in the front room. By now she was so used to thrift that, when Mr Lal relaxed and increased the housekeeping allowance, she saved the extra money in a tin moneybox. Three years later she produced it proudly and said she wanted to bring her parents out from India. Mr Lal agreed. It was a natural thing to do in his culture. The house would clearly be too small but he had other plans. A couple of shrewd investments had brought exceptional returns. To the rental hovel in Railway Street he'd added units in Sydney, retirement villas on the Central Coast, a healthy share portfolio and selected art. He was set up for life. He could afford to build the house he'd always wanted. He did not need to work.

The next year was a flurry of change. House plans were commissioned. Bureaucrats at Immigration and the Trundle council had to be dealt with. In these confrontations, his years of hard-nosed business experience paid off. Officials soon discovered that this undersized Indian chap had infinite patience, could uncover every loophole in the regulations and would never sway from his stand. Shanti's parents were granted their immigration papers and arrived a few months before the new house was finished. Camping in the living room didn't worry them. The family felt closer, living cheek by jowl that way. Shanti smiled more. Vim would sprawl like a princess on her grandmother's bed, showing off some assignment she'd put together on the computer. Vijay, who had by now turned twenty, was usually to be found in his bedroom, strumming a guitar and keeping out of his father's way. Even he came out to join the family, trying out chords to fit some tune his grandfather would croon in his cracked old voice. Walking in on such a scene, Mr Lal would feel an unfamiliar emotion then—belonging; that was it. He couldn't wait to move everyone to the new house. It would be their reward, and his, for a lifetime of self-denial and struggle.

Yet today, as he sat alone in his office with its computer, fax and photocopier, he felt no elation at fulfilling his goals. He'd lost the fire that had propelled his energies in his pen and paper days. His business affairs had acquired their own momentum and his money multiplied as fast as he could spend. He'd just been on the phone to Sam Playfair, who handled his rental property in Railway Street. The place had stood vacant for two months and the agent implied no prospective tenant would look at such a run-down place. Nor was Mr Lal's own new house the happy home he'd envisaged. Shanti seemed tired, and had several times murmured that there was a lot of housework to do now. All the more reason surely for her to make use of the dishwasher and the washing machine but, no, she went about her chores the old way, even saying she missed the old-fashioned copper she'd had to boil up when she did the laundry. Her parents had their separate quarters now. They had their own bathroom, toilet, shower—even a kitchenette. Yet they were talking wistfully every day about India. The old man had developed a nasty cough and was deafer than he'd ever been.

Then Mr Lal had concerns for his offspring, who had become young adults while his back was turned. He'd bought the dog in memory of two children begging for a pet, but neither Vijay nor Vimla wanted to feed or exercise the creature, whose present fate was to make a thorough nuisance of itself. Vijay's guitar, which used to annoy his father, was now muted by soundproof walls. Mr Lal would listen in vain for music as he walked past his son's room. It was as though Vijay no longer lived at home.

Only Vimla was delighted with the house. She loved the size, the space, the luxury of every fitting. The huge mirrored bathroom especially pleased her as she stood preening and posturing. In India, parents would surely turn their minds to appropriate matchmaking as Vim matured. Mr Lal uncomfortably observed her thrusting breasts and curving hips. Sexual symbols, carved in sandstone everywhere in India, were disconcerting reminders that while his daughter still wore school uniform her body was a woman's. How he disliked those long flirtatious phone calls she had with unknown boys! Discreetly he asked Shanti to discuss hem lengths and fit of bodices but his wife shrugged and said this was Australia, a girl in a *sari* would be laughed at. Besides, Vimla took no notice of anyone, what would be the point of giving advice? In a few months she would sit her final exams and be ready to embark on her career. At least they had one ambitious child. Even in a little town like Trundle, there would be a place for Vim.

Bimbo's barking drew his attention to a visitor. From the window he recognised one of the ladies from next door. She was of heavy build, and walked in a leisurely way. She paused to pat the dog and examine the young plants in the bare landscaped garden. This must be a follow-up to his previous exchange with the irritable neighbour.

Marie, who had eyed the building progress of the house next door with curiosity, was glad of an excuse to visit. Carrying the empty glass jar, she walked along the cement driveway flanked with pebble-covered garden beds, and knocked on the wood-panelled front door. The Indian who opened it was presumably the man who'd been to see Ronnie earlier. He stood in the marble-floored entrance hall, dwarfed in the space created by the cathedral ceiling from which dangled a chandelier. A staircase behind him curved upwards to the second floor.

'Come in please.' His words sounded abrupt but he was smiling as he beckoned to his wife who came shyly from the shadows. She was a plain woman of passive manner; something about her made Marie think she was unwell.

Discarded footwear formed a tidy row just inside the door. Marie kicked off her slip-on shoes and placed them in line, wishing her naked feet didn't look so large. She followed her hosts across cold marble into an elaborate sitting room where several large leather couches, chairs and occasional tables made little impression on the space.

'Sit down please,' said Mr Lal.

'Thank you. You have a lovely home!' To Marie, this was hardly even a white lie for while she would not have chosen such a style herself she could empathise with poor migrants who had no doubt struggled to be successful.

'I've often wondered what your house was like.'

The man and his wife sat side by side, saying nothing to her chatter.

'And thank you for the sweets. I have a sweet tooth, I'm afraid. I've brought back the jar. My sister mentioned your visit.'

'I chose an inconvenient time,' said Mr Lal diplomatically.

'Ronnie's a nurse. She works shifts—afternoons, nights—she doesn't sleep well, and the barking drives her mad.'

Shanti nodded as though she sympathised.

'Bimbo must be tethered because the fence has collapsed. This is why he barks. I bought him for my children.' Mr Lal sounded quite wistful.

'The rooster's a bit of problem too.'

'My wife's mother is homesick, you see. When the rooster crows she says it is like waking up in the village. She has a little garden now, for marigolds. She likes flowers.'

'How kind you are!' Suddenly Marie had a picture of this household with its varied age groups, their needs and problems. It was hard to see Mr Lal as an adversary. He looked surprised at her compliment.

'It is my duty. Meanwhile, as we are discussing mutual concerns, there is the tree.'

'Ronnie did mention that.' Marie did not repeat her sister's opinion of tree management.

'It is only a matter of trimming, not removal.'

'The leaves are falling every day,' murmured Shanti. 'They make black stains.'

'Surely we can resolve these problems?' Marie took matters into her own hands, wishing Ronnie would not make big issues out of small affairs.

'It is to be hoped.' Mr Lal, sensing the closure of a business deal, was alert.

'The fence does need replacing. But Ronnie won't have Colorbond.'

'Why not?'

'It's—not what she likes. How's this? We'll agree to pay half share of a timber fence. Wood's more natural.'

'It is less durable.'

'None of us will live forever. Let's have the new fence built and untie poor Bimbo. While we're at it, I see no reason why you shouldn't trim the overhanging branch. Just do it when Ronnie's at work.' Marie leaned back with an air of mischief and conspiracy.

'So we come to the rooster?'

'To tell you the truth, Mr Lal, *I* rather like the rooster crowing in the morning.'

'Bring tea, Shanti.' The Indian looked pleased with progress.

His wife complied, while Mr Lal and Marie began to discover they had certain interests in common. Marie said she was hoping to open up a shop in town. When he learned she had knowledge of antiques and valuables he sought her advice about buying a quality carpet for one of his spare rooms. She told him she knew dealers in the city who would give him a good price if he mentioned her name. She promised to drop in their card. In no time they were chatting like old friends.

Donning the brown suit he kept for business affairs, Mr Lal set off to walk to town. As he closed the iron gates behind him, he looked back proudly at his house. Year by year, as he'd dealt in real estate, he'd gathered ideas for his dream home. Here it was, complete with posts and pillars, archways and balconies where, in his mind's eye, he and Shanti were supposed to sit, taking tea and reviewing the events of the day. So far this routine hadn't been established. Shanti spent much of her time resting on the bed. Clearly she ought to see a doctor but she wouldn't go.

One item on his day's agenda was to arrange a house call on his wife's behalf. As well he was going to see Sam Playfair. The Railway Street house was still untenanted—an unsatisfactory state of affairs. He walked briskly along Alexandra Avenue. He enjoyed walking. In his garage was parked the new red car Vimla had persuaded him to buy, but he hadn't so far learned to drive it. In his opinion, buses, trains and his own two legs were non-depreciating and adequate means of getting from place to place. In their hearts both father and daughter knew that the Fiat was destined for Vim's use. Above him, clouds, birds and the leaves of rustling trees went unnoticed. He saw structures, bricks and mortar, the state of his neighbours' properties.

Certainly his own house was the newest and the biggest. The bank manager's carport was falling down. Sam Playfair's guttering was rusted out. The sisters' place was shabby and needed painting. Yet no one in the street, apart from Marie whose call had been to do business, had paid a welcome visit to the Lals. He'd always felt their isolation in the town was to do with low status, but the new house apparently made no difference. He had a long memory for racial slurs, though many years had passed since rude remarks had come his way.

He reached Main Road in less than fifteen minutes. Trundle served both the local population and farmers from surrounding areas. So far it had managed to survive government cutbacks that, elsewhere, had led to closures of small hospitals, banks and the railway. Its long main road was bounded at the north end by the Travellers' Arms hotel with its pretty wrought-iron fretwork and five decapitated cypress trees in front. At the south end stood the RSL Club, in its vantage point overlooking the river. The Club needed upgrading. Its discoloured cement exterior had last been painted in 1976. Among the rest of the buildings it did not look so out of place. There was a general atmosphere of peeling paint, faded canvas awnings and old stock as Mr Lal strolled past the shops. Butchers and bakers, hairdressers, fast-food outlets, hardware stores, newsagents and bargain shops plied adequate trade in Trundle; but as for designer clothing, classical music, fine furniture, frivolous gadgets or computer wares, it was necessary to make a day trip to one of the bigger centres up or down the coast.

Mr Lal passed *The Trendy Trinket* and waved to Marie, who was wiping down a table near the window. He called in to the surgery and booked a house call for Shanti. He deposited a cheque at the bank and bought a new ledger book at *Priceline*. Mid-afternoon shoppers went up and down the street, greeting one another and dawdling in pairs and groups. No one spoke to him. As he walked on to the land agent's office the town clock was striking three.

He asked to see Sam Playfair, who came out from his tiny office, his round face conveying a geniality he did not feel in relation to the Indian's rental house. The place had been on the market ever since the last lot of tenants absconded, leaving a filthy mess and a backlog of unpaid rent for Sam to explain to his disapproving client.

'This is a timely visit!' His warm, freckled hand enveloped Mr Lal's. 'Matter of fact just got off the phone from someone who might take Railway Street.'

But in spite of his good cheer he seemed to have some reservation.

'It is high time it was re-let.'

'Trouble is, the lady concerned could be a risk.'

'Is she unemployed?'

'No references. People by the name of Halpin. Husband and wife, two kids. I knew Nora back in school. Local girl. Left town years ago, went up North somewhere. Now they're back. '

'Not got a reference,' mused Mr Lal.

'I'm having difficulty with your place. The better tenants can pick and choose. Have you been past lately? If you renovated...'

'Sign up these Halpin people,' said Mr Lal. 'If they don't pay the rent you can evict them.'

'That's a bit tricky... Young family, all that.'

'Business is business.' This was one English expression Mr Lal liked. The language had many strange, even incomprehensible sayings, but this one, at least, was clear.

'It's a gamble,' was all Sam would say to that.

The purposes of his trip to town accomplished, Mr Lal felt well satisfied as he left Sam's office. Young people just out of school milled around him, shouting, shoving and pushing, and the Indian stood back in a doorway, waiting until the unruly groups moved on. Some hoodlum in the crowd might see a target in dark skin. But no one took the slightest notice of him. He followed at a distance, seeing them turn off into the milk bar, the chip shop or McDonald's. There, the smell of cooked meat caused him a moment's disgust, until the sight of his daughter suddenly displaced his objection to beef. Vim was swinging her hips in a skirt that showed off three-quarters of her long legs as she wandered along with a boy. His arm was around her shoulders and she laughed up at him in a coy, flirtatious way. Mr Lal had a strange desire to hide from her. He felt paralysed to act. Vim didn't see him. With her boyfriend, she turned in at McDonald's door, while Mr Lal walked home, uneasy and deep in thought.

After the interchange with Mr Lal, Sam sat thinking. He had the role of fall guy when it came to the unpleasant side of the rental business, and he had misgivings about Nora Halpin, who he remembered as precocious and frequently in trouble. She was supposed to be calling back, and he shrank from the prospect of hearing that hoarse voice, those wheedling words; *Aw, c'mon Sam, giz a break!* Sam had no say in it. Mr Lal had no intention of making repairs to that dump in Railway Street; it represented rent and that was all.

But the caller wasn't Nora, but another voice from the past. Sam and Bryan O'Brian had gone to school together. Bryan had moved on to bigger places, but he came back to Trundle from time to time; usually when he wanted a favour or had some doubtful deal in mind.

'My old mate! How's it going? I'm passing through. Can I shout you a few drinks after work?'

Sam guessed that Bryan had a business proposition. That meant money, on which subject his wife Kitty was becoming monotonous. Bryan on his last visit home had turned up with a showroom-shiny 4-wheel drive and a new lady friend. Dixie was a cheerful blonde divorcee. She wore plenty of eye make up and gold jewellery and talked about cruises, holidays and good times. The three of them had enjoyed one of those long lunches businessmen claimed on their tax returns.

Sam tidied away the files and papers on his desk and saw it was time to head to the Club, where he was meeting Bryan. He phoned Kitty and said he'd be late. The last half-hour of his working day dragged on. He sat at his desk, bored, tracing his forehead lines and rubbing around the crown of his head where he was starting to lose hair. Nora phoned at a quarter to five and he decided it would be a weight off his mind to be rid of the property. He made a diary entry to have her sign the lease and collect the keys, asked his secretary to lock up and strolled out to Main Road.

He'd always lived in Trundle and thought no more about its features than his own. A place like Canberra was carefully planned with a manmade lake and thousands of hand-planted trees. Trundle seemed to have happened accidentally. Many of its buildings served dual and unrelated purposes. The small art gallery was on the second floor of the Water Board's offices, the library operated from a room in the Council Chambers, and you hired videos either at the garage or from the news agency. Sam did not find these associations quaint. He did not think about his home-town at all, except when someone like Bryan came back. There was nothing fancy about Bryan's background. He came from Railway Street, where his old mother lived to this day. But when he breezed into town, dressed to kill and driving the spoils of his profitable existence as a so-called *entrepreneur*, the prospect of drinking with him made Sam step up his pace. He had no wish to arrive hot and out of breath to face his old school mate.

Above a flowerbed squared off by white-painted chains, the town clock sat perched on its pedestal. Five o'clock was striking as Sam crossed the dizzily patterned carpet in the club foyer to show his membership card at the desk. Portraits of stern-looking past presidents observed his progress down the corridor that led along to the bar. The bistro, off to the left, smelt of chips and sausages. The faint reek of tobacco grew stronger as he paused outside the poker machine room; clubs were among the last bastions where smokers could indulge. Each machine had its acolyte who sat perched on a high stool, gazing into the spinning reels with that look of intimacy and communion usually associated with falling in love. The atmosphere here vibrated with the busy whirr and rattle of commerce as the machines gulped in money and spewed back coin. Jingles played in every key and rhythm. A deep concentration ruled the room.

Just then a bell shrilled, announcing a jackpot winner and at once every player in the room stared enviously around to see whom Lady Luck had smiled on. Sam had been brought up to stay away from gambling. Now he experienced a surge of exclusion. He'd felt the same as a twelve-year-old, when Bryan used to boast about what went on with Nora behind the bicycle shed at school. The reckless longing of those faces reflected greeds and passions he'd never let himself indulge in. He walked on to check the bar. Bryan wasn't there. Acknowledging the nods of the regulars, he arrived back at the foyer just as Bryan came in sight, taking the stairs two at a time. Sam sucked in his solar plexus and stepped forward to sign the visitor in.

Some time in the small hours of that night, all the residents of Alexandra Avenue heard an ambulance siren. Lights bloomed in windows up and down the street as people reassured themselves the emergency concerned some other household, not their own.

Sam sat up in bed, startled into after-dream recall. Something dangerous had come so close its hot breath still panted in his ear. His wife stirred and murmured. She soon dozed off again, but he lay awake, replaying his day's dealings. Bryan had cheap blocks of land for sale on the coast near Pelican commune. There would be a decent cut for the selling agent but, as usual with Bryan, there was a catch; a building veto which left the benefits of ownership unclear to Sam. He'd said he'd think it over. Bryan had offered to wait a week or so before approaching another agent.

Ronnie Gale had been another victim of uneasy dreams. The siren had catapulted her straight out of a recurring nightmare where someone was trying to persuade her to climb inside a coffin. Now her heart was pounding from the shock of sudden awakening as she sat upright, the flashing red light of the stationary ambulance in the Lals' driveway casting bizarre shadows on her wall.

Marie had burrowed out from her untidy nest of bedding and was peering out into the night. At her neighbours', lights were on all over the house and the dog was howling. After a short time the vehicle reversed and drove away, leaving in its wake a strange, uneasy peace. As she crawled back into bed, she impulsively seized her favourite teddy bear and took it beneath the covers, the way a child shuts out phantoms of the darkness.

3

Ronnie was back on day shift. For a few moments she stood on the porch, appreciating the pastel sky and dewy grass alive with foraging birds which took wing as she slammed the car door and started the engine. She backed down the driveway, glancing at the silent brick house next door. The disturbance last night had clearly been a medical emergency.

It was only a short run to the hospital and she arrived early to find the night staff writing up Mrs Lal's urgent admission. She had haemorrhaged and was scheduled for a biopsy and surgery. According to the night nurse, Shanti was anxious and shy, and not wanting to be examined by the male doctor.

'These ethnics! Probably bled away for years and done nothing about it. Now it's probably too late.'

'More fact, less speculation,' said Ronnie. The staff nurse pulled a face as her supervisor strode away to do her morning round.

Curtains sealed off the Indian woman's bed. Though they'd never spoken, never even met, Ronnie felt sorry for her. She had the passive manner of a captured animal accepting the futility of struggle. Ronnie checked her for bleeding and said she would have to sign a consent form. It was hard to be sure how much she understood or whether she knew she had any rights.

'We can't let you eat or drink before you go to theatre. Press this bell if you need anything.'

'My family…?'

'Of course they may visit.' Ronnie smiled at her. 'But you'll be very drowsy from the anaesthetic.'

'Thank you.' Shanti had no questions.

'Do you understand about the biopsy? It will tell the doctor what to do. They may have to take away your womb.'

Evidently shamed by the mention of intimate parts, Shanti closed her eyes as though removing herself to her household where she could supervise her children's breakfast, her husband's clean shirt and her father's cough. In this alien and foreign environment, why would she spare a single thought for herself and what might happen next? Ronnie pressed her hand and briskly continued her rounds of the surgical patients.

Her next port of call was the west wing where long-term residents were housed. Apart from a couple of young people whose disabilities did not fit the criteria of hostels or group homes, the patients were senile or incontinent elderly. Here the staff were on first name terms with their charges. There was a less rigid sticking to the rules and regulations of hospital efficiency, but today, as Ronnie strode along the corridor, they were already hounding resentful old folk to the showers for their pre-breakfast soap and scrub. The new nurses' assistant, Sandy Smith, in over-large white rubber boots and apron, was trying to wrestle the flexible shower head from her naked charge just as Ronnie looked into the bathroom to investigate the noise. Sandy slipped and fell; water sprayed over the supervisor as she reached to turn off the tap.

'Dress this patient, get yourself dry and report to me!'

It wasn't a good start to Sandy's or anybody's day.

The Lal family arrived as a solemn group by nine o'clock. Shanti was already sleepy from her pre-med. but roused herself enough to scold Vim for missing school and remind her father to buy a refill for his nebulizer. As she was transferred to a trolley and wheeled from the ward, the Lals stood staring after her even when she was out of sight. It would be some hours before the outcome of the operation would be known, and they were advised to come back later in the day. Mr Lal declined, politely asking where they might wait.

They were offered chairs in a sitting room where the family settled to their vigil. Shanti's parents sat bolt upright, conveying an infinite patience. Their son-in-law impassively gazed ahead, occasionally running his fingers through his hair. Vimla flipped the pages of a magazine, paced across the room, sat down again. Vijay wandered in his half-indolent, half-graceful way to the windows, where he stood staring at the staff car park. Their solidarity was a palpable force, and staff hesitated to disturb them. The word from theatre was much as expected—invasive cancer of the pelvic organs. Even now Shanti was undergoing radical surgery.

Ronnie knew she was the wrong person to deal with the family. Unlike Marie, she'd made no overtures of friendship and did not expect them to welcome her under such worrying circumstances. But that was no reason to deny them basic courtesies. Sandy Smith would do. The girl couldn't speak out of turn on medical matters, and her shyness might be acceptable. She'd been pulled out of West Wing and was now put to practise stripping and remaking a bed in a cubicle where she could do no harm.

'Nurse Smith!'

Startled, the girl knocked a pile of pillows to the floor.

'You know the whereabouts of the coffee machine and the public toilets?'

'Yes Sister.'

'Then go and show the Indian family where to find them. Finish that bed first, and mitre the corner.'

The girl's dull brown hair half-obscured her eyes and the over-long uniform made her look dowdy. How nervous she was! Her hands were trembling.

'Go along now,' allowed Ronnie, quite kindly, and Sandy fled.

She felt sorry for the waiting family, looking at her with expressions of fear and mistrust. A hospital was an intimidating place: blood, needles, tubing, the disinfected smell. Clever purposeful people came with their forceps and scissors, steel kidney dishes and surgical packs, and who knew just what suffering they might bring?

It was a wonder Sandy was here at all. She had no ambition to train in one of the university-based nursing courses. Nurse assistants, she'd been told, were really not required any more. Just what did she have to offer? Sandy remembered looking directly at that woman across the desk. *I like people who are old and sick. I could do little things that make them feel a bit better.* The starchy woman told her not to get her hopes up. And then, out of the blue, Sandy was offered a temporary job. Just as she could hardly register her luck, she'd ruined her first day. Another mistake and she'd likely get the sack.

These poor people! How worried, upset, afraid, alone they were.

'What is the news?' the middle-aged Indian asked. Four pairs of eyes beseeched her to bring them some reassurance, some reprieve.

'I'm not a proper nurse. Sister sent me to show you the drink machine and the toilets.'

It seemed the silent people must have no bodily functions, no hunger, no thirst. The father was in a world of his own. The old ones sat like statues. The girl in the tight jeans had apparently gone for a walk. Only the nice-looking boy smiled at her.

'Could we get some tea?'

'I'll show you the machine,' said Sandy. It was a lovely smile, slow and full!

They walked together along the corridor and he did not say anything except, 'Do they sell chocolate anywhere?'

She confessed it was her first day here, she didn't know.

He had change for the tea but not enough for the Mars bars in the other machine. Sandy had some money in her pocket and, as he took it, he looked at her as though he really liked what he saw. He said his name was Vijay Lal. She said hers was Sandy Smith. They carried the paper cups back to the waiting room.

They saw a lot of each other in the course of the next week. The presence of the Lals at Shanti's bedside remained a constant as each member of the family absorbed with shock the realisation of how ill she was. Mr Lal conferred with the doctors, requiring full information on the disease, its progression, statistical survival, forms of treatment and the like. Shanti's parents visited, bringing home-cooked delicacies when it was obvious the hospital food wasn't to her taste. Vimla bounced in each day after school, carrying her haversack of textbooks and her day's news. However, it was Vijay who stayed longest with his mother. He came to the ward as soon as he was allowed, and stayed all day. When treatments or medications interfered, he strolled in the car park or took a wander downtown for an hour. He would always return, telling of everyday doings at home or reminding her of small events that sometimes made her smile. If she drifted off to sleep he still sat, glancing at a book or just staring into space. He often acknowledged Sandy with a glance and a few words as she changed the water jug and collected the meal tray.

He was fond of reading. She would glance over his shoulder, and noted that meditation and guitar chords seemed to be his two main interests. There was never a chance to exchange more than a few sentences, for Sister Gale would arrive as if she had radar, her look conveying what she thought of lazy girls who wasted time. It was always then that Sandy would trip on a cord or bump herself on the locker. Once a plastic dinner plate of uneaten food slid off the tray. She dropped to her knees to clear up the mess, feeling sick and apprehensive in the old way she'd learnt in childhood whenever trouble was brewing. That time, Vijay crouched beside her and helped her pick up the bits of meat and potato.

Shanti's drip had been removed, she was off morphine, and was supposed to be taking assisted walks. But all these signs of progress did not seem to register with her. Although she knew what was wrong with her, she'd asked no questions. It was as though she experienced the hospital as an unbidden dream from which she would thankfully awake. A doctor or one of the trained nurses would try to talk about further treatment. Shanti would thank them politely, close her eyes and shield herself beneath the covers. When the day's report was read out to oncoming staff, a note said that Mrs Lal's denial of her illness was holding back her convalescence. She ought to mobilise and verbalise. Sandy, trying to look unobtrusive, stood at the back of the little group. She was not required to offer any input and kept to herself the scene she'd witnessed earlier between Shanti and Vijay. In anguish the mother held out her hand to her son, who clasped it as though they were parting lovers who know that nothing lies ahead but pain.

As usual, Sister Gale seemed able to read Sandy's mind.

'You've been working in that room today, Nurse Smith. Are you in possession of any information?'

Sandy mumbled, 'They know.'

'They know? What do they know?'

'They know she's going to die.'

'Nurse Smith! *We* don't know that. How could they?'

'I don't know. Because they love each other.' Sandy, by now in tears of shame and humiliation, ran off to the change room. She sat huddled in a corner, awaiting dismissal. But that did not happen. When she dared emerge, red-eyed and wearing her cotton skirt and windbreaker with the broken zip, Sister Gale looked sympathetic. She actually said, 'I know it's hard, dear. We must learn not to take it all so much to heart.'

The supervisor was weird. Now the day didn't seem so awful, particularly when Vijay stopped Sandy as she walked towards the exit gate.

'Want to go for a thickshake?' he asked.

'I don't mind.' She smiled as, side by side, they wandered towards town. Ahead, among the knots of pupils walking home from school, she saw Vimla with a boy. He had the build of a footballer and carried her haversack while they exchanged flirtatious looks. How could she laugh so merrily when her mother was so ill?

Vijay did not comment. When his sister turned in to a take-away, he walked on and found a shop further along Main Road.

'What flavour do you like?'

Sandy considered. She was not in the habit of being asked such questions. She read through the chalked choices—*chocolate, strawberry, banana, vanilla, pistachio, raspberry, mango, rum*—then went through the list a second time.Vijay did not hurry her. He seemed to understand the importance of the decision. Finally she said *banana* and he *chocolate*. He ordered double scoops of ice-cream, and brought the frothing masterpieces to the orange-painted booth, where they faced each other as though they were alone in a little row-boat like that one in the faded lake poster on the wall. They compared flavours, swapping straws. Vijay still preferred the chocolate. Sandy thought both could be recommended.

'Do you like being a nurse?'

She nodded, but reminded him she wasn't; not a real one.

'What's a real nurse?'

She thought he was joking, then saw he took a word like *real* seriously. She had to think before suggesting a real nurse would have a medal and certificate and would know what to do in any medical emergency.

'I just like helping the sick people,' she said.

'*That's* real.' He sounded sure, dismissing certificates in a way that made her wonder if he'd failed his HSC. She didn't like to ask.

'What sort of job do you do?' She liked his devotion to his mother but wondered how he had so much free time.

'I'm still finding out. Life should be deliberate. Most people are unaware and lead unconscious lives.'

She sucked on her straw in silence.

'My father would like me to take any job, packing groceries, selling hardware.'

'Do you still live at home?'

'We have a house in Alexandra Avenue. You could visit me if you like. Sandy, do you think my mother will get better?'

'Of course.' She liked to hear him use her name. It was strange, the way people asked questions when they already sensed the answer; and the way you replied, saying what they wanted to hear. Of course there was the other language, conveying in a look its message of fear, hope, concern. What dark eyes he had!

'So you'll come and visit soon?'

The dregs of the milkshake gurgled as she gave a lingering suck. 'I don't mind,' she said. 'I better get off home now.'

Vijay walked her to a shabby wooden cottage, ten minutes out of town. She didn't invite him in, her stepfather being due back from the pub any time.

When they left the take-away bar, Gordon wanted Vimla to come back to his place. His mother was at work and the house was always empty after school. The first time Vim had gone home with him, she'd felt dawning excitement as Gordon led her straight to his bedroom—a typical boy's room with its unmade bed and dirty shoes and clothes dropped anywhere. They'd wasted no time. They both took off their shoes and socks; Vim unbuttoned his school shirt and reached for his zip. He pulled at her clothes while desire veiled the unromantic surroundings. Breathing fast, Gordon crab-walked her to the bed, pushed her down and lay on top of her.

The veil slightly lifted; his pillow had a funny smell and Vim had a close-up view of his acne. His nipples were harmless brown circles while hers reared up, dark and greedy to be stroked and sucked. *I'll get the rubber,* he said, his voice thick and frantic. He fumbled in the drawer and rolled on a bright blue condom. *He'll do it now,* she thought. It wasn't her first experience but they must all be different. A gasp pressed from her throat as he began to push. There was discomfort, and she was about to push him away, then suddenly *Yes!* And she hugged his naked back, wanting this game to whirl her everywhere until she was dizzy. Sex, the secret pact, the forbidden conquest. He gasped, groaned, rolled off, collapsed beside her. That was it. *Don't go to sleep.* She shook him vigorously. *Your mother might be early.*

Now he was always after her.

'I have to visit my mother.' Boys were so selfish when it suited them. She still had a love-bite from the last time. At school that was a mark of esteem but concealing it from her parents was another matter. Sex was a trading card. Boys wanted more and more, they ended up bargaining and begging. She wasn't one of those stupid chicks who'd go and get pregnant before they'd even passed their HSC. Vim's future was a red-ruby carpet, and she was Oscar material: clever, good-looking, with loving parents and a nice home. Her sights were set on the red Fiat in her father's garage, a job in journalism, money. Romance and love could wait. Her present encounters were along the lines of data-collecting exercises, and if she was getting a reputation, who cared?

Gordon was disappointed but he walked her to the hospital and tried to kiss her at the entrance. She pulled away from him.

'My mother's *sick*!' She sounded indignant, as though he'd made a pass at her at a funeral. She went off without a backward glance. She hated the hospital. It was the pits. Why would anyone choose to *work* there? The smell of the corridor was enough to make her spew. The sight of her mother made her want to cry.

'Hi, Ma!' She kissed Shanti, who opened her eyes and peered suspiciously at her daughter's neck.

'What's this?'

'Nothing. Just a bee sting.'

'Not a bee sting. What did you eat for lunch today? Did you do your homework?'

'I'm nearly eighteen, I'm not a baby.'

Shanti's fingers weakly combed the tangles of Vim's glossy hair. 'How are things at home?'

Vim shrugged. 'When are you coming home?'

'Soon, soon. I'll be better in a while.' She closed her eyes. Vim shook her arm.

'Why don't you get up and walk around? You won't get strong, lying in bed.' Vim's tone was petulant. Shanti hardly seemed to care for anything. 'When Daddy comes, will you ask him if I can use the car?'

'You know what he said. After you pass the HSC.'

'But that was before. I've got my L's. If I had the car I could come and see you twice a day.'

'No, Vimla! After your exam is soon enough.'

'Why is everything so horrible?' Vim flung herself onto her mother's bed and embraced her in a fit of passionate weeping. Shanti, used to her daughter, summoned enough strength to stroke the downcast head until the overwhelming emotions passed. She grimaced and pulled away, and Vim looked up, tear-stained, repentant. 'Did I hurt you?'

'They cut away some inside parts. It's very tender all down here.'

'I don't want you to be sick; please come home!' Now she began to sob.

'Now now.'

Vim absorbed the soothing words, the gentle tone, and gradually her crying stopped. Shanti passed across a packet of paper tissues from her locker.

'The food comes soon. They have meals at half past four. Very early.'

'At least you'll *have* a meal. Who knows what we'll have? Some weird thing Nani cooks up. I might get take-away again.'

'That food is no good. Eat what Nani cooks for you.'

'I don't like Nani's cooking.'

'I don't like this cooking. Make the best of it. I'll soon be home.'

Vim slid off the bed and hoisted her heavy school bag onto her back.

'These books weigh a ton. I'll be crippled carrying this weight. *Please* ask about the car?'

Shanti gave a weak smile. 'Bad girl! Walking is good for you.'

'Love you, Ma!'

'I love you too. Go on home now, they'll be wondering where you are.'

Outside, Vim cast away all thoughts about her mother, tiresome boys and the load of homework that she carried on her back. Beyond the rule-ridden institutions of school and hospital waited her real life. It was true that Main Road was drab, and that Trundle offered a humdrum future for an ambitious girl. She ceased to notice the ordinary gardens and suburban houses as she walked on, her imagination illuminating rich and wonderful worlds of glamour and adventure.

4

Mr Lal stopped in at Kitty's teashop next morning. He sat down on one of the rickety chairs, his expression so preoccupied that Marie ventured to ask about his wife.

'Recovering. You know she had an operation? The doctors say she's on the mend.' But he sounded unconvinced, adding, 'They recommend further treatment but Shanti has a mind of her own, you see. It is hard to convince her.'

'How worrying for you!' She placed the teapot, milk jug and sugar basin with a solicitude he seemed grateful for.

'And for her parents and the children,' he agreed. 'Vijay stays in his room when he isn't at the hospital. Vimla comes home later every day. I don't know where she goes.'

'I see her sometimes, walking past.' Marie made a point of sounding noncommittal; saying nothing about the company of boys who usually surrounded his flirtatious daughter. 'Mr Lal, do let me know if there's anything I can do? We're neighbours, after all.'

The Indian nodded and stirred his tea round and round, his thoughts clearly elsewhere.

'Poor man,' commented Kitty after he paid his bill and left. 'I hear it's cancer.'

'It sounds as though his wife's refusing follow-up treatment.'

'Indians have their own ideas about medicine.' Kitty reached into the pocket of her floral skirt and took out a photo. 'I had this from Holly yesterday. Here she is, in the back row, in the *sari*. The hospital's in Dehra Dun, near the Himalayas. She's been there six months.' Kitty gazed at her daughter's image as though it held an encoded message.

'How did she come to be chosen for volunteer work?'

'Our church has missions in Africa and the Pacific, as well as Bangladesh and India. Of course Holly isn't qualified for anything. I don't know what they get her to do. She doesn't say.'

Kitty spoke of her daughter's unshared life with fond resentment. It was much the same tone as Mr Lal had used about his children. Parent and child… It was the one relationship Marie regretted never knowing. Hugh's grandchild lived at Pelican with her mother. Wouldn't he want Marie to make contact and perhaps repair the past?

She had a more pressing matter to resolve. While Kitty was at lunch, she phoned Sam, who confirmed that the vacant shop was still available. By mid-afternoon she'd been down to his office, written out the cheque for the first month's rent and signed the lease. On her way back, she saw an elderly couple whose well-groomed style contrasted with the casual shorts and sunfrocks of Trundle shoppers. She hurried over, recognising her old friends Honor and Laurie Stedman. They were in town from Pelican to do their fortnightly shop and seemed genuinely happy to see her.

'I wish I could stay and talk,' said Marie. 'I must get back to work.'

'And we have hair appointments. Marie, *do* promise you'll come out and see us soon?'

'I'd love to. In fact, why not this weekend?'

When Kitty heard of her friend's bold move to open her own shop, she seemed a little envious, but offered to help in setting up the stock.

'We won't be competing?'

'Of course not.' Souvenir tea towels and plastic key rings were hardly the treasures Marie had in mind for *Victorian Gilt*.

'We can hunt the garage sales together.' Marie's spirits were high. Could it really be so simple to make a dream materialise?

There was no sign of Ronnie when she arrived home. She slung her bag and coat across a chair and rushed straight to the piano. Music reflected her cheerful mood, and she was able to shed her inhibitions and play as she could, triumphantly and joyfully. When the clock chimed, she sprang up, anxious to be on her way to the commune before Ronnie came home and started organising their weekend. She quickly tossed a few clothes and toiletries into an overnight bag and scribbled a note to her sister. Then, like a child planning to run away, she set out to drive to Pelican.

A warm spell lazed over the town, enticing people outside to stroll or chat across garden fences while sprinklers played and lawn mowers droned. A wafting barbecue aroma reminded her of food. With luck, Laurie Stedman would have the fridge stocked with his culinary talents. She drove on past the river, where cows stood riveted in the golden light of evening. Through the open window blew healthy smells of dung and grass. How many years had passed since she'd made her first journey, so unexpectedly to meet a man who'd changed her life? Privately she was that same girl still. Now, she desperately wanted to make amends; to meet Hugh's daughter, Rowena, and be allowed to participate in little Pippin's life. Hugh would have wanted that.

She was taking a risk. Rowena must resent her. She might be as erratic and spiteful as her mother. With an unpleasant feeling of anticipation, Marie followed the old road to the commune.

She was soon on the home stretch to Pelican, where the road tapered away to a bush track winding through woodland. Lugging her weekender, Marie set out. An eldritch glow shone through the trees now echoing with the whistles, chirrups and caws of settling birds. She remembered walking the track hand in hand with Hugh, while they wrestled with their attraction, trying to find the non-existent answer that would be fair to everyone and cause nobody pain. No wonder she'd avoided coming back. The experience had taught her that she shared her good-hearted nature with another, dark persona. She chose to be with Hugh, and in so doing she had wounded a small child's heart and sowed seeds of hatred in his wife's.

The mysterious illumination had given way to twilight when she came to the diversion from the marsh. One track led to the beach; the other to the collection of low buildings at the top of the rise. The prospect of seeing her old friends and finally resolving the past made her go faster, a stout figure labouring a little as she began the uphill climb.

Sam Playfair had been mulling over the proposition put to him at the Club by Bryan. In retrospect, it was the rationalising of a greedy man. He forgot about it until Kitty drew his attention to their leaky guttering. At the end of her tirade he felt thoroughly demeaned and angry. The issue hardly seemed to be about house maintenance. His wife's cold words and sharp looks rather reflected her opinion of him these days. Since Holly had left home and Leaza, their teenager, was demonstrating a will of her own, Kitty seemed disenchanted with both motherhood and marriage. His sweet, accommodating wife was suddenly a shrew. Her love was showered on their nine-year-old, Joel, who had every gadget and toy he set his heart on. Sam was lost. He hadn't changed. He'd tactfully suggested she ought to see a doctor, thinking it might be one of those woman-type phases, but all he got for that suggestion was a double dose of rage. He felt even more wary of discussing their problems. Anything for peace! All marriages went through rough times. Best just go softly, give her what she wanted, and hope for better days. Which led to his phoning Bryan and agreeing to act as agent for the land sales. These were low-lying blocks on the coast near the Pelican commune. Bryan promised to pick him up on the Saturday morning and drive him out to take a look.

Sam, who had a rust problem in his Holden Sunbird, experienced daggers of envy as he swung himself aboard the high-slung Land Cruiser. He felt like a general overseeing the foot soldiers as Bryan revved up, alarming pedestrians who scurried for the pavements. Bryan grinned. He pressed the CD controls, shocking Sam as the thud of bass line careered through his body and plunged into his belly.

'Six speakers. Graphic equaliser. Ten stack replay feature,' Bryan rattled off as they passed the wide-verandahed pub on the corner. A landmark, it now catered for commercial travellers, regular drinkers and some patient dogs sitting and scratching while they kept hopeful eyes on the saloon's doorway. Rusty pick-ups and old V8s were angle-parked, windows wound down. The road crossed the railway line, bypassing a few old houses and sheds as it led on to open countryside. One finger on the steering wheel, Bryan reached for the mobile and dialled.

'Dixie? Hi, lover! Sam and I are headed out to see about those coastal blocks. We'll need a pretty name when we subdivide... *The Mudflats* hasn't got quite the right ring. Put your thinking cap on and I'll book that cruise you fancied.'

Whatever Dixie said made him laugh suggestively. 'I'm playing our song, sweetie. See you later.'

He accelerated. Stones spurted from the tyres and crows flapped away from roadkill they were gourmandising. The bush on either side of the highway had survived a minor fire. Natural cycles of destruction and regrowth already clothed stripped eucalypts in a tender reddish haze. Sunlight flickering through the undamaged canopy had a hypnotic effect on Sam, who closed his eyes and leaned back. He didn't want to think about the euphemisms or lies of omission that might result from this journey. Instead he listened to the music; Country stuff about loneliness and the love that used to be. Sam found himself thinking over that recent scene with Kitty. A memory of her as a girl came to his mind. In school she'd been the teacher's pet: never late, never in trouble, homework neat and handed in on time. She'd run the Sunday School class at their church. During their engagement he distinctly remembered her saying she only wanted Sam, children and a house in Trundle, near her parents. Later, when she opened her little shop, she managed to fit work and family duties into a smooth operation.

Why was she different? What did she want? His life wasn't exactly a fun fair. There was nothing thrilling about leasing shops, valuing farms or playing the go-between for tight-wallet landlords and their troublesome tenants, like Nora Halpin. Christ, she'd aged! An image of her tough, bruised-looking face made him shift restlessly.

Bryan had been lost in his own reverie.

'People laughed at me, reckoned I was throwing money into a bog when I bought this land. You just watch all those city greengrocers and pizza bar owners jump at a chance to own a cheap bit of the coast.'

'You say the land's zoned non-residential. What good is it?'

'Ownership, mate! Land title. Nobody would want to build on the outskirts of a dump like Trundle. Anyway, councils have been known to change their zonings.'

Brian rubbed his thumb and finger together in a gesture of graft. Sam felt offended. Trundle was his birthplace. He liked the town. But why provoke an argument? He turned his attention back to the music. People must lead generally miserable lives, by the sound of this CD. He certainly wasn't enjoying this ride to view some shady deal. His thoughts roamed through money worries, Kitty's moods, kids leaving or turning into surly strangers overnight…

'Here we are!' Bryan swung the wheel so sharply that Sam wondered if he'd dislocated his neck. They proceeded to take a rodeo ride along a rutted track until Bryan stopped abruptly and raked on the hand brake. The racket of the engine and the CD player gave way to the solemn peace of the bush as the two men stepped down and looked around. Whip birds, frogs and the waters of a rushing stream played like tranquil music, inviting them to enter a place of contemplation.

'It's a pretty place,' conceded Sam, giving his baggy pants a hitch.

'Got a bit of a trek ahead,' Bryan said. 'The fifty acres we can carve up are down on the coast.'

'Near Pelican commune?'

'Where the nutters hang out? Yeah. Actually, they made a damn good investment. Their land's well above the water.'

'You mean yours has a flood risk?'

'Only on king tides.'

'So that explains the zoning.' Sam wished he'd come dressed for a bush walk. Despite the hot weather it was damp underfoot and his leather shoes skidded on loose dirt and leaf mould.

'Anything can be fixed these days. Bit of drainage, that's all.'

Sam imagined the type of people who would buy such a doubtful investment as Bryan described. They would hardly be shrewd businessmen; more likely folk with a little nest egg put by. He didn't like to think of it being lost on a folly.

Bryan was clearly not troubled by such doubts. He strode ahead, his Akubra at a tilt, and at the top of a slope stood poised like an explorer claiming the entire vista as his own. The pathway forked here. Below, bush thinned to marshland dappled with reeds and water holes, beyond which glistened a quiet sea.

'The commune's up that path.' Bryan waved towards a collection of low roofs higher up. 'We take the low road. Come on, old boy, you're dragging the chain a bit there.'

He bounded on ahead while Sam picked his way carefully. There was a salty tang, and the plaintive mewls of sea birds. Within ten minutes they'd crossed the marsh. Certainly Bryan's land, fronting onto the wide beach of low tide, looked in these summer conditions to be an ideal retreat for any jaded city dweller. Frowning at the sunlight, Sam wandered about, rasping his fingers across his chin as though confirming an irritation he did not express. Bryan was eyeing him.

'I'm only asking you to list them. I'll take care of the advertising.'

'If I list them I'm endorsing them.'

'If you don't, someone else will, mate. They'll be the ones laughing all the way to the bank.'

'They're pretty enough, but basically they're useless tracts. I mean, you can't farm them, mine them, build on them. What do you do with them?'

'I don't know mate! People buy anything. Look, this is legal. If city blokes want to come up here and stick up a tent short-term they can.'

'How would you get through? It's a fair hike with camping gear on your back.'

'It's not my problem! Sam, I'm not here to argue with you.' Bryan adopted a businesslike tone. 'If you want the agency, great. Actually there's another bloke I know who's dead keen. Well, I prefer to deal locally, but...'

Sam eyed the empty expanse of ocean; he wished he were a solo sailor in his own boat.

'OK, Bryan, let's head back. We'll sort out the details in my office.'

As they turned, he saw several people coming along the beach, and recognised Marie at the same time as she waved. He didn't know the young woman or child. Must be from the commune. He didn't wait to chat. Trundle's grapevine rambled into every household. Now Kitty would be informed that Sam had been at Pelican. He imagined his wife's reaction if he turned down Bryan's financial proposition. He hoisted his pants again and followed Bryan to the car, noting how well his moleskins fitted. Even the splashes of mud on his elasticised boots had that casual designer flair.

Still in her dressing gown, Marie sat down at the Stedman's dining table, where Laurie was setting out a full English breakfast. Already he was sprucely shaved and cologned. Honor too upheld their standards; she wore a tailored frock, stockings and Cuban heels. The Stedmans had never seen fit to get about like hippies in the bush.

'Remember the old days?' Sunshine caught the gold-brown tinted lights in Honor's swept-up hair. She was referring to the founding days of the commune, where, in the late '70s, alternative lifestylers arrived in the area. They could hardly have been a more diverse group, except that all sought a different way of life based on the land. Pelican was the name they adopted for their new home.

Marie smiled, sharing the mood of nostalgia. She could hardly recall the naïve girl she'd been. Young and inexperienced, she'd felt out of her depth among those with drug habits or free love theories. Perhaps that was why she'd turned to the Stedmans for company and advice, or spent her time with married couples and their kids. That was how she met Hugh. In scanty shorts and a tie-top, she did her share of daily chores, or in wet weather joined their circle around a log fire. They sang Dylan songs, burned incense, read Castaneda. It was a time of energetic building. Everything had to be started from scratch: steps hewed from the clay, dwellings erected, gardens dug and planted. As a commune, everyone was entitled to have their say; a process that could seem intolerably slow and indecisive.

Honor and Laurie Stedman must have then been in their fifties. Both were well-educated and widely travelled people. Honor had the particular distinction of knowing Gurdjieff's system, having lived and studied under John Bennett at Coombe Springs in England. Before that she'd followed an Eastern system of spiritual development under an Indian swami. She liked to tell stories about those days. When she invested her savings in a large parcel of the land, peace of soul and growth of consciousness were her motives in choosing this place as her retirement home. Laurie, her mild-mannered second husband, did not care much where he settled, as long as they were together. He did not feel her passion to keep Pelican on a spiritual course, though his unpretentious daily life reflected an essential kindness and good will.

The other main investor had been a Dutchman, Richard Van Rjien. Likewise a well-travelled man, he came to the commune in his early thirties. He too was widely read in esoteric and spiritual teachings, but his soul and his personality seemed to be at war. A clever, go-getting *entrepreneur* with disdain for non-intellectuals, he was intolerant of those who enjoyed a simple faith, and took particular delight in pointing out the flaws both of individuals and the creeds they clung to. He had money, and his superior manner made him a respected but disliked figure at the commune. Before long it was plain that a pecking order was trying to take over; in particular, he and Honor disagreed in a way suggesting that, as idealists, they might have left the world behind, but their natures were firmly in residence and keen to engage in human conflict.

'Tell me what's going on these days,' said Marie. 'I'm surprised to find the place still here.'

'Pelican is what it was always meant to be. A community. We're not motivated by profit, we are conservationists, we have room here for the weak who seek healing.'

Honor sounded so adamant that Marie felt reproved, while Laurie patted his wife's hand.

'Times change, my dear.'

'I'm not exactly in my dotage, Laurie. I know times change. It's the direction of change that I object to.'

'Are you unhappy about something?' Marie asked.

Honor's face was flushed. 'It's That Man, Marie. He has Greedy Plans Afoot, but I have the antidote.' Whatever this mystery entailed she was not prepared to divulge. Laurie spoke mildly to Marie. 'Richard Van Rjien has a plan to open up our land here; to build some kind of high-class resort for the public. Tourism with a difference, perhaps.'

He did not sound opposed to the idea but his wife bristled with anger.

'Tourism with a difference! Can you just imagine it! Japanese honeymooners snapping photos, Americans looking for the golf course...'

'It's hardly realistic.' Marie's tone was soothing, for she could see that such a change would threaten her ageing friend's security. 'Developments like that cost millions.'

'Don't think that would stop him! He's got more contacts in the financial scene than you can count. He's saying we've become redundant.'

'How can people be redundant?'

'He means the concept of Pelican. He says we serve no social role now.'

'Do we?' prompted Laurie, and his wife's indignant back straightened.

'We might need a new direction and that's exactly what I propose.' Her blue eyes fixed on Marie. 'I have a friend in London—an eminent doctor with a keen interest in alternative medicine. Running a healing centre might be right up his street. We've been corresponding.' She would not be drawn further.

The talk drifted back to the early days. Marie knew that, of all the nonconformists at that time, she'd made the most radical statement by leaving the commune with Hugh, a married man and father. She felt compelled to re-state their reasons for abandoning his wife and child.

'We truly loved each other. It broke my heart when he died. I own that one does more harm than one ever intends.'

Laurie was not a man to absent himself from human failings, and nodded in his understanding way, Honor offered her veined hand with its pearly polished nails and several large rings to reassure her.

'The only human being who's done no harm has surely lain in a coma since birth. Hugh's wife was a difficult woman.'

'The remorse I feel is for his daughter.'

'It's true, poor little Rowena thought her father simply didn't care. She's a grown woman now, and she's lived with her unfortunate mother and her problems. She must have developed insight.'

'Hugh never saw his grandchild.' Marie was close to tears but Honor was determined to be positive.

'It's not too late for you, Marie. You're Pippin's step-grandmother. What if I take you to meet them this morning? She knows you're here.'

As they wandered along the leafy paths of the complex, Honor pointed out changes that had happened over the years. A pretty Asian girl looked up from sweeping a verandah to wave as they passed the most elaborate chalet.

'Who's that?'

'Richard's wife.'

'Richard!' He'd always seemed too aloof to need intimacy.

'Tuti's charming. Far too good for him!'

As if sensing adversarial vibrations, Richard came out from the chalet and eyed the two women. He'd gained some weight and his hair had thinned, exaggerating his domed forehead, but the supercilious manner was evident still.

'Ah, Maree!' He'd always seemed to enjoy mispronouncing her name. 'What calls you to Mecca?'

'Just visiting, Richard. Won't you introduce me to your wife?'

He smiled with an air of ownership, placing his arm around Tuti. She laughed and shyly waved a graceful hand.

'She looks happy,' said Marie.

'So she does.' Bypassing this mystery, Honor led the way to a small garden chalet where a little girl, perhaps four or five years old, ran about tossing a ball to her mother.

'That's Pippin.'

As Marie watched Hugh's grandchild, she was overcome by all her unfulfilled urge to love and nurture. She'd thought they were impossible longings she'd had to displace onto dolls and teddy bears. Honor gave her a gentle push forward and emotion blurred her vision, so that her first impression of Rowena was an angular figure, a tangle of long hair and a noncommittal greeting. But perhaps she sensed the good intentions of the woman who'd lived with her father for so long and made him happy.

'I suppose we could all go for a walk?' she proposed. 'Pippin's been pestering me to take her to the beach.'

'Oh yes!' said Marie, who hated walking. 'Oh yes, I'd like that very much.'

5

They were short-staffed at the hospital and it was late when Ronnie reached home. Marie might have put dinner on to cook? No, the house was in darkness. She read Marie's note and tossed it in the bin. Typical. They'd had an understanding to go through the junk in the living room and start stripping the wallpaper. Now she was off on a jaunt to see old friends. 'Back Sunday.' So be it.

She flicked on the living room light, registering the look of desolation. She'd lived alone, both before and after Max. At least she'd made those places her own. Here, she had to accommodate not just her sister's vagaries but the insubstantiality of ghosts. The cold fingers of her parents' lives prodded her as she looked at unused cups and figurines locked in the china cabinet, ornaments lined up on the mantelpiece, cavernous vases that had never sheltered a love-posy of fresh flowers. The time was overdue to do something about that repellent brown floral carpet and stained wallpaper. Marie had promised!

She pulled the door closed with a slam and looked into Marie's room. Unblinking dolls and teddies gaped back at her. Plump pillows were askew and soft blankets drooped to the floor as though Marie's warm person had just stirred and reached to flip the pages of the decorating magazine lying on the quilt. The fading flowers in the pretty crystal vase released a sickly scent.

In her own room, she hung up her jacket and sat down on her bed. The walls were done in flat ivory paint, the doona had a complex paisley cover. On the desk, study books and the laptop suggested intellectual effort. The CDs in their rack reflected a taste for chamber music. The resident here would have neatly-folded underwear, shoes in pairs, a practical, well-pressed wardrobe. The library books, a biography of Disraeli and a recent Australian novel, weren't due back for another week. On the bedside table stood a clock and angle lamp. Ronnie considered a packet of Panadeine, a torch, Clarins moisturiser. *Who am I?* she thought, kicking off her shoes and swinging her legs up on the bed.

The silence was irritating. She put on Beethoven's Eb piano and wind quintet and lay down again. She'd settle for an easy tea; scrambled eggs and toast. She had the weekend off and, thank God, the howls and barks next door had eased since the fence went up. Marie wasn't a bad diplomat, giving credit where due. Handled by Ronnie, there would probably be a lawsuit underway by now. The Lals certainly had their problems. An image of Mrs Lal's drawn face came to her. Nursing took and took from you. Sometimes she wished she'd chosen any other profession but it was a bit late to change now. It was hard to walk away from suffering and switch on the mood for fun. Fun! She'd forgotten what the word meant. Doubtless Marie and her friends knew.

A cramp woke her. She must have dozed. Another dream, this time of Max, demanding his running shoes. Funny how he'd made such a point of not caring about their age difference. It must have always been an issue, buried under good intentions. What had alerted her psychic watchdog to think of Max? Choosing the Beethoven earlier, she'd noticed a Joan Armatrading CD he'd once given her. The past lived on, in music, in gifts, in certain streets and place names. Sometimes she felt so lonely. With Max, she'd made the fatal mistake of adopting his ways, his friends.

All that was gone. Moving back to Trundle had compounded her feeling that she had no friends. She thought of her sister, at that moment no doubt lapping up company. Well, there was one advantage to her absence. Ronnie had the place to herself. That could save a lot of argument about what ought to go from the living room. There were spare boxes in the shed. Ditching the past was long overdue and Ronnie was in the mood to do the deed. She'd be up and on the job first thing. To hell with the past! Marie was in for a surprise when she came home.

By ten o'clock next morning she'd been to town, made an appointment with a second-hand furniture dealer, hired a wallpaper stripper, collected paint cards and bought a tin of undercoat. Having a project filled her with vigour. No sleeping pill; no bad dreams. No wonder people saw a demolition derby as entertainment; wrecking what you didn't want was quite a buzz.

The dealer had promised to call before lunch. By the time he came, she had packed up every unlovely ornament and picture, pulled down the blinds and curtains, and stacked the tapestry firescreen, fire irons and coalscuttle. Everything except the piano was to go. They'd start from scratch with clean walls, new carpet or perhaps polished boards and a good rug.

She accepted the dealer's first offer. He and his offsider loaded up the van. As they prepared to drive away Ronnie waved.

'You've forgotten these.' She indicated the ornaments and *bric-a-brac*.

'Sure you don't want them, lady?'

'I don't want them.'

He packed them with the other goods and sped away.

Her first project was to take up the old carpet. It was tacked down in strips—not difficult to prise free. Newspapers from the fifties acted as an underlay. Briefly she sat back on her heels to skim the cheap prices and dated fashions of the day. The pontifical editorials would be unacceptable to a modern readership. Were the fifties really so long ago? She'd been born at their tail end herself, in the April of 1959; Marie arrived in the new decade in late February 1962. Their mother would have sat in her kitchen to nurse the new baby and keep an eye on her jealous three-year-old, while she turned these same pages, reading the sale columns, eyeing the household appliances, wishing perhaps she could afford to go to town and deck herself out in some of the smart apparel worn by fashionplates.

Under the newspapers, Ronnie uncovered money—ten shilling and pound notes. She counted it up. Twenty pounds. The old currency made her unexpectedly sad. It seemed to convey all the fears of her parents' frugal existence. Who could guess what that hidden hoard was to save them from? No doubt it had meant much scrimping to collect the money in the first place. She left it on the kitchen table to show Marie, later, and carried the heap of newspaper out to the incinerator, where she set a match to it and watched it burn away to ash.

She was starving. Physical work was always her best antidote to brooding. She made coffee and sandwiches before setting to work to strip the wallpaper. It was a big job but she'd break the back of it by Sunday. Then would come the fun part of redecorating.

Humming that lovely *Andante cantabile* from the Beethoven, she felt empowered. She'd never realised how rooms and objects inflicted such memories. Her mother had died after a relatively minor illness. Another woman might have put up a fight. It was as though she'd considered the future, and shaken her head. Ronnie had seen that often. The ones you might expect to die could defy all odds, while others faded before your eyes. They asked no questions, accepted any treatment, lay passively, neither raging nor weeping at the injustice of illness.

She had such a one under her care at present. Cancer patients usually went through the whole gamut of emotion: fear, anxiety, anger, sorrow, a determined curiosity regarding all their treatment options. Mrs Lal showed none of these reactions. Her docility wasn't a good sign though it made her an easy patient. It was to be hoped that Sandy Smith's intuition was at fault. That girl, clumsy and plain though she was, had a rapport with her patients. She had the makings of a compassionate nurse. Pity she couldn't train locally. Modern tertiary education for nurses had its point; Ronnie herself had sent for the course outline for extramural studies in administration. But as far as young ones went, there was nothing like on-the-job experience and a dose of the healthy discipline that Ronnie had been subjected to, back in her training days.

Marie sang along with her Abba tape as she drove home on Sunday afternoon. She'd kept every tape she'd ever bought before CDs came out. Some people wrote diaries to record their lives; her memories were stored in things. She knew exactly the kind of shop she wanted to set up. Discarded objects handled with love could resume their original significance and value.

Waterloo! Knowing my fate is to be with you! She felt like a teenager, dressing up to the nines and heading off with Kitty to a Saturday night disco. Her life had done a sharp about-turn. The years of regret and mourning were over. Now she was renewing friendships and planning a brand-new business. Hugh's daughter was warming to her and little

Pippin was adorable. Thinking of the pleasures a grandmother could look forward to, Marie put her foot down. Who'd know, on these back roads?

Abba's comeback had been a huge success. Now it was her turn. *Waterloo! Finally facing my Waterloo!* She was on the home stretch into town before she knew it. The shops were closed and Main Road was deserted, but spring declared itself in cultivated gardens, where pink and port-wine magnolias flowered, fallen camellias lay in drifts and golden forsythias speared the blue backdrop of sky. The sweet cascade of jasmine welcomed her home. Something was different there; a mound of wallpaper sagged on the porch and the house smelled of chemicals.

'Ronnie?'

Her sister, in a work-worn tracksuit, was relaxing on the window seat in the living room, which had been stripped bare. Their parents' lives were erased. A dustsheet moulded the shape of the piano. Everything else was gone: carpet, furniture, ornaments, pictures, curtains, blinds and wallpaper. Ronnie raised her glass.

'Welcome home! Grab a drink. I'm too tired to move.'

'What have you done? Where's all the stuff?'

'I've saved you the trouble and got rid of it.'

'Ronnie! I didn't agree to that! I wanted to pick out some mementoes.' She wanted to cry. The happiness of the weekend had gone.

'You didn't say. I had a dealer pick up everything. He didn't offer much, there was nothing of value.'

'Mum and Dad didn't think so. I just wanted a few things.'

'Well, I didn't know.' Her sister sounded impatient. 'You'll have to go and buy back what you want. You can use what he paid.' She laughed. 'Guess what? I found some money Dad stashed under the carpet. The mean old bastard must have forgotten about it. Can you still change old currency?'

'I've no idea. You shouldn't talk of poor Dad that way.'

'Poor Dad my eye! Mum had to manage on the smell of an oily rag. That carpet was laid in the fifties. I could tell from the dates on the newspapers.'

'I suppose they've gone too?'

'Well of course. Why keep newspapers? I burnt them. You're in a mood! Get yourself a brandy. Was the weekend a flop?'

Marie walked away. It was so like Ronnie to take over, then expect gratitude. She'd be bewildered if Marie said she felt violated, as though someone had smashed the vases on her parents' graves.

On Monday she visited the second-hand shop and explained the situation to the dealer. He led her through to the back room where he kept unpriced stock. Removed from their home, the piled furniture now had the look of junk. Marie sorted through the smaller items. In a way Ronnie was right. Marie couldn't imagine the china ducks in frozen flight on her bedroom wall, or the Dewar's Whisky ashtray on her dressing table. In the end she decided to buy back a cut-glass fruit bowl and a stained tapestry cushion she thought might clean up. Perhaps her mother's hands had stitched it. Taking her opportunity to browse, she poked around the other stock, selecting a silver teaspoon and a promising decanter. One box of bric-a-brac reflected an oriental slant. She picked out an ebony elephant she liked and thumbed through a few books. One, a reference work about the Taj Mahal, might interest Mr Lal. She added it to her purchases and paid the dealer.

Had she over-reacted to Ronnie's efforts? She'd meant well. They'd hardly spoken this morning. Some deep difference between their personalities was creating misunderstandings every day. It wasn't a pleasant way to live. Ronnie might find conflict stimulating, but it wasn't Marie's way. In all her years with Hugh, they'd rarely argued, and never had a serious fight. The thought of Hugh reminded her of the commune's attractions. It would be fun to participate in the plans to revitalise its purpose. Honor had hinted she would be welcome to rejoin. Unless Ronnie changed her attitude, she might find her sister taking steps to accommodate herself elsewhere.

The weekend wasn't referred to again. The careful truce on the home front was only set aside when Ronnie brought home the news that Mrs Lal's condition had deteriorated. Doctors wanted to transfer her to a distant hospital for radiotherapy and chemotherapy, but she remained silent and refused to eat.

'Surely she's not going to die?' said Marie. Although she hardly knew Shanti, she'd seen she was the hub of the family. How would Mr

Lal cope if he was left with an estranged son, a wilful daughter, and disoriented old people who'd come halfway round the world to rejoin their daughter?

Ronnie shrugged. 'As far as I can see, she has no will to live. There's no cure for that.'

Marie turned away. 'You sound very hard.'

'Maybe my job makes me that way.'

'Then you ought to get a different job.' Marie walked out of the room.

She was wondering whether to pay a call next door. Perhaps it would be better to write a little note. She could compose a tactful message; just a few sentences on a greeting card, offering her support. She would slip the envelope, and the book she'd bought, into the letterbox on her way to work in the morning. It was hard to know what was appropriate, particularly when she knew so little about their culture, but friendship must surely be a universal need.

Marie's emotions were a minefield, decided Ronnie. Her sister had gone off to her room in another huff. She didn't understand why a nurse couldn't afford to wallow in tea and sympathy. You never got used to death. One kept up a professional front, monitoring signs, relieving suffering, helping the relatives through their waiting; yet another's death was only a pass call on one's own. It was impractical for Marie to talk of changing jobs. A frivolous career change mid-life wouldn't keep her in her old age. Her faith in universal manna was childish.

Ronnie showered and went off to her own room to read. She browsed through the administration course outline. Somehow it didn't grab her. One was expected to climb the ladder, of course; she ought to keep up if she wanted promotion or even job security in these days of hospital cutbacks and closures. She was lucky to have a job at all. Why think of tossing it? Yet the posters of Paris and Rome she'd pinned above the desk filled her with wistful imaginings. Others who felt as she did simply packed their bags and headed for those cities of their dreams. What had stopped her? Career, marriage, a sense of duty to her sister? She imagined booking plane tickets, resigning, and simply taking off. *By the way, Marie, I'll be away six months, just popping over to Europe.*

Dreamland! Reality was the hospital and painting the living room walls.

She read a few chapters of an old Simenon detective story, swallowed a sleeping pill and switched off the light. Waiting for sleep to come, she imagined herself wandering through cathedrals, art galleries and parks in the romantic cities of her fantasies. She'd be travelling light, this slim smiling woman in casual summer dress; a rucksack on her back and all the time in the world to explore. She'd walk in the Tuileries, visit Notre Dame and stroll beside the Seine. She'd feed the pigeons by Rome's fountains, see the Sistine Chapel, and climb the ancient hills.

But her dreams were uneasy when she drifted into sleep. She was supposed to bury a woman who seemed co-operative until Ronnie told her to get into the coffin. Then she resisted. Ronnie offered her three aspirins and still the woman went on arguing. Ronnie was frantic because she couldn't carry out her orders. The woman wouldn't die.

Startled awake, she lay staring into the darkness. Who was that woman? Marie? Herself? She'd have to get off those sleeping pills. Maybe bad dreams were a side effect. The Lal's dog let out a few forlorn howls. For once she didn't mind. At least one fellow dreamer shared her night terrors.

Her sleep was disturbed again at dawn. She heard the Lal's gates clang shut, a car engine, and then the dog's volley of protest at being abandoned. When she turned up for the morning shift, the night staff reported that Mrs Lal had been moved out of the ward and the family summoned. Ronnie quietly entered the single room. Here the stricken Lals formed a tableau by the bedside. She felt uncomfortable, having no facile words of comfort to offer. They would have no interest in medical facts, such as that a sudden deterioration like this wasn't uncommon, or that the poor woman's condition was far too advanced for a cure. With invasive treatment she could only have lasted months and she'd chosen not to fight. She lay peacefully, seemingly asleep. Her parents looked doubly aged by shock and bewilderment. The daughter's face was blotched and her eyes bleary with weeping. The son, obviously devoted to his mother, clasped her limp hand, while her husband remained standing at the far end of the bed. He glanced at Ronnie but did not speak, and she could think of nothing useful to offer him. Quickly checking the patient, she left the room.

The normal hospital routines went on. Meal trolleys rattled past, people on intravenous therapies wheeled their drip stands along the corridors. Convalescents read, knitted, and tidied themselves for visitors. Medications were given out and the day's reports were written up. Ronnie, on her rounds from ward to ward, continually thought of the Indians at their vigil. They would not know whether the dying woman even cared that they were there. By midday she was unconscious. Her dying was without struggle; its pain was for those who loved her. It had seemed unlikely their wait would be a long drawn out affair, but each time a nurse went to check and turn the patient, there was little change. They shouldn't have been called in so soon, thought Ronnie. She told Mr Lal that, if he wished, they could all go home and wait for further news.

'We will stay,' was all he said, but his look was eloquent. She ordered tea and sandwiches to be taken in to them. The tray was left untouched. Perhaps eating and drinking in Shanti's presence struck them as disrespectful. They looked weary and confused as they settled back into the waiting. Ronnie checked the doctor's orders on the chart and spoke to the sister in charge of the ward.

'We'll give Mrs Lal her morphine now.'

The charge sister sounded dubious. 'She hasn't needed it so far.'

'Well we can't ask her if she's in pain.'

'But she's not conscious.'

'Her doctor has charted morphine p.r.n. and in my judgement it's time to give it, sister. Will you check the drug please?'

Ronnie administered the injection herself. The watching family asked no questions. Soon Shanti's unconsciousness deepened and her breathing became shallow and irregular. She passed away at 2.30, just in time for her death to be written up in the dry shorthand of the report and relayed to the incoming staff, one of whom was Sandy Smith. The girl looked her usual dishevelled self, hair hanging over her eyes and a ladder in one stocking. Ronnie bit back her reprimand and instead beckoned the assistant nurse aside.

'When the family leave, Mrs Lal will have to be washed and made ready for the morgue. You can assist. I assume you've never laid out a patient?'

Sandy shook her head. As usual, she looked terrified; whether of the supervisor or of death Ronnie couldn't tell. She opted for the latter.

'It's part of every nurse's experience. You can just observe if you like. I'd like you to take a message in to the family before they leave. Mrs Lal's personal effects have to be collected from the front office.'

Sandy went off reluctantly to speak to the Lals, who were still taking their leave of Shanti. Ronnie well remembered how awesome and alarming her own first brush with death had felt. Yet a corpse was only an abandoned house without a ghost to fear. Every young nurse had to face that moment for herself.

The supervisor was glad to go off duty and head for home. Marie wasn't back from work. Ronnie had a bath and was relaxing on her bed when a familiar car stopped. She went to break the news of Mrs Lal's death to Marie, who immediately looked stricken.

'You hardly knew the woman.' Ronnie intended comfort but her sister burst into tears. She'd visited the Lals and formed an impression that as a family group they were vulnerable.

'Those poor old folk, without a word of English. And the children at that awkward age. As for her husband…'

'He was quite composed.'

Marie shook her head. 'I've spoken to Mr Lal a few times, at Kitty's shop. He's not easy with his feelings, but it's plain he's a sensitive man.'

She glanced over to the looming house next door.

'Poor man, there's his dream, and what use is it to him now?'

'The lives we'd lead if we weren't ourselves!' But as Ronnie wryly dismissed the fate of dreamers, she was thinking of those journeys she'd never made.

Marie disagreed. Her present life was fuelled by a hope that, through Hugh's daughter and Pippin, she might yet experience family life and mothering.

'Everybody needs a dream,' she said.

'You run the risk of losing it.'

'That's what I meant, Ronnie. If the children leave home and Shanti's parents go back to India, that big house will be empty. He'll be alone.'

'Aren't we all?' Ronnie shrugged. She was tired of the topic.

'Is that how you feel?' Marie was upset. 'We're not alone! I was, when Hugh died. But not now. We're sisters, we have each other, don't we?'

Her honest eyes blurred with affection and tears. Ronnie gave her sister's plump shoulder an awkward hug.

'Oh, let's have a brandy! For heaven's sake, no waterworks. Of course we have each other.'

PART 2

THE TAJ MAHAL OF TRUNDLE

PART 2

1

The settled residents of Alexandra Avenue owned single-storied homes set off by well-tended grounds and mature trees. Ronnie's and Marie's cottage garden in April was a sweet-smelling confusion of scattering rose petals, daisy bushes, hollyhocks and end-of-summer bedding plants. The Lals' house, next door, was a marked contrast. Its iron gates were closed against visitors. The side fence and long concrete driveway created a self-contained, remote atmosphere. Bougainvillaea, robbed of summertime's cerise blaze, framed the entrance porch with thorny branches. In spite of lights at several windows, there was an impression tonight that no one was at home.

Inside, the family went their separate ways. The old woman Sunita counted out her husband's evening medicines. Vimla, no longer a schoolgirl, watched the evening news while she filed her nails. Vijay's girl friend was ironing shirts in the laundry while he, in his room upstairs, fiddled with Shearer's slur and reach exercises on his guitar.

The head of the household was rarely seen these days. Since Shanti's death, Mr Lal spent most of his time in his own room, the door closed. His normal routines had gone. During the day he pushed aside neglected financial dealings, napped, or sometimes turned the pages of the book he'd been given by his neighbour. Marie's thoughtful gesture made him feel there was at least one kindly heart in this unfriendly town. The book contained a history of the 17th century Mughal ruler, Shah Jahan, who had ordered the building of the Taj Mahal in memory of his favourite wife. The historical detail, intricate photography and impassioned verses of court poets of that era addressed his heart; verses which described so intricately and in such detail the Shah's emotions when his beloved Mumtaz died. Even the magnificence of his concept failed him in his grief. The Illumined Tomb proved that mourning afflicted all, however rich or powerful.

If Mr Lal's days dragged, it was the nights he dreaded. Sleepless, he would reflect on his marriage and accuse himself of the lost opportunities of his past with Shanti. Sometimes, to escape his loneliness, he would lift down her ashes from the wardrobe. So light she was; weighing no more than a large packet of rice. He would sit with the container on his knee and speak to her. He felt she was listening, as she always had. So he sat tonight, contemplating the package. In his imagination he summoned her from the shadows, hearing her *sari* rustle as she squatted to place offerings and carry out *puja*. They had migrated together, thirty years before. He'd known his own course and overridden the fears of a simple girl. When the day came to leave her homeland, Shanti had clung to her parents and wept, but his decision stood.

Now he cradled the package in his hands, privately pleading for some sign from his wife's spirit.

'Six months, Shanti! Look at me now, I who never showed weak feelings. You should be here! Why did you leave me? I am ten years older than you. I should die before you! Have you deserted me and gone home to India?'

He imagined her spirit soar free above the holy places. He had only this memorial, her ashes in his hands. He couldn't abandon her to a pigeonhole at the crematorium. Such earth-bound confinement, the custom in this country, was inappropriate for an Indian.

For a long while he sat reflecting. All those years of building his business and making his money, he'd hardly thought of India. Strange how memories were returning now. Its religions were honoured in the architecture of mosques and temples; palaces and forts acknowledged its rulerships and wars. History was worn into the very street cobbles and gazed from the sombre eyes of its people. By comparison, he had sentenced Shanti to a raw and untried landscape. No wonder she'd clung to her past, a traditional wife who ran the house and raised the children, and eventually demanded her old parents must be brought to be cared for in the new country. Fortunately that application had been approved without exercise of the xenophobic slogan, *Australia for*

Australians! That catch-cry from a past decade reminded him of uneasy moments when the colour of his skin drew hostile attention. Had Shanti ever suffered similar insults? She was a humble woman; perhaps she hadn't expected others to value her. It was fitting she should go home to rest. He hadn't the energy to consider such a trip yet, but the idea gave him hope.

'We'll go later,' he promised as he returned the box to the wardrobe. 'We always said we would.'

The silence in the empty room overwhelmed him and he wept, whispering through his tears, 'Shanti? If I can find a way to sleep tonight, speak to me with a sign. Tell me you are really here?'

Sandy woke to the rooster at calm first light. Each morning she opened her eyes and lay in bed, reassured by that homely crowing. It made her new status (for eight weeks now, the live-in girlfriend of Vijay Lal) seem real, for most of the time she felt quite disbelieving. Here she was, plain and ordinary Sandy Smith, living in style with the Lals.

Several weeks after his mother's death, Vijay had waited for her outside the hospital and invited her to his home. At the gate an undisciplined black dog growled and nearly knocked her down but the rest of the visit went very well. She'd never set foot in such a house, which was in the posh part of town. Vijay played her some music, his long fingers teasing sweet sounds from the acoustic guitar like some TV star, she thought. She told him he was very good. Although she'd met his father and the rest of the family during their hospital vigils, Vijay now introduced her properly. His sister, in the throes of sitting her HSC, was only too pleased to take a break from her study books and chat. The elderly people smiled at her, and even the dog wagged its tail as though it wanted her to stay.

Vijay and Sandy began going out together. They went to the pictures and to the Chinese restaurant in Main Road. He took her to a coffee shop where he sat perched on a high stool and played his guitar for half an hour for free; to gain exposure, he said. She didn't invite him to her place, explaining she didn't have a proper family since her Mum had died. There was just her stepfather and stepbrothers at home. Vijay didn't feel rebuffed, much to her relief. Between the grog and the racist jokes, it could have been a very awkward visit. A few weeks after that he borrowed the car and drove her out to park at a peaceful spot beside the river. She'd packed a picnic lunch. They didn't swim. She'd deliberately left her togs at home, deciding she didn't want to show off her white skin and bony knees. In any case, Vijay said he didn't like cold water, even in mid-summer. They sat under the trees in the shade, his arm casually round her shoulders. She was just concluding he must quite like her when he asked if she'd like to move in with him. So taken aback she'd been she'd just said the first thing that popped into her head, which was *I don't mind.* Adding, *but won't your father?*

Vijay said no. His father didn't care about anything these days. The family hardly saw him. In any case, whatever Vijay did was wrong, so it didn't really matter what he thought.

When she met the family in their home setting, Sandy concluded they were, if not strange, then somewhat different. Nobody drank beer, listened to the races, watched the footy, swore, ate pies or hamburgers, or treated her like a servant. Here she was at least looked on as a person. Compared to normality as she understood it, she thought she much preferred the many adjustments living here required.

Of course Vijay was at the heart of all these changes. He lay beside her, sound asleep. Timidly she withdrew her arm, which had pins and needles from his weight. He didn't welcome affection at this hour of the morning. She edged out of bed, collected her clean clothes and went off to the bathroom to get dressed. Steam on the mirror proved that, no matter how early she woke, the old woman Sunita would be up before her. Life-long habits didn't die. Already she would be in the back yard, stooping to collect eggs and pull greens for the hens. She and Sandy communicated with goodwill; a wave or smile that served as their common language.

Sandy shed her pyjamas and hung them on the drying rail next to Vim's glamorous underwear. She surveyed her misty image in the mirror, visualising her small, pink-tipped breasts encased in the leopard-spotted bra, and black lace stretched across her bony hips. Whatever would Vijay say to that? He didn't ogle girls and she'd never heard him speak crudely, like her stepbrothers, as though sex was the be-all of existence. Vijay was not the world's greatest lover, but neither was she. Sex was a shy, infrequent meeting in the dark—just one of the many puzzles that left her on the edge of some exhilarating excursion. She stepped under the comforting flow of warm water, inhaled a sensuous whiff of Vim's new shampoo and began to lather her wet hair. She'd always wanted a sister. Now she almost had one. Yes, life was full of change. That awful supervisor, Sister Gale, now lived right next door. There was a lot of housework and shopping to do. Sunita's spicy food gave her constant stomach upsets. The unruly dog nearly pulled her arm out of its socket whenever she took it for a walk. Vijay was completely unpredictable. But, back at home, people would be demanding to use the bog, yelling for her to hurry up, stop using up the hot water, give others a go. This was a better life. Here nobody minded if the shower ran all day.

Before she left for work, Sandy went to peg out her hand washing. Sunita, her face sombre, was now starting on her domestic chores. She scrubbed the cooking pots with salt and washed by hand, in spite of the automatic machines in the gleaming laundry. Sandy guessed she might be homesick and grieving for her daughter.

'Morning!' she called cheerfully and Sunita persuaded her stiff body to stand straight. She waved. The day was fine and the hens had laid. Her husband was out of bed; they could hear him clearing his nasal passages. The rich golds and flaunting yellows of marigolds set against a heaven as blue as any Indian sky must have caught her eye. She pointed them out, beaming to her fellow early riser as they shared a smile like conspirators.

Vimla despised household preoccupations. She disdained cleaning and had never cooked a meal. In spite of the shock of her mother's death, she had resolutely studied and done brilliantly in the HSC. She had secured a job as cadet reporter with the local press. World news and current events were matters she considered worthy of her attention and her two morning routines involved watching the news and grooming herself to look like the attractive TV presenter she hoped one day to be. Now, in cream-coloured jacket and trim tailored skirt, she ran up the stairs two at a time and burst into her brother's bedroom. When he made no response she rattled the newspaper, bounced on the edge of the bed and dragged the blankets onto the floor. Groaning, Vijay grabbed the sheets.

'Go away!'

'Who said he'd be up at dawn to meditate?'

'God would have woken me if it had been meant. Give me my blanket.'

'You're so lazy! Sandy's been up for ages. Sit up and read Mr Booth's editorial.'

'I don't want to.'

'I'll read it to you. The government wants to privatise the railways. Our train service could be lost.'

'I don't care! Please please go away.'

But Vim began to read aloud. When he moaned and covered his ears she simply raised her voice. 'We must call a public meeting, and get a petition circulating. I have to work but you're free, aren't you?'

'Certainly not.' Vijay had no intention of drafting letters, addressing envelopes or canvassing the district as Vim no doubt planned for him. Her passion for causes was hard to bear, especially before breakfast. No wonder she went through one boyfriend after another. Who could handle such a firecracker? Who wanted to be dragged from sleep and bossed about like this? Sandy was discreet, tiptoeing about, not daring to disturb him. Vim's idea of feminine behaviour was to batter him with his pillow. There was nothing else to do but retaliate, which he did, tickling her while she writhed and shrieked, 'Mind my new jacket, I'll kill you if you crush it!'

Sandy came in, looking apologetic, as though this wasn't her room too.

'I've lost my purse. Oh no! I'll be late. Sister Gale will murder me. Have you seen it, Vijay?'

'No. Did you leave my breakfast ready?' Lately his clothes felt tight and he'd decided he was going on a purifying diet, a decision he already regretted after only one day.

'Yes. An apple and an egg. I kept to the kilojoules you said. Are you sure you haven't seen my purse?'

'Only one egg?'

'Why do you wait on him like a servant?' Vim delivered a sound punch to her brother's belly so that he set her free and rolled away.

'My sister will die a spinster!'

'Better than having a lazy fat husband like you!'

Their game began again while Sandy crawled across the floor, searching under Vijay's scattered clothing. The missing purse had been kicked under the bed. She retrieved it, looking flushed.

'I'm dead meat now. I've missed the bus.'

'Stop worrying. I'll drive you.' Vim was glad of an excuse to claim the car again.

'Thanks! But you'll be heaps early for work.'

'I'll impress Mr Booth. See you in five. I'll just go fix my hair.' Vim scored the winning blow and ran off, laughing. Sandy stooped and shyly kissed Vijay. 'You eat that breakfast.'

Vijay reorganised the pillows, sighing with relief. The girls were on their way. Peace would soon return.

While Vim backed the car from the garage, Sandy scurried to feed Bimbo and pack up her sandwiches, the shopping list, the old man's asthma prescription and Vijay's dry-cleaning. She remembered it was the garbage pick-up day, wheeled the heavy bin down the drive and climbed in beside Vim, sighing as she buckled the seat belt and leant back.

'I wish I didn't have to go to work today,' she murmured.

She was often tired. Her back ached from lifting stroke patients and carrying heavy shopping bags. The death of Mrs Lal had left a vacuum she tried to fill, for she liked to be of use.

'You should make Vijay get a job.' Vim backed rapidly from the driveway, collecting an unfriendly toot from Ronnie Gale, who was also on her way to the hospital. Sandy shrank lower in her seat, but Vim just revved the engine. If the last year had been a time of hard work and unhappiness, this year was going her way. She'd topped the school, got the first job she applied for and had almost secured the Fiat as her own. Having a girl of her own age around the house was another bonus, although Sandy's relationship with Vijay puzzled her.

'What actually do you see in my brother?' she enquired.

Sandy took a while to reply. She didn't understand Vijay. He did not seem to want what normal people wanted. He said he had everything he needed, why should he go out to work? When Sandy thought about this, she saw that it was true. His father provided him with most requirements, while she filled in the missing ingredients. She had soon discovered that the merest hint of commitment made him so restless she would hardly see him for days. What they had in common she couldn't say. She had no interest in meditation or artistic goals. Everyday work suited her. Someone had to do it and it was good to feel needed. The patterns of nature gave her such pleasure. She could sit and stare at clouds swirling, water eddying, the industry of spiders, ants and bees; yet Vijay didn't even see them. They were an odd pair, for sure. Hadn't he said to her, only last week, 'I wonder why we like each other? I'm so unreliable, and you're quite dull.'

She thought she was dull, too. But did he need to say it? All the same, he relied on her now. She earned money, did his laundry, ran his errands, listened to his dreams. What if he did lie in bed and never lend a hand to help? He knew so many interesting facts. He could be so sweet and childlike. He did not ask her to change. He wanted her to be happy. 'Don't you like living here?' he asked, upset when she inquired how long it might be before they found a flat of their own. She had to admit she liked the grand house, the aromas of spices, the way different age groups shared this one hospitable roof.

The deserted air of Main Road gave Trundle the feel of a ghost town. The hospital came into view. Sandy began to gather up her things.

'Thanks awfully for the lift,' she said.

'You didn't answer my question,' Vim reminded Sandy as she parked.

'You mean Vijay? I s'pose I love him. I better run.'

Vim was thoughtful as she drove on to work. The matter-of-fact conviction in Sandy's answer made no sense to her. How could her idle, ordinary brother inspire love? How could plain Sandy feel such a deep emotion? Vim was positive she would both give and demand far more than Sandy was willing to settle for, if that torrent of passion, so much more than the sex she'd known with callow boys, ever claimed her own heart.

2

Mac Booth, editor of *The Trundle Times*, stood at the office window, noting the punctuality of his junior reporter as she exited the front seat of the red car. An unfit bachelor in his late fifties, he was on his way to the monthly Rotary breakfast. This morning he'd made an effort with his dress. He'd discarded his baggy cords in favour of decent trousers, whose creases he'd reset by sleeping on them, and was wearing a plain shirt with buttons straining like the desperate reach of a man plunging over a precipice.

From the driver's door a pair of long legs dangled in space as Vim reached back to gather her possessions. She came to earth, settled her short skirt on her vigorous hips, and marched towards the stairs. Mac wasn't surprised to see her on deck an hour before starting time. He'd sensed a fellow news-hound as soon as the young woman presented herself for her interview. She hadn't been in the job long. Her confidence and drive had won her the position, to which she applied herself with the utmost co-operation; making the tea, reorganising the files, willingly going wherever she was sent on work experience. If families only received a quota of energy, she'd got the lot. Her ethnic background might produce subservient women, her father and brother might seem unworldly, but Vim knew where she was going. The girl had vision. Her goals sparkled in her eyes; her rather sharp nose was keen for the scent of opportunity.

'Good morning,' the editor greeted her as her heels tapped assertively on the wooden floor.

'Mr Booth! What are you doing here early?' inquired Vim as though she regularly checked on the staff's arrivals and departures. So far she showed none of the traits of a worker who counted the hours to pay day.

'There's a Rotary breakfast on. I'm sounding out reactions to this business of the rail cutbacks.' He thought of himself as one of the boys and spent much of his free time socialising at the pub or club. His drab living quarters had little to offer. He wasn't a drinker, but often got wind of a news story over eggs and bacon or a mixed grill at the bistro.

'Can women join? I'd love to!' She clearly liked the idea of committed citizens who couldn't wait for normal work hours.

'I suppose you could apply.' Mac smiled as he fiddled with his sideburns; it was a habit he found reassuring since the bald crown developed. What would the fellows say if he showed up with Vimla in tow? Her carriage, strut and perfume announced a young woman aware of her sexual powers; and Mac had an idea she would stop at nothing to advance her career. Heaven help the man! His usual wariness with women was at full throttle.

Yet there was innocence about her. He guessed she'd never been knocked back, disillusioned. At present she could probe into life's tragedies with impunity. People did not mind her blunt questions; perhaps they were glad to hand over their stories to so uninhibited a girl. Her turn would come, of course. It was a pity life was hell-bent on tumbles, even if his particular trade thrived on bad news.

'Won't you be late?' she reminded him, bossy as a wife.

'I'm on my way. You can hold the fort.' He couldn't help laughing as she marched to her desk like a war correspondent on a mission of international significance.

Vijay had gone back to sleep when the girls left. He was reawakened by the roar and banging of the garbage truck. The incessant activity of his fellow humans was a trying fact. He could not understand the purpose of a life wasted in boring work. People amassed wealth and goods, only to die and leave it all behind for others to squabble over. Such an existence had to be illusion. Nobody appreciated the effort it took to remain untainted by such a lie. How hard he had to work to maintain clear sight! Everything conspired to tell him he was at fault. His father thought so. Vim called him lazy. Even Sandy was casting hints.

He lay in bed and wondered why he existed. He was sure it wasn't to pass exams, progress up a corporate structure, found a family dynasty or amass the trappings of success. People did not seem to notice how time passed, life reached its end and souls took their leave as though they'd never occupied a human form. His mother had made her quiet departure with no apparent review of what had been her life. His father, once a preoccupied man taken up with material concerns, now wandered the house like a ghost. As a child, Vijay had rarely been allowed into his father's office, much less been taken on his knee. In that converted bedroom, papers and ledgers were piled high and numbers covered every sheet of paper. Bills and receipts, bank statements and tax returns consumed his father's time while the rest of the household had to creep about in silence. Figures clearly did not make his parents laugh or want to play with him. Such work did not seem to warrant a lifetime's focus.

Schooling was another disappointment. Vijay was an average student. His sister usually topped her class. Clever as she was, he could not see what use it was to her. She seemed content to fossick among the debris of pointless local news, as though school fairs and marrow competitions mattered.

Vijay observed and stood apart. There was no one he could go to, no priest or guru to guide him in life's meaning. He tried to explain his lack of motivation to Sandy but she said nothing when he told her he had no idea who he was. She couldn't understand why he saw family and society expectations as a trap.

'It's all conditioning.' He tried to explain. 'In this country you're a success if you have a lot of money and drive a Porsche. If I'd been born in Africa I'd be expected to kill a lion. In Vanuatu the elders would test my manhood by pushing me headfirst off a fifty-metre bamboo tower. Do you see?'

She said she did and suggested they rent a video. At least they shared a taste for Science Fiction. Sandy enjoyed the danger and the threat of invasion. Vijay approved of the technology: transporter beams and replicators that made money redundant.

He knew his father judged him to be a failure. How unfair! He was only twenty and had found nothing worthy of effort. Music was a possibility, but his talent was only average. He practised diligently and still heard unsatisfactory sounds when he turned to his guitar. He'd dipped into New Age values. They interested him and he'd read old copies of Sai Baba's and Krishnamurti's ideas. Their general message sounded wise but implementing their teachings was another matter. He'd tried meditation. It was a process full of distraction and boredom for him. He made himself sit cross-legged in his room, waiting for something that never happened. If only he could find a group, or even one single individual, where he could receive advice.

He tried not to care when he saw the disappointment in his father's eyes. When Sandy suggested he could take on pupils, he had to face the fact that she saw music as a money-spinner. He had to shut out her hopes when she admired the red car, or asked if Vijay ever planned to marry and have children. He offended her if he said he felt like going out alone. He had to endure the way she clung during sex as though she'd never let him go. He longed above all else for a vision that would give some point to life. He was afraid he would die without ever finding out.

His stomach rumbled, reminding him of breakfast. Yawning, he rummaged in the wardrobe, not bothering to pick up the clothes he knocked off the hangers. He couldn't find the loose shirt he wanted. He wished he'd never raised the subject of dieting. He felt very hungry. He would see what Sandy's allocation came to, and add a few extras of his own.

He pulled on his bathrobe, went downstairs and began to search the pantry for his favourite honey. There was a sound behind him and he turned and saw his father. Mr Lal must have just awoken. His hair stood on end and his clothes were crumpled. But today his eyes were alight with a peculiar fervour. It was unusual that he'd come downstairs; more so that he warmly embraced his son and began to confide in him.

'Vijay! I have seen a vision. Your mother sent it to me in a dream. I am going to build a model of the Taj. I have seen it, gleaming white, many rooms stocked with merchandise from home. Silks, *saris*, sandalwood: museum of relics, paintings, sculptures. And a restaurant serving Indian cuisine. I will create a centre for people to visit and learn about our culture.'

'Cool!' said Vijay. This was the first confidence his father had ever shared with him. He was uncertain what was expected now.

'Yes, this is your mother's vision. Life continues. I feel her presence, day and night. We speak, not in words, she finds me in some etheric way. Oh, I feel so comforted then. Do you understand?'

Vijay had never heard him use this tone of voice, as though father and son had much in common. Pity and affection filled him. The little man looked lined and weary, very mortal himself apart from the burning glow in his eyes.

'I'll help if you like,' he heard himself promise and added cautiously, 'though it would be a lot of work.'

Mr Lal seized his son by the arm. 'Come upstairs. I want to show you a book detailing the construction of the Taj. I have been studying its origin. It's a topic I find fascinating. Do you know of Shah Jahan? From 1628 to 1658 he ruled a vast empire stretching from Afghanistan to Assam. He married Mumtaz Mahal. She died in childbirth, with their fourteenth child. The Shah was broken-hearted. The court writers produced couplet upon couplet, describing the pall his mourning cast upon his kingdom.' A tragic expression settled on his features as he quoted. *"The face of the world was scratched from both sides, causing two oceans of blood to meet each other.'*'

Mr Lal paused for breath, while Vijay, wondering if the history lesson was over, dipped his finger in the honey jar. This was not a day to think of dieting.

'Suffering has been transformed,' rejoiced his father. 'If Shah Jahan had not been bereaved, there would be no Taj Mahal. Death is the great leveller, Vijay. Shah Jahan grieved as we do. As you do, my poor boy! But now what do we remember of that? Tourists will pay homage to this monument to love. Come now, I want to show you my plan. I've drawn a quick outline.'

Vijay hadn't been to his father's room for months. The neglected atmosphere shocked him. The air smelt stale as though the sheets were never changed or the windows ever opened. Garments lay on the floor, the bed coverings looked chaotic and papers were scattered everywhere. Mr Lal picked up the photograph from the dressing table and offered it for his son's inspection.

'She is here, you know. Her body has left us but we have the memories.'

Vijay stared at his mother's patient face and tears filled his dark eyes. His father however was excitedly gathering his sketches. He opened a book at a floor plan of the famous building.

'See here, the glorious Taj! Notice how the gardens draw one towards the entrance?' He was flipping pages depicting gateways, towers, mosques, porticoes, arches, domes, chambers and cenotaphs.

'Where did you get this book?'

'From Mrs Marie Mortimer. She is a very kind lady. Listen to the poetry! *'When the hand of perpetuity laid that foundation, Impermanence ran fearfully to hide in the desert.'* Such power in a monument!'

Vijay was struggling with the novel experience that he was needed. It was clear to him that his father, now wildly quoting poets of the past, was in a disturbed state. Their roles seemed reversed.

'One thing is a puzzle though.' Mr Lal frowned. 'Elephants.'

'Elephants?'

'Why were they in the vision? Two white elephants flanked the entrance steps, but look at these pictures. There are no elephants anywhere.'

'Mother liked them. She used to say she wished she could go home, just to see them parade.'

'Did she really? Then elephants there will be. Now I have much to do today. I must go and see the bank manager. I will have to liquidise many assets and arrange a loan. I must get started immediately.'

'Not before breakfast,' said Vijay firmly. 'You haven't eaten anything. Get dressed and we'll have something together.'

His father nodded like an obedient child. Vijay felt most uneasy; almost off his food. For once, Sandy would have approved of his moderation.

The appointment at the bank was promptly scheduled.

'I'll come with you,' Vijay said. 'Will I call a taxi?' Vim had the car, and Vijay, who did not enjoy driving, liked walking less.

'No, a short stroll will do us good.'

'If you like.' His father's thrift usually annoyed him. Today however he felt tolerance was called for. 'I'll get changed.'

Vijay surveyed his wardrobe for appropriate attire while Mr Lal put on his suit and packed his briefcase with hastily assembled notes about his fantasy. His bank manager was aware of the scope of his commercial acumen, but this was an unusual proposal. It must be presented persuasively. He would need a loan, for no capitalist stored his wealth under the mattress these days.

The two Indians proceeding towards town at noon were a contrast in every way. One was short and thin, the other tall and plump. The older one wore a brown suit and went briskly. Beside him, walking with a lazy lope, the young one wore black trousers and a zip-front jacket. Each was lost in a world of his own. Neither one noticed how the leaves crunched underfoot or how quilted clouds adorned the benign sky. As they passed the Playfairs' garden, neither saw the white cat sunning itself on the porch, its alert eye on the sparrows on the lawn.

It was a twenty-minute stroll to Main Road, where they passed the RSL Club, just repainted in calamine pink paint and sporting brass lettering and potted palms in the renovated glass foyer. Shops with tattered awnings and drab window displays carried on a desultory lunch-hour trade. Browsers eyed the merchandise, picked up the supermarket specials or sat at Formica-topped tables, lunching on meat pies or salad rolls. Mr Lal imagined the restaurant that would grace his complex. He visualised its atmosphere, so subtle and so ambient, its *papadams, samosas* and *roti* so fresh, its southern curries so hot, its chutneys and pickles so delicious, its side dishes of coconut, plump raisins, cucumber in yoghurt, banana in lemon juice, all so inviting to the palate. Diners would discover a true culinary experience far surpassing any pizza parlour, Chinese takeaway or McDonald's.

Along from the wine shop and the medical centre was a new health food shop, its polished window displaying pyramids of plastic containers, glass bottles and coloured flyers promising stamina, health and long life. Nearby was Marie's shop, *Victorian Gilt,* its lettering also fresh and its display window artfully arranged. It had been open for four months; conservative Trundle shoppers window-gazed and usually walked past. Travellers and tourists, delighted by so quaint a shop in this country town, so far provided Marie's main trade.

At the bank, the two men were asked to take a seat until Mr Bexley returned from lunch. Mr Lal began to rehearse the interview in his mind, while his son stretched out his legs and puzzled over the faint and dogged strumming of guitar chords behind the manager's closed door. G, C, D7, G. Bart Bexley kept an acoustic guitar at work, and devoted his lunch breaks to music practice. He was a frustrated performer who raised his pleasant tenor voice in local light opera productions, headed the carollers at Christmas time, and secretly wished to join a country band. The *Teach Yourself Guitar* manual was hard to follow. While he fumbled through its lessons, his stubby fingers trembled and his kindly face perspired. He sang the words of sad folk songs in his mind—today, *I Wish I were Single Again.* Not that he did; he thought of himself as a happily-married man who was fortunate in his wife, his children, and his calling in life. Contentment marked his face, and he looked on every transaction at the bank as a further opportunity to make supplicants' dreams come true. For they were invariably empowered by some vision that only money could make real. Where he could, Bart loved to assist in the acquiring of a modest home, a car, a holiday. In this way, he had partaken of a thousand destinies and he was genuinely upset if he had to decline a loan request or issue a repossession order. His clients in Trundle were on the whole a stable lot and he'd turned down promotion to a livelier centre. In this quiet town he could afford to have friends as well as clients.

Punctually at one o'clock he returned his guitar to its case and welcomed Mr Lal and his son into his office with a genial handshake. The father's accounts were significant and Bart leaned forward receptively to inquire into the nature of the present visit. Mr Lal decided not to go into the details of Shanti's psychic communication. Instead he stressed how the building of an Indian cultural centre had commercial advantages for Trundle's tourist market. Beyond the Taj Mahal's façade would operate a thriving industry, including shops, stalls and exhibitions.

Bart carefully examined the portfolio of photographs and scribbled plans laid out on his desk. Surely this unorthodox investment must have been researched.

'Do you have a business plan? This town needs new developments. If they do reduce the rail links we'll be scratching to exist at all. This could give tourism and local employment a boost.'

He smiled at Mr Lal. He was no fly-by-night. He was an accountant and a wealthy man; all achieved through years of sacrifice. No doubt about it, these Indian chaps weren't afraid of hard work. 'There's the ethnic significance of the project as well,' he continued, warming to the vision of a Taj Mahal just up the road from the bank. 'You could have concerts, musical performances, that sort of thing.' He could visualise *sitar* players and veiled dancers.

Mr Lal relaxed at this receptive opening. 'The first step is to get approval for the finance.'

'How much? I'd need the approval of Head Office for a project of this size.'

'My equity is guaranteed.'

'I don't question that. You're talking big money, Mr Lal. Have you considered asking Council for a subsidy? Rotary might fund raise. Why not put it to them?'

'I'm not a member. I've never been invited.'

'It's an insular town.' Bart looked apologetic. 'I'll nominate you if you like. I think this idea is great. Unfortunately it's beyond my authority. Head Office will want it backed up with figures.'

'Naturally!' This was a topic both men were at home with.

Assets, equities, securities and strategies were tossed back and forth while Vijay repressed a yawn and wondered what brand of guitar lay hidden in the music case. In his mind he went over some chord progressions for a song he was writing until, startled, he heard his name spoken in a tone of evident pride by his father.

'Vijay is a fine performer. He will be happy to arrange some music lessons for your son.'

'Thanks!' Bart beamed. 'I might even enrol myself. Meantime, you follow up on the preliminaries. Write to Council. Have a look around for a suitable site. Get a proper business plan drawn up and we'll take it from there.'

'Right!' Mr Lal stood up. 'I'll call at the land agents' on my way home. Are you ready, Vijay?'

The three men parted in an atmosphere of bonhomie.

3

Marie Mortimer said she ran her antique and old wares shop on luck and a prayer. Her dream of opening her own business was realised but exchange of money was another matter. Passers-by might eye the romantic wedding gown or quaint toys in her window but rarely wanted to buy a lace collar or a carriage clock. The bell could stay silent all day. Then someone from out of town would walk in and buy a Royal Doulton dinner set or cedar chiffonier, saving her fluctuating fortunes for another week. Luckily Bart Bexley was a flexible bank manager and Marie was clever at juggling her accounts.

She'd had a lot of fun with Kitty Playfair. They'd rummaged for bric-a-brac at garage sales and markets, inspected deceased estates and found old-fashioned hats and garments at the Op Shop. Marie had provided many pieces of choice stock from her own possessions. Kitty said her friend had window-dressing down to a fine art, but clearly thought she wasn't businesslike. Where was the market these days for such refined pursuits? She did not understand Marie's pleasure in the way she spent her days, starching linen, cleaning jewellery, creating memories of the past. To wait discreetly at her counter, to serve the few who cherished quality gave her a sense of peace and rightness.

To while away the rest of the afternoon, she set a Chopin record on the turntable and began to mend a torn lace collar. She loved her shop, even when she was alone there. Arriving at the door was a pleasure. The leadlights glowed with mystery. The bell tinkled, introducing the rich air of aged wood, lavender bags and herb sachets in muslin pillows. Each section projected a personality of its own: the music room, the children's corner, the wedding day, the boudoir with its carelessly dropped cambric and *broderie anglaise* lingerie. Marie sometimes sat there on the Victorian loveseat, daydreaming of another era as she saw herself unfold the painted screen, pour scented water into the china bowl, take up the hair combs and run her fingers on the silky-grained surface of a dressing table whose dents marked treasured memories.

Her favourite display was the dolls. In wicker chairs they watched. Worldly Colette strutted in plum-red velvet, her blonde hair piled high like a courtesan's. Marianne, innocent in her gingham frock, balanced a basket of wildflowers on her posed wrist. The boy doll tipped a cheeky cap and whipped his top. Jacintha the Jumeau wasn't up for sale. Marie hated parting with the toys, even the tattered rocking horse or the teddy bears. She had some long-nosed Steiffs that were gaining in value but her favourite bear, Hugh's last gift to her, had pride of place on the counter top. She would never sell it. People said time healed all wounds but it wasn't so.

Nothing prepared you for the loss of a loved one. Ronnie said her sister lived in the past but then Ronnie was blasé, switched off to feeling. Her failed marriage had made her cynical. Marie preferred to spend her free time at Pelican, where relations with Rowena, Ben and Pippin had improved to the point where she'd considered cutting her ties and moving out permanently to the commune. There was the link with Hugh, her friendship with the Stedmans, and an air of revived energy now that Honor's friend, the English doctor, had confirmed his interest in heading the commune's proposed healing centre. He was due to arrive within the month.

Marie was musing over these matters when the shop bell tinkled and Mr Lal and his son walked through the door. Mr Lal approached the counter while Vijay wandered around, curiously examining the unusual displays.

'Very nice music,' said the Indian.

'Dinu Lipatti's recording of the waltzes. He was one of the great Chopin exponents, I always think.'

'It is a melancholy tune.'

His words reminded her it had been months since she'd visited her neighbours and she felt a stab of guilt. 'I've been meaning to call in but I've been so busy—'

To remark on the forbidding impression of his closed iron gates seemed rude.

'So I can see. You have done a great job, Mrs Mortimer. I wish you prosperity.'

'Please call me Marie. How is your family coping? I hear Vimla topped the district in her exams.'

'Yes. She did well. She has a job with the local newspaper.'

'Already! She knows where she's going. And your son?'

'Vijay!' His son approached, holding an ebony elephant he had picked out.

'Where did you get this?' said Mr Lal to Marie.

'It was in a box of stuff at the local second-hand shop. My sister sold something I meant to keep so I went to buy it back. It was the same day I found that book for you. Perhaps you never looked at it? It was something about the Taj Mahal.'

'Is this some kind of message, Father?' asked Vijay.

'It is more than coincidence.' Both men seemed strangely fascinated by the ornament. 'You see, Mrs Mortimer—Marie—although my wife is dead our link has not been severed. I don't know if you understand me.'

'Of course I do! My husband died some years ago, yet it still seems like yesterday. People expect you to be sensible, accept, move on...' She had gathered up a tattered teddy bear from the counter. As she cradled it he thought she looked like a large, lost child. 'Hugh gave me this. If you offered me a million dollars for his gift I wouldn't take it.'

The freedom with which she expressed emotion seemed to release his own.

'I feel my wife is still here, in this world around me.'

'Do you?' she cried eagerly. 'Oh, I feel the same about my Hugh. How often I think it's him, walking ahead of me in the street, standing on a corner somewhere. I dream of him, you know.'

'I must tell you of the dream I had last night.' Mr Lal began to pour out details of his vision, explaining how Marie's book had been the inspiration for his present project.

'I'm delighted you found it useful,' she told him, while he decided her patient listening manner reminded him of Shanti.

'Perhaps you will come over next Saturday?' he invited. 'I can lay out my plan in detail for you to comment on.'

'I'm sorry, I'm spending the weekend at Pelican. Family and friends to see.'

'Is that the commune on the coast?' Vijay's interest had been sparked.

Marie nodded. She had her eye on a browser who was looking through the clothing rack, but Vijay persisted.

'A commune—that's a place where work and money take second place to a life of meaning?'

'I guess that's the idea.' Marie smiled at the intent young man. 'If you're interested, why not go and see for yourself? Will you both excuse me? I have a customer.'

'We'll take this.' Mr Lal presented the elephant for wrapping. He was amazed at the chain of events that were unfolding. In a single afternoon he'd had encounters with two warm and friendly business people. Shanti had often told him he worked too hard, that was why he made no friends in Trundle. Perhaps it was so. His project was impelling him towards a new life. He saw himself moving among people, enlisting advisors and workers, being seen as a leader in the community. The scheme was a gamble. He was putting up his whole life's security against a vision. Yet risk is more invigorating than certainty and his step was assured as he and Vijay left Marie's shop.

He still had to call on the land agent. Vijay said he didn't want to come. To be strolling around Trundle with his father, chatting to the local people, was a first in his experience. The mention of Pelican had whetted his curiosity. He'd heard a bit about the place. Perhaps he might pay them a visit and find out what went on there.

'Sandy finishes work at three,' he said. 'I'll hang around and take her for a milkshake in town.'

'Buy her something. She's a good girl.'

His father took out his wallet and handed Vijay several notes. They parted on the best of terms.

When Mr Lal walked in to the land agent's office, Sam was busy with a client; a tall man with aloof and aristocratic features and the high forehead that suggests intelligence. Ten minutes passed before the men parted company in a mutually affable way that suggested the nature of their business was profitable. Sam's expression came back to earth as he saw the waiting Indian.

'The man I want to see!'

Mr Lal nodded politely at this patent lie.

'Trouble with your tenants the Halpins, I'm afraid. Arrears. I had a bad feeling about them.'

'Never mind about that,' said Mr Lal. 'I want your advice on another matter.'

The landlord's indifference was out of character. Surprised, Sam ushered him to the chair just vacated by Van Rjien, a Dutchman from the Pelican commune. Now that had been a tasty business nibble! Choice land coming up for sale, with none of the disadvantages of Bryan's shonky flood-prone sections.

'What can I do for you?'

'I need land, several hectares, prime position naturally.'

He launched into his vision, while Sam's inner calculator raced. Prime site, panoramic views, access to beaches, draw-card for tourists. And, best of all, spare no expense. Here was the reprieve Sam needed. According to the fellow he'd just interviewed, choice land at Pelican was coming on the market. Van Rjien had said there were a few loose ends still to tidy up with other shareholders; implying that as his investment was one of the largest, he expected no real opposition. Sam would be in line for a good commission, subject to a sale proceeding. Perhaps the determined little Indian could hurry the sale up by some tactical negotiation. A mine of wealth was opening up at Sam's feet, and he nodded in an enthusiastic way.

'All I can say to you is, this is your lucky day!' *And mine!* he thought.

'You are suggesting I go to this place and speak directly with your client?'

'Just say I sent you. See, they're a funny lot at that commune. High minded. Fancy ideas. Environmental, all that kind of thing. Like, they won't sell to just anybody. They'd want to know all about your project. Seems to me it might be right up their alley.'

'Then I will visit them.'

'Speak to this man.' Sam scribbled Van Rjien's name and mobile phone number on his business card. 'And while we're talking, what do you want to do about those Halpins? Evict?'

'We'll see.' Mr Lal tucked the card into his wallet and stood up. 'I'll consider what to do.'

'I'll hear from you.' Sam also stood up, his posture one of general relief.

Outside, hordes of schoolboys and girls surged along Main Road, munching snacks or giggling as they eyed books and magazines on display in the sex shop window. How pleasantly this day had passed! Mr Lal set off to walk to Railway Street, reflecting on his interview with Sam. He would go to Pelican and see this land. The prospect of two businessmen sitting down to bargain appealed to him. Most of his assets were in popular retirement areas or tied up in shares. Throughout the country there must be thousands of successful investors, yet he'd never found his way into those networks. He'd been a loner, secretly and carefully building up his portfolio; buying here, selling there, rating markets and assessing risk. Like any artist or tradesman, he sometimes longed to talk shop. He wanted to belong.

Had he ever? He'd come away from India as a young man ambitious to escape the poverty of his childhood. How well he remembered those hungry times! His mother was wrinkled and bent, long before she was old; so too his father, sick from ceaseless labour. *Never enough, never enough!* Those words were like some old song always haunting his memory. He had kept his vow to work and save and turn life around. His family had minded when he left. His mother had clung to him. His father called him a deserter. That breach could not be healed now. He'd sent money, had even suggested they could join him in the lucky country. But his parents died before his wish could be fulfilled. Such memories made him regretful.

Railway Street was a slum area that ran beside the rail line, with a rubbish tip fenced off at its far end. A faint odour of garbage pervaded the air as he turned into the street. He strolled past the row of close-packed, shabby weatherboard houses, whose paling fences leaned like comrades on one another. Brown or weedy grass patches passed for front lawns, where gnarled shrubs and stick-like trees baked in the afternoon sunshine.

'Afternoon!' An old chap in a sailor's cap greeted him from his porch.

'Afternoon!' returned the Indian. Nostalgia had permeated him as soon as he had turned into the street. Odd. He'd never lived here. The first and last time he'd visited was all of twenty years before, when he'd first moved to Trundle and used his small savings to put down a deposit on the dilapidated cottage he'd rented out ever since. In all that time he'd spent nothing on the place. It was time to assess for himself the nature of Sam's continual hints.

Outside his rental property two ragged little girls played hopscotch on the pavement. The house looked derelict. The letterbox had fallen over and the front yard was littered with junk mail, empty bottles, and a rusting supermarket trolley. Looking further, he saw how the paintwork hung in scabby patches, the porch sagged, the step was broken and several window cracks were patched with masking tape.

The mongrel tethered at the side of the house sprang to the end of its chain and set up a savage barking. At once a woman stepped out onto the porch. She shouted at the dog and eyed Mr Lal with an unfriendly eye. Presumably this was the Mrs Halpin whom Sam spoke of with such reserve. Had he encountered her in town, with her hostile look, her shabby clothes, and her rough language as she ordered the children inside? They went, grumbling. The woman gave Mr Lal a final stare of warning and slammed the door.

He'd seen enough. Now he knew what he recognised—not Railway Street or Nora Halpin, but his own song of childhood. It rang in his ears as he returned along the dingy street, where thin cats and growling dogs sniffed rubbish bins that were left on the kerb, week in, week out. *Never enough, never enough!*

An inquisition was underway at the Halpins.

'Did that darkie talk to youse lot?'

They denied it but Nora had a point to drive home. 'Don't talk to no strangers. Don't take nothin'! No lollies, no money! You hear me now?'

They'd better hear her, because she knew. Relenting, she let them back outside to play. All the same, she took her fags out to the porch, and stood there dreaming in the sunshine while she kept an eye out for any foreigners who might fancy her kids. *Don't trust no one.* Even old Ernie next door had an eye for kids; not her girls though. She needn't worry there. He kept his chocolate bars for little boys. She'd watched and seen.

Nora sat down on the broken step, lit up a cigarette and took a deep drag. Memories drenched her as she absorbed the familiar feel of the grainy old wood, so like the porch she'd often sat on as a kid. Railway Street with its tumbledown, close-packed houses felt like home. The people were the kind she knew: old Ern, Mother O'Brian and that homebody son of hers who spent his life making queer things nobody wanted. The dump at the end of the street was like the one she'd explored with the Neavis kids, whose father went in and out of clink. They slunk round the streets in a pack, nicking what they could.

She'd known, even then, that once the world picked out its troublemakers, they got the blame for everything. If the milk went missing or someone posted swearwords in letterboxes, Nora's Mum would say, *Those Neavises, they deserve a good kick up the backside.* The real culprit, sly Mandy Palfrey, whose parents had a concrete garden pond with a fishing dwarf and a plaster frog, got a smile and a pat on the head.

The Neavis kids, if they came to school at all, usually came hungry. Nora had to share her lunch with them, not because she wanted to but because they singled her out and whined until she gave in. She didn't like them. No one did. They were bottom of the class and they smelt. Their clothes were dirty. They frightened her when they hung around as though they could see something about Nora that they recognised.

It couldn't have been Nora's home. The paint might have been peeling, a few windowpanes cracked, the grass untidy, but it was always cheery; food cooking, the radio going, the flies in summer humming their song. Mum was a goer, she ran the house, paid the bills, worked down the Club in the bistro for extra money. She took Nora sometimes. She had to sit down and shut up, they didn't let kids in the Club but she'd peep through the swing doors and see the people smoking, drinking, listening to the races and playing the poker machines. Nora loved their twinkling lights and tinkling tunes and the sound of coins spewing into the metal trays.

The bad times started when she was thirteen and Mum dropped dead with a heart attack.

Nora tried her best. She cooked and did the washing and went to school, but nothing felt real. She started going with the boys, breaking rules, getting a name at school. She left the day she was old enough and got a job in Trundle's lingerie factory. She liked the powerful machines, the way the needle flew in and out and the overlocker whizzed along.

The boss made a pass. It was an old story but she hadn't heard it then. He said she was a little trimmer and put her on overtime. After that he had her every way she'd ever heard of and then some. He was at it all through the autumn collection. She swung her hips at every man she set eyes on; men on building sites, men driving trucks. They guessed what she was up to; winked and whistled. She felt powerful, until his wife found out. Nora got the boot. She toughened up after that.

She had her share of blokes, dumps, moves, fights. For a while, she and Tag had worked out. Pity his brain had gone addled since the accident. He'd got a raw deal and now when he hit out at life that was just Nora's bad luck if she happened to be in the way. She could fight him back and often did. For a few minutes it made her remember what it was to feel powerful and desperate and alive. But the kids got upset. She could cop a black eye anyway. It was only pain and she'd known worse kinds many times before.

Get over it! Tag was away at the pub. Easy tea tonight. Flicking the butt away, she fished out some change and called the kids.

'Hey, youse lot!' she yelled. 'Go down the shops and buy us some chippies?'

They ran off, shouting. She grinned. They'd soon be back, paper parcels clutched like prizes. Lots of salt and tomato sauce. Life wasn't bad on a sunny afternoon in Railway Street.

4

Kitty took her recipe for *pot pourri* to *Victorian Gilt* and stayed for afternoon tea. She often came by on one pretext or another, for she was lonely since Marie had left *The Trendy Trinket* to try her luck on her own. Her friend puzzled Kitty. She'd never done things by the book. Hugh was a good example of that. Yet here she was, uncensored, contented, with memories of a loving marriage and the confidence to risk her hand on antiques in a town like Trundle. It seemed unfair.

'Come round for dinner and cards this weekend?'

'I can't, Kitty. I'm heading up to Pelican on Friday.'

Marie went to the Playfairs less frequently than she used to. There was a chill in the air there. Sam was too quiet and Kitty, who used to be so predictable, had gone ash blonde and was wearing clothes unsuited to a woman who worked on the church committee and sang in the choir.

Kitty's shrug suggested this was just another disappointment. She could convey a thousand reproaches with a sigh. 'Sam will probably be out, anyway. He's never home, these days. I think he's having an affair.'

'Sam?' Marie dismissed the image of her down-at-heel, balding neighbour lost in the throes of passion. 'What an idea!'

'It has been known.' Kitty's tone suggested that the past should never be forgotten. 'I've some good news, Holly's coming home.'

'So soon? I thought she had another year to go.'

'She's pulling out. I don't know why.'

'Well, Trundle to India; quite a transition. Perhaps it's all a bit much?'

'People are the same everywhere,' said Kitty, whose own travel experience involved a trip to Coffs Harbour for her honeymoon. 'Anyway, I don't care why. We can be a normal family again.'

'Of course.' Sometimes it was better to tell Kitty what she wanted to hear. 'Look what I found at a deceased estate sale.' She held up a 1920s ukulele.

'My grandfather had one. Joel's inherited his musical ability. He wants an electric guitar for his birthday.'

'Isn't he too young?'

'You sound like Sam. It's what Joel wants.'

Kitty returned to work and Marie read her *pot pourri* recipe.

Dry first in a sunny room, rose leaves, lavender, lemon verbena, or any kind of sweet-smelling leaf at hand. Then add half a pound of orris root, four oz. of cloves, two sticks of cinnamon, two oz. allspice, one oz. of bergamot, one drachm or less of musk. The spices should be all pounded and mixed with rose leaves, the old-fashioned, sweetest scented flowers, old cabbage, moss or shepherd roses.

'Tell me, my pets,' she addressed the dolls and bears. 'Where am I to buy bergamot, in Trundle?' Propped in attitudes of benevolent attention, they stared past her into space.

Back home, Mr Lal made an appointment to see Van Rjien, then phoned Sam, astonishing him by saying he had decided to renovate the house in Railway Street.

'Please find out exactly what needs doing,' said the Indian, adding, 'within reason, naturally.'

Sam welcomed any excuse to work on at the office. Kitty's moods were hard to take and absence was his solution to the problem. 'I'll arrange an inspection. It will give us a lever with the rent arrears.'

'No hurry about that,' said Mr Lal, leaving Sam bemused.

In his room, the Indian began to list the tasks involved in his project. Soon pages covered with his methodical script overflowed from his desktop and drifted to the floor. He couldn't remember feeling so energetic for years. How wonderful it was when grief gave way to inspiration! Those old poets understood the heart of man.

Longing to share his elation, he reached into the cupboard and took down Shanti's ashes. He cupped the box in his palms and spoke softly to her, recounting the day's events and thanking her for his restored sense of purpose. He told her how he'd bought the ebony elephant she had perhaps caused to be placed like a sign for him in the antique shop window. He pointed out its sturdy form, set beside her photograph. He said he missed her. Still, it was as the poet recorded in chronograms acknowledging the death of Mumtaz Mahal. *'A valuable pearl had slipped away; the flute of joy had its joints severed; the mine gave forth no more rubies.'*

Yet death brought forth its own fruit. 'It's true, my love,' agreed Mr Lal. *"If the oyster gets washed ashore from the ocean, pearls remain as its memento.'*

'If a mine gives forth no more rubies, and is depleted, its rubies still sparkle like the sun.' You, my beloved, sit in the canopied litter bound for the Gardens of Paradise; yet stay with me a while longer and guide our project. Together we'll give this gift to future generations. People will remember our mutual deep devotion. When you were with me, I rarely said I loved you. I took your wifely favours and service as my right. Your absence has given birth to my heart. I can no longer hide my feelings. I have become weak. Yet, how strange it is, I feel so alive, so unafraid! I know you understand. I think you knew me better than I knew myself.'

He often wept when he let himself reach out like this to her. Today the awful sense of loss did not oppress him. He replaced the box in his cupboard and decided to organise his lists. It was clear to him that he'd better get started with plans and permissions straight away. He would spend the next day making phone calls and setting up appointments. He would need the co-operation of town authorities before there was any point in proceeding; while publicity of the right kind might ease his way. A daughter on the staff of the local paper was an asset. Together, he and Vimla could write an arresting article for publication.

Meanwhile, Vijay, who had volunteered his help, could chauffeur his father to Pelican, for Mr Lal had never learned to drive—his way, perhaps, of keeping out of the mainstream. As he picked up his pen from the dressing table, he patted the little elephant and smiled. Surely he was right in thinking it was a sign from Shanti.

That evening the Lal household came together for their evening meal. Even Sunita and her husband, who often ate apart, were drawn to the table by their son-in-law's high spirits. Mr Lal was full of plans.

'Vimla! Tonight we will compose an article for submission to the newspaper. Vijay! We have an appointment at Pelican early on Thursday. We will go together. Your mother wishes us to unite as a family in this project. And while we are here, let us all thank Sandy, who sits here so quietly, who buys our food and helps manage the house.' He reached over and gave her shoulder a kindly pat. 'We are all grateful for your help.'

Sandy's pale blue eyes, whose outlook was usually familiar with life's struggles and hardships, lit up, although she wanted to run away from all those smiling faces. People never thanked her; she felt embarrassed and disturbed. Fortunately Mr Lal resumed instructing his children, who were exchanging dubious glances across the table. Sunita however was pleased. This was the way a man should behave! The natural order had seemed reversed in this household, with women who acted as men, going out to work and earn, while the males stayed shut away indoors, never meeting in the sunshine to smoke and joke and discuss men's business. Only good and proper outcomes could result from this change. Soon the men would work, young couples would spend time together, her old arms would then feel again the joy of holding a tender, newborn baby.

Straight after dinner Vim was summoned to help with the proposed article, which she promised to type up on the computer and present to Mac Booth. She decided to edit her father's prose, which had taken on the influence of the court poets. In essence, however, all the angles of a good story were covered: human appeal, ambition, risk, cultural interest, a touch of the bizarre. She was shocked by the story of the deceased queen, Mumtaz Mahal, who had died giving birth to her fourteenth child. Only seven of her offspring had survived. Surely here was scope for a secondary article on women's issues. Her boss would be impressed.

First thing on Thursday, a journey of significance was underway at the Lals. The whole household was on deck. The high gates stood wide open and the car engine revved while Mr Lal, in a business suit, stood in his driveway making frantic hand signals to the driver, who seemed none too practised behind the wheel. The red Fiat missed the gatepost by inches. The driver stepped out to adjust the seat, and stood smoothing back his curly black hair while he waited for Sandy to come running to catch her lift to work. Mr Lal climbed into the passenger seat; the young man resumed the chauffeur's position, while a bent old woman shuffled down the drive to secure the gates with a slam of importance.

Main Road was deserted when the car reached town. Stunned by his dawn summons, Vijay was silent. His father might be on some quest but he felt sure Pelican held an equal significance for himself. Enquiries he'd made in town about the commune had been met with shrugs or dismissing jokes.

The town clock was chiming seven as he dropped Sandy off at work. She seemed less worried than usual to be a few minutes late on duty. She knew the supervisor had a day off and her substitute wasn't always punctual herself. In the geriatric wing, where Sandy now worked, she thought it did no harm to let the old people have a sleep-in. When Sister Gale was on deck she expected to see everybody up and dressed and the ward ship-shape. She took no notice of old folk who begged to lie in bed in preference to having their withered bodies soaped and scrubbed.

Sandy was popular. She was slow and quiet and her bitten nails never inflicted accidental scratches. She would interrupt her tea break to take an anxious old lady to the lavatory for the tenth time. The insults of her patients touched her heart, for she sensed they were an indirect raging against unjust forces that had stolen from them their homes and independence. The ones she cared for were lost in a time warp. For them, it was too late to live, too soon to die. She understood loneliness. She often missed Vijay when he neglected her for days or weeks, but there were other times that made up. Last night they'd lain awake, talking for hours. Vijay had made love with her before he went to sleep. Afterwards she'd savoured the darkness, hearing his breathing, feeling his warm skin against hers.

She waved shyly to him now, then ran up the hospital steps. As Vijay prepared to take off, his father made an unexpected suggestion.

'I have never eaten at McDonald's. I'm a modern man—how can I expect to run a successful enterprise when I know nothing of popular taste? Are non-beef items on the menu?'

Vijay, who liked pancakes with maple syrup, nodded. He parked between two semitrailers and followed his father through the swing doors, where slowly revolving fans stirred the warm air, sending a homely smell of food and coffee through the almost deserted restaurant.

The only other occupants were a couple of red-eyed truckies replenishing their energies with breakfast. Mr Lal observed the surroundings keenly, taking note of the ovens, frying vats, drink dispensers and cash registers. He fingered the little packets of salt, jam, and whipped butter; examined the plastic cutlery and paper napkins; studied the framed prints and touched the pot plants to see if they were real. Vijay carried their tray of pancakes to one of the yellow laminex tables, where Mr Lal sampled the food and nodded his approval.

'I never expected to find myself in such a place, eating breakfast with my son. The smell of beef has deterred me. It didn't seem the right place for me. I've looked in and seen families and young people, laughing, making jokes. Do you and Sandy come here often?'

Vijay shook his head. He, too, had envied the solidarity of families crammed side by side on the green benches as they shared cartons of chips and thickshakes. He could never remember eating out with his parents, and he'd avoided asking school friends home for meals, knowing they would be wary of foreign food.

'Do you like the pancakes?' he asked.

His father nodded. 'What would your mother have thought of this?' He stared around the restaurant. 'She didn't want to come to this country, you know. She wanted to live near her parents, but I was determined to leave. Well, she obeyed my wishes. That is how she was brought up. That is how she was.'

Mr Lal touched his son's hand, acknowledging their mutual loss. Soon he began to talk about the restaurant he intended to build within the Taj complex. Vijay finished his breakfast in silence, surprised by his father's openness.

The traffic through Trundle was increasing when they set off for Pelican. The road ran parallel to the railway line before it bridged the small river and headed on towards the coast. Unlike the chains of tourist accommodation erected near so many of the sandy beaches to the north, the land was relatively undeveloped. The bays here lacked that tropical atmosphere, being edged by saline marshes, mangrove swamps and oyster beds. The road wound lazily on, flanked on one side by flat fields of rushes and on the other by the river. Intermittent stands of native bush were reflected in the greenish water, their images quivering in the slow-moving surface currents. Between these bushland groves were dotted a few houses. In the subtly tinted landscape they inhabited, the purple lasiandras and bright yellow cassias blooming in their gardens had an eye-catching impact, like migrants walking out in their national dress.

Vijay, who had abandoned materialism not long after gaining his licence, was a slow driver. The car proceeded cautiously towards the coast, gathering yellow dust from the unsealed road. There had been little rain for months and the terrain was passable, though at bridged points in the road were signs with names like Boggy Creek. Painted measuring posts along the way identified previous flood levels. Presumably the river overflowed its banks regularly.

Taking the gradual decline that wound down through thickening bushland they reached the end point of the road. Ahead lay access suited to a four-wheel drive vehicle. As though disdaining this challenge, the little car stalled; Vijay had confused the clutch with the brake pedal.

'We'd better walk now,' decided his father.

A hand-carved sign identified the way to Pelican. Mr Lal set down his briefcase while he rolled up his trouser cuffs. He ensured the Fiat was securely locked. Together he and Vijay set off along the track.

They were equally unused to walking in the bush. Unless trees grew in parks, Mr Lal did not like them. They undermined drains, disrupted sward-like lawns and caused him endless problems in his rental enterprises. He felt unsafe, suspecting a host of foreign insects lurked among their shadows. In his opinion, only strange individuals would choose to live here. He asked himself how any businessman could conduct his enterprises in such remote surroundings. His spirits rose, for it seemed to him that he would need to offer little persuasion to the man he was on his way to see. In his mind he rehearsed his approach to the Dutchman. He would describe the Taj; its importance to himself personally and to the town as a whole. He would explain the necessity of siting it on the land under negotiation. He would offer suitable financial recompense.

Vijay was not a nature lover either. He rarely heard the birds singing, saw the flowers in bloom or noticed whether it rained or was fine. He was curious about his fellows, not in Vim's way, as a recorder of drama and disaster, but impartially. In a city, he would have gravitated to the seedy districts, sat about past midnight in the clubs and bars where his fellow night-owls would be making music, drinking, dancing, picking up their casual lays or supporting their addictions with whatever transactions they thought necessary. Though he'd rejected the trappings of education and financial success, he did not expect the offbeat course offered better solutions to the puzzle of existence. In any case he couldn't be bothered to leave home. He didn't mind Trundle.

Mr Lal and his son walked along the deserted track that soon led to deeply shaded bush. The croaking of marsh frogs was incessant. Secretive rustles gave away the presence of tiny animals or reptiles. Wing-beats of flashing brightness marked the sudden flight of birds. Occasionally they passed a sign that reassured them they were on the right course but there was as yet no sign of any settlement. Vijay felt curious. An unusual energy drew him forward, as though destiny lay just round the next corner.

The trees thinned out. Ahead, wetlands made a transition between the bush and the distant sea. Mewling birds flapped above the reeds, a few long-legged kinds stalking for food. There were signs of industry now. Proper wooden steps had been placed to make the way easier. The buildings of Pelican were visible at the top of a slope towards which the Lal men trudged. Intent on his interview, Mr Lal looked for signs of life. He asked directions from a gardener who was digging friable ground in a fenced plot.

'Mr Van Rjien lives over there,' the Indian told his son, as an older woman came out of a six-sided building with a tented roof.

'Can I be of help? I'm Honor Stedman. We don't get many callers at this early hour.' Her smile was welcoming.

'I have an appointment with Mr Van Rjien, concerning land for sale.' Mr Lal felt at home in this community of early risers. In India, people did not sleep through the most refreshing hours of the day but his son regularly proved that things were different here.

'There's no land for sale.' Honor sounded definite. She walked briskly and her voice was youthful, but as she led the way along well-kept walkways draped with flowering creepers, she muttered to herself in the way of the elderly, *What's That Man up to now?*

'Go along with this lady and find somewhere to wait,' said Mr Lal to his son, who went off with Honor, assured that he was welcome to look around.

Richard Van Rjien invited his visitor into the house. It was a simple cedar structure where oriental rugs, carvings and artefacts suggested a man who had made many journeys in his life. His light-coloured tropical suit, pungent aftershave and faint accent all confirmed a foreign background, though one different from his smiling Asian wife, a girl considerably younger than himself. He introduced her as Tuti; his manner one of ownership.

'Coffee? It's one of the few pleasures I allow to rule me. On the whole I don't depend on anything. That way, one is never disappointed. However, we can rely on Tuti's coffee.'

He intended some joke, though Mr Lal could not see what it was. He nodded his thanks and stood waiting to be offered a chair. However, as Tuti left the room, Richard sidled over to the bookcase, which was packed with hardbound titles in several languages. He ran his fingers along the shelves as though considering in which category he placed his visitor.

'You must read extensively,' said Mr Lal. He would bring out his book about the Taj Mahal in due course. Van Rjien took down a leather-bound text and showed it to his guest.

'What do you think of this?'

Mr Lal did not recognise the script, but there was no mistaking the nature of the pornographic illustrations.

'It is not to my liking.' Embarrassed, he moved away and Richard, smiling, returned the book to the shelf.

'Not a reader?'

'I am a businessman. Buying, selling, this is what I understand.'

He felt shocked that any man would keep such lascivious pictures so openly in his living room, where his wife might chance to browse. He wished they could get to the point of his visit. When Tuti returned with a wicker tray set with coffee cups, Richard finally offered Mr Lal a seat and poured from the percolator himself. Tuti presented the milk jug, smiled and withdrew.

Richard picked up his cup and pontificated. 'I'm a single-minded fellow. That's my recipe for success. I've amassed my wealth and acquired my wife. Now I'm devising an expansion plan for Pelican. Not everyone here agrees with me. Do you have enemies, Mr Lal?'

'Not that I'm aware of.'

'I do! Clear vision excludes all who see things differently. I sound self-centred, don't I? The beauty of selfishness is that it's honest. I'm nothing special. I'm warped by flaws, riddled with self-pity. You're a wog yourself, you'd understand the nature of the outsider?'

Further offended, the Indian sipped the bitter drink in silence. He was doubting the wisdom of this journey. This man was more than strange.

'Consider a poor Dutch boy!' the monologue continued. 'Growing up in Indonesia, constantly moved from pillar to post, a misfit, laughed at, bullied. Don't you think I should have turned to drink or drugs? Surely I should be a law-breaker... At least develop some terminal disease? But I'm a great success! Now why have I achieved what most men only dream of, given my unpromising nature and background?'

From his low-slung chair, Mr Lal looked up at his overbearing host. The man's bulk towered over him and his peculiar concentration on himself gave no leave for interruption. It was a wasted journey. So far he'd been insulted, bored and subjected to moral indignity. A kind of hostility underlay Richard's genial remarks, as though he would take pleasure in thwarting Mr Lal's wishes, once he had bothered to hear what they were.

'I don't waste time,' continued Richard. 'I don't bemoan what I lack or envy what others have. I attend to what is relevant.'

At this point, his desperate guest seized his opportunity to enter the conversation.

'Yes, relevant! I'm told that what I lack, you wish to sell. Land...'

Richard smiled down at him. 'Let me tell you how I came to acquire a wife, my friend. It's an interesting tale.'

Not waiting for Mr Lal to confirm this opinion, he went on. 'Having spent years establishing myself through study, travel, business, perusal of the literatures of various cultures and so forth, I decided I should be married. I'd never allowed women to divert me so I was a novice. I considered the kind of wife to suit me, knowing the type of husband I'd be. I decided on an affectionate girl, free from antagonism. I'd seen enough of conflict. My parents fought like two street dogs. I registered with an Asian marriage bureau of repute. They saw me as a good marriage prospect, of course. I was wealthy, healthy, strong, clear-minded and free from obvious vice. I examined some hundreds of photographs and case histories before I chose Tuti. I knew the village she came from in Sumatra. I'd once passed through with my parents. She could cook, sing, dance and was educated. She belonged to the group called *Subud*, whose philosophy I'd read about during my analysis of world religions. She had the happy nature of those who believe in a deity. The exchange of introductions took place; I paid a flying visit to her homeland to reassure myself she was suitable. As I'd hoped, she perfectly fitted the mould of Indonesian women, who are graceful and well trained in wifely duties. In due course we were married. She is all I hoped to find; obliging and quite understanding of my preference not to have children. As a father I'd be a dismal failure. Mind you, in bed...'

Deciding he could stand no more of this endless and inappropriate monologue, Mr Lal sprang to his feet and picked up his briefcase. 'We are wasting one another's time.'

Richard was unruffled. 'We have reached your limits? Well, let us come to the point. Why are you here?'

'To inspect a certain block of land. Here is the agent's card.'

'What do you want the land for?'

'To build a replica of Taj Mahal.'

Richard laughed loudly.

'It is a commercial enterprise.' Mr Lal was now determined to have his say. 'Money is no object. I intend it to be a tribute to my dear wife who died recently. Mr Van Rjien, I am not here to discuss my wife or yours, however. I merely wish to see the land. Though I doubt it would suit my purpose. This location is out of the way and undeveloped.'

Richard took the low chair facing Mr Lal's. 'People call some of my own schemes far-fetched, but it never occurred to me to build a palace in the back-blocks. In this country the bizarre flourishes! *The Taj Mahal of Trundle...* It has panache!'

Mr Lal stood up. He spoke with dignity.

'I need not account to you in relation to my investments. However, my Taj will be faithful to its cultural background. Its shops will carry nothing but the finest wares. Its museum will house only genuine exhibits. Its restaurant will serve excellent food. I shall employ only the best architect and builders. I shall travel myself to India to ensure that all materials are appropriate. I shall commission artisans there to complete those details I would not dream of entrusting to foreigners.'

'I'm face to face with an entrepreneur of my own ilk,' Richard murmured. 'I must clarify the position. The land is communally owned.

However, I own a major shareholding, along with Honor Stedman. I believe we should sell off a parcel. Unfortunately, Honor's dead against progress. She has some idealistic notion of a healing centre. She has taken it on herself to drag some doctor here from England. There's a meeting this coming weekend to iron out these issues. We'll see how my suggestions fare.' He stood up. 'I too have a proposal. I think your idea could blend in with mine. What do you say we inspect the site? It's only a short stroll from here.'

Mr Lal stayed seated and said nothing.

'You'll be impressed! Commanding position, natural setting, extensive views. Undeveloped, of course. I hear that Council has zoned in an exclusive subdivision near us. There'll be a wealthy clientele on hand. I can put you on to a first-rate architect.'

'No hurry,' said Mr Lal. 'I have other options...'

Van Rjien grinned at him. 'Quite so! Tuti!' He beckoned and she came obediently, to massage his shoulders through his jacket. Richard reached up and patted her small hand.

'She insists I'm a good man, even though I deny it. See how her hands are unadorned? She could have jewels. She only wants this wedding ring. She refuses my offers of fashion clothing. She doesn't want a car. She'd live with me if I were a pauper. Tuti deserves a palace of her own one day.'

The Dutchman seemed to have come to the end of his disclosures. Mr Lal felt he had the tactical advantage and said his goodbye. A return visit sounded very likely. He went to find Vijay, who had toured the grounds and chatted with several of the younger members. He was with Honor, who was explaining the commune's principles to him.

'How did it go?' he asked when his father found him.

'There is nothing settled.'

'Nor will there be,' Honor said. 'You've been misinformed and I fear you've had a wasted trip. Our land is jointly owned. We have no intention of turning Pelican into a sideshow for rich tourists, whatever Richard thinks.'

'My interest has nothing to do with any plan of his,' was all Mr Lal chose to say. There was clearly a long-standing conflict here. Laurie wheeled in a tea trolley just then, and the talk shifted to lighter issues. Vijay said nothing about his impression that here he'd finally met a group of kindred souls. Mr Lal did not express his doubts concerning the commune's distant location and its offbeat members.

Each withdrawn into his private thoughts, father and son drove home.

5

On Friday afternoon the melodic chimes of the town clock struck five as Main Road shops closed. Only the food suppliers would stay open: the Chinese take-away, the Vietnamese hot bread shop, and McDonald's, its red and yellow emblem signalling welcome to drivers on the long haul north.

Marie was glad to be heading to Pelican tonight. There was a contentment to the dreams and memories in her shop that was lacking in the life she shared with Ronnie. She locked up and walked in her down-at-heel shoes past the closed stores whose window displays conveyed a sad, rejected air, as though the chrome kettles, the children's school shoes and men's business shirts had no individuality and would never be treasured. Security lights shone in the empty bank. The entrance to the adult shop was sealed with a large padlock. The jeweller's window had been stripped of its valuables. Outside the real estate agency, Sam exchanged a greeting, climbed in his old car and drove away in the opposite direction from his home. Marie remembered Kitty's words. Perhaps Sam did have a secret life. Who was she to typecast others? She was no spring chicken herself, yet she missed Hugh's caresses and reassurances. All that was over forever; yet, should the right man come along, she'd gladly welcome another chance at love. The recognition made her feel unfaithful to Hugh.

She had parked near the newspaper office. Now, only a red Fiat awaited its driver. Vim presumably worked on upstairs, culling the news that mattered. One light shone single-mindedly in the otherwise deserted building.

Marie tossed her baskets on the back seat and set off in the direction of Pelican. Interesting developments were taking place there. Rowena was less wary and Pippin was starting to accept her stand-in grandmother. The land issue had yet to be resolved. Honor's latest news was that her friend, the British doctor, had booked his ticket and would be arriving soon to take charge of the healing centre at Pelican. Marie wondered if the poor man knew what kind of conflict he might have to face. The Stedmans had promised to wait dinner for her; the gossip should prove interesting, and she couldn't wait to hear about the new arrival. Nowadays people wanted alternatives beyond pills and surgery to reclaim their wellbeing. In a little place like Trundle, the health food store would have been bankrupt in times past; but it had a prosperous look now. A holistic health retreat at Pelican could well up-date the commune's goals and refocus the loose-knit group.

Ronnie understood conventional health networks. She might have useful comments to make. But any mention of Pelican brought that expression of impatience to her face, as though Marie's friends were crackpots.

Marie was nowhere in sight when Ronnie arrived back from work. She sat down on the old wooden steps to enjoy the last afternoon sunshine for a few minutes before she bothered to find her key and open up the house. Recently she felt a growing need to be on her own, though she tried not to express her longing for solitude to her sister. After all, they shared the house and she could hardly object to Marie's clutter or her erratic working hours. Her way of doing things was nothing new. There weren't the shocks a spouse or a stranger might announce. And they were both busy people. Sometimes they didn't see each other for days. Marie was usually off with some friend or another, or at that commune she was always on about. Obviously people liked her. She'd always been popular; one of the crowd. Ronnie was the loner. Family units were like that. Why feel envious? Poor Marie drooped like one of her heat-exhausted blooms. Her clothes were from the '80s, she hadn't had a good haircut in years, she had a dated look about her as though she had no idea how to keep up with life.

Forcing herself to move, Ronnie unlocked the back door. The smell of fruit peels and scraps explained the drone of trapped flies. The stove was awash with boiled-over coffee. Dead flowers drooped in the pretty Lalique vase. She'd pour a good stiff brandy, but there wasn't any. Pulling on rubber gloves, she cleaned the bench and made a cup of tea. The living room, refurbished attractively in modern style, had been shut up all day. Feeling she could hardly breathe, she pushed up the windows, confronting the Lal's edifice. She liked it even less than when it had first been built. The Lals were a peculiar family; naturally Marie got along with them, even that strange nurse, Sandy Smith, who was in tow with the indulged-looking son. Ronnie twitched the curtains shut, their brass rings jangling. Another of Marie's successes! She should be home now. She must have gone off to that commune straight from work. Now, contrarily, she felt deserted and alone. All the weekend maintenance was left to her again. The housework, the garden... It wasn't fair. Sleepless nights were getting to her, yet her mind churned with jobs she had to do. The hospital expected her to write a submission concerning the threatened rail crisis. Rumour had it that the health system was included on the government's cost-cutting agenda. Trying to forget just how tired she was, she reached for pad and pen and sat staring into space.

She was glad to see the back of hospital routine for a few days. Call it burnout, but nursing was just a means of income. Some of her colleagues remained compassionate and kind and others worked mechanically, seeing suffering as part of the job. Marie called her hard; let her dress a bedsore or lay out a corpse and see how delicate life really was!

It was another night of broken sleep. Sunshine striping her paisley quilt woke her next morning, as pigeons babbled gently outside the window. She dozed, and that damn dream replayed again. The woman, the coffin, the aspirins, the sudden switch from amiable co-operation to refusal and rising panic. Sleep-ins were a mistake. Far too much to do. Throwing on the man's check shirt and army pants she used to ward off prickles, she grabbed breakfast and went out to attack the lantana with a tomahawk.

Autumn's legacy was dead wood, seeding weeds, and rampant growth. A mad weaver had run riot with jasmine and morning glory runners. She chopped them off the fences and out of the borders. The hydrangeas hadn't been pruned for years. She left them with a few bud eyes. The deformed geraniums had outlived any value. Their roots gave way easily. Bamboo was there for the long haul, but a pickaxe finally tore out the roots. Honeysuckle was surprisingly tough; the fish fern gave like worn-out cotton. She ripped sweet pea vines off the trellis and straightened her back to spy elusive growth. Everywhere, insects shocked from their hiding places searched desperately for shelter.

She mopped her face, gathered the prunings and, fuelled by triumph, piled them beside the gate. Serve Marie right! Let her run off for the weekend if she wanted to. She wouldn't like Ronnie's response. Not one bit.

She went inside to shower and change. She still had to go out and pick up some groceries and brandy. Then she'd vacuum and do her washing. The lawn could wait until Sunday. She wanted to type up that submission. Lucky she felt so wound up. She couldn't have relaxed if her life depended on it.

On Sunday, Marie set off from Pelican later than she'd intended. Although she'd done this short walk many times, she always found the solitude mysterious. Palm fronds rustled and the surface of the wetland shivered as the breeze crept through its reed mantle. The lonely sea was robbed of colour. The sounds of the bush played like a symphony: bird melody, frog timpani, the flute-like whispering of foliage. Small as it was, the settlement stood for much that made her life worthwhile. The weekend, with its natural peace and friendship, had let her forget the tension at home. She had spent time with Rowena and Pippin. Honor had primed her on Victor Argyle's background; her effusive admiration balanced by Marie's private query as to why such a successful doctor would abandon his practice for the backblocks of Australia. She had weighed up the pros and cons of selling part of the communal land, and decided in favour of the idea. Honor might be inflexible, but in reality numbers at Pelican continued to dwindle. Development might benefit the isolated little group, and she could see no reason why Honor's therapy centre and Richard's commercial venture could not co-exist. Marie had a small investment in the land herself; anything she could recoup would supplement the shop's erratic earnings very handily. As she trudged towards the car, she reflected on the fruitful discussions, where it had been agreed that members past and present would be invited to attend a weekend meeting to vote on the issue soon.

Her thoughts mellow, she reached the town and turned into Alexandra Avenue. As she parked, she saw an unfamiliar mound of prunings stacked high in front of her home. A sense of unreality, as at a crime scene, made her stumble across the verge and plunge her arms deep into the trails of dying greenery and flowers.

'They were past it.'

Ronnie called from the shadows of the front porch. She was standing there, some drink in her hand; she never seemed to be without one lately.

'You ought to be grateful,' went on the hateful words. 'You leave all the work to me. So I've done it. My back's killing me.'

Slowly Marie turned, letting the foliage fall in a stricken pile. Her garden had been savaged. Ronnie must hate her.

'Why?' Her voice was a cry. Ronnie didn't answer. 'Why would you do this to me?'

They were face to face across the no-man's land of the narrow driveway. Ronnie took a gulp from her glass. Still she said nothing. Marie sighed, a huge breath of inexpressible sadness. 'You know how I loved it. What a bitch you are!'

She walked inside and slammed her bedroom door, weeping in private at this misery she had to call her home.

The outlook was worse next morning. Without its soft garb of creepers, the periphery of the garden was a view of dirty bricks and fence boards. An ugly heap of stones replaced the careful disarray of Marie's trailing rockery plants. Impressionistic corners hazed by ferns and foliage were now reduced to bare earth. The graceful arch where roses had tumbled was just a rusty hoop of wire.

Roses were pruned back to their stumps. The hydrangeas were gawky twigs. The borders were stripped. Preparing herself to face the final damage, Marie tried to frame some possible account for Ronnie's destructive act. She'd loved the garden too. To tear to pieces all their careful work was senseless. Was Ronnie going mad? Angry memories flooded her. She thought of the childhood hurts, the unkind words and painful pinches Ronnie had got away with because Marie had been afraid to tell. Yet they'd been such good friends. It couldn't be Ronnie who was laughing at her, leaving her behind and running off with the big kids while her little sister dragged home alone, her sandals scuffing through the dust, tears making everything blurry and unreal. Ronnie would be waiting, smiling, taking her hand, helping her get the buckles undone and her wet pants into the wash hamper before the adults found out.

That was the confusion. Ronnie could be so generous with her toys, lollies, money. If anyone picked on Marie at school, Ronnie was ready for fisticuffs. There were two sisters. Though it helped to pretend the cruel one wasn't real, that left Marie with a feeling that, behind some bush, around some corner, pain and hurtful words lay in wait.

Who was Ronnie now? The well-organised woman with her bills and her electrolysis appointment fixed under a fridge magnet? The vulnerable woman who turned briskly from pain, saying, when a stray dog came looking for a home, *No pets! It's too painful when they die?* Or the hard woman who glared at Reality and berated Marie because she wouldn't shoulder the whole world's pain? The woman in control, whose eyes warned you not to come too close? The woman who could destroy her sister's garden without remorse?

Marie went outside to search out the remains of growing things. She picked a flower of black-eyed Susan, a tip of golden honeysuckle, one blue-violet morning glory missed by the slaughter. Slaters and ants ran busily over the brown earth. A butterfly alighted on a single blood-red rose. Marie looked at the sad posy in her hand and began to sob.

On Monday morning, Sam Playfair's office telephone rang continually, as he was besieged by enquiries about Bryan's bog sites. His advertisements had worked. Bargain-hunters made appointments to inspect. One even offered to post his deposit, sight unseen. Sam explained the sites weren't zoned as residential; even hinted at a problem with the water table, but there was no discouraging the buyers.

He decided the rash acquisitions of his fellow man were none of his business, for he had other problems on his mind. He shouldn't have let that house in Railway Street to Nora. She'd returned to Trundle with her hopeless *de facto* and her pair of kids, and wheedled her way into his office. Her once-bright face was awfully scarred, but she'd honed her tactics on the grindstone of survival. Her familiar manner implied some old bond between them as she promised to be a good tenant. He'd let her sign the lease and had been pestered by her complaints ever since.

He didn't like the idea of eviction. He'd done a quick inspection, Nora pointing out the broken oven, burnt-out hot plates and leaky cistern as her reasonable excuse for withholding the rent. Sam had relayed the news to Mr Lal, who had recently agreed to repairs. But the Halpin's rent remained unpaid.

The phone rang yet again. His wife, Kitty, suggested lunch at the Club. Right on twelve o'clock, she crossed the street and came towards his office. Kitty was always punctual. She despised lateness, along with careless mothers and lazy fathers. Duty was her recipe for a problem-free family. Through the plate glass, Sam watched his wife. The gentle, fair-headed girl he'd married inhabited his heart. He was always surprised to notice she was now a matron, middle-aged. She'd begun experimenting with what she called My New Look. Had her hair ever been so cropped, so blonde? What was she doing in that short strapless outfit? Sam ran a comb through his hair, hitched his pants and went to meet her.

They walked along to the Club, where the lunch menu was unadventurous and cheap. As he queued, plastic tray in hand, Sam eyed white bread sandwiches and rich chocolate cakes, but Kitty was watching so he chose a low-fat salad plate and a whole grain bun. She was always at him about his diet since their children had grown up. Leaza was a dreamy sixteen-year-old who took interminable showers and lived in her bedroom, playing pop songs and reading romances. Holly was in India. She'd beaten a dozen other applicants to travel as an aid worker funded by the church.

At the time, the whole family had been excited. To travel so far from home!

The blue oceans and pink and lemon continents of the atlas were suddenly real. Their ports of call were listed on a travel itinerary; their diseases posed a threat against which Holly had to be inoculated.

Her first letters home spoke of the heat, the dust, the power failures and the unsafe drinking water. Her photos showed no smiling locals in quaint villages. Kitty framed one picture, of Holly with a group of other volunteers. She stood it on the piano, alongside other mementoes of schooldays. Portraits and photos of the children were everywhere. Sam could accept that the days of ballet lessons, Brownies and Santa were over, but Kitty fretted. She devoted herself to Joel, their youngest, and, in Sam's opinion, she spoiled him. As for her husband—well, her caring was evident, but he wished it needn't involve so much cottage cheese and lettuce.

They carried their trays to a table and Kitty sent Sam to the bar for lemonades. He sat opposite her, preparing to unload some of the morning's frustrations, but Kitty got in first, her words rushing past him like uneasy pedestrians fleeing from a collapsing building.

'Poor Marie, that beast of a sister's wrecked her garden!'

Kitty had never liked Ronnie since she'd dropped a rubber funnelweb spider down Kitty's blouse in sixth class, and sat laughing at her hysterics.

'Marie's so upset. It's wicked! If Ronnie were my sister, I'd soon put her straight. But Marie hasn't got much gumption. She'll never make a go of that shop. It's not Trundle. Well, I tried to tell her, but she's off in her own world. I'm not surprised that sister's not married. No one could live with her for long. Serve her right! But a woman like Marie shouldn't be alone. Sam? Do you think?'

'Think what?' His attention was on a young couple canoodling at the next table.

'I said, Marie ought to have a man. Well, I did try. Remember how I went to no end of trouble, arranging that dinner with Vern Hackett? Marie came in those dreadful clothes, and her hair looked like she'd been through a cyclone. And she did know he was coming, because I dropped plenty of hints.'

The couple couldn't take their eyes off each other. Honeymooners, perhaps.

'Don't look like that, Sam! It's a shame, I know, but some people won't be helped.'

'Probably.' He was out of the habit of listening. 'Anyway, business is on the move. Cheap coastal blocks. You can start getting quotes on that carpet you want.'

Somehow he wasn't surprised when she hardly acknowledged his news. Kitty wasn't happy. Whatever she wanted, he couldn't provide it. At least Holly was on her way home; perhaps that would bring back the wife he knew.

After lunch they walked back to Sam's office, their steps adjusted to the unconscious rhythm of many years together.

'I might be late tonight,' Sam said.

'Don't work too hard.' It was a platitude, like the little kiss that skimmed his cheek. He did not know that Kitty had withheld the most upsetting piece of news about her friend; that Marie intended to go and live at Pelican commune. The fight with her sister had brought matters to a head, and Marie had sounded resolute.

Kitty wandered back to work, uncomforted by her hour with Sam. He seemed switched off. Everyone was leaving her. Tears filled her eyes.

Kitty blinked them away, held her cropped head high and stepped out like a woman who knows she is needed and valued.

PART 3

STRANGERS IN TOWN

PART 3

1

On the morning of the public meeting, dawn bestowed its impartial calm on the sleeping citizens of the town. It was followed by an apricot-coloured sunrise, wonderfully gilding the faded signs, tattered awnings and peeling paint of shop facades and redefining the landmarks of trees and hills. The moments of its rebirth seemed to endow the centre with significance. Beneath that light it was easy to imagine Trundle as an arena where civilised issues were at stake; where men and women examined their souls and strove to create lasting memorials to their brief existences.

The brilliant sky gave way to a grey morning. In Alexandra Avenue, alarms shrilled and clock radios blurted out cheerful music. Kindly or irritably, people with things to do greeted one another. Shower jets steamed, cornflakes rattled into bowls, frying bacon and fresh toast aromas drifted on the May breeze.

At the slum end of town, the unemployed of Railway Street slept on until the sensation of a minor earthquake dragged them from their dreams. Only old Mrs O'Brian, who'd been there forty years and raised her two sons to the background music of trains, did not notice as they streaked past the back garden fences. Ernie Hood, the sailor who'd found his way to one of these run-down houses to retire, had yet to get used to the racket, which rivalled the spectacular fights of the Halpins, his neighbours. As the vibrations of the train subsided, he pulled the blankets higher and conjured images of the little boys he loved to fondle in his dreams.

Next door, Nora Halpin lay tenderly exploring the extent of her bruise, while her good eye assessed the hole in the bedroom door, placed there the previous night by Tag, who'd taken exception to Nora's goads. He was still asleep, dishevelled and unshaven yet, in sleep, more like the old Tag she'd joined forces with to do battle with a tough world. Before his accident they'd had a chance of winning. He'd had work. Now he drank too much; so did she. Half the benefit went on beer and smokes. She had a god-awful head. The kids were quiet for once. It must have been a big barney last night. That still wouldn't get the rent paid and her notion to work it off on the quiet with the agent, Sam, wasn't worth a follow-up. He'd run a mile! They'd once been in the same class. Not that she'd fancied the shy, well-behaved type. And he'd been scared stiff of her.

Nora stared at the hole in the door. She'd have to hide the damage when Sam came back to inspect the repairs. There'd been tradesmen in and out, fixing this and that. Now she'd really have to do something about the rent. Tag wasn't any help. She wished the day would go away.

The morning train brought a visitor, Nick Questro, to Trundle. A freelance journalist, he was following the effects of the government's user-pay and general cost-cutting measures on rural towns like Trundle. He intended to draw his own conclusions from the public meeting, scheduled for that evening, as part of the hard-hitting essay he had underway.

He strode towards the town, limping slightly from the injury he carried from a car accident, and ferreted out the local newspaper office. It was a small place on the main drag. A handful of staff—the editor, Mac Booth, and an attractive dark-skinned girl sitting at a desk across the room. He could feel her stare as he went on explaining his assignment.

'How long have you been on the road?' asked Mac, a touch enviously. Nick was his desired *alter ego*: free, good-looking, ready to go where he pleased and nose out the stories he was interested in.

'Quite a while. I've covered several inland towns, now I'm working down the coast.'

'Good copy?'

'I think so. Sad to see the worst-affected places. Business in the doldrums, banks closing, the people demoralised. I hope Trundle puts up a damn good fight to keep its transport links.'

'We will. Bureaucracy usually wins. But we'll try.'

'The local member's onside?'

As the men chatted, Vim's gaze stayed fixed on Nick.

'Who's that girl?' he murmured.

Mac grinned. 'Vimla Lal. A very bright young lady. She started a few months ago.'

'She's lucky, landing work here. You wouldn't have many openings for staff?'

'Very few. We're a small turnout and I'm not going anywhere!'

'Don't fancy a short sabbatical?' There was some kind of offer in Nick's light remark.

'Why would you want work in a one-horse town like this?'

'I'm keeping clear of Sydney.'

'Why's that?'

Nick hesitated. Going into the details of the past still dragged up so much pain. He'd found real love, a marriage made in heaven, with Jenny. That had all disappeared one day, with no warning, while they were driving back from holidays. He'd got off with a shattered leg. The semitrailer driver hadn't had a scratch. And Jenny had been killed. Fourteen months down the track, the court case was still pending. Likewise the compensation claim. What else was there to do but keep moving, hoping that one day he'd want to live a proper life again?

'I lost my wife last year,' he said.

The editor didn't pry. 'Sorry to hear it. But work—no, there's nothing going here.'

'I'm not surprised. No long service leave for us journos! I'll push off now. Can you recommend a place to stay?'

'There's one motel, down by the river. The pub's a bit noisy.'

Nick nodded. 'I usually land the bedroom right above the bar. Thanks for your help.'

'See you tonight at the meeting then.'

As Nick turned to leave, he came face to face with Vim, who stood smiling by the desk, so close to him that he took a step back from her.

'Mr Booth? My article. You wanted to see it.'

'Finished already? This is Nick Questro, a journalist from Sydney. He'll join us at the meeting tonight.'

'Sydney! How long are you here, Nick?'

'Just a few days.' He nodded and escaped. Women were not on his agenda. Just as well, perhaps. It was a long time since a girl had looked at him with such unconditional approval.

Lights blazed at the community hall, where groups of citizens stood about, exchanging pleasantries. Usually this was the venue for scout meetings, aerobic classes, World Vision slide evenings and light opera productions, sung to the accompaniment of an ancient piano with a crackled veneer case.

Tonight, both sides of Main Road were lined with cars. Residents were out in force: the mayor and councillors, business people, police, clerics, lawyers, doctors, accountants and teachers mingling with shopkeepers, tradesmen, citizens and ratepayers. Catholics were in one huddle, masons in another. A few town characters held forth to anyone they could waylay.

'I'll find parking.' Vim dropped off her father and Vijay, and drove on in the anticipant state that had enveloped her since she'd met Nick. Vijay followed his father up the steps. He didn't care about the fate of Trundle's trains. His father was keen to speak on the need to attract tourists, and his sister would scribble notes and quotes as though her most passionate concern was the transport system. For his part, he was bored. He withdrew to a corner, picked up a faded handbill and began to study the cast of *South Pacific*, in which Bart Bexley had played Emile De Beque the previous summer.

Vim came running into the foyer just as the meeting opened. By now the hall was packed. Standing at the doorway she scanned the chairs until, near the front, she spotted Mac, and beside him the fair-haired journalist, his black, collarless shirt somehow defining him as a city man. The meeting was called to order and the chairman delivered his introduction while Vim edged her way along the aisle, jotting down points on the critical role played by rail transport into Trundle. Ronnie Gale stepped up to speak. She spoke on the consequences to those on low incomes, when any public amenity became a profit-driven business. A pastor and a representative of the Salvation Army both stood up to reinforce her points. Action groups put forward their proposals—a poster competition, a protest march, a subcommittee to promote tourism. At this point Mr Lal took his chance, stood up, and gave an account of his own plan to enhance Trundle's tourist image.

All this time, Vim continued to watch Nick as he made a note or murmured in Mac's ear. She had almost reached the front when a sudden clatter interrupted the present speaker. People craned their necks, wondering about the confusion at the front. Mac had pitched forward and fallen to the floor, where he lay facedown, his bald patch shining pink beneath the lights.

'Mr Booth!' Vim pushed her way towards Nick, who knelt beside the editor and rolled him over. Mac's face was a bluish colour and he gave a faint groan, then seemed to fall unconscious. Ronnie had rushed forward and was now checking pulses and calling for an ambulance. She began resuscitation while Nick used his mobile phone, then took over the breathing while she worked on chest compressions.

'Mr Booth!' Vim fell on her knees beside the others. 'Is he dead?'

Mac groaned again, and Ronnie signalled Nick to help roll him on his side.

'He's had a heart attack,' she said, and Nick saw Vim's dark eyes flood with tears.

'I'm sure he'll be all right. The ambulance is on its way.'

Comforted by his gentle tone, Vim stood aside, watching while the ambulance personnel assessed Mac and carried him away on a stretcher. Now people stood in groups, uncertain whether the meeting was concluded.

Nick placed a hand on Vim's shoulder and guided her outside.

'Mac told me he wasn't feeling too good,' he said. 'Thought it was indigestion from the pie he ate for tea. He'll have to change his diet now. A heart attack's serious.'

She knew it was. Mr Booth had looked terribly ill. Even her own heart had pounded alarmingly at the sight of him.

'I think I'll go home,' she said.

'Are you sure about that?' Nick sounded challenging. 'Who's going to write up the outcomes of the meeting?'

She was silent.

'A good journalist has to overlook personal reactions. Or is that too hard?'

She tossed back her hair. 'I'll manage. But I don't see how there'll even be a paper this week.'

'I'll visit Mac in the morning. Perhaps I can hold the reins until he's better.'

'I thought you were leaving?'

'My schedule's flexible.' He smiled at her obvious pleasure. 'The meeting's ready to resume. Maybe I can walk you home afterwards?'

Miraculously revived, Vim made careful notes for the rest of the proceedings. She gave the car key to Vijay and told her father she had some final writing-up to see to. Nick was waiting by the steps for her. Together they turned off Main Road and wandered on along the deserted streets of her suburb. She shivered and Nick laughed. 'That's a silly dress for this time of year. Step it out, you'll soon warm up.' He rested a brotherly arm around her.

He took long strides, and she liked the fact that he made no concessions because she was a girl. She was not used to walking late at night. Moonlight shed a mysterious light over the scenery she knew so well and the erratic breeze kept raising goose pimples on her bare arms.

'This morning I enquired about temporary work on the paper,' Nick said. 'I reckon Mac might welcome the idea now.'

'Poor Mr Booth!' But her attention returned to the news that Nick planned to stay in Trundle. 'Can I show you round town tomorrow?'

'You get the write-up done in the morning. I'll pick you up at lunchtime.'

They turned in to Alexandra Avenue and soon reached the Lal's home, where lights announced the others had returned.

'See you round.' Nick casually waved and walked off while she unlatched the gates. Bimbo pounded down the front path and stood beside her. She waited, fondling his head, until Nick's footsteps were no longer audible.

Vijay, unusually keen to drive out to Pelican again, was chatting with his father when she went inside.

'How did my speech go?' Mr Lal asked his daughter. 'Did people like the idea?'

Vim, used to his one-track mind, gave an automatic nod. 'It was fine. I won't stay up. I'm tired.'

She went to her room, where she began checking the notes she'd made. Her copy would be ready and the newspaper would come out on time.

Mac sat propped on pillows, stunned by the news that he was lucky to be alive. When Nick Questro walked in to the ward, wearing his camera bag, Mac managed to smile.

'Come to take my picture? Seems I ought to thank you.'

'Everybody should learn CPR.' Nick had a flashback to Jenny, lying on the wet road as the ambulance men worked on her. 'You look better than you did last night, Mac.'

'Don't remember much about it.' The doctor's words were running through Mac's mind. Myocardial infarction. We'll send you down to Newcastle. You're a bypass candidate. It was like an episode of *ER*.

'I have to get back to work,' Mac had said.

'Surgery's the first step. You'll need physio, medication, and a diet. You'll be a new man.' His pager had sounded and he'd walked away.

Mac had been quite content with the old man. He didn't want a diet, much less an operation. On the other hand, he wasn't keen on dying. In this uneasy frame of mind, he heard Nick suggest that he take over as editor for a few months.

Opportune, this fellow turning up. He had sub-editing experience on a major daily paper and he wouldn't be after Mac's job.

'Seems I'm for the knife,' he said unhappily. 'I'll be off work for a while. So yes. If you're prepared to stay, the job's yours.'

'Thanks. A country paper sounds right up my street.' Nick stood up to leave as a nurse came to check Mac's readings. 'I'm available till August. You can fill me in how you like things done. I'll spend some time on it with you tomorrow.'

Nick walked back to Main Road in a thoughtful state of mind. The past twenty-four hours had shaken him up. He'd saved a life, landed a job, and an attractive young lady had eyes for him. He had no intention of responding, but looked forward to her showing him round town.

Vim, in short skirt and high heels, stood outside the office as the town clock struck midday. All night she'd lain awake, thinking about Nick's smile, his city air and the mystery of the night as she'd walked home with him. He was coming towards her now.

'I've just been to see your boss,' he said.

'How is he?'

'He'll need treatment, but he's OK. I might be doing his job for a while.'

She knew it was wrong to hope that Mr Booth would be off work forever.

'What would you like to see?' She wondered how to spin out Trundle's sites of interest.

'Everything!' He seemed cheerful today. The lines of humour around his mouth gave him a look of experience, she thought. Together they began to walk, while Vim pointed out the Council offices, the club, the library, the picture theatre. She was running out of ideas, and only fifteen minutes had passed.

'There's the old storehouse by the river. It was being turned into an historic museum, until the money ran out.'

'I've seen enough museums.'

Marie's antique shop caught his eye and he lingered at the window.

'Worth a browse?'

'No,' said Vim, who hated old things. 'There's the park. They built that fountain last year.'

Nick let her conduct him to the small oval across the street. Vim noticed how muddy the duck pond looked and how Nick kept darting his glance about.

'Will you take my picture?' she asked impulsively.

'If you like.'

Though she wished the idea had been his, she was pleased when he took not one but several snapshots of her, posed beside the troop carrier with its commemorative brass plaque. There was nothing else to see. They wandered on.

'What do you usually do for fun?' she asked.

Nick mentioned the theatre, art exhibitions, book launches, restaurants, the opera.

'I'd really like to travel overseas,' he added.

'Then why don't you?' Surely at his age you did what you wanted.

'Business matters pending.' He did not confide in her.

'I've never been to an opera.'

'We'll have to rectify that one day,' he said lightly, and she smiled up at him, feeling he had made her a promise.

A bridge and railway line spanned the river as they reached the industrial sector, where an appetising smell from the biscuit factory mingled with fumes from engineering works and machine shops. Along Railway Street stretched a row of half a dozen shabby houses. Beyond them lay the tip and the scrap metal yard.

'You don't want to look around here,' she decided.

'Yes, I do. It's quintessential country life.'

'They're just old dumps,' Vim said, not mentioning that one belonged to her father. She was glad Nick had seen where she lived. Her father's house, in her view, was an ideal home. She hoped when she married that she would be provided with one every bit as spacious. Nick's taste made her curious. She wondered if he might be very poor.

'What kind of house do you have?' She blushed as he laughed.

'I'm a nomad. Let's wander.'

In her high heels it was all she could manage to keep up with him. The houses here were all the same, with tiny front gardens, rotting board fences and sagging porches on which stood ancient sofas, their stuffing poking out. An old fellow with a goatee and a nautical cap puffed at his pipe in the uncertain breeze. Next door, a little girl swung back and forth on a leaning gate. It collapsed, and the child's wails brought a worn-looking woman out to investigate. She helped the girl up and gave her a rough pat. 'Bloody kids!' she volunteered, to no one in particular.

Next door, a man was tinkering with machinery that occupied almost all the tiny yard. Nick stopped to question him. Soon the two were deep in conversation.

Vim stood back to study Nick while his attention was engaged. A longing she'd never felt before intoxicated her. She was no longer solitary. Her happiness was tied to this stranger who had not even existed in her life before yesterday. The family bonds that had accompanied her childhood were frayed and ready to snap, if Nick so much as beckoned.

'I might come back and investigate these inventions of yours. Sound interesting.' Nick glanced at Vim. 'Time's getting on, we'd better get you back to work.'

'It's strange there, without Mr Booth. Could I visit him?'

'Sure! He's going to fill me in on the job tomorrow.'

'So you'll be my boss?'

'We'll have to pull together. I need a place to stay. A motel's no good now.'

'Come and stay with us!' She could hardly contain her excitement.

He seemed puzzled. 'I was thinking of a flat.'

'We have heaps of room.'

'Maybe.' He was weighing things up. 'It would help out.'

'I'll ask my father tonight.' Vim floated along Railway Street.

She was rapping at his motel room before eight o'clock next morning. When Nick opened the door, he had a towel wound at his waist and water dripped from his hair.

'You can stay with us!'

He was charmed in spite of himself. She reminded him of a time when love had been naïve, impulsive. He gave a shiver.

'Better come in. Put the kettle on while I get dressed.'

He soon came back, buckling his belt, and set out cups.

'Coffee? It's only instant.'

'I like instant.' She would have accepted rusty tap water with delight.

He brought the coffee. They sat side by side on the sofa bed.

'Now you're sure your father doesn't mind putting me up?'

'It's fine.'

'Temporary, you understand. Tell me, Vim, how did you land a newspaper job here?'

'Exam results. I came top.' She sounded as though it was her usual place.

'There wouldn't be much promotion here. Where would you like to work, eventually?'

'In the city.' She sat swinging a shapely leg, and her body seemed to melt and flow towards his, stirring up sensations that made him ask, 'How old are you?'

'Nineteen last November.'

'I'm forty-two.'

Her arm brushed his, making the curly hairs tingle. He'd forgotten how that felt.

He stood up decisively. 'Let's get going. I'll just pack up my things and let them know at the office.' He paused. 'You really did check this with your father?'

'Of course.'

Which was in one sense true, for these days Mr Lal only had thoughts about his Taj, and frequently did not pay attention to other matters of conversation in the household.

2

Since the garden episode, the sisters were on cool terms. Marie kept to herself her plans to move to the commune, and tried to do her fair share of the household duties. However, this weekend she was determined to go to Pelican, where a welcome for Victor Argyle, the English doctor, was being arranged. Ronnie did not see the urgency of the visit.

'You were supposed to help me wash the windows,' she said.

'Leave them. I'll do them next week.'

'Pigs will fly!'

Marie shrugged, picked up her weekend bag and drove away.

A phone call on Saturday destroyed Ronnie's own plans. Half the rostered staff were off sick, and the registered sister on geriatrics was down with the same gastric bug. Ronnie was needed to stand in on Sunday. She went to work reluctantly. As Sister Gale arrived on duty, a word of warning circulated. The staff worked to the clock and the patients cowered. Sandy had a very bad time.

'Did you leave that wet draw-sheet on the floor, Nurse Smith?'

She had. The stumbling, senile old lady had taken all of Sandy's concentration.

'Then pick it up, and disinfect the area. Haven't you heard of cross-infection?'

How slow this girl was! Ronnie often surprised her perched on the side of a patient's bed as she helped with a knitting pattern, peeled an orange or read out a letter or a *Get Well* card. Ronnie was well aware there was more to good nursing than carrying out allocated tasks in the allotted time. Sandy quietly comforted the fearful, fed the paralysed, or held the weak hand of a dying patient.

Ronnie had been like that once. She resented Sandy's well of caring. Her own was dry. The job was a dreary interlude between paydays. The whole hospital scene felt depressing; a *déja vu* peep at her eventual future. She knew she was impatient and abrupt but seemed unable to control her manner.

She followed Sandy to the sluice room, where she was filling up a metal bucket with hot water. She avoided looking up and did not speak.

'Nurse Smith...' She realised the girl was in tears. 'You want to be a good nurse, don't you? Is something wrong?'

Sandy shook her head and Ronnie felt unreasonably rejected.

'In that case, get the floor mopped.'

As she walked away, she was close to tears herself. Why did everyone, even her sister, misunderstand her? Marie had virtually attacked her over the garden; had shouted and cried and dredged up resentments she must have carried since childhood.

You couldn't un-say words. The two had maintained a polite distance since then. Fortunately Ronnie had done a run of afternoon shifts which meant their paths had hardly crossed. The house was an unpleasant place of closed doors and echoes.

And dreams. That same one. So natural, so friendly, until the moment came. The other woman wouldn't co-operate, never mind the cool satin lining and the quality polish of the casket. Trying to force the aspirins into her mouth... She spat and frothed, hitting out. Ronnie had to beg her, Quickly, quickly, time is running out...

She felt so tired as she went on with her rounds. It was one of those days. The old people were like children playing up for a new baby-sitter. Craziness had its quirky side but today she found it painful. There was Rose, pursuing deaf George along the corridor. Ribbons in her wild white hair, her catheter bag dragging like Mary's lamb, she hummed her siren songs. *My word nursie, the boys loved me!*

While George made his escape, she dug ragged nails into Ronnie's arm and was steered to the day room, a sad holding pen where inert bodies lolled sideways against their safety restraints. Ronnie's uniform reminded them they'd once had rights.

'Get me a banana,' screamed Nonnie. 'A horse you are, untrained horses!'

Ronnie wheeled her away to the lavatory. John was there, trying to climb into the bowl. Ronnie pulled his trousers up. He looked horrified; clinging to the cistern while an unknown adversary fiddled with his fly buttons. He'd been a pilot. His wife still called him her darling while she mopped up his dribble and held his flaccid hand.

'Oh come on, John.' Without compassion, this kind of work was hell. A brown puddle was taking shape under Nonnie's wheelchair. The old woman looked satisfied as she watched it spread. Ronnie left her and dashed to answer the phone. Someone on the end of the line burst into tears and begged her to relay a message. Ronnie located the woman's husband. He was upright at his bed table, fighting to breathe, in the late stages of emphysema.

'Gladys can't come today.'

He burst into tears and cradled his head on his arms.

'She said she's sorry.'

Will you tell him that I love him? But somehow Ronnie couldn't. She hated the way love struggled on even in this burnt hill station; love, which had once seemed to her a light and lasting thing. Now she thought it was an illusion born of need and loneliness.

She was behind in her schedule. There was the medication to give out and no one on hand she could delegate responsibility to.

Later, she wondered at exactly what point she'd chosen to bale out. She was too seasoned a nurse to forget basic safety regulations; to allow the simple mistake that could have caused a patient's death. She'd rushed through the round, failed to have her drugs properly checked, confused syringes and administered a high dose of insulin to the wrong patient. Fortunately there'd been a doctor on call. She'd had to submit an Incident report and knew she could expect a disciplinary interview and a black mark on her record. The staff nurse on Surgical tried to cheer her up when she heard the supervisor was so upset she had to go off duty. *We've all done it once*, she murmured. But she was wrong. Ronnie had never done it.

The house was deserted when Marie returned on Sunday afternoon.

Practice for the doctor's group welcome and her concert had gone well. Reviewing the pleasant weekend, she was walking to the house when Sandy waylaid her.

'Can I ask you about that commune?' she said. 'What do you do there?'

'You have to pay your way. There's work to do: feeding the hens, growing vegetables, building, selling the crafts. Older members have private incomes.'

'I like gardening.'

'Why do you ask?'

She was a shy girl, perhaps easy to manipulate. Marie doubted these questions were just for her benefit.

'Vijay wants to go and live there.'

'I see.' And Sandy would follow, hoping for security, until one day (perhaps it would take a thousand compromises for she had a patient look) she would become angry and resentful. 'You're happy with Vijay? How did you meet?'

The girl smiled. 'He bought me a milkshake. We sat and talked for ages.'

'And now you live with his family. Do you like the Lals?'

'Oh yes. I like the big house.'

'And you earn the money?'

'At the hospital.' Mention of work reminded her of the supervisor and she looked nervously at her watch. 'What time does Sister Gale get home?'

'Not yet.'

Sandy looked so relieved that Marie laughed. 'I know she can be a dragon. You must stick up for yourself.'

'I know. What sort of people live at the commune?'

'All sorts.'

'Not praying all the time?'

'Good heavens no! I plan to move there myself. I have a granddaughter there.'

Sandy looked relieved. 'You'd be there?'

'Yes. Now, promise me you'll talk to Vijay. Does he realise how hard you work? Does he know you're unsure about moving?'

Sandy shook her head.

'Then talk to him. You may end up liking the place more than he does. You seem quite different types.'

'That's why we're suited,' Sandy said. Just then, Ronnie's car pulled up and the girl froze. 'I better go!'

Marie watched her rush away. How nice it must be to have a daughter who visited and talked over her problems!

She waited on the porch. When Ronnie made no appearance she decided to walk out to the car. Her sister just sat on in the driver's seat.

'What are you doing?' Marie asked. Ronnie didn't answer. She looked peculiar; in shock.

'What's wrong?' Marie opened the car door and Ronnie stumbled out. She stood there in the middle of the driveway.

'I nearly killed someone.'

'Here, come inside. A car accident?'

'At work. I gave the wrong drugs. I'm resigning.'

Marie stared at her. 'Isn't that a bit drastic?' Jobs for middle-aged women weren't easy to find.

Ronnie shook her head. Tears filled her eyes and her mouth quivered like a punished child's. Marie filled the kettle. While the water seethed she rinsed teacups. She made the tea. Ronnie sat down. She tried to pick up the cup. Her shoulders shook with sobs. When Marie went to take her trembling hand, Ronnie pulled back as though she had no right to comfort. Tea splashed on the cloth.

'I don't know what's happening to me.'

Marie clasped her firmly; this woman who spoke in the voice of a despairing child.

'Didn't I tell you, Ronnie?" Her voice had the tone of a kind, no-nonsense mother, who would scold and comfort and solve impossible problems. 'You're all uptight and silly. You need time off. You try to do it all alone. You can't.' Ronnie kept on sobbing. 'You just can't!' Marie gave her a handkerchief, and held her sister until Ronnie collapsed against her.

They sorted it out together next morning. Marie deferred going in to the shop. She brought Ronnie breakfast on a tray. Her sister lay quietly, the bedclothes hardly disturbed; there was nothing to her but the lined face with its lost expression. She agreed to go and see a doctor. She agreed to go on sick leave. She agreed to put off resigning.

'I have an idea where you can recuperate,' Marie told her. 'We'll talk about it later.' Ronnie agreed to that as well. She said she was sorry about everything and Marie comforted her and begged her not to cry; it didn't matter, it was over, in the past, forgotten.

3

When Victor Argyle, at the end of his marathon journey, landed in Australia and checked his bags through Customs, he looked to be a prime example of his own philosophy. A dark-haired, strong man in his forties, he exuded health and energy. As he scanned the crowd, Honor Stedman, waiting with Laurie, waved and hurried forward to greet him.

'Victor, we're so thrilled to have you here!'

Used to her exclamatory ways, he smiled down at her. Honor had been his honorary aunt, sending him Christmas and birthday cards; her letters with their foreign stamps had given him trading material at boarding school. She'd attended his wedding, and for decades had kept up correspondence from her quiet retreat at the commune. It had been Honor's persuasive talk of a new health clinic that had sown the seeds of his interest in a sea change. His interest in the holistic approach had been growing for many years and the chance to apply his theories had other timely advantages. His finances were severely strained as he kept his wife Elizabeth and their five children in the luxuries expected of a doctor's family, including private schooling, pony clubs, and a large eighteenth-century house that needed continual repairs. His colleagues, surgeons and physicians, were traditional doctors. They looked on alternative therapies as backward superstition, and eyed Victor strangely when he mentioned his interest in homeopathy, meditation or naturopathic remedies.

His marriage was no better. His wife Elizabeth complained that he grew more and more detached and impossible to talk to. He could not explain that these defences, developed to keep at bay the female patients who sometimes turned his medical attentions to fantasies of an entirely different nature, had taken him over. In fact, he did feel detached from everything except his children.

He had been enticed by Honor's conviction that the commune must expand to serve a wider community. Like a boy setting off on an adventure, he'd made plans to come ahead to Australia, leaving the family to follow when the house was sold. The novelty of the new landscape brought back the light to his sombre brown eyes, and he laughed a lot on the journey north.

Pelican itself came as a surprise to him. He'd concocted some impression of the community that bore no resemblance to the place itself. There was certainly no sign of a lay-about lifestyle in the trim gardens and neat chalets, nor any evidence of the casual sex relationships he'd somehow assumed went on in communes. He wasn't sure whether he felt relieved or disappointed. Sexual impulses, particularly his own, made him wary. He preferred them safely contained within the social framework of home and family life, where temptation was minimal and where grateful or lonely female patients did not suggest with looks and sighs that they found him a very attractive man.

He was keen to get to work right away. However, it seemed nothing concrete was in place.

'We'll have you set up in no time,' was the best he could extract from Honor, who added that there would possibly be some opposition from a certain problematic Dutchman.

'I'm sure we'll sort it out,' said Victor, who had not travelled 17,000 kilometres in pursuit of new problems.

The group had arranged a welcome, in the form of an Indonesian-style meal followed by musical entertainment. A middle-aged woman, Marie Mortimer, gave a short recital. The piano was hardly of Albert Hall quality, but Victor complimented her when she had finished and she blushed.

'Thank you! We're all so excited that you're here.'

'My wife and children will be joining me soon,' he said in a businesslike manner. 'Do you happen to know of a house I could rent in town?'

For Elizabeth had been specific in her instructions. *I'm not bringing the children halfway across the globe to live on some commune!*

'As a matter of fact, my home's available.'

'That would be out of the question,' he said, recoiling from an image of yet another lonely woman manoeuvring him into her fantasies. 'I meant a vacant house. I have a very large family. Five children.'

He saw he had misunderstood as she began a long-winded explanation, to do with her sister being ill, and the pair of them moving to live at the commune.

'It might suit you, until you get a feel for things here. You could move your family straight in.'

'Is it furnished?' It would be months before his own goods were sent by ship.

'Yes, with all the main items. And the rent would be low.'

'Why would that be?' His suspicion was slow to die.

'You'd be doing us a favour. We don't want to leave the place empty. If we rent to strangers we'd have to put everything in storage.'

'I'd like to inspect it.'

'Of course. Any time.'

She said they had a spare room, if he wished to spend a night in town, exploring the facilities.

Victor spent the next few days walking the bush and beach tracks. Between hikes he sounded out the views of other members, trying to piece together an overall concept for his clinic. He discovered that views ranged widely; from a simple rest facility to Richard Van Rjien's elaborate blueprint for a multimillion-dollar tourist complex.

'A health and fitness clinic could be integrated with the other attractions,' Richard pointed out, as lunch progressed to coffee and the offer of cigars.

Victor declined the cigar but did not dismiss Richard's idea. It was grandiose; there must be money backing this man's talk. His plans were backed up with facts and figures, and his manner was persuasive. Perhaps that was how he'd landed such a pretty little wife. She'd first caught Victor's eye as, slim and supple in a *sarong,* she'd moved between the reception tables. The pair seemed to have a happy marriage. The reminder of his wife and family, so far away, made Victor feel nostalgic and confirmed that he must get on and find a suitable house for them.

Nick Questro was also looking for accommodation. It did not take a genius to see why Mr Lal was not warm towards his guest. Wherever Nick was, Vim followed, exuding clouds of perfume and charm. Her father observed in watchful silence. The journalist was cool and businesslike, but he too decided that the sooner he moved out, the better.

At the Lals' home, he had been introduced to a neighbour, Marie Mortimer. The topic of conversation was a local commune in which everybody had some interest. Vijay asked questions, Sandy added several of her own, Mr Lal kept turning the conversation to some land for sale there, while Marie herself announced that she and her sister was vacating their house and going there to live.

'I'm moving too,' said Nick, ignoring Vim's glance of dismay.

'Sam Playfair's the local agent. Tell him I sent you.'

'Thanks. I will.' The networks of small towns amused him. 'This commune? How does it survive? I'd have thought it was an anachronism.'

'Plans afoot,' said Marie. 'Changes. Come out and visit us. We always welcome visitors.'

'I might.' Nick stored away the invitation. He guessed there weren't too many spots of interest around Trundle.

Vim was downcast at dinner. Sensing she was hurt by his decision to move out, Nick spoke to her gently. She was not to know his past and he had no wish to tell her about the accident or his own slowly-healing scars. He had no intention of misleading a girl, less than half his age, who was ready to throw herself at him.

His host began to talk about his plans to build a replica of the Taj Mahal. The man had evidently passed through the first stage of paralysing grief, and sought some way to actualise his mourning. A sudden image of Jenny struck Nick; but this time it was not the indelible horror of that last sight, her body lying sprawled on the wet road. He remembered her as joyful, as she laughed and tossed a tennis ball for their blue heeler, Marquis.

'The Taj is a great story,' said Nick. 'I'm sure Vim will keep me up to date.'

Mr Lal nodded. He was clearly pleased by the news of Nick's impending departure.

Strategic retreat beckoned. A stop at the local rental agency was first thing on Nick's agenda.

Holly Playfair had walked out on an argument with her mother. Kitty thought she ought to be interviewed by *The Trundle Times*. She said it was the least Holly could do, after all the money the Overseas Aid Committee had invested in her.

'I don't want to,' said her daughter who, the previous Sunday, had been bombarded after church with questions about her work at the mission in India. She couldn't face another cross-examination. The tension she felt at home was bad enough.

Her family's wastefulness appalled her. They threw food away, left on unnecessary lights, spent in a week what an Indian household had to manage on for three months. Leaza was a spoilt and lazy adolescent who thought education was a drag. Joel was enrolled in Cubs, gymnastics and music lessons. He was nine years old and he owned a bright red electric guitar and amplifier he could hardly lift. Kitty's mind roamed from one expensive purchase to the next. She was putting in new carpet, worth more than a basic home in India. Sam worked hard; yet how could his job compare with the lot of poor labourers bent double under heavy loads?

Holly had been brought up to believe in charity. To help the poor was a worthwhile act. But the poor of India hadn't wanted her. Worse, they'd seemed happy, while she was miserable.

Now, as she walked with Joel beside the river, she saw a man standing thigh-deep in the sluggish current. Something about his concentration made her curious. Whatever he was doing, he was totally absorbed. Holly stopped to watch him. He was tinkering with a water wheel whose blades slowly rotated. He looked like a figure in a landscape painting— his toil in harmony with universal elements. Holly recognised one of those adjustments that had disturbed her even though she'd not identified it. In response to India, where everything took so long to happen, she'd slowed down. Back home, she'd been jolted by the pace of freeway travel, instant meals, and television shows where pain and humour were mere grist to the mill of information.

Now the man was wading out to reposition his device. His posture was intense and childlike, reminding her of Joel as he squatted there on the riverbank, poking at some insect with a stick. The man tugged his model this way and that. There seemed to be a stuck blade. He glanced up and saw her. Holly called out to him.

'What are you making?'

'A power generator. It's meant to be floated on a barge with submerged paddles. The current's no good today.'

He waded back and stood shivering as a cold breeze funnelled down the road. He began to lug the wheel towards the riverbank.

'How do you transport it?'

'On my bicycle.' He grinned. 'You'd be amazed what I can shift. I've towed a washing machine uphill with this gearing I designed.'

'Are you an inventor?' piped Joel, who liked to dismantle objects to find out how they worked.

'I suppose so. I haven't sold any so far.'

'Why do you make them then?' Joel was a modern child, well indoctrinated in commercial principles.

'It's fun.' Peter attached ropes to a contraption on the bank and began to wind. The wheel, like retrieved treasure, was slowly winched to shore. Joel was impressed.

'What else have you invented?'

'Heaps of things. Why don't you come to my place and have a look? I live in Railway Street with my old Mum.'

He seemed to be speaking to Holly through the medium of the little boy, as though shy to approach her.

She watched him lash the wheel to his trailer. His preoccupations were odd and his transport shabby. This was the sort of homemade taxi service an enterprising Indian might set up to earn a few rupees. His brown legs silt-stained, he crouched on strong calves to knot the ropes. His beard curled crisply in a way that Holly liked. The wind was sucking at her dress and blowing her hair all about. Norms of modesty she'd found so old-fashioned in her host country made her gather up the billows of her skirt. Peter cocked his head, smiling up at her.

'My name's Peter. I haven't seen you before. New here?'

'I've just come back from India. I'm Holly, this is Joel.'

'India? That's a place I reckon they could use my water wheel.'

He finished strapping the contraption to his cycle and patted the passenger bar.

'There's room for the lad, if he's allowed.'

Holly smiled at him. 'We've nothing else to do.'

Joel climbed aboard and Peter pedalled away, the trailer swaying in his wake. For the first time since she'd arrived home, Holly felt happy walking behind his peculiar transport, the breeze making her eyes water and messing up her hair. Outside Railway Street's close-packed houses, urchins squatted, playing marbles. Old folk sat quietly in the weak autumn sunshine, a mother yelled at her kids, a stray dog sniffed around a garbage bin. There was an air of living in the present. This was the life she'd known for the past year; a day-by-day existence where plans were simple and pleasures basic.

Peter dismounted at a house as shabby as the rest and lugged his trailer into the front yard.

'I'm back, Ma!' He murmured to Holly. 'That's her, sticky-beaking at the curtains. She knows everybody's business. Come and have a look round.'

He began to explain other curious inventions lying about; a solar-powered pump, a ratchet device to move heavy loads.

'There's no work around here, so this is what I do with my time. Some of these might be useful in third-world countries.' He added shyly, 'I'd like to help people there.'

It seemed he was used to being written off as an idle dreamer but Holly was touched that his thoughts bent towards others less well off.

'What was India like?' he asked.

'Most of the time I hated it. I didn't help anyone.' She expected him, like everyone else, to brush aside her words. People wanted to hear tales of her wonderful work among the under-privileged. The truth was that, for every letter she'd sent home, there'd been several so full of despair and self-pity she'd tossed them away. She'd never understood how basic were the ingrained habits of an upbringing or how many assumptions she'd made. Trivial things drove her crazy. In Australia, she could wear shorts and tank tops, work on her tan, read the magazines for teenagers. She was used to milk in cartons, McDonald's, air-conditioning; chemists who stocked tampons and insect repellent, batteries that worked and matches that would strike. Back home, an appointment was something people tried to keep. Buses and trains left on time and usually arrived at their advertised destination. A woman wasn't expected to drape herself from neck to ankle in case some man's desire was crazily provoked. It was the migrants who didn't speak the language.

'At least you tried,' he suggested, as though telling her to keep faith in herself. She wanted to spill out the disappointment of the whole experience and shook her head.

'I was useless. I never found out what I was supposed to do. They told me to tidy up and sort equipment. They said I should give basic English lessons, but nobody came.' She was close to tears as she remembered the humiliation of it all. 'The people didn't trust us. They only came to the mission as a last resort. I saw horrible things like weeping sores and fractures that hadn't healed. Babies died of dysentery. There were stillbirths and deformities. I couldn't wait to leave.'

Instead of judging her, he smiled. 'But you tried,' he said again. Holly felt herself relax. It was good here with Peter and the brick-red geraniums and the washing blowing on the line.

'Have you always lived here?'

It was a home where the grass would grow and the gutters slowly rust unchallenged.

He nodded. 'My brother Bryan's moved on and Mum's no spring chicken. She won't admit it, but she needs someone around. She must be going mad with curiosity! Come and say hello.'

Joel ran off to join a game of marbles as Holly followed Peter along the cracked front path. Something she needed was here; though what it was... Who knew?

4

Sam Playfair perused the *Payments Received* ledger. The Halpins' name was absent. As he'd feared, Mr Lal's renovations had not made a whit of difference to the arrears situation. He would send out a final notice and Nora would ignore it. He scratched his neck. The rash under his collar was growing worse.

He was glad of the interruption when Nick Questro dropped by at his office. Sam looked through his rental listings. There were a couple of flats that Nick thought would do and the agent suggested an immediate inspection. He was pleased to put aside the paperwork and get out in the fresh air for an hour. Nick explained that during Mac Booth's absence he would be acting editor for *The Trundle Times*. He asked a lot of questions as they drove; a journalist's habit, Sam assumed, as he was quizzed on the town's population, work force, and a host of similar statistics. At least the fellow was easy to please. He said he'd take the first flat on the list, and they drove back to the office to complete the paperwork.

'What do you know about a place called Pelican?' Nick asked casually as they pulled up in Main Road.

'Why do you ask that?' Sam felt uneasy. He'd never expected those unusable lots of land on the coast to sell, but Bryan had written glowing advertisements. Sell they had, like the proverbial hot cakes. Sam was dreading the winter. A few good downpours of rain and his phone would be ringing hot again; this time with irate buyers complaining they'd been sold a pup. It wasn't the sort of information he wanted a nosy journalist to get hold of.

'Everyone I've met since I arrived seems to have some interest in the place. I've been staying with an Indian family. The chap apparently wants to build a palace there!'

'I wouldn't know,' said Sam evasively. But he was glad to hear this piece of news. If Mr Lal and Van Rjien had struck a deal, Sam was happy to be middleman.

In the office, Nick signed up and paid and Sam handed over the keys. This was one tenant he wouldn't have to chase for the rent.

Nick emerged into the main street with a feeling of relief. For the next few months he would be settled. Trundle was just the sort of town he needed while he sat in limbo, with a court case looming down the track. A manslaughter charge was pending against the semitrailer driver, whose lawyer was arguing for a lesser charge of dangerous driving. Meanwhile the insurance companies were playing their usual delaying games. Time had watered down Nick's first anger and feelings of revenge. Now he felt a helpless sorrow for everyone. Jenny was gone. No prison term could return her to him. The driver himself had a wife and young family and had gone to sleep at the wheel in the course of a punishing run from the far north. There were no fair outcomes.

At least he could turn his mind to a job. He'd seen Mac again and sorted out the routine. He had a few ideas to give the paper a new slant. Local births, marriages, deaths and the annual regatta were all very well as news items, but Nick felt he could play up the wider social issues underlying the slums of Railway Street and the government sell-off of public services. He'd finished his own piece on rural communities. Now he planned to tutor Vim to look beyond routine reporting and find the potential human drama Nick sensed everywhere. Railway Street was worth a return visit and an intriguing air of mystery surrounded the outlying commune. As he passed the antique shop, he went in for a quick look round and recognised Marie as the neighbour who'd said she was going to live at Pelican. He drew her into conversation while she sketched a quick map of the commune's location and repeated her invitation to him.

'You'll hear plenty of stories, if that's what you want! Honor Stedman can tell you all about the Gurdjieff movement and John Bennett. And Victor Argyle is a man worth interviewing. Homeopathy's just one of his specialities. I believe he attended certain Royals in England. Now he's just joined us to found a holistic clinic. And we have our own expansion plans as well.'

'Mr Lal and his Taj Mahal?'

'Well, that's one suggestion. Richard Van Rjien's the man to talk to. I believe he has something even grander up his sleeve. The community will be meeting to vote in a few weeks. So pay us a visit. You'll certainly come away with stories.'

Storing this information, Nick went on to the office. Trundle was full of surprises.

At work, he went through Vim's articles with a red pen. A good reporter couldn't write according to whim. He had decided to steer their relationship to strictly professional ground. She'd made no attempt to conceal her crushed feelings that he'd decided to move out. An attractive girl smitten with puppy love and serving him breakfast in a satin negligee might tempt any man. It wouldn't have surprised him in the least if she'd come creeping into his room at midnight. And, if so, who could predict the outcome? The key in his pocket had a reassuring feel as he summoned her to go over his editing.

'We'll put this on the front page.'

She looked pleased as he pushed the town meeting report to the features tray. Her write-up on events was clear and factual.

'What about my other article?' she asked.

'It's interesting. You wrote it jointly with your father?'

'Yes. He wanted the poetry.' She looked embarrassed.

'A few lines are OK. They suit the theme. The whole thing needs a trim. I just have a problem with the slant. I mean, the Taj Mahal is only a dream at this point. This says it's reality.'

'It will be! My father's determined.'

'I'm sure he is. But where's the land? Where are the blueprints? Has Council given the go ahead? Is the money in the bank?'

She looked downcast and he smiled at her.

'Let's just file it for now. Meanwhile, would you like to go out with me?' Quickly he rephrased as her eyes sparkled. 'I'm going back to Railway Street to get some first-hand interviews. Folk there depend on public transport, and they put up with the noise and the pollution. We'll take a wander and see what we can find.' The phone rang and he signalled she could go, adding gently as he reached for the receiver, 'By the way, I found a flat. I'll move my gear tonight.'

Vim stepped across the rutted tyre tracks left by trucks and followed Nick into the scrap yard at the end of Railway Street. Everything about him confused her. Why had he brought her to this derelict dump where crushers and bobcats basked as though digesting a recent kill? Where was the news in oil drums, tin baths or rusty car bodies?

Nick bounded ahead. He limped just a little when he hurried. His interest was in some tramp who was sorting through the rubbish, placing bits and pieces in a sack. Vim stayed near the gate, afraid she'd get muddy. Nick poised his camera, the scavenger hitched up his pants and hoisted up his sack.

'Quite a character,' Nick said as he rejoined her. 'Now let's find the inventor.'

Peter was delighted to talk about the dearth of jobs in Trundle. Nick made a tour of the various contraptions in the yard and, when Peter's mother tottered out to investigate, invited her views on the rail crisis. She said it was six of one and half a dozen of the other but she didn't mind having her picture taken. She fetched her teeth and stood beaming beside her son.

'Peter's a good boy,' she murmured to the journalist. 'Bryan, he's my other boy, slips me a few dollars when he bothers to call in, but Peter's the one who minds out for me.'

Next door, Nora eavesdropped by the new fence. To Nick she volunteered that the trains could go to blazes; she hoped she'd never hear one more race past her bedroom. Trains were no good to her; she had no money to go anywhere. She had such chatty views on welfare, jobs and rental dumps that a barefoot, bristly man in a grey singlet and shorts came out to investigate.

'Tag, get over here in the picture!' Nora ordered and the pair lined up and turned on a grin.

Ernie Hood, watching the performance, next aired his views.

'Give me a ship!' he said. 'Trains? Don't give a tuppeny damn about them.'

He delivered a potted history of his seafaring days while Nick snapped several pictures. Vim felt more and more bewildered. Who cared what these down-and-outs thought? Mr Booth never interviewed types like this for the paper. Nick was ignoring her. He was more interested in tramps and layabouts, that much was clear. He'd apparently finished his interviews.

'Ready to head back?' he asked lightly. She did not bother to reply. Turning to march ahead, her heel caught in the uneven pavement surface so that he had to steady her. For a moment they stood touching while she regained her balance.

'You should wear sensible shoes,' he said in a teasing voice. She felt her body yield and wished his arm might lie lightly around her forever.

As Nick and Vim left Railway Street, Nora Halpin heard the postman's motorbike. The arrears notice from Sam was no surprise to her; she didn't associate mail with pleasant surprises. Filled with contempt, she skimmed the rental agency's letter and tossed it into the gutter. After a few moments she retrieved it, realising she couldn't ignore the eviction warning. Slowly she went back up the path and sat on the porch step. She rubbed the scar over her eye and wondered what to do.

It always came down to this. No good landing it on Tag. That kick in the head he'd collected playing footy years ago had knocked him off the air for good. He'd changed. His cheek and backchat had gone sour. The booze made him nasty, laying into her and the kids, swearing and carrying on so all the neighbours knew their business.

Coming back to her hometown had seemed like a good idea. Trundle was a quiet place. They'd get somewhere, she said to Tag, as she remembered the wide main street, the slow river, the trains rushing through. Why was it all so much smaller and rundown now? Tag had taken one look and grumbled. *Another dump.* He had his pride.Yes, she'd believed it too.

She didn't want much. Somewhere to live and raise the kids. A packet of smokes. Beer. A bit of a laugh. Why was it so hard, so different from what you'd think? Didn't seem to matter where she went, trouble wouldn't leave her alone. People didn't like her. They avoided her or looked away. She could put up with a bit of bashing, so why couldn't they cop the sight of a bruise?

That slimy Sam, for example. Sending her a notice, all official, as if he hadn't just been a pimply kid no better than she was. Now up himself good and proper, asking for references and a month's bond as if she was Lady Muck in a Cadillac. She'd had to lay it on with a trowel to get a place out of him. And now this fancy letter. *Dear Mrs Halpin. We wish to draw your attention…'* And he signed his name with a doodad instead of proper writing.

Mrs Halpin my foot! She was Nora and no bugger was going to put her and the kids out on the street. She checked the arrears figure and winced. The benefit wouldn't cut that out. Where did you get money in a hurry? The Sallies were all right for clothes, even food at a pinch, but they didn't pay the rent for you.

An idea struck her. So novel yet so simple was the answer that she rushed back to the street and grabbed one of the give-away papers that usually lay forlornly until the rain and wind did the housekeeping. Today, there would be a job intended for Nora Halpin and no one else. She found it, too, under *Barmaid Wanted*. It couldn't be hard to pull a schooner and chat up the fellas. She dashed in to old Mother O'Brian's to beg the use of the phone, got an appointment in town, and rushed home to dress up. Tag was snoring as she ransacked the wardrobe. Nothing looked suitable. She didn't care. In town there would be the right shop with the right outfit at the right price. It was suddenly one of *those* days; exciting, fun, like when you were young and you knew life was on your side. Someone out there wanted her, they were going to pay her, stone the crows, she felt proud.

She walked along Main Road, visualising herself in various costumes that might do for bar work. She settled on the right image just as she came to Marie's shop. On the spur of the moment she pushed the door, and a little bell tinkled softly. She knew the shop kept second-hand clothes, though whoever wore those funny old feathers and furs was a mystery to her. There were piles of junk inside: worn-out bears and dolls, hats, a brass bed, old plates and cups that didn't even match. The service wasn't too good. The woman at the counter must have seen her but she took no notice. Maybe she was deaf. Nora couldn't muck around. The appointment was in half an hour.

'Do you sell outfits here?'

'We have some,' Marie said politely, though Nora didn't look to be in line for an old ivory lace wedding gown or debutante's coming-out dress.

'I'm looking for a cowboy set.' The server seemed a bit uncertain so Nora explained. 'The kind with a fringe across here—' (she slashed an imaginary line across her breasts) 'and here—'(she sketched a hemline mid-thigh) 'in suede or leather stuff.'

'I'm sorry,' Marie said, 'I have nothing along those lines.' Nora looked so disappointed she added, 'Were you going to a fancy dress party?'

Nora cackled. 'Bloody oath! I'm going after a job or we're getting chucked out.'

'That's terrible!' Marie sounded as though she genuinely thought it was and Nora found herself pouring out the tale of Tag and the football accident and the way they had to keep moving because people hounded them for money. 'But I've got a job,' she said positively. 'I'm going to the interview now. I want something decent to wear.'

'That always helps, at an interview.' The poor, desperate woman looked so worn and weary it was hard to tell her age. Perhaps in one of the trunks she could find an outfit. Anything would be better than the stained tracksuit pants and stretched old T-shirt with its manifestly untruthful motto: *I'm the greatest!*

'Wait a minute. I'll slip the lock.' Marie put up the *Back in 5* sign and beckoned Nora to follow her to the back room. There she started to search through piles of old clothing while Nora looked around, amazed that anyone could own so much rubbish and have the nerve to call the place a shop. The owner had apparently never heard of three piece lounges and telly tables. She was a good old stick anyway, trying her best to help. She was holding various bits of clothing up and tossing them aside impatiently.

'Here we are! I thought I remembered this.' She shook out the red fringed dress, which shed its creases as though being stuffed away in a trunk for years was just a bagatelle in its long and gracious life.

Nora looked doubtful. It had the fringes. That was all. It was a bit on the baggy side. She felt the fabric, which snagged on her rough fingers.

'It's soft,' she said.

'Silk,' said Marie. 'Pop it on.' She took one look at Nora's underwear and went back to the trunk. Soon they were both confronting the mirror, while Nora asked tentatively, 'What d'you reckon?'

'I think you wear it well. The colour suits you.'

Nora looked pleased. She would have preferred something with zips and press-studs, in black denim you could wear with high-heeled boots. A thought struck her.

'It looks funny with these.' She pointed to her dirty jogging shoes.

'They won't do.' Marie moved on to another trunk. The shoes she produced had little low heels and a bar across the top. At least they had a bit of a sparkle and the old girl was trying to be nice, running a comb through Nora's mop of hair, dabbing powder over her scars, even tying a little band of ribbon round her forehead. Nora gazed warily at her image. The reflection made her afraid. She was someone else; one of those rich people you see in shops, buying expensive clothes, parading in front of mirrors. Suddenly she longed fiercely to be one of them. If Marie had taken back the dress, Nora would have clawed her face.

'What's the damage?' she asked in her hoarse, smoker's voice.

'What would you say?'

Nora was doing a quick count up. This place was a cut above the usual op shops. Still, old was old.

'The Sallies charge $3 for a dress and $2 for shoes.'

'In that case, $5,' Marie agreed.

'Oh, and there's the underwear.'

'Don't worry about it. It's just old lace.'

Nora scrabbled for coins in her battered handbag.

'Take this.' Marie handed her a little beaded bag.

'Got anything I can stick me old gear in?'

Marie helped pack up Nora's discards and was rewarded with a confidential grin.

'Tell you what I'll do for you some time. We'll go on the train and I'll show you where they have real furniture and dress shops. Might be good for business.'

Marie thanked her and wished her all the very best with her interview.

It was strange to prance along Main Road in her get-up. She didn't wear dresses as a rule and the feel of a skirt swishing about her legs was most unnatural. The shoes pinched; joggers made your feet spread. But the red silk attracted glances, and people had a more friendly expression than usual. She held her head up high and hurried off to her interview. It went well. She was well versed in beer labels and looked as though she could punch out the lights of anyone who decided to get rough. She said there was no problem with night work. She didn't know what Tag would say about it. He was so jealous, he seemed to think every bloke in town was after her. But he'd have to wear it. The proprietor looked at her determined face and offered her the job.

At home she hid the red dress and shoes in a drawer and changed into comfortable clothes. When the kids came in from school she told them the news.

'Your Dad and I are getting our picture in the paper. And I got a job.'

At once they clamoured for toys, clothes, a trip to Wet and Wild. To keep them happy she gave them the last money in her purse to go down the street for takeaways. They ran off, squabbling over what to buy. Tag wandered out, yawning and scratching. 'Want a tinnie?' Nora suggested. She had to tell him sooner or later and something told her he wouldn't pick on her today.

5

Mr Lal's plans were also crystallising through an unexpected turn of events. The bank manager had kept his word; prior to putting forward a nomination, he made sure the Indian was invited to the next Rotarian breakfast. There, owing to the failure of the booked speaker to show up, Mr Lal agreed to speak about his unusual project. The centre of attention, Mr Lal elaborated on details for the Taj complex, drawing so many questions that he forgot his reticence. Bart Bexley had to wait his turn to inform Mr Lal that Head Office had turned down the loan application.

'But why?' his client asked. 'Surely my equity… My standing with the bank…?'

'The gist of things is simple. They don't believe a Taj Mahal in Trundle is a feasible idea.' Bart looked as disappointed as though he'd been rejected himself.

'They might consider an alternative: a shopping complex, a supermart.'

Mr Lal shook his head. Naturally he had other sources of revenue to explore. A prudent man did not patronise only one barber whose razor might grow blunt. One possibility would be to dispose of other property investments. There were drawbacks to that idea. The market was in a flat cycle, and in any case months would elapse before capital would be realised. An association with the Dutchman, which he'd rejected on its first airing, now came back to him. In that event, several problems might be turned to advantage. There was the question of a site. There was Richard's own resort project to provide a guaranteed clientele. There were his contacts, which, in all cultures, eased the birth pangs of great enterprises. There was a human factor. Mr Lal did not put words to it. He simply felt he should examine Richard's scheme in conjunction with his own. The ready company of an entrepreneur and an architect awaited him at the commune.

The power of thought was indeed remarkable. In a trice Mr Lal finalised the whereabouts of his palace, complete with its guard of elephants; it would be built at Pelican, commanding 180-degree sea views. Decisively he took leave of Bart and went home to strike the deal with Richard.

The Dutchman received his mobile call in a cordial way. Without a trace of antagonism or his peculiar humour, he invited the Indian to pay another visit.

'I've been thinking of you,' he said. 'Come on out and browse. I'll show you the site. While you're here you may like to look over my own ideas.'

Vijay agreed to drive his father there next day. Now, as Mr Lal prepared for bed, his mind seethed with ideas, visions and things to do. When he awoke, he had enjoyed sound and restful sleep. He drew several deep and energising breaths, and gave Marie's little elephant on the dressing table an affectionate pat. Her various kindnesses had drawn his family together. The girls liked her. She listened to their confidences and was a welcome caller to the household. What a misfortune that she was moving away to the commune! A man could provide the trappings of security; only a woman could centre a family. His house had become a strange place. Its inhabitants seemed to be in a state of waiting. His daughter's manner troubled him. Vijay was without goals. Sandy was too young, Sunita too old for them to be that stable reef against which the restless moods of daily life could dissipate. As for himself, he only had money and security at his disposal.

And his plans. The Dutchman was open to some sort of collaboration. It would be prudent to have formulated every detail in writing, when they sat down together to draw up their agreement. Mr Lal began his morning toilet. Any discourse with Shanti would have to wait. He had many items on his agenda. He was hungry, the sun was shining; this must be a day to profit by.

They set off from Alexandra Avenue straight after breakfast. This time the way seemed shorter and the settlement less isolated. Vijay left his father to go about his business and went to explore the commune. He was made welcome as he watched a kiln firing and chatted to the gardeners who were digging in compost and planting the winter crops of cabbages and broccoli. Later, he fell into conversation about music with a young couple, Rowena and Ben. Ben was a songwriter. He played acoustic guitar and, after hearing Vijay play, said he'd like to form a duo. Rowena seemed rather like Sandy, although she was more outspoken. In this atmosphere devoid of clocks and routines, Vijay felt peaceful as he twirled the daisy chain that Pippin had threaded for him.

'She looks happy,' he said, and Rowena nodded.

'It's a good life for kids.'

'Stay for lunch. You're welcome anytime, mate,' Ben said, draping Vijay with a brotherly arm.

Mr Lal had gone directly to Richard's chalet. This time he received a friendly greeting and was offered a chair. The Dutchman sat opposite, leaned back and came straight to the point.

'I'd like you to join me as a business partner.'

'There is much to be considered,' began Mr Lal but his host was unrolling large blueprints; securing their four corners with a handy set of brass elephants whose symbolism seemed too strong for Mr Lal to overlook. Richard's plump finger traced a guided tour of a futuristic complex, part of which contained an unmistakable outline. Mr Lal adjusted his spectacles as he stared at his Taj, somehow transported onto Richard's page.

'It's only a provisional addition, but I like it!' Richard said genially. 'So would the tourists. They want the exotic. Fantasy, escape—that's what a luxury holiday's all about. Yes, I do like it. An Indian experience without having to set foot in the reality of India. We both know what that entails!'

Mr Lal did not smile. Richard continued, his finger indicating an arcade of boutiques on an aspect labelled *Entertainment Wing*. 'See. Plenty of shops.'

'You have misunderstood,' said the Indian. 'I intend to present my country's culture. Its history, its spiritual resources, its way of life.'

'The real wealth? We'll cater for that. Rich people don't want tourist trinkets. Stock sandalwood chests and inlaid marble tables, and watch their pens race across the face of cheques.'

'You misunderstand!' Mr Lal began again, but Richard interrupted.

'Locating your scheme here is a stroke of genius. Can you imagine your wares selling in the main street of Trundle? That's where you go for laxatives and underwear.'

Richard had not only taken over the project, but was revising it before Mr Lal's own eyes. The Indian decided against collaboration.

'No. I want to buy communal land,' he said. 'Is it for sale or not?'

'I want it myself. We'd be in competition.'

'What do the other people have to say?'

'Little people. They think small. They don't know what they want. I'm a major shareholder. I've made enquiries about you, Mr Lal. We could do worse than work together. We both need a wealthy clientele. I don't much fancy going broke, do you?'

Mr Lal was well aware that the Taj project was risky. The bank had turned him down. On the other hand, Richard liked his idea so well that he'd commandeered it. Mr Lal could hardly take him to court to claim a vision as his own. The Taj was anyone's dream.

'Let's take a look at the building site now. A palace would sit nicely with my ideas.' Richard rolled up the plans. He set the elephants one behind the other on their display shelf. Mr Lal eyed them thoughtfully.

'I suppose it will do no harm, as I am here.'

It did not do to interfere with karma, though any past link with Richard must be seriously to his discredit in the world of spiritual accounting.

They walked over to inspect the land. It was a superb block, its elevation impressive, its view over bush and sea panoramic. The isolation of the site would be solved if he joined forces with Richard's scheme. Tourists preferred places that were off the beaten track, as long as they had every luxury on hand. Motorists on their way north would see the sign and turn off the highway out of curiosity. Access could easily be opened up.

Although he thought Van Rjien a peculiar fellow, he recognised a man akin to himself in commercial flair. Sometimes life required the tolerating of partners and personalities very different from oneself. Richard was wealthy and had plenty of contacts. As well, Mr Lal sensed a different individual concealed behind the screen of Richard's odd manners. Many of his books indicated a thoughtful scholar. Despite his air of ownership, he could not hide his devotion to his wife. He must be hard working and single-minded. Without him, Mr Lal would have to risk a lifetime's savings on his dream. After all, a partnership was not to be dismissed. He maintained a cordial attitude as the two men walked back from the building site.

'I am keen to finalise matters,' he admitted. 'Time is passing. Therefore, what do you propose?'

'Give me a few more weeks. Once the people here understand our venture, they will be steered into agreement. We are setting up a general meeting and group vote soon. I'll have my architect on hand, and we'll sort out details then.'

Ronnie, now on medication and sick leave, slept late and went to bed early. She had sorted a few personal possessions to take with her to Pelican, but seemed unable to help with the work of clearing the house for tenants. Victor had no objection to them storing goods in the spare room, but it was Marie who had to run her shop, pack, attend to meals and work on the agenda for the commune's general meeting. Meanwhile Ronnie sat outside, gazing pensively at the ravaged garden.

While the doctor did not want to pay rent for the house until his wife and family arrived, he had already spent a few nights at the sisters' home. He said that he wanted to familiarise himself with the schools and general facilities. Ronnie paid him no attention. It was Marie who found a man's presence disturbing. She lay awake, aware that she was separated from his bed only by the thin partition of the wall. It was awkward deciding whether to flush the cistern at night and she found herself peeping into his toilet bag, wondering what brand of aftershave he used. In the morning she made a point of combing her hair and wearing an old silk dressing gown she'd uncovered from her days with Hugh. As forgotten objects surfaced out of drawers and cupboards, she was lost in memories. She would sit turning the pages of an old wildflower catalogue, smelling a bar of lavender farm soap, or tearfully examining snapshots of herself and Hugh in dated dress.

Victor however was focused on getting his family to Australia. Once he pulled out an airmail letter to show her drawings and little letters from his children. He became increasingly impatient when it seemed there was a hold-up with the house sale. Marie, who found packing just for herself and Ronnie was a trial, sympathised with his wife, coping alone with so major a move.

'There must be so much to do, bringing your whole family across the world,' she suggested.

Victor looked surprised. 'Oh, Elizabeth's a good girl, she'll manage.'

Marie demoted Victor a little. Successful men seemed to take a lot for granted. Hugh had never been like that. He was tender, thoughtful, appreciative. But, trying to remember exactly what these attributes meant, she found an insidious mist obscured her memory and she twisted her wedding ring, unable to recapture Hugh's love within its circle.

Until the family arrived, Victor said he would camp out at the commune. He cited transport as the reason.

'Won't you be buying a car?' she asked.

'I'm low on funds until the money from the house comes through.'

She was surprised to hear an eminent doctor was so short of money. 'I can give you a lift any time,' she offered. 'Once we move, I'll have to make the trip daily.'

He did not seem particularly interested, although he thanked her politely. She lay in bed that night, thinking again of Hugh. Was there no time limit to mourning? Victor had awakened memories of marriage, intimacy and sharing. *I'm overtired,* she lectured herself. Within the week she would be living a friendlier existence. Her friends said they were sorry she was moving. Kitty was planning a farewell dinner. But when Marie said she would like to invite the Lals, Kitty had frowned.

I don't think so, Marie. The man's not one of us. Sam's client. Better not mix business with pleasure.

Marie didn't press the point, though she was troubled. Holly might offer charity to Indians; to dine with them was clearly another issue. It must be true, as Mr Lal had said, that Marie was the only neighbour in Alexandra Avenue who had even bothered to introduce herself. The group at Pelican, small as it was, had a cosmopolitan background and welcomed strangers. She couldn't wait to rejoin them.

PART 4

PELICAN

PART 4

1

They drove to Pelican the following weekend. Ronnie sat staring at the bush and isolated homes beside the river, where phantoms of the material world fragmented in the ripples.

'Tired?' Since the crisis, Marie had assumed a motherly role, seeing to the meals on trays and the hot baths scented with lavender oil.

Ronnie nodded. 'It's the Ativan.'

'Don't talk. I'll just play a tape.'

Ronnie closed her eyes. She dozed until the jolting last stage of the drive shook her awake. Through the open window flowed a deep and restful stillness punctuated by the chime of birds and the tolling of frogs.

'We walk from here. Here, let me carry the bags.'

It was quirky terrain they were entering; several landscapes crammed together in quick succession. Unlike the native bush along the way, the trees ahead had a tropical look. Sunshine highlighted the fanned foliage of palms. Soon the lush growth opened out to woodland with lacy casuarinas and tough coastal shrubs. In turn they changed, as the slope declined, to swamp vegetation. Bulrushes stretched away, their low profile thinning to reed beds interrupted by cabbage palms. Mewling birds planed overhead for molluscs. A purplish haze covered the marsh, beyond which lay a view of gentle harbour; little more than a paddling place for toddlers and old people.

'Not far now.' Marie, who had been picking her way around muddy patches fed by the tidal creek, stopped for a rest. Ronnie waited. In that desolate place she could have curled up like a swamp bird in its hollow of grass.

As they resumed the climb, the land crossed vegetated dunes. Marie turned off where wooden steps led up to a few low buildings that looked like pens or stables. Garden plots with rich-looking soil were carefully netted against possums. Ahead appeared a low, hexagonal building, its roof peaked like a circus tent's.

An elderly woman, limping, came out to greet them. Marie set down the bags and embraced her friend.

'Honor! What have you done to yourself?'

'Sprained my ankle.' She held out her hands to Ronnie, observing her with youthful curiosity. 'Welcome to Pelican. Marie's talked of you so often.'

Ronnie nodded. She felt a need to be by herself. There was a surreal brightness to the light. A golden-haired child, clasping a scarlet ball, scampered across the emerald grass towards Marie, who bent with a loving gesture and scooped her up.

'Ronnie, meet Pippin. Hugh's granddaughter.'

Unable to deal with strangers, Ronnie put on her sunglasses. 'It's so bright,' she murmured. 'I feel giddy.'

'Do you need a drink?' said Marie, and Honour grasped her stick and turned towards home.

'Would you like lemonade? I make my own. It's rather good. Laurie's fond of it. I'm worried about him, Marie. That nasty cough just won't go away. He needs an X-ray but try and convince *him* of that...'

Her rambling conversation bypassed Ronnie. 'I need to lie down,' she said faintly.

'Of course, my dear. The guest chalet's number nine. It's all ready.'

'I'll show her, Honor. Keep off that ankle.'

'I will. This silly fall has quite disabled me.'

The springy buffalo turf ended at a flight of stone steps artfully framed by bamboo. Beneath canopies of foliage, the sisters followed walkways to the sleeping huts. Marie stopped at a wooden cottage complete with curlicues, window boxes and a lead-lit panelled door. Inside, leaf-screened windows filtered a subdued light. The floorboards released a subtle linseed aroma. There was a gas-run refrigerator, a modern bathroom and sleeping alcoves on two levels.

'These are separate guest quarters,' Marie said. 'The members are arriving later, for the voting on our future, but they'll use the dormitories. You make yourself at home. As far as I know there's no other visitors at present.'

'What about you?'

'I'll bunk with the members. Don't worry about me. Just get yourself right.'

Taking the first bed in sight, Ronnie collapsed and smiled forlornly up at her sister.

'Never wake me!'

Marie placed fruit juice and a dish of nuts beside the bed.

'Have a good rest. There's food in the fridge. See you later.'

Ronnie closed her eyes against the stippled light. In seconds she was asleep.

Marie felt a sense of homecoming as she went back to the Stedman's chalet. Pelican was her old stamping ground, where she'd made good friends and fallen in love with Hugh. She felt a special link to those idealistic days. Now Pelican was to face the challenge of change, along with the chaos that would involve. The weekend would be eventful. Over the years, many residents had invested funds. Now they were being called to listen to development plans and decide on the future of the little settlement.

As Marie reached the main building, she saw that preparations for the influx were already underway. Honor explained there was to be an Indonesian *selamatan* of welcome, followed by a day of meetings, proposals and a general vote.

'Join us for lunch,' she suggested, as they made their way back to her chalet. A wind chime tinkled somewhere and the scents of cedar and linseed were in Marie's nostrils as the older woman chattered on. 'Your sister won't be joining us?'

'She's asleep.'

'Already? As you say, she's a woman in need of healing. Well, I think she'll find that here. We'll offer what we can.' And Honor's blue eyes shone with a look of penetrating kindness.

As late afternoon wore on, others began to arrive and the laughter of reunions grew. There was a festive air as people aired their news of births, weddings or illnesses. Honor was in her element as she dispensed welcomes and sleeping arrangements.

'What an influx, just like Congress at Coombe!' She was referring to the Gurdjieff centre near London, where she had studied the teacher's spiritual system under John Bennett. 'The dorms are almost full. Marie, will you stay with us tonight? The sofa bed's quite comfy. Oh, there's Isobel Gulbransen!'

She hurried off as quickly as her ankle would allow. She was in her seventies, but her thick hair retained its golden lights and her vitality was obvious. Her second marriage was a happy one. Laurie's down-to-earth nature balanced her sometimes-dogmatic convictions. The couple's placid affection reminded Marie of her own good years with Hugh. She stood apart from the guests, afflicted by the loneliness that overwhelmed her, until Pippin ran up to her and took her hand. Hugh's grandchild seemed to love her. As the little girl led her from friend to friend, Marie wondered if there might be a healing for her, too, in this peaceful place.

By evening, dozens of people were wandering around the commune and making their way towards the *selamatan*. Ronnie had no desire to join them. She picked at the cheese and fruit in the fridge, and took out the tablets she'd been prescribed weeks ago. Perhaps she could try a break from drugs. It was true enough that there was an air of tranquillity here. She flicked the pages of a magazine; reading had become a task beyond her concentration. Much later, she woke from a doze to hear the sounds of people calling their good nights and preparing to settle for the night. The voices and laughter reassured her as she nestled under the doona and went back to sleep.

It was sometime in the small hours when she got up and found her way in darkness to use the bathroom. Returning to the bedroom, she was startled when the bedside lamp snapped on and a man sat up in bed. In the dim light she thought she recognised his face but could not place him.

'Well, this is a surprise!'

He looked attractive and about her own age. Quickly she whispered, 'Wrong room, I'm so sorry...!'

He was propped up on an elbow, patting the edge of the bed. 'Well, why rush off? I don't bite. Stay for a minute?'

Without a thought she crossed the room and lay beside him. Switching off the lamp, he placed a gentle arm around her. She could feel the soft stuff of his T-shirt rub her cheek as she nestled in to share the longest and most delicate embrace of her life. Eventually, as the sensuous communication ended and they curled up together like contented children, he gave a sigh of pleasure.

'That was very nice. Thank you for choosing the wrong room.'

'My pleasure.' She felt free and very light. 'Will you please tell me where we've met before?'

'We did CPR together on Mac Booth when he collapsed. Remember?'

'Of course! Mac's gone down to John Hunter hospital for a bypass.'

'And you're Ronnie Gale, the nurse? I was in your sister's shop. She said you were taking leave and coming here to Pelican.'

Ronnie wondered what else Marie had told him; discretion wasn't her strong point.

'I just need a break. What about you?'

'Nick Questro. I oversee the local rag while Mac's off.'

'But what brings you out here?'

'I'm nosing out a story.'

She laughed. 'Well, don't use this one! I'm not in the habit of barging in on strangers.'

'Did we feel like strangers?' He sounded pensive and she was glad, though she eased out of bed.

'I'm going! To my own bed, this time.' The moonlight showed her to the door as he called teasingly, 'Sleep well, Ronnie Gale!'

For the remainder of the night, as the leaf-curtain beyond the window gradually resumed its form and colours, she lay awake, reflecting on their unsought and magical encounter. It was hard to say whether an hour or three had passed since she'd turned left instead of right and found Nick Questro. There'd been no goal, no sense of time, no self-interest nor any end point to that beautiful communication. Searching her own vocabulary in vain, she turned instead to Marie's, wondering if at Pelican it was possible to stumble across normal boundaries and meet in finer ethers.

2

The members' meeting was scheduled to begin after breakfast on Sunday.

The encouraging warmth of the social gathering on Saturday night had been a good omen, Marie felt. The candles had shed their kindly light on old and young as anecdotes and news went the rounds of the little tables. As the plates were removed, entertainers took the floor. Richard had remained in the background, smiling and indulgent while his wife, graceful in her *batik* dress, danced to the recorded sounds of *gamelans* and gongs. Even Honor had enjoyed herself, although she'd come alone, despite Laurie's protests. When Marie's turn came to play, she hoped Mozart would make allowances. The short recital drew applause and again Victor Argyle made a point of complimenting her. If the Sunday meeting continued on this note, Honor's mountains would be molehills.

Marie chaired a committee to record the wishes of all members, including small investors in Pelican land. In the morning, she left Honor to see to Laurie and follow at her own pace, and hurried over to the meeting hall. Richard, Victor and a stranger were already conferring there. The Dutchman was clearly in command. He gestured in suave illustration of some point to which the other two responded with thoughtful nods. As a group, they exuded the unconscious conspiracy of men used to having their own way.

The doctor, radiating the vitality of a man who has managed a ten-mile jog and a splash beneath an icy waterfall, saw Marie and waved. Richard and the third man walked over to her.

'Ah, Maree! Meet my architect, Waldo Grocholski. Maree is on our committee.'

The stranger crushed her hand in a hairy paw. In his tartan bush shirt, old moleskin pants and tramping boots, he looked the amiable type to create havoc and thrive on a disreputable life.

'Good morning.' She turned to Richard. 'Aren't you being a little premature in appointing an architect?'

'Not at all.' He was suave. 'Nothing has been decided. I see others are arriving. Shall I help set out the chairs, Maree?'

The Sunday meeting began straight after breakfast. Marie reported no opposition to the use of communal land, providing the chosen development would benefit the group and its shareholders. Victor Argyle stepped forward to present an outline for the health centre. There was nothing sensational in his ideas but he spoke with such persuasion, and looked so healthy himself, that his talk drew a long round of applause. Marie was kept busy scribbling notes and resolutions for the minute book, as questions to do with finance, personnel and equipment were discussed.

There was a break for morning tea. Richard's proposal was next on the agenda and he began setting up his props while Tuti stood nearby.

'Is he going to saw her in two?' said Honor, loudly, so that Laurie, who rarely expressed disapproval, shook his head at her.

As proceedings resumed, Tuti stepped forward and whisked away a cloth draped over the large whiteboard. Richard began to describe a plan far beyond anybody's expectations. He wanted to create a magnificent resort on Pelican land.

Tourists would relax in luxury. Victor's health centre, along with heated pool, sauna, spas and gymnasium, would occupy one wing. An entertainment centre, topped with satellite dish and observatory, would attract the country's best talent. The coastal setting would be exploited to provide boating, fishing and diving facilities. Perhaps the most outstanding feature of all was the open cheque Richard presented to the group. Apart from his pledge to meet seventy-five percent of development costs, he offered a suggestion that it was perhaps selfish to retain for the tiny group Pelican's assets. They should open their doors to the rest of the world. At the end of this address, people applauded at length.

'What did I tell you?' Honor, flushed with anger, refused to join the others who surrounded the whiteboard, examining Waldo's preliminary sketches. But Marie felt excited. The scheme involved the kind of expansive thinking usually reserved for the rich and powerful.

'That Man has to win. He doesn't want a healing centre; that's a sop to conceal what he's up to.'

'What is he up to, my dear?' asked her husband mildly.

'He's an empire builder, Laurie. Don't worry! I can see through him. He'll take over and Pelican will simply disappear. Industries with no interest in our values will step in and buy us out. Is that why we moved here? He'll be the death of us.'

Laurie took her arm. 'You may be right.'

Marie left him to soothe his wife. She wondered how many others in the group shared Honor's misgivings, but the atmosphere was light and happy. As she listened, she realised people did not really care how the land was used. Their interest in Pelican was personal, with ideals and friendships rating far above prospective change. A few, like Honor, had the questing makeup that pursues answers to life's purpose, but most were simple or lonely individuals, happy to belong somewhere. Some came from strict church backgrounds and had developed a violent resistance to organised religion. Yet seeds of faith and aspiration left them wanting some replacement.

The lifestyle at Pelican, in its peace and lack of distraction, allowed talents to flourish. Artists and craft workers had found markets for their pottery, fabric painting and ornaments. The gardens were developed and producing. A few livestock had been bought. The older couples introduced a balance for young couples pressured by suburban jobs and families. The majority of members came back to Pelican for interludes of refreshment and retreat. The implications of Richard's scheme were beyond people whose most ambitious project was financing a house or one-man business.

Voting was to take place later in the afternoon, after a group inspection of the building sites. Determined to put a stop to Richard's elaborate proposal, Honor was ready for a fight, but Marie dissuaded her.

'Why don't I ask Richard for a delay on the vote? We all need more time to think.'

Perhaps Honor should be supported in her caution. The little community at Pelican would very likely disappear if developers and tourist consortiums moved in. Honor and Richard would never be able to compromise. As an intermediary, Marie might effect some meeting point between the two.

Tuti showed her to Richard's study. Her husband, seated at a desk, adopted the delaying tactics that were so disconcerting to people wanting to deal with an awkward issue.

'Ah, Maree. See, pussy is sulking.' He indicated the little cat on his knee. Its ears lay flat and its tail was slowly lashing to and fro. 'We are trying a new kind of food, better for the teeth, but he wants the old sticky brand. Well, we have ways to make you change your mind, Homer.' He cradled the cat. 'Observe! I wait till he's all relaxed and unsuspecting...Then, I let him drop. He doesn't like it. Sometimes he draws blood.' He parted the neckline of his open shirt and pointed to the pale skin on his chest.

'I'm surprised he comes anywhere near you,' said Marie, who detested cruelty to animals.

'It must be the suspense. He likes to be teased.' He tickled the cat on its white throat and although its tail kept moving it began to purr.

'Richard, could we discuss this morning's proposals? We feel an impulsive vote may be unwise.'

He laughed. 'Honor fears I will win?'

'Quite frankly, we were astonished by the scope of the outline.'

'Did you like it?'

'I'm not sure. Some of us seemed to. But there was no prior consultation with the committee. You see, it downplays the health resort to a minor amenity. Victor's come halfway across the world. I don't think he'll want to put his energies into massaging wealthy tourists or running aerobic classes.'

'*Au contraire*—Victor understands the resources that would come with a large-scale venture. He would be salaried, for one thing. Any visitors will recuperate all the better with saunas and spas and a gymnasium.'

'Have you asked yourself which visitors could afford them? The resort would be far beyond the average person's means. Excluding the poor is not what we had in mind at all for Pelican.'

'Club Med. lacks spiritual standing?'

'Why make a joke of it? Do you want to see Pelican overrun with tourists?'

'Well, why not? We're all tourists in this life. Let us be so in style!'

'You're so sure of yourself?'

Richard shrugged. 'I think, *wait and see.* Our doctor is quite happy with the revision of facilities. He has already offered input. As for my friend, Waldo, he's a first-rate architect.'

'We're a community,' Marie reminded him. 'We set up a committee to gather group opinions. You're simply overriding us with grandiose plans and a big cheque. Is that really what you mean to do?'

Expecting him to defend his stand, she saw him smile and nod.

'I'm a trying fellow! I like to lead. Usually people find it's easier to be a follower. No one else has complained about my plan. Really! I've had only compliments. But we'll soon find out when I ask for pledges for the balance of the money. Talk is one thing, cold cash another. Let us bank on a democratic outcome? Tell me, Maree, have you seriously considered my project? I don't need the prop of a pseudo-spiritual agenda. I merely open my eyes and see potential. If other members try my approach they may like the view.'

His gibe was aimed at Honor. Marie pointed to a bookcase lined with volumes on mysticism and spiritual systems 'For someone who reads books like those, you contradict yourself.'

He smiled like a chess player who acknowledges a wily move. 'Gurdjieff was one of Honor's gurus, you know. He had such strange techniques for breaking through the mechanisms that rule our behaviour. Insults, rudeness, deprivation: they were the tools he used to wake a sleeping consciousness. Of course, some devotees went mad or committed suicide. But, for those who stayed the course, nothing worked better. Our good sister Honor studied that system at Coombe Springs, under Bennett. As she so frequently reminds us. She must have many fascinating memories of those days. She can confirm the value of an annoying person like myself!'

There was a sudden disturbance as the cat took its chance and made a dash for the open window.

'Homer thinks he's free now. We all pursue illusion. Wait and see. Pussy will be back at feeding time.' He leaned back, yawned and stretched. 'I like to have a short siesta after lunch. The group inspection is at three? And the vote at five?'

'We have no objection to you gathering feedback or provisional numbers. We won't be rushed into a final vote.'

He shrugged. 'Procrastination? What's the English proverb?'

'Richard, we won't be rushed. Provisional or nothing.'

Conceding, he shrugged. 'My wife brews excellent coffee. Would you like some, Maree?'

Feeling somewhat like the cat, Marie declined the offer and left the study.

Tuti stopped her at the door. 'May I ask for your advice?' she said. 'Of course!'

'Do you think Rowena would let me look after Pippin sometimes?'

'I expect she'd be delighted. You're fond of children?'

'Oh yes! I come from a very large family.'

'Then you'll be well-equipped, when it's time to start your own.'

Tuti looked down. 'Richard doesn't want children.'

'Many men say the same thing. It's up to us women to keep the world going. He'll come round. He mustn't have his own way in everything!'

Marie waved and went back to report to Honor that the meeting with her adversary had led exactly nowhere.

People were gathering in the main hall for a farewell meeting. A voting box collected opinions, while sponsors willing to back Richard's project were negotiating pledges in a side room. Already a number of the group were willing to put up their small nest eggs of savings or to raise loans and mortgages in favour of the project. Meanwhile Victor stood by, giving his commitment to opening a temporary health clinic straight away. An air of solidarity descended on the group as those returning to their lives away from Pelican made the most of their last hours together. Friends hugged and kissed, addresses were exchanged, visits promised, and a few tears shed.

At the start of the working week, Marie set off for Trundle, reflecting on the weekend as she drove. In retrospect, she thought Richard's scheme had a fantastic element far beyond the capabilities of the small group. Certainly alternative suggestions and riders would delay a decision for some time yet.

She opened the shop punctually. As usual, Mondays were slow; by late morning the bell had not uttered a single tinkle. Business in the antique trade was in the doldrums; while the letter delivered after lunch advised that Bart Bexley, in the nicest possible language, was asking her to reduce her overdraft.

She wondered what to do. In a crisis, Ronnie was usually good for a loan but Ronnie wasn't there. Her prescribed medication, and Pelican's tranquillity, seemed to have eased her tension, but she was in no state to discuss money. As for the usual trade-tricks, advertising or a sale, they wouldn't work in Marie's specialised shop. She'd have to sell a few of her personal treasures, though the idea felt like pulling teeth. In a sentimental mood she wandered round the displays, talking to herself as she sometimes did when trying to solve a predicament.

Nora, calling in on her way to work, heard Marie talking to the teddy bears and decided the old girl was definitely off the air. She rummaged in the plastic bag that served as her handbag and dumped a little parcel on the counter.

'How did the interview go?' Marie's enquiry was sincere; the poor woman's problems had been on her mind.

'I got the job. Thought I'd let you know.'

'That's very good news.'

Nora pushed the parcel forward. 'Reckon I owe you one for the dress. The kids found this down the dump. Don't know if it's any good.'

'You don't owe me anything.'

Nora, marching to the door, spoke with new assertion. 'I got my pride you know.'

Marie examined Nora's gift. It was a human figure with the head of an elephant; a souvenir brought back to the antipodes to decorate a mantelpiece. Its expression was gentle and benevolent. Marie sat him in pride of place near the empty cash register, beside Hugh's teddy. But despite her liking for symbols, custom remained thin. At lunchtime she took her break and walked along to Kitty's shop. Business looked brisk there. The new wrought-iron tables and chairs were fully occupied by the midday crowd, and a busload of tourists queued to buy souvenirs.

Marie walked on along Main Road. Kitty wouldn't receive pay-up letters from the bank. She gave modern people what they seemed to want. The charm of the past was in small demand in Trundle.

Perhaps I'm an anachronism, Marie thought. In old fashions, clothing, furniture and knickknacks she liked to think she was nurturing values where profit was not the main criteria of worth. Imagining the hum of carriage wheels, the tap of horses' hooves, the rustle of floor-length gowns, she returned to a slower pace of life when conversation was an art and entertainment home-made. She valued the past, even the pain of losing Hugh, for his death and its acute sense of loss had made her know how profoundly she was alive. *What can I say about Hugh now? I miss him. The words seem dulled and I even ask myself, Was it ever really so?*

She was startled when Mr Lal, emerging from Sam Playfair's office, came up to her. Standing in the sunshine, they chatted for a few minutes, then walked back to the shop, where she showed him Nora's present.

'Ah yes, Ganesh. Lord of beginnings, undertakings and examinations. He is usually invoked to remove obstacles and ensure successful enterprises.'

'Then perhaps he'll mark a turn in my affairs. Unless I do something about my overdraft you may have to visit me in prison!'

Mr Lal saw nothing funny in insolvency. He felt an urge to help her, but to offer money was a personal gesture he felt uncertain he should make. Perhaps she had something he could buy.

'As you know, I'm interested in collectors' items,' he began.

'Oh, you can't have him... Not the Lord of beginnings and undertakings.'

'Don't forget examinations.' He smiled at her expression of distaste.

'I was never much good at those.'

'You mentioned a couple of carpets. May I inspect them?'

Marie gave a sigh. 'I know you want to help. I'm a bower bird, that's my trouble.' Impulsively she reached over and pressed his small hand with its pale, trimmed nails. 'There's no one I'd rather sell to. Come out to the back room. I have a Hereke Silk and a Persian Shiraz you might like to see.'

A pleasurable fifteen minutes passed while they examined designs, looked up references and considered price. An amiable deal was struck. Mr Lal had a fine rug for his room and Marie could soon appease the bank manager.

'People think I'm a fool, selling antiques in Trundle,' she confided. 'I love beauty, you see.'

'When Shah Jahan designed his Taj, he was not concerned with current fashion.'

'Well, you understand, you're a dreamer too. You'd do better with an adventure park, you know.'

He disagreed. 'I want people to remember my wife, and our small roles in our adoptive land.'

She was childlike in admiration, seeing only the best in him. 'And you will be remembered. Most people live that hope through their children.'

'Children don't always fulfil one's hopes.' He sounded despondent.

'You have your son and daughter. I've no one.'

He said kindly, 'That is no dishonour.' Though in his culture it might have been a different matter.

'It's a regret. To see a child grow and develop must be one of life's marvels.'

Mr Lal was doubtful. 'My son lacks direction. As for Vimla...'

'She's a very bright young lady, with brains, good looks, a career...'

'She seems to expect something more.'

Marie laughed at his perplexity. 'All girls expect something more! We're made that way.'

'And do you find it?'

'We usually settle for contentment.'

His thoughts, still on Vim, made him shake his head.

'Don't worry about her. She'll lead an interesting life; her career might take her far afield. Perhaps you'll go to India together one day.'

'She shows no interest in her origins.'

'She's young. Give her time. Of course I've only read of India. Forster's novel had a character; a Dr Lal, in fact. A good man. Oh, I forget the actual story. Something to do with that hysterical sexuality that can wreck lives. But what I do remember is the haunting atmosphere.'

He smiled. 'You must verify this for yourself.'

'I doubt it. I'm a homebody. My sister's the one who longs for faraway places. I've never wanted to go far, except in my mind. I'd settle for a family, but it's too late for that.'

'Surely it is never too late?'

Marie laughed, concealing her regret. 'I'm afraid, Mr Lal, that would take a miracle!'

3

Mr Lal pondered his financial options. To undertake his building project alone would be foolhardy. The real estate market was depressed and the stock market bearish. If Van Rjien would not come on board as a partner, he would have to build elsewhere; perhaps right out of the area. The prospect disappointed him. He would have one last try at a deal with the Dutchman. He put together his figures, his blueprints, and his terms of contract and once more set out for the commune with Sandy and his son. Vijay needed no persuading; he'd made his interest in the alternative lifestyle plain.

At Pelican, he parted company with the young people and went to the Van Rjien's chalet to present his offer. His host considered the draft contract, laid it on the coffee table, and pressed his fingertips together.

'So what is the decision of your members?'

Mr Lal had come to the point more rapidly than Richard wished.

'The wheels turn slowly here. There is progress. However, I await final confirmation that we can proceed.'

'This is not much good to me.' In business, the Indian was decisive. 'Do you want to sell the land or don't you?'

'Absolutely. The group's behind me, more or less.'

'What is 'more or less'? Enough time has passed. I require 'yes' or 'no'.'

'Agreement is held up by one old woman. Her name's Honor Stedman. She's a stubborn reactionary who thinks she has the power to stop progress.'

'And this old woman runs your life?'

Van Rjien flushed. 'She has one foot in the grave. I would put her to crochet caps for refugees. Unfortunately, along with myself, she holds a majority shareholding in Pelican. She is opposed to tourists.'

'Perhaps I should go and see her?'

'Why would she take any notice of you?'

'My Taj is not a typical tourist venture.'

Richard nodded. 'I suppose it's not a bad idea. You could play up the aesthetic pretensions and the sentimental *raison d'être*. She'd like that. Yes, sell her the idea if you can. Tuti, are you there?'

As his wife stepped into the room, his expression became doting.

'My sweet, could you prepare a little dinner party for some friends tonight? The Stedmans, Mr Lal, and perhaps the English doctor? He has Honor wrapped around his little finger and he supports our ideas. We'll call this a welcome meal for him. So! I'll go and extend the invitations. My friend, refresh yourself. You'll stay the night? We have a spare room. Tuti will show you.'

Richard offered his hand in a congratulatory grasp; it had the plump feel of freshly powdered baby's skin.

The Indian was reviewing his first impression of the man as a rude and dominating decision-maker. Perhaps in a boardroom Richard might rule the roost. Some powerful figures, merciless in the public arena, expressed weakness in their private lives. The man was almost childish. The pornographic pictures, the bullying manner, his embarrassing doting on his young wife were immature. His ploy to trick Honor was the device of a crafty little boy. Mr Lal would not manipulate an old woman. He did not mind the games involved in business but his nature was not devious.

Yet Tuti seemed very fond of this childish husband. Curious, Mr Lal stepped into the kitchen where she had begun preparations for the impromptu dinner.

'Do you have regular guests here?' he asked.

She shook her head. 'Richard hasn't any friends. Sometimes a visitor comes on business.'

'What actually is his line of work?' He knew he was prying but she said she didn't know. 'He works on the computer all the time. Trading shares. It is very complicated.'

'What about you? Is Pelican a good place to live?' He was surprised that a young woman could bear such isolation.

'My husband thinks so.' Her submissive manner did not seem to be an act.

'You must both visit next time you are in town.'

'Thank you. If Richard agrees.'

Compliant though she'd been, Shanti had known her mind and could express it forcefully. Mr Lal believed it correct that people arrive at their own values. Of course rules and regulations were useful. Society depended on them. But he hadn't indoctrinated Vijay or Vimla, as Tuti appeared to be trained, in the dutiful ways of her culture. Perhaps he should have been clearer with his children. Now his son refused a man's responsibilities, while Vim was determined and manipulative. He blamed himself, feeling he'd failed as a parent.

'Do you have children, Mr Lal?' Tuti might have read his mind.

'Two. Grown now. Do you come from a large family?'

'Five boys, three girls.' She sounded wistful.

'I remember how I missed my family when I migrated. It was better once I had children of my own.' He meant to cheer her and wondered why she looked sad.

'Richard has no desire for a family.' She sliced vegetables with economical and graceful movements.

'Men have been known to change their minds.' Perhaps the talk was taking too personal a turn. 'A few weeks ago I'd no idea I might be in partnership with your husband.'

Tuti said no more. The Indian returned to the main room to wait, until Richard returned in good humour.

'We can proceed as planned. The Stedmans and the doctor will be here at six. Rehearse your story!'

'I will explain my project to this lady. I can say nothing about yours. I don't feel sufficiently advised as to its scope or nature.'

Mr Lal spoke pleasantly enough. He excused himself and went off to find Vijay and explain the change of plan.

Honor had known Victor Argyle since his childhood. He was the son of her best friend and, throughout her copious travels, she'd kept track of his progress through correspondence, for she was a diligent letter-writer. She'd been on a trip home to England when he'd married Elizabeth, and had sat misty-eyed at the wedding, regretting her own unhappy marriage and lack of sons and daughters.

At least she could say she was entirely contented now with Laurie.

'You must miss dear Elizabeth and the children!' she said to Victor, who had stopped by for afternoon tea with the Stedmans.

'Naturally.'

'They must be longing to join you.'

He was less sure about that. Elizabeth's letters were brief, with an air of much that was unsaid. He was starting to doubt the endless delays over the house settlement. Meanwhile his funds were dwindling at an embarrassing rate and his family was due to take up occupancy of the sisters' house in Trundle.

'So when are they arriving?'

'Any time soon.' He went to look at the many photographs hanging on the chalet walls. They captured a series of decades: Laurie and his children from his previous marriage, a youthful Honor with her sister Valeria, a wartime Honor in nurse's kit, her own wedding portrait with Laurie.

'How young you look there!' he said. Honor's age exempted him from his usual reticence. When he allowed it to show, his charm was powerful and Honor, a girl at heart, responded.

'Naughty boy! I was all of sixty there. The photographer draped a silk scarf across the lens to play down my wrinkles. Don't I have the air of Vivien Leigh after a long bout? But what an actress! I suppose you're not old enough to remember her live performances? I saw her once. *Streetcar*, I think. Or was it *The Glass Menagerie*? What about a sherry?'

'Tea will do, thank you.' He was smiling as he looked around the room. Her *décor* was as scattered as her conversation. Watercolours and oil paintings hung beside curling Christmas cards and an out of date calendar. Dead flowers drooped in a silver vase. A superb horse sculpture reared next to cut-glass kittens and a china Pierrot.

'I'll see to it. Laurie's tied up in the kitchen. Today of all days he had to make lemon curd. We were given the lemons and he can't abide waste.' She went to stand up and grimaced. 'This wretched ankle's keeping me tethered. Surely with all your training you must know a magic cure?'

'Show me.' She displayed a pretty ankle and he knelt and carefully tested the joint.

'See how stiff it is?'

'Massage and physio should fix things. I'll drop by daily and give you a treatment.'

'Bless you!' She patted his dark hair. He welcomed her affection for he thought of her as an aunt.

'You leave the tea to me. Stay there.'

She settled back amid her nest of books, tapestry, and sewing.

The kitchen was a fug of steamy fragrance. Jam pots lined the bench, where Laurie stood straining pips from his brew.

'Make yourself at home. Tea's in the caddy there.' Laurie worked neatly, a military touch to his orderliness. 'I'm nearly done. Don't mind a bit of cooking. Creative in its way. Nothing like my wife's talent, still...' Laurie was immensely proud of Honor. 'She sculpted. Ever seen that photo of the bronze she has in the Royal Academy? I'll show you when I'm done here.'

When they returned to the living room, Laurie displayed the photo album.

'These are all her work.'

'Oh Laurie, don't bore Victor!'

'I'm not at all bored. I'm impressed.' Several heads were cast in an attitude of suffering, proudly borne. 'Who were your models?'

'Local people; Zambians. When I went out to Africa I was like all the British, expecting the romance of Schweitzer. What did I become? A nanny for little colonials.'

'I believe you played a part in the war effort too?'

'We had to stop that dreadful little man.'

Laurie and Victor smiled as they visualised the Kaiser in retreat from Honor's flinty gaze. The three were finishing their tea when Richard tapped at the door to issue his dinner invitation.

'A small gathering, just yourselves and my associate, Mr Lal.'

'We've met. I didn't know he was your associate.' Honor sounded suspicious.

'Tonight will be your opportunity to ask, and ours to answer any question. We look forward to it.' Richard nodded and withdrew.

'What's he cooking up now?' She looked with appeal at Victor. 'I beg you, don't be taken in by him! Stick to your own concept, or the health centre will be swallowed up in his grandiose ideas.'

'I'm sure you needn't worry.' Victor was more used to offering than taking advice. Recalling the figure Richard had mentioned as a likely salary, he slipped into the bedside manner that had soothed the anxieties of a thousand patients. 'There would be some advantages to working the clinic in with wider parameters. Let's consider all the options. I'll get going. We'll meet at dinner and make a start on that ankle in the morning.'

Laurie saw Victor to the door, leaving Honor to consider the prospect of Richard's resort. Her mind unreeled images of raucous tourists, gluttonous meals and cocktails garnished with entire fruit salads, destroying her beloved Pelican.

As six o'clock approached, the Stedmans were putting the final touches to their grooming. There were few social occasions at Pelican; even a meal at the Van Rjiens warranted a fuss. Honor checked her face powder and picked a white hair from Laurie's jacket but his sudden burst of coughing worried her.

'I hope that's not a relapse of bronchitis. Perhaps we shouldn't go?'

'Of course we'll go!'

'Why won't you have a proper check-up? You worry me.'

'You worry yourself.' He patted her arm. 'It's just a tickle. By Jove, you smell good. Is it the Chanel?'

She nodded. 'No point in hoarding it. Nothing lasts forever.' He drew her to him and they stood close until the clock chimed. She smiled. 'Time to confront the enemy... No, tonight I'm completely open-minded.'

'Why's that?'

'Our worst fears have a way of coming true. I'd better set them aside. Cough mixture, Laurie!'

At the Van Rjiens', Tuti, elegant in her long skirt, her hair immaculately groomed, had emerged from the bedroom. Richard inspected her, tucking a wisp of hair behind her little ear, where he pressed a kiss. Then he went off to change. He returned wearing a tropical suit that made Mr Lal anxiously check his own cuffs for spatters of mud.

'I wasn't prepared for this invitation,' he reminded his host. He liked a degree of formality; owned an immense extension table at home, with the idea of entertaining twenty guests for dinner. But it had never happened.

'Use our bathroom,' offered Richard. 'There's a clothes brush on the dressing table. You'll find a spare razor in the cabinet.'

Thanking him, Mr Lal went to freshen up. Modestly averting his eyes from the marriage bed, he collected a silver-backed brush and withdrew to the *en suite*. The bathroom cupboard was stocked with Tuti's cosmetics, expensive male colognes and talcs. On another shelf was a row of patent medicines and ointments. It was their privacies that made people seem most human. He could imagine Richard pacing about at night, grumbling and belching, much as Mr Lal himself had spent distressed nights walking the floor, full of sorrow and self-pity.

The guests had arrived. He recognised Honor, resplendent in beaded top and long crepe skirt. She was hardly the old woman Richard had described.

'Mr Lal, how nice to see you! I've been talking with your son. A thoughtful young man, isn't he? He's keen to join us. Of course he's welcome. Our purpose is to provide a retreat for visitors.'

'Is that our purpose?' said Richard. 'If so, it must be out of date, judging by the fall-off in our numbers.'

'I'd say we've had quite an influx: Marie, Ronnie, Victor, now Mr Lal's son and his little girlfriend.'

'They'll all be fly-by-nights,' Richard predicted.

'Here's Victor.' Laurie intervened in his diplomatic way. 'What are you cooking up, Tuti? It smells very good.'

Setting provocation aside, Richard assumed the manner of genial host and offered pre-dinner drinks. Tuti soon called them to the table, where Richard expounded on the vintages of a select red and a white wine. Mr Lal, at a loss for small talk, occupied himself with the chicken curry. He listened without much interest as Victor discussed the philosophy of homeopathic medicine. The residents of Pelican must have inheritances or invested funds; certainly no one held down a proper job. Some quest had apparently driven them to abandon normal lifestyles. Of course holy men and women in India sometimes withdrew from the world, seeking God. He had yet to discern much holiness at Pelican and Vijay had never impressed him as devout. How could business possibly proceed among such unconventional people?

His attention returned to the present as he realised that Richard was looking at him expectantly.

'Isn't that right, Mr Lal?'

'I beg your pardon?'

'Won't you explain your proposal for the benefit of our friends?'

In halting sentences, the Indian spoke about his dream. Even to himself, it had a touch of the bizarre now. His faith in Shanti's guidance was shaken. The troubles over finance and land made him dubious. Perhaps in one foolish gesture he was about to throw away the hard work of a lifetime.

'You may think I am mad,' he concluded.

'Of course we don't,' said Richard, briskly. 'We understand the significance of dreams. Isn't that so, Honor?'

'I must confess I've done my fair share of searching,' she agreed.

'Tell us about your gurus. That swami chap—you keep his picture on your mantelpiece.'

'Swami was a remarkable man.' Honor afforded Mr Lal a respectful nod as though he might be a relative of the teacher. 'I followed Gurdjieff''s system, too.'

'The heroes we appoint, hoping their wisdom will rub off on us!'

'Back in the old days, when we were founding members, Richard, I remember you were also in search of God.'

'God has been elusive. After the doctrines are studied and the books examined, the basics resume importance. I have my Tuti and my building project. Mr Lal and I hope to pool our resources. You may yet gaze upon a Taj Mahal.'

'It's an improbable dream.' For Honor, Pelican was an ideal that had nothing to do with buildings or finance.

Richard was determined to persuade her, for he felt the Indian had done a poor job of selling their scheme. 'Dreams!' he mused. 'What is life without them? I'm sure even Tuti has a little dream? Tell us, my love?'

The polite attention of the dinner guests fixed on the shy girl, who spoke softly, addressing Richard as though they were alone. 'I do have one dream,' she said.

'You see?' He sounded justified. 'Tell me what it is. I shall buy it for you tomorrow.'

'I want a child.'

There was an extraordinary adjustment to the mood of the host. Expressions of rage and resentment crossed his face, while Tuti's resolute words appeared to terrify her. She stood up, looking afraid and lost. 'Excuse me,' she muttered, and rushed from the table.

'Well, that was an odd one!' Richard quickly recovered his composure. 'Is the moon full tonight?'

'Go to her, Richard,' said Honor.

'She'll come back when she's ready. She has to serve dessert.'

He was quite correct. Tuti returned, carrying a fine fruit salad from the kitchen. Nobody referred to the incident as the conversation eased its way towards more diplomatic subjects than the heart's desires.

4

Sandy was impressed when she was shown around the commune. The gardens were well tended. Rowena seemed hospitable, and Pippin attached herself to Sandy. The little girl grasped her hand as though they were best friends and Sandy, who had a period overdue, let herself be taken to see the pottery and woodwork sheds, feeling strangely passive and contented.

Later, Vijay suggested a walk to the beach. He was in a mood for novelty, and guessed the suggestion would please her. She often trudged for miles, lugging heavy shopping bags. As a rule his summers were too hot or his winters too cold to exert himself for no reason.

A steeply descending track led down to the bay. Vijay twisted his ankle in a vine and had to sit down to recover. Beside him, Sandy pointed out several different bird species. She was full of plans to explore the tidal inlets, gather driftwood, and dig for crabs. She said she could learn to cook on the old wood range and help out in the gardens. Perhaps one of the potters would show her how to make a bowl.

'What are you going to do here?' she said.

Her plans were practical. His own impulses were less easy to put into words.

'Get to know people. Discuss life and ideas. There's a spiritual essence here.' He tried to expand on the sense of companionship, of like-minded friends, but soon she cut him short.

'Can we go to the beach?'

He clambered to his feet. The slipping, sliding descent did nothing to improve his aching ankle. Sandy went ahead. By the time he limped onto the sand, she was calling him to inspect a rowing boat anchored above the tide line.

'It must be for anybody,' she said. 'Let's go for a row.'

Sandy sometimes shocked him when she helped herself to fruit or flowers from neighbours' gardens.

'It's not our property. Anyway, I don't know how to row.'

She laughed at him 'Anybody can. It's easy.'

'No!' He resisted when she tugged him like a toddler to the water's edge. Her skirt hoisted up, she gambolled like a gawky child.

'Slowcoach!'

It hurt, Sandy making fun of him. Slowly he rolled up his trouser legs and took a few steps into the waves. Mud squeezed unpleasantly between his toes. He stood still while Sandy skipped around, flicking him with water.

'Stop it!'

His rage flared. He turned his back on her and hobbled up the beach. She ran after him.

'I was only joking.'

'Well don't. You know I hate the sea.'

'Why?'

'I can't swim. At school, we had to take lessons. Everyone knew I was afraid. They held me under. I thought I'd drown.'

'I didn't know. I'm sorry.' He didn't resist as her hand curled into his. 'It's nice at Pelican. Do you really want to live here?'

'Yes. I do.'

Through the veil of her hair she gave him one of her mysterious glances, and in a grudging tone he said, 'What about you?'

She shrugged her thin shoulders. 'I don't mind.'

She'd said exactly that when he'd suggested living together. He let go of his bad mood.

'I think we should go back. I hope I can make it. My ankle still hurts.'

'What a fuss!' But she slowed down and waited for him on the climb to Pelican. They spent the evening with Rowena and Ben, who invited them to stay overnight. The decision seemed to make itself; Vijay and Sandy would try the life at the commune.

In the morning, they drove back to Trundle under brooding clouds. Vijay, high in spirits, told his father of their plans. Even Sandy added a few supportive remarks. Vijay sensed a change in her, as though she understood him better and compared his sensitivity to the brashness of people who felt nothing deeply.

Mr Lal could not share in their high spirits. He would be left at home with his ailing in-laws and an unruly dog. Vimla was no company to him; she was either at work or shut up in her room. He was planning a trip to Sydney soon. Perhaps he could tempt her with a change of scene.

After the rainstorm, Ronnie went on one of her solitary bush rambles. Rays of weak sunshine turned the foliage to an acidic green and lit up the gathered raindrops. When Nick's voice hailed her, it was as though her thoughts had materialised.

'What are you doing here?' He'd given no warning that he was coming.

'Thought there might be some outcome from the voting.' He fell into step beside her. 'Nothing's decided yet?'

'The Mills of God run this place.'

He laughed. 'Actually, I'm skipping town. A young lady's taken a fancy to me. It's awkward—the last thing I want.'

'So here you are.'

'Here I am.'

The sound of rushing water grew loud as they made their way to the bottom of the slope. The ground was slippery; the air smelt damp and peaty. On the banks of a clear brown pool, pale day blooms stabbed the shadows.

'Fancy a dip?'

She hesitated. 'No bathers.'

He pulled a sarong from his haversack and she stepped away to change while he stripped to his boxers. Together, they walked across smoothed stones into the freezing water and let the cascade sluice over them. Shivering, they waded back to the bank. She noticed the long scar on his right leg, and the hollow area on the thigh. Without thinking, she ran her fingers softly along the livid line.

'What happened?'

'An accident. I lost my wife.'

He turned away to dress.

'I had another reason for this visit,' he said as they wandered back to the commune. 'I wanted to see you again.'

'Here I am.'

She waited, but he did not elaborate. A silence fell between them. When Nick finally spoke, he seemed removed from the intimacy that lay unexplored between them.

'Read much?'

She was disappointed. 'Normally I do. I've been on medication. Can't concentrate on long works.'

'I'm reading Japanese short stories. I'd like to try my hand at fiction.'

'Really?'

'You?'

'Can't say I've ever thought about it.'

They walked on in silence.

Nick accepted an invitation to stay on to dinner with the group. He did not want to leave. The image of Ronnie's hand, caressing his disfigurement, had moved him strangely. Since Jenny died, he'd avoided women. Even his reading had been tailored to sporting conquests or tales of exploration. He'd only just returned to fiction as though facing some risk he had to overcome. Literature's power amazed him afresh. A long-dead writer who conjured the blue of morning glories and the rasp of cicadas could confer on him honorary citizenship of Japan, a land he'd never visited. But he was uncomfortable with the reminder that love seemed to be inextricably bound up with suffering. In these stories, father and son, husband and wife, or lovers all paid some price. Later, after walking with Ronnie towards the chalets, he'd meant to make some move, but having no idea what he wanted instead said a casual goodnight. She gave him a questioning look, and walked away.

Nick took a shower, read for a while and settled down to sleep. The wind was rising again. Twigs scraped and clattered on the roof. He scratched an insect bite, went to close a window and stared at Ronnie's mellow pane of light. Her bed wasn't ten metres away, through a couple of thin walls. They might well be adults, unattached, but through that illumined window Nick seemed to see Jenny, telling him to move on from a solitary life. Roughly he pulled on a tracksuit and went to tap on her window.

'In the mood for company?' He waited.

'Come in.'

She was a mere form in the dull light. He stepped inside and closed the door. Hesitating, he climbed into bed beside her and the base creaked. She pulled off her T-shirt and nestled against him.

'This could be dangerous.' He felt compelled by a strange reserve to joke.

She was quiet. He felt her warmth and closeness. His sense of distance melted into intertwining, sighs, soft sounds. They were rocking on the slow, warm tides of sex. They dozed and woke, clinging like safe children. Before Max had deserted her, she'd known the urgent lovemaking of a demanding young man. She couldn't understand this man's lack of presssure. Wondering if he found her inadequate, she asked, 'Is there anything you want?' and heard him just laugh and say, 'What—a cup of tea?'

She forgot expectations and relaxed, drifting in and out of sleep. The leaves that screened her window were visible again when she asked sleepily, 'Are we ever going to consummate this?'

Nick, thinking of Jenny, just smiled at her. Ronnie thought he was turning his mind to the plans and duties of a normal day as he eased out of bed and dressed.

'Go back to sleep,' he murmured, kissing in a way that said the interlude was over.

She wasn't in the habit of impulsive liaisons, but felt no regret. She was entirely contented as though, if a genie were to appear and offer her a kingdom, she'd simply yawn and snuggle down, explaining, 'Thanks all the same, I have everything I need.'

The weekend had been a bitter disappointment for Vim. Free to play with her family away, her schemes concerning Nick fell apart when his empty flat confronted her. She went home and flounced about the house, ignoring Sunita's suggestion to walk the dog. Each time she dialled, Nick's phone rang on and on.

'You weren't home yesterday.' She thought he would offer some explanation but he changed the subject.

'I'd like to see your follow-up on the meeting resolutions.'

'Resolutions?' Longing had erased almost all her scheduled work, including the previous town meeting. She found her scribbled notes. *A walk-a-thon. Children's colouring competition. Fundraising. Petition by citizens and ratepayers to the local member.* She dialled and set up an interview with the committee chairperson, trying to muster interest in a journalist's concerns.

Nick Questro had written up his piece on Railway Street. It was a commentary on hard times in country towns. Considering his photographs of Nora and Tag, Ernie, Mrs O'Brian and her out-of-work son, and the scavenger from the dump, he thought he'd effectively conveyed Trundle's underside. Poverty, unemployment and old age made a change from the insular interests of local news.

Methodically he laid out copy and proof read the week's columns, thinking of the night he'd spent with Ronnie. Then a small smile lightened the often-dark expression that had become habitual since Jenny's death. He was grieving for a real person and a genuine love, and had little understanding of Vim's young heart.

Irritated, he noticed that she was out of the office again, and determined to give her a dressing down on the subject of lateness.

An official-looking letter lay in his mailbox when he went back to the flat. The date and whereabouts of his Sydney court case erased all Trundle matters from his mind. He sat alone, reflecting on the illusion of ever receiving true compensation in the way these cold typed words represented. Fingering the still-tender scar that ran down his leg, he visualised Jenny, bloodstained and motionless on the road. His cheeks were wet. After a while he stood up and marked on his wall calendar a large, deliberate cross against the given date. It was time to face the driver who'd wrecked his life. He would hear the fellow's sentence, get his payout and let the nightmare rest. There would be goods to sell up and decisions to make about the house. He wanted a clean break. Probably travel. He felt relieved.

He ate a scratch meal and was watching the evening news when he heard a tap at his door. Vim was standing there. He caught the drift of some wafting perfume.

'What on earth do you want?' He did not hide his annoyance.

She blushed painfully. 'I wanted to explain why I didn't come back to the office.'

'We can talk about that in work hours, I don't want you calling on me. It's not professional.'

'Professional?' Standing under the porch light among the cobwebs and dead leaves she was on the verge of tears. He felt sorry for her.

'I've got something for you. Wait there.' He came back with the photo he'd taken of her in the park. 'Listen, this is a small town. We work together. Neither of us need people spreading gossip, now do we?'

'I didn't think.'

'Go on home now.' He was determined to see her on her way.

As she drove home, she poured into the memory of that cautious conversation each rich hope and deep yearning of her heart. Surely things weren't as bad as she'd imagined? He had the negative of her photo. He might have had a second copy taken off. If he wanted discretion, she was willing. She cosseted the memory of his touch as he'd steered her down the steps and walked her to the car.

At home, she picked at a cold meal and went upstairs in search of company. She was baffled by the news that her brother and Sandy were moving to the commune. She thought it extremely odd that they were even partners, for there were no public demonstrations of affection between them.

She found Sandy on her knees, sorting Vijay's clothes.

'Sandy?' Vim sat on the side of the bed. 'How did you hook Vijay? There's someone I really like.'

'You could buy him a milkshake,' suggested Sandy, apparently reflecting on Vijay's courtship.

Vim laughed. 'He's a grown man, Sandy. An adult. I can't tell if he likes me.'

'Why don't you ask him?' Sandy lay down on her stomach and began to feel under the bed.

'Because that's not the way you do things.' Sandy seemed to have no feel for the manoeuvres of courtship.

Sandy was counting. 'Sixteen odd socks! Where do you think their pairs are?'

'I should play hard to get.'

'And half the buttons are gone off his shirts.'

Vim fell silent. Shirt buttons, socks; she'd never associated them with love. On reflection, the thought of touching Nick's clothing as Sandy now handled Vijay's was a pleasing liberty.

'Do you really want to move?' she asked.

'Not at first. I was walking through the bush and that supervisor from next door was right behind me. It was like that stalking video we watched. I felt like running. Guess what? She just waved and smiled at me.'

'But do you *want* to go out there to live?'

Sandy just yawned. 'I don't mind. It's what Vijay wants.'

Before she went to sleep, Vim examined the photograph from Nick.

She turned it over, still disappointed there was no personal message on the back. At least it proved that Nick had wanted to please her. He'd changed. He'd ignored her write-up about Shah Jahan to use his own story about Railway Street. Why publicise slums above the lives of successful people like her father? Trundle wasn't impoverished.

Vim lay in bed, inventing her new image. Nick could have all the discretion and distance he wanted. If Sandy's romance could accommodate the sorting of socks, Vim could be ready with businesslike gleanings from the *Save Our Rail* committee. She propped her photo against her bedside lamp, reassured by the image of herself by the troop carrier; a soldier, prepared for war.

5

By June, the voting to decide the use of joint land at Pelican remained split. Regular calls from Mr Lal to Richard confirmed their merger could not yet be settled. Frustrating as this was for the two businessmen, the delay suited Honor, who advised Victor to set up his clinic in one of the spare chalets meanwhile. One of the disused cabins was appointed for his use, and a team from the commune volunteered to hold a working bee.

On a weekday afternoon, an odd team of mopsters trailed through the bush. Rowena, Tuti, Sandy and Ronnie toted brooms and dusters; Vijay and Ben carried tools to deal with the cobwebs, grime, the broken step and sticking door. Wrapped up in knitted ponchos, Laurie and Honor sat side by side on a fallen log, dispensing moral support and thermos tea.

'We'll make you a home away from home, Victor!'

He nodded courteously, concealing his doubts. With his money dwindling and his wife strangely silent, he was at present camping at Pelican while he awaited news.

Unaware of his problems, Honor clung to her belief that the commune should remain unchanged. The next day, she sat out in the winter sunshine to compose one of her regular letters to her sister. She was a born communicator and kept in touch with numerous friends. Some relationships stretched back to girlhood, or were scattered through the many countries she'd visited during her questing life. Envelopes addressed to Britain, Africa, and India were regularly despatched from Trundle.

> *My dear Valeria,*
>
> *A brief update on progress here. Victor is proving the wonder we both know him to be. Due to his acupressure and massage, I am*

almost my energetic self again. If only I could say the same for Laurie. He is the most obstinate man! He barks away like a poor old dog, and all he says is, Rum and honey's the go!

Our little community struggles on with a few new arrivals. As for the plan to make of Pelican an up-market resort, I feel Richard will not have his way, after all. As usual, we are at loggerheads. He likes to rule, on the home front too. We had dinner there recently, and a domestic scene sprang out of nowhere when his poor little wife tried to make her wishes known. Maternal urges stirring. Richard is too hungry for attention to share his life with any rival, even a baby.

Do you remember Rosa Braun, that beautiful young cabaret singer we both knew in London? She had men wrapped around her little finger. She's in her fifties now, and here in Australia. Had a bad run of health; cancer, I believe, and sounds down on her luck. I've suggested she pay us a visit and try Victor's therapies. His family hasn't arrived. He doesn't say why; some hitch over the house sale, perhaps? His clinic's slowly getting underway in temporary quarters while we wait to hear the fate of the land. Delays do infuriate me! Patience has never been one of my virtues. But you know that. My fondest love to you and all the family, Honor.

She laid aside the writing pad to immerse herself in the chime of birdsong, the chirrup of insect, the interplay of light and shadow. Beauty existed everywhere. Gurdjieff, despite his oddball methods, had driven one lesson home to her. Human beings were mechanised; awareness involved effort. It might be easy to observe the mental conditioning of others, but to control one's own was the challenge of a lifetime. Swami's way had been simpler. *Be here now,* and variations on that theme.

Honor noticed Richard as he came walking in his hunched, hurried gait along the path. In her peaceful state, she saw him in a forgiving light. Today her enemy was a pitiable man, diffident and shy. His rudeness was a technique to ensure that no one liked him. He dominated others because he did not expect them to give freely.

'Richard!' she called impulsively. 'We so enjoyed dinner with you.'

He looked up, startled, as though she'd called him from deep reflection.

'You and Tuti must come for a return meal. Would you like to take a pot of lemon curd? We've more than we can use.'

'Tuti will collect it. I'm looking for Victor. Is he at the clinic?'

'I expect so. Ronnie is helping him set up.'

'Good, good. I'll see you later.'

He hurried on. Honor sat back and closed her eyes. Laurie found her like that and gave her an anxious little shake; something in her slumped posture and slack mouth upset him. But she looked up like a happy child.

'I was dreaming.' He saw that her golden hair rinse had faded; the strands at her roots were quite white.

'Come along inside.' He helped her up. 'You've had enough sun for one day.'

As Victor set out his sparse assortment of medical books, he was thinking of all the valuable equipment he'd left in London. Honor's letters had conveyed a setting far different from this run-down bush hut. He felt at a loss to understand what had inspired him to come all this way. For years he'd visualised a way to integrate complementary methods into the medical model. He believed in natural remedies; the massage, herbs, and nutrition that so many of his colleagues sneered at. But why travel to the ends of the earth to get started? Honor's vision had led him to expect proper premises, trained assistants, and a salary of sorts. He'd been given a dusty hut with tree spiders nesting in the rafters. He wasn't at all comfortable with the Australian bush. At least he'd seen no sign of snakes.

Hearing footsteps, he glanced up as Richard walked in without knocking.

He gave the small room a cursory inspection.

'No one else here?'

'As you can see.'

Since talk of managing a modern health centre under the Dutchman's sponsorship had ceased, the doctor was unsure how much credibility to accord Richard. However, he spoke cordially. 'As this is what I've been supplied with, this is where I'll start.'

'Any customers?'

'It's bound to be slow at first.'

'Well, I'm here to set the ball rolling.'

'You want a consultation?'

'A little snip, actually. I want a vasectomy.'

Victor stared at him. 'Sorry. I can't do surgery,' was all he said, but he was remembering the awkward dinner scene when Tuti had gone running from the table.

'It's a minor matter, isn't it?'

'Good heavens! Your Medical Board would have something to say if I turned up from England and set up as a bush surgeon.'

It was the end of the matter, he thought, but Richard persisted.

'How would they know?'

Victor ignored the question. 'Take your wife along to the surgery in Trundle. They'll fix you up, providing you're both quite sure about it.'

'My wife! What's she got to do with it? A man decides matters concerning his own body.'

With growing dislike, Victor offered his advice. 'She'll have to consent. If not, there are plenty of temporary birth control measures these days.'

'I want to be done with the matter. I don't want children. Why should I father brats she'd give all her love to?'

'Children can bring great joy.' Victor's ambivalence towards women eased whenever he saw a baby tenderly asleep at its mother's breast.

'Joy to whom? Tuti knew my attitude before she married me. She'll get over this whim.'

'A normal, natural urge,' corrected Victor. He wanted to conclude the fruitless exchange and stood up. 'I can't be of help.'

Richard looked around at the inadequate facilities. When he spoke his manner was that of manager to tradesman. 'It seems you're sorely in need of funds. I'm quite prepared to pay well for your service.'

'I'm sorry,' the doctor said abruptly. 'I can't help. And I most strongly advise you to discuss this with your wife.'

Repressed anger flared in Richard's words. 'My wife's a mystery; yours too, it would seem. I wonder why she's taking so long to follow you? Overstretched bonds are liable to break. Good luck with your clinic. You'll need it!'

He turned and walked away.

Victor sat thinking. His wife and children were on the other side of the world. His money was running out and his vision had disappeared.

Without imagination, this whole venture was madness. If he could get his hands on the fare, he'd book a return flight home as soon as possible. But even that was not an option.

Richard's offer of money had shocked him; in all his years of practice, he'd never come across a bribe. Nor had he ever felt a moment of willingness, before he turned it down. He needed funds urgently. Slamming the rickety door, he broke into a run, pushing his limits in a burst of physical effort that would have done credit to a man half his age.

Marie was waiting for him in the clinic when he came back. The thought had crossed her mind that Victor's family, for whatever reason, might never materialise in Trundle. If that were so, the house should be quickly handed over to Sam Playfair and proper tenants found.

Her intention to speak firmly to him on the matter of unpaid rent faded as he smiled at her. He looked exhausted. His dark hair was blown about and sweat dripped from his face.

'What can I do for you?' He did not remember having an appointment with her.

'It's about the house.'

'I'm not using it yet.'

He seemed defensive. She persisted. 'Your family's still coming?'

'All's under control. Just a matter of days.'

It was the kind of reply she would make herself, if pressed by a creditor.

'The matter of rent…You know how it is.'

'Of course. I'll see to it. Please excuse me now.'

His words were polite enough. But she saw he was upset as he almost pushed her out the door, locked up and strode away so that she had to run to keep up with him.

'I wanted to discuss publicity for your clinic, Victor. The committee expects me to organise it.'

'Later. I'm going to take a shower.'

'When then? This afternoon?'

'I'm going for a row then.'

'In that case, I'll come too.' She could be as determined as he was.

He broke into a jog, leaving her standing. Well, she was not to be brushed off like a bush fly. In fact she was looking forward to a boating expedition on Pelican's tranquil harbour. It was something she used to do all those years ago with Hugh, when their love affair was a secret and they sought private places to be alone.

Victor strode across the salt marsh, whistling as he considered the factors of tide and wind for his row. The towers of cumulus lining the horizon suggested a weather change before the afternoon was over. He planned to stay out for an hour or so, and was preparing to launch the little craft when Marie, in a big straw hat, came stumbling over the sand towards him. Now he remembered some vague thing she'd said earlier, about publicity.

'I wouldn't come if I were you. Looks like choppy weather. We'll discuss that matter later.'

'Oh no!' she laughed. 'You're not putting it off again, Victor. Besides, it's years since I've been in a boat.' Sandals in hand, she hitched up her skirt, waded into the shallows and clambered aboard. The dinghy rocked. With a spring, Victor came aboard, not sure why pursuing females always seemed so hard to avoid. He decided to stay inside the bay and make the trip as a short as possible.

'Do you row?' he asked.

'When I was young. I don't exercise now.'

She sounded quite proud of the fact. He guessed she was the type to eat anything, not caring for her body.

'It's a good habit. I keep up a strict regime myself.'

'Anyone can see that you're fit.'

He did not want admiration and picked up his stroke, planning to terminate the outing as soon as possible.

'Oh, look!'

Marie indicated the pelicans dipping majestic heads in search of fish.

'Fine birds,' he said.

'They have a colony there.' She indicated the promontory jutting from the mainland. 'I've always wanted to go there. Let's take a look.'

He hesitated, then steered the bow where she pointed. A focus to the trip would be the best way to end it. 'We'll have to be quick. There's a southerly change coming.'

They beached on pebbles with not a pelican in sight. As Marie wandered off, Victor eyed the whitecaps. 'Don't be long,' he called. 'We'll head back in five minutes.'

He sat down to wait. The place had a deserted, treeless atmosphere. Cliffs reared up, eroded caves along their base. Waves slammed against the rocks in forlorn rhythm.

'Yoo-hoo!' Marie was trudging towards him. 'Guess what? There's a colony of pelicans round that bend.'

'Jolly good. But we need to get a move on.' He frowned. Now she'd turned her ankle. By the time she'd rubbed it, adjusted her sandal and lumbered aboard, the current was against them and the boat was hardly moving.

'We'll pull together,' he suggested, regretting it as he saw she had no idea of co-ordinating their stroke. The dinghy was now unbalanced and lurched about.

'Grab the oars!' He moved over to adjust the ballast.

'Oh. The wind's got my hat!'

As she let go, a rowlock came free and flipped into the sea, followed by the oar. Floating away, it bobbed up and down near Marie's hat. Furious, he pushed her aside and grabbed the remaining oar. The boat began to circle. Rowing back was no longer an option. Rooster tails blew off the waves and the sky was darker. Scowling, he let the tide carry them to the sand and ordered her out. She watched as he dragged the dinghy up the beach.

'What an adventure! Are we stranded?'

She must be a complete idiot. Striding away he heard her calling, 'What about the boat?'

'I can hardly pick it up and carry it.'

He looked back at her, hobbling over the pebbles like a child abandoned by playmates. Anger always turned him silent. He blamed her for forcing him into this trip, and himself for making that silly mistake with the rowlock pin. Now a cliff climb would seem the only course to take.

'I'll go on ahead and bring someone back to help.'

She was gazing fearfully at the steep cliff path but he felt braced by the challenge. About to rid himself of her trailing presence he gave a cheerful wave. He hadn't invited her company; nor did he like her soft, vulnerable body and slow gait.

'Take your time. See you back at Pelican!'

Pleased to forget her, he set a fast pace, assessing the return trip would take half an hour. With a decent helper, he'd have the boat back at Pelican by evening.

Slithering down the last rough path, he went straight to the community room to get help. Vijay was there among the group. Victor recounted the tale of the disastrous outing and asked for a volunteer to go back with him.

'I'll come,' Vijay offered. He secretly admired Victor's physique. Life at the commune was proving Sandy to be far fitter than he was. She could trudge for miles, while he was full of aches and pains. Victor glanced at him.

'I need somebody fit, thanks all the same,' he said, nodding when the architect said he'd go.

Vijay wandered back to the sleeping quarters, was curt with Sandy, and soon went by himself to the beach. Everything was grey and a cold wind, preceding rain, cut through his clothing. He could see the shape of the promontory where the stranded craft lay. The men were probably there by now, battling the elements. He wondered how people knew how weak he was. Even Sandy babied him; telling him it might rain, he should take a coat. Nobody cared if Waldo and Victor got soaked. They had no trouble in the world of men.

He kicked stones along the sand and wondered why he'd expected Pelican to be any different. A friendly call drew him from his brooding. Wrapped up in parkas, Rowena, Pippin and Ronnie fell into step beside him.

'Victor and Marie went out in the dinghy. There's no sign of them.'

Ronnie was scanning the horizon as Vijay explained Victor's story. The group stood together talking when Marie's distant figure came into view, limping down the hill path. They hurried along to meet her. She was tearful and out of breath as she slumped down on the sand and pulled off her sandals.

'Let's have a look.' Ronnie squatted beside her. 'We'll have to get some antiseptic on those blisters. Whatever happened?'

'He just went off and left me. It was miles. Where is he, anyway? I thought I'd die!'

'Victor had to go back for the boat,' said Vijay, defending his hero.

'I hope he drowns.'

There was a grumble of thunder and scattered raindrops began to pit the sand.

'I suppose it was an emergency.' Ronnie had never viewed Victor in Marie's doting light 'We'll help you back to your chalet. Come on, you need checking over.'

'Not by him, thank you.' Marie accepted their support and together they went back to Pelican.'

Her feet soaked and her blisters treated, Marie fell into self-reproach.

'It's my own fault. I knew he didn't want me to go.'

'Then why did you? It's not like you, mooning after a man like him.'

Marie flushed. 'I wasn't mooning.'

'Yes you were. Even if he wasn't married, he's hardly your type.'

'You can say that again! But he seemed so nice.'

'He is nice. But he's a very self-centred man.'

'Hugh would never have left me on my own like that!'

'Hugh was different,' said Ronnie gently.

'I'm losing him.' Marie's tears flowed again.

'What do you mean? It's years since he died.'

'He's fading, Ronnie. Sometimes I can't remember what he looked like. I found a snapshot of us on that coach tour to Alice Springs. We were just a couple in out-of-date clothes. What did we say? How did we feel? It's all slipping away. This ring… It has no meaning now. My life has no meaning.'

As though some lifelong emptiness must be faced, Marie began to sob. Pippin stared and Rowena sat down on the bed and put her arm around her stepmother, while Ronnie watched her grief. Her sister had always found playmates who outdid her and made fun of her. Hugh, a deeply kind man, had protected her from destructive people. No wonder she clung to his fading memory. It was the frailty of love that made Ronnie wary, as an uncalled-for image of Nick Questro floated through her mind.

'You're wrong!' Rowena said. 'Of course your life has meaning. We need you, don't we Pippin? Show Nanny how much you love her.'

Reassured, Pippin clambered up on the bed and pressed fervent kisses on her grandmother's cheek again and again until Marie managed a laugh. Returning to Pelican had been a brave step for her. Running her shop, buying and selling, balancing the budget—all these time-consuming activities held away introspection. Here, like bubbles slowly surfacing from a noxious pond, the mind could retrieve its sorrows and regrets; and the soul's quiet voice could express a new direction.

Next morning she drove back to Trundle, her stuttering car announcing some imminent disaster. Loudly encouraging and reproving it, she made it to the garage workshop where the engine promptly died. It was a fair walk to her shop and as she limped along, blisters stinging and legs aching, she wondered what to do. The mechanic's estimate of the repair bill had made her gasp. She'd never been one to put money aside; for her, it was just a commodity and handy tool and she could not understand meanness or miserliness. Yet there were times when she wished she had a cash box hidden up the chimney or bullion buried in the yard. Without transport she was stranded. Victor still held the lease on her house and she had no intention of asking any favours of him. She turned in to Kitty's shop and explained her predicament. As usual, Kitty was a fund of good and sensible advice.

'Come and stay at our place. You know you're welcome.'

Remaining in town was an attractive prospect. The embarrassing outcome of her boating expedition could fade and a break from her roles at Pelican appealed. As for the money, she would simply have to trust that it would come.

She rearranged her window display and telephoned a few old clients to advise them of new stock. As she replaced the receiver, the little shop bell tinkled and Nora Halpin looked in. She seemed to have appointed Marie as her honorary friend. It was hard to ignore her black eye but Nora made no reference to it, chatting for a few minutes, then waving cheerfully as she went on to buy groceries. Her existence reminded Marie that her single state was not such a bad outcome. The thought of the Halpins' home life horrified her.

On Nora's heels followed Mr Lal. He liked Marie, and their common links to Pelican now gave them much in common. Today, after enquiring after his son and Sandy, he produced a catalogue and flipped its pages.

'I have a companion watercolour to this one.'

The painting he indicated was called *The Month of Ashadha*. Marie was entranced by the glowing colours and multi-layered scenes of court life. Lovers approached a canopied bed, yogis sat apart, a warrior paced, master and maidservant conferred.

'This must be quite lovely in the original,' she said.

'It's one of a series based on the twelve songs of our Indian calendar. Ashadha is the whirlwind season. This brooding sky! Its moral advises the wise to stay at home. Only the demented venture forth and face the storm.'

'I can vouch for that,' said Marie, thinking of her rugged tramp across the hills.

'I have decided to sell my painting.'

'But why part with such a treasure?'

'Partly for the money. I must explore alternatives or my project will not get off the ground. Also because I am not fulfilling the artist's purpose.'

'Meaning…?'

'Such art was never meant to be hidden in a bank vault because of its value.'

Marie nodded and Mr Lal fixed her with an intent gaze.

'You can help me with contacts. My wife has sent me here. She hasn't yet gone to the Gardens of Paradise. I pay great care to her guidance.'

Marie remembered he'd been a widower less than a year.

'Tell me about your wife,' she suggested. He began to describe how they'd met, their journey out from India and their long marriage.

'Her ashes rest in my bedroom. One day I will take her home to India.'

She understood his sadness. Yesterday had shown her that, even now, she too mourned for Hugh. There could be no time frame to grief; the neat idea of closure was a fallacy.

The phone was ringing. Mr Lal stood politely aside while she took the call.

'Stop in at my home soon,' he suggested when she had finished. 'Then we can discuss the best way to effect a sale.'

Marie said she would be pleased to do so. Her call had been an enquiry from a buyer in search of a cedar chest. She knew she had one in her bedroom at the old house. It would be easy enough to drop by and remove it. Her financial worries were about to be relieved.

After work Kitty drove her home to Alexandra Avenue. The untidy garden and overgrown grass confirmed that Victor's family was no closer to taking up residence. Marie used her spare key to investigate. Inside, there wasn't a trace of occupation, although the power was on and there were a few scraps of food in the fridge. Victor had evidently called in recently.

With her friend's help, it was an easy matter to carry out the small chest and fit it in the back of the station wagon. Marie hesitated, then scribbled a note of explanation to Victor before she slammed and locked the door on the mystery of the unfriendly man and his missing family.

They dropped the chest back at the shop, then drove to Kitty's. The bounce of new carpet and the aroma of lamb already roasting in the automatic oven announced a homely welcome. Donning her apron Kitty was transformed by domesticity. Marie watched her friend peel vegetables and check the answerphone messages. Leaza wanted oatmeal and egg to mix a face pack. Joel was reminded to do his guitar practice. She sent Holly out to buy gravy mix and offered Marie a glass of sherry.

'Thanks. But can't I help?'

'I'm used to managing. Relax and enjoy yourself.'

Which Marie did, reflecting on the warm family atmosphere of Kitty's home.

In her own case, the affection of a child and grandchild had been a vain hope just six months before. Now Pelican had answered her dearest wish, to be needed and accepted by a family of her own.

PART 5

THE MONTH OF ASHADHA

PART 5

1

On a winter's day, Mac Booth caught the train home to Trundle. Beyond the window, in country back yards and paddocks, men drove tractors, women pegged up washing, children waved; activities that for Mac were newly profound and sweet reminders of existence.

Outwardly he hadn't changed much. He'd lost some weight and carried a long scar beneath his shirt. Recent months had reminded him that death was no longer just a news item. He knew he was lucky, but this homecoming meant far more to him than luck. He felt grateful and blessed beyond belief. He was a man truly saved by technology and the gift of a surgeon's skill. He could feel his heart at work in the diligent pulsing at his wrist. Magic! He'd done plenty of reading during his recovery period. After leaving hospital he'd stayed locally with a cousin; a nurse who was able to keep him supplied with research articles on cardiac surgery. A few patients made strange claims that along with renewed vessels came personal insights; even changes of direction. And he did feel very sensitive now, due to his near-death encounter and subsequent trauma. As he left the train at Trundle and stood on the platform, he felt weak and almost ethereal. He had to close his eyes for a moment, just to get his bearings.

Carrying his small bag, he walked slowly through the gates and along past the river towards Main Road. It was a dull, windy day and the few shoppers hurried along, heads down, cardigans and coats clutched tight. Home! His drab little flat beckoned like paradise. Other people's ways soon palled, especially when you had invalid status. Their beds, their food, their conversations soon grew irritating. Town pride began to jar; the faces of TV presenters weren't familiar. One felt out of sorts, trying not to complain, being grateful. At night, in the darkness, a twinge was enough to call up dread. No wonder they called it a heart attack! Attack was aggressive, sudden, and without compunction. By chance, pure luck, he'd been saved. He kept thinking that. Saved! He could as easily be underground with the grass already greening his grave. He could be incinerated and scattered to the wind. He'd never made a will, much less considered his preference after death. Ah well, he had more time! He felt an assault of love for his mates, his job, the Club, the dull old shops, the quiet brown river, Trundle… Suddenly he felt a bit faint, and had to hail a cab to take him home.

The doctors' instructions were pretty clear. Daily walking, brisk. A low-fat diet. Regular medical checks while the balance of diuretics and other medications kicked in. No heavy work during the recovery period. And so on. Feeling a quite new and tender solicitude towards himself, he began the walking at once. At home, he went through the dietician's instructions and made a shopping list. He phoned the hospital and made an appointment. For some reason, he put off contacting the newspaper office, which was obviously running smoothly without him. He'd picked up the current issue and noticed a few changes in style and layout, read a few paragraphs and set it aside, ignoring a peculiar impulse to breathe in the familiar paper smell. His mind was turned off to information. In contrast, he was newly aware of tastes and scents; as sensitised as a baby to colours, shapes and shadows.

A few days passed before he opened his door to Nick, who smiled and extended his hand.

'Heard you were back.'

'News travels fast,' said Mac. 'I've been meaning to call you. Sorry. Look, come on in.'

The transitory appearance of the dingy flat reminded Nick of his own digs. Most lone men didn't bother much with decor.

'You look well. Pleased to be home?' He wasn't prepared for the look of bliss on Mac's face.

'Absolutely. Paper running smoothly?'

'For sure. I'll be down in Sydney for a week at the end of the month. A court hearing I have to attend, and other business. No problem. I've already planned a couple of features and Vimla will handle the day-to-day stuff. No need to rush back.'

'Thanks. How's our young lady?'

'We've had our moments. She's settled down lately.'

Nick didn't elaborate and Mac didn't enquire. He wasn't interested in drama. He didn't care if he never read another newspaper. He had everything he wanted, right here, now.

'Any big news while I've been away?' he asked without much interest. Strange, the effort to relate. He felt he'd been out of the world for a long time and had inadvertently been dropped down in some past reality.

'Not a lot. The *Save Our Rail* committee had a protest march. Mitch O'Malley won the pumpkin contest.' Nick grinned. 'A new type of health centre, run by some English doctor out at Pelican. I'm going out this weekend to do a write-up.'

Nick had interests both professional and personal for this visit. At Marie's persuasion he'd agreed to visit. As well, he'd heard the council was concerned about breaches of residency near the commune. Squatters were saying they'd bought land under the impression they could live there. And then there was Ronnie Gale. She was on his mind.

'Good, good.' Mac could have cried with relief when Nick left. Perhaps one day he'd feel such things mattered. For now, he peeled an orange and reflectively tasted a segment, enchanted by its flavour and the symmetry of its design.

Winter's mists and rain had not discouraged Vijay, who had adopted the doctor as guide and model. Whenever he saw Victor stride towards the beach he would follow, carrying his mat and his book on yoga positions. As Victor pushed off and rowed away, Vijay would undertake his exercises, studying each picture and imitating the postures. His loose joints allowed him to assume some positions, such as sitting cross-legged, quite easily. Others, which required strength, were much harder but he persevered.

Victor paid him no attention, hardly noticing the routines of the other residents. It took a few weeks for him to realise that Vijay timed his activities to Victor's. Whether he was swimming in the morning, hiking at midday, or rowing in the afternoons, there was Vijay, loitering nearby. He did not like to be spied on and the young Indian was watching him closely. Victor changed his routine. His shadowy companion pursued him, never speaking, always at a distance.

Victor confronted him one day on the beach. A cold wind blew and spits of rain were falling yet there was Vijay, upside-down, his legs curved over his head like a hedgehog rolled up for protection.

'Why are you following me about?'

Vijay returned to a supine position and gazed up, smiling. 'Because I admire you.'

'I don't understand you.'

'I'm weak. See for yourself.' He held up smooth arms. 'I have no muscles.'

Relieved, Victor felt a little sorry for the young man. 'Is that all? I was starting to think I had a private detective on my tail! Look, my clinic's open, so come and see me in the morning. A fellow from the newspaper wants to see me in action. If you'll be the guinea pig, I'll give you a physical and a training programme.'

Vijay's large brown eyes grew liquid with gratitude. He nodded as Victor strode away, adding, 'And stop following me.'

He was preoccupied with ideas for the clinic, and frustrated by his lack of funds. Marie had organised a newspaper write-up. With the Press coming, he wished he looked more professional. This bush shack wasn't exactly what he'd visualised. He didn't have a proper massage table. Herbs and homeopathic tinctures were expensive and he thought with regret of the costly spectroscope and imaging equipment that sat mouldering away in London. In the back of his mind lived the hope that Van Rjien's resort would go ahead, with himself running the associated health facilities. From time to time Richard implied he had agreement pending but, since denying the man that strange request, Victor felt the Dutchman had withdrawn.

At least a few clients were turning up and he found Ronnie's help gave him a semblance of professionalism. She was the kind of nurse he preferred: up-to-date, efficient, minding her own business. She said she was glad to give him a few hours each day, it would pass the time. She seemed an active type and he felt he shouldn't count on her presence for long.

When he'd asked for her help, Ronnie had been curious to observe his methods. She knew that surgeries were full of chronically sick people. When tests came back clear, doctors were at a loss. Perhaps alternative therapy had a place.

'Who have we today?'

'Mr Chan is bringing his boy again.'

'I wonder if the lad's improved—the *calcarea carbonica* ought to have cleared up his ear infection and the eczema but I can't find an appropriate remedy to try for bed-wetting. If only my books would arrive! Elizabeth was supposed to despatch them weeks ago.' He did not add that, for the past week, phone calls to his home number had failed to connect, and he hadn't had a letter for a fortnight.

'Laurie has an appointment. And Rosa.' She mentioned the last name discreetly for Rosa Braun was proving the kind of patient Victor found most difficult. Since arriving at Pelican, she had begun to take more and more of his time during her consultations, telling him rambling stories from her past and seeking his attention out of clinic hours. A few times Victor had terminated the consultation and passed her on to Ronnie; *the counsellor,* as he'd appointed her, to her amusement. 'And Nick Questro's interviewing you.' She felt strange, saying his name aloud.

'The newspaper fellow? When he comes, will you bring him over, and young Vijay too? He wants a fitness programme.'

Ronnie, maintaining the façade of professional, agreed. She hadn't seen Nick for a fortnight and was trying to convince herself he was a fly-by-night and best forgotten. Her resolve failed as soon as she saw him. He was carrying a small bag and she realised how much she wanted him to stay. He smiled at her.

'What have you been up to?'

'Not a lot. Victor's opened the clinic so I lend a hand. A few clients have turned up.'

'Officially, I'm here to do an interview. Your sister persuaded me these woods are full of stories.'

'Maybe.' Marie was a dramatist. Ronnie wondered what his unofficial reason was for the visit. Longing for time alone together, she said, 'If you drop off your bag, I have a message to deliver. Shall we meet up at the track?'

The bush path felt slippery underfoot. They walked enclosed in dim and private intimacy. A fecund odour rose up from the leaf mould and the rushing of the swollen stream grew loud.

'No lingering under the waterfall recently?'

'It's rained every day this week.'

'That terrible hailstorm in Sydney!'

'Shocking.' Ronnie laughed at the trite exchange. 'Weather's a pretty safe topic.'

She stopped walking and turned to face him. Urgently he took her in his arms. A surge of desire bound them in a long, deep kiss before Nick drew back, breathed deeply, sighed.

'Can I stay with you tonight?'

She said nothing, her body language answering as she rested her head against his chest, content to be close. Gently he patted her shoulder. 'Come on. We'd better front up for this interview.' Hands linked, they strolled on until the clinic came into view.

Victor was courteous, explaining his theories on complementary medicine while Nick scribbled notes. The journalist found it hard to take the interview seriously, given the rundown premises, lack of equipment and the fact that Vimla's brother was apparently to be his demonstration client. Why Vijay? He'd seemed perfectly healthy during Nick's brief stay with the Lals. They were an odd family all round. Vim hardly spoke to him these days and had stopped pestering him out of hours but he thought there was some other agenda behind her coolness. As an employee she seemed dreamy and unreliable. Sometimes he had to make her rewrite copy over and over, as though she hadn't heard his initial directions. Or, busy at his desk or on the phone, he would feel her intense gaze, the same way she'd latched on to him that first day at the office. Surely he'd made himself clear. Yes, a strange family, the Lals.

He made notes on stress mechanisms and holistic healing principles, and was trying to secure a deal on the printing of publicity brochures, which Marie had hinted at, when Vijay turned up. Victor assessed the young man. He pronounced him below the minimum percentile of fitness, informed him he must cut out all sugar, white bread, cake, biscuits, sweets, snacks, coffee, tea and alcohol, and outlined a regime of aerobic exercise. As the young man was leaving, Nick asked him if he'd seen squatters on the new subdivision. At once Vijay spoke up, full of indignation. He and Sandy had met a fine Greek couple living in a tent on land they'd purchased. They were being hounded by the council, who said they had no right to be there. The girl was pregnant and they had spent all their savings on the land.

Nick looked at Ronnie, adopting the offhand tone that suggested he had wind of a good story. 'Want to take a stroll and see if we can find these people?'

'My nurse will be available after lunch,' said Victor firmly, for Rosa Braun was his next patient. At once Vijay offered to escort the reporter. They set off, the young Indian extolling Victor's virtues and setting a pace his mentor would have applauded.

There was a group meal that night. People gathered afterwards, exchanging news and enjoying the improvised duets from Ben and Vijay. Ronnie sat curled up in a corner seat, wondering what the night would bring. It was a long time since she'd fallen for a man. After her divorce and solitary withdrawal there'd been a few one night stands; she'd found them meaningless. Celibacy was the only option. Men seemed to read her mind for there'd been no more approaches. She knew Nick wasn't looking for a quick fling. She could understand his reserve. Her own cherished independence now battled a longing to feel love again.

Soon she slipped away from the group and went for a shower. In bed, she read and reread the same page of a book until she heard his footsteps stop outside.

'It's open,' she called.

He came straight to her and, kicking off his shoes, lay down beside her. Expecting the gentle embrace she'd found so tender, she was surprised as he kissed her passionately, tugged off her nightwear and threw his own clothes aside.

'Hey!' She felt at a loss. This intensity unnerved her. 'Slow down! We've got all night.'

At once he drew back and lay still and she suddenly understood that he was terribly anxious. 'What's up?' she asked. 'We don't have to do this, you know.'

'I want to. I want you. Since Jenny, I haven't...' His voice was full of grief. He gave a bitter laugh. 'I'm sorry! I come to you to make love with another woman on my mind.'

'Not another woman, Nick. Your wife.'

'I can't forget it. Every day I'm still back there with Jen: the crash, the blood, the pain. It felt like the end of everything. It was horrible. The case comes up soon. I'll have to sit there and go through the whole thing again, blow by blow. Some fellow will go to jail. I'm actually sorry for the bastard. What good's it going to do?'

'I know how it is. Why don't you tell me about her?'

'Jen? I don't know what to say. Why do you want to know?'

'You loved her. She's here now. What was she like?'

As he lay beside her in the dark, he began to describe Jenny's looks, how they met, their plans and dreams, random memories. He went through the accident, her death, the nightmare of his own surgery, his need to escape the scene of their lives together and travel anywhere from one sterile motel to the next. Sometimes his voice sounded choked and, when she touched his face, she could feel tears. His pain filled her with tenderness. As they drifted into sleep she had her arms around him, rocking him gently.

Some time during the night they woke and turned towards each other. As their kiss stirred passion, it was clear a barrier had gone. He was a slow and sensuous lover, exploring her body to awaken erotic imprints that were quite new to her. And when they made love and he climaxed, it was her name that he cried out.

In the morning they lay lazily chatting in the way of contented lovers.

'After your hearing, what will you do?'

'The house is rented but I'll probably sell up, clear the mortgage. I should get compo and insurance money for the car. I'd thought of taking a year away; Europe, maybe. I don't know now.'

'I always dreamed of Italy. Posters are the closest I've come.'

He seemed surprised. 'You're free, aren't you?'

'I suppose so. I couldn't see myself that way before. So you're leaving Trundle?'

'Mac Booth is back. I saw him on Friday.'

'How is he?'

'Fine. In no hurry to get back to work. Who can blame him?'

'And how's your young admirer?'

His smile was wry. 'Vim? I think she's got the message. The Lals are an odd lot! Young Vijay wanting to be Mr Universe and his father with that improbable building scheme.'

'We all dream. Life's not much without that.'

'What's yours?'

'That would be telling.' She yawned and stretched. 'Pass my T-shirt? I hope you're not the garter and suspender type? I must be a sorry disappointment!'

He kissed her lightly. 'You're not a sorry disappointment, Ronnie Gale.'

In the shower, standing under the relaxing flow of water, she thought of Nick's plans to leave Trundle and travel, warning herself how easily the sense of dependency could surface.

Nick hitched back to town after lunch. Ronnie strolled with him as far as the road, longing to ask when he'd be back. The return walk was a lonely one. She felt strangely open, as though her feelings were visible to everyone. Avoiding company, she lay down on her bed until it was time to give Rosa her daily injection.

Rosa was resting in the patients' chalet, her wig sitting neatly on the bedside table beside her tapestry. A tall, gaunt woman recovering from cancer and the side effects of chemotherapy, she seemed unselfconscious as she smiled up at Ronnie.

'You have had a visitor.' Her clasp surprisingly strong, she took Ronnie's hand. 'I can see he is more to you than just a friend.'

Her tone suggested she was at home in the waters of deep feeling. Whatever subject she raised (the war, lovers, migration, illnesses) she infused with a passion which could be disconcerting. She seemed to draw out one's secrets.

'In the past you have been hurt, abandoned? I think you are afraid of losing this man?'

'He plans to go away,' Ronnie admitted. Her mind found Rosa's words extreme and fanciful, but she sensed tears not far away. This probing intimacy made her uncomfortable and she prepared the mistletoe injection, saying briskly, 'Victor wants to reassess your treatment regime tomorrow.'

The mention of Victor had a startling effect on Rosa. She sprang up from the bed and stood close to Ronnie, who took an involuntary step back. 'We women are born to love and suffer,' she breathed. 'To find such a man here... How strange! It is Fate.'

Her evident belief that in some way her life and the doctor's were irrevocably bound did not surprise Ronnie. The signs were there, in Rosa's impromptu clinic visits, her lengthy stays and Victor's evasive and abrupt reactions. The poor woman had created some fantasy around him, disregarding every fact of his life and her own. Perhaps a brush with death made one immune to appropriate response.

'He's expecting his wife and children any day,' Ronnie reminded her, but Rosa seemed not to hear her.

'Ronnie!' Again she loomed close, her scalp shining palely through the downy hint of regrowth. 'It is wrong to conceal one's heart. I want to share my own with you. Please take this...' She pulled a little diary from her bedside drawer. 'I want you to read what I have written. I want you to know me as I know myself. Take it, please!'

Ignoring Ronnie's reluctance, she forced the book into her hands.

I have always believed in love. Yes, as a young and beautiful girl I had my share of lovers, both men and women. I don't say love is the domain of sexuality, that other loves are pallid. I have loved the petals of flowers, the bark of trees, the shape of river stones. Art, work, public adulation, these too I have loved. Cancer found its entrance when I forgot to love. I absorbed depression, helped it grow. They tell me I am obsessive. I say to them, I feel.

My skin grew yellow, my eyes dull. I was a walking skeleton. My hair fell out. Drugs and rays poisoned me. To walk a few steps was beyond me. 'This is my time to die,' I thought. To discover that life is nearly over is a terrible realisation.

They tried to confine me but they do not know me! Ordered to rest and await the end, I dragged myself from the hospital. People were shadows, fllickering beyond my reach. My old friend Honor wrote to me and told me of this place called Pelican, where a healer might bring help. And so I came here.

This reprieve is wondrous! Yes, I hold the gifts of life and hope renewed. This place of healing is my salvation. He is a gift of grace. To find love here, how strange! He comes to me in my dreams, a fine-looking man ten years or more my junior, tall, fit and in his prime. Can this be? asks the heart. I tell myself, Rosa, you are not a girl! But what has age to do with the heart? Love courses through my weak limbs, bringing to my womb the ache of desire. How his form attracts me! I store the memory of his aftershave and memorise the pattern of his paisley tie. Oh that I could be the one entrusted to launder his shirts for I would hold them close and inhale his aroma.

The turgid *voyeurism* of her style was persuading Ronnie to leave the rest of the notebook unread. She would have to return it unobtrusively, when there was no chance of Rosa demanding to know her response. A final entry puzzled her. Gifts were spoken of several times in succession.

Love opens the heart and frees the giver. He is a quiet man, he makes no demands. Poor man, devoted to healing, he has been abandoned by his family and taken for granted by ungrateful people here. Can't I see his distress as he apologises for his humble clinic and the shortage of resources? I, Rosa, will be the giver of the gift. What he needs, he shall have!

Perhaps Rosa had money, though Ronnie had not formed that impression. When she next saw Honor, she asked casually, 'Is Rosa a wealthy woman?'

'Poor dear, she hasn't two sticks to rub together. I believe she was working as a housekeeper before she fell ill. She never went for wealth or stature. She fell for awkward men, the kind who don't last.'

'So you've known her a long time?'

'Certain people reappear along life's path, don't you find? Is she benefiting from Victor's treatment? She's convinced he's cured her.'

Ronnie made a noncommittal reply. Rosa's diary was an enigma. Ronnie slipped it under the door of her chalet when she knew Rosa was at dinner, presuming the book was some kind of therapeutic release for the ravaged convalescent woman.

2

Vijay embarked on a fitness regime as enthusiastically as he'd started his pursuits of enlightenment and musical excellence. He did push-ups, worked out with bar bells, and learned yoga. He jogged and took long walks every day. Sandy accepted his new creed but had no interest in redesigning her body. To her it was a useful object. At least he no longer puffed and complained on their rambles. But she was tired of Victor's name. Vijay seemed unable to discuss anything without referring to his hero.

Sometimes when the other residents were settling down by the fire, he and Ben would improvise guitar duos, but quite often, worn out from training, he would go to bed straight after dinner. Sandy was left to curl up by herself, an outsider among these people who'd known one another for years. At least Rowena seemed friendly. She had a fund of tales gathered from her unconventional upbringing. Sandy was impressed. There was nothing exciting about work in the old folks' ward. Rowena asked very personal questions, saying Ben was getting boring; did Sandy have any good ideas to spice up things in bed? Sandy shook her head. She hid her suspicion she might be pregnant. It was hard to guess how Vijay would react. She wasn't one to risk a confrontation, and often adopted her most inscrutable expression and said she was going to bed.

Tuti, the third of the young women at Pelican, was equally isolated. The considerable age gap between her husband and herself meant she was usually attending to his interests rather than socialising. She would have liked nothing better than to visit the girls, talk about children and babies, cooking, feminine gossip; but Richard, in his doting way, kept a strict eye on her whereabouts. Neither Rowena, with her sulky look, nor Sandy, with her vague ways and odd partner, were in his opinion likely to exert a good influence on his wife. His idea of talking usually became a monologue concerning his business or the psychological quirks of

Pelican's members. He saw most of them as hangers-on; ineffectual people, easily led. He disregarded the voters' clear message that he had not gained majority support, and spent his time revising blueprints and investigating building codes and zoning.

Tuti was in a quandary. They'd been married for five years. Richard had taken a businesslike approach to courtship, first through an agency, then corresponding for a time before making a trip to Indonesia to meet her. She was expecting a strong, self-confident man, just like his photograph. He meant to convey assurance but, seeing how he perspired, she sensed how shy and insecure he felt.

He began to list the assets she could expect to gain from their union, yet she was thinking he seemed vulnerable, as though no woman could ever want him for himself. He described his material wealth, financial acumen, good health and education, yet all she observed was his dry mouth and the way his hands began to tremble. She felt a wave of love; maternal, generous love for this pompous gentleman who bore some unknown, deep hurt. To reassure him was beyond her upbringing and his dignity so she sat quietly, her feelings masked. He seemed to be telling her he did not want to father children; the world was already overpopulated and in any case he did not understand play or laughter and would not be fit for such a role.

Although such words were beyond her understanding, she remembered a family of Dutch administrators who came to the district while she was a little girl, secure and happy within her village life. Those cold, strict parents had looked down on locals and their superior children had been kept apart. Richard might have been just such a little boy. The knowledge made her tender. How could he know the joy and pride of loving parents? She resolved to teach him. She was young; she could wait for babies. He wouldn't be rough or stray off with other women. She liked the idea of travel and living in Australia. Certainly her friends envied her.

Abruptly he proposed marriage as though he'd shown all his cards. She saw his great relief when she nodded. His confidence was restored within the second; he even sounded a little condescending, as though a refusal would have shown her up as a person of poor judgement. It took months after the wedding before she came to understand his dual faces. In public he was aloof and spoke as though he owned her. But only she had access to his private, inner wants.

Her tender giving wrenched from him the utmost admissions. He desired her, loved her, needed her. She was his all; she held the power to supply everything the past had denied him. Of these two husbands, she knew which one spoke sincerely and she was content. But on the issue of children, he had not budged at all. Even the mention of a baby turned him moody or, worse, angry, as though she had some plot to displace him. She felt desperately in need of good advice and, thinking of Honor, said to Richard, 'I'll go over and collect that pot of lemon curd.'

A voice declaiming from the Stedmans' porch stopped her in her tracks. Peering through the foliage she saw the elderly woman, apparently addressing thin air.

In fact Honor was making a tape to send to her sister; usually an enjoyable task, but today she felt distracted and her thoughts refused to flow. People were giving her the impression that she had become redundant. Marie had replaced her as Pippin's stand-in grandmother. Victor, though courteous, gave out no information about his family and seemed to support Richard's grandiose ideas. Rowena no longer asked her advice. Even Laurie used a calming tone, suggesting she might try letting matters run their course. Thinking back to all the moral battles she'd thrown her weight behind in the past, she realised she was weary now. She sighed and pressed the *rewind* and *record* buttons for the third time.

> *My dear Valeria, Laurie hasn't been well. Bronchitis, but it's been a nasty go of it and he's not out of the woods yet. I can't help wondering how you manage on your own, after forty years of marriage? At least grandchildren must be a comfort. You don't complain but I wish I could spend time with you face to face. I might think about a last trip home. Today I have a sense that life is much too short and one must spend it wisely, what remains of it. I have a fancy to make contact with England's rocks and bricks. I want to hear larks and nightingales. Perhaps I should just check this taping machine is working...*

Taping machine! She caught herself using out-of-date expressions as though she belonged in the age of crystal sets and silent movies.

Impatiently she rewound to do the last sentence again, only to discover she'd mistakenly erased everything. It would have to wait. Resting her head against the cushion, she closed her eyes, and Tuti, still hidden by the bushes, did not like to interrupt her rest, and stole away.

She waited until she had served dinner and her husband had pronounced the meal to his liking, then asked casually, 'Is Victor a proper doctor?'

'I believe so.' Richard shrugged. 'He could be a quack. Who would really know? Why do you ask? You're not unwell?' He touched her neat hand fondly.

'Every woman needs to have medical check-ups,' she reminded him.

'There are doctors in town. I prefer you not to consult our healer.' He did not want Victor to have access to his wife's body. 'I'll make an appointment and drive you in, if you think it's necessary.'

She nodded and he said no more, preferring not to enquire into the details of feminine conditions. Instead he signalled for her to leave the dishes on the table, embracing her and pressing urgently against her. She led him to the bedroom and undressed him and he lay down naked, his arms stretched passively along the pillows while she fondled and aroused him. After several minutes he groaned and took her in his arms. He could be a patient and persistent lover; sure of her love once she moaned and surrendered to his touch.

He drove her in to Pelican the following afternoon, leaving her at the surgery while he went off to attend to other business matters. She sat nervously in the waiting room, remembering how, after the dinner party, she'd washed her contraceptive pills down the sink and gone to bed with a feeling of control that had excited their lovemaking for several weeks. Now she felt ill; physically nauseated and mentally afraid. Silence was her way but a baby couldn't be concealed with closed lips and a downcast gaze. As a very obvious mother-to-be was called for her consultation, Tuti picked up a magazine and began to look at pictures of baby wear. Soon she too would be a mother with a baby to feed and dress and love. She did not fear giving birth. Painful though that might be, it would be nothing compared with the risk she knew she faced when her husband understood what she had done.

Richard stepped out from the bank and looked along Main Road, where tattered awnings drooped in the still air. He was surprised that he'd allowed such a run-down town to become his home. When he first came here, he'd been in his early thirties; a worldly man, widely travelled, with sufficient experience of novelty to know its limits. The prospect of living in this little backwater appealed to him then. As an only child, he'd inherited a good sum of money from his father and invested wisely. Methodically he purchased shares, property, franchises, laying the foundations for an independent income. His material future seen to, he decided he was not yet ready to marry. This mid-life passage he would devote to his inner growth. He expected there would be a straightforward methodology a man in search of God might follow, but perusals of spiritual literature, theology, and the teachings of world religions left him confused. Parables annoyed him, dogma could not be substantiated and the strange experiences of mystics baffled him. However, one identifiable thread advised men and women with his goal to go apart from the world for a time. They retired to the wilderness, the desert, monasteries and convents where, if they were patient and fortunate, some enlightenment descended.

Just as he decided to follow this course, he heard of Pelican and came to Trundle to investigate. The Stedmans made him welcome. Laurie was a quiet man but Honor was happy to tell him of her past quests and travels. The values she expounded seemed to reflect what he was looking for and the commune's setting was beautiful and remote. As he wandered through the unbroken landscape and met up with other founding members, he began to feel he could belong here. He'd been uprooted regularly as a child; wandered incessantly as a young man. A kind of home was a new prospect. To be alone yet in community among idealists seemed to him a pleasant setting to receive whatever spiritual insights might descend. The land was very cheap. He sold a parcel of shares and was welcomed as a major shareholder to the commune.

The ensuing years involved planning, hard physical work, and much negotiation. Used to having his own way, he frequently stormed out of meetings where discussions went round in circles and impractical ideas were mooted. Wondering if his own books failed to deliver some essential information, he borrowed Honor's. She too had a library of writings by famous saints, mystics, and gurus, yet not one of these books could show him the meaning of enlightenment or the way to God. The gentle pace of life at the commune left him with much time to brood. He felt lonelier than ever here, in this lovely place, among his group. He did not call them friends. In fact, he did not know what friendship was. He even began to hate himself. His good manners were a façade. Throughout a painful season, he realised the face he showed the world was self-seeking, cold, unloving. He would wake from nightmares, tears wet on his cheeks.

Honor had listened with sympathy when, on one occasion, he confessed how miserable he felt. 'You've entered the dark night,' she said matter-of-factly. 'How can we progress until we see exactly what we are?' She pulled a faded booklet from her shelf and offered it to him. 'Read St. John of the Cross.'

'I've had enough of books. I regret my decision to come here. I was much happier travelling. This life is a waste of time.'

'It's hard, this facing up to the self,' she said gently.

'What self?' He felt angry; his logic challenged by a woman and his worth doubted by himself.

'Spoken like a good Gurdjieffian!' She laughed. 'I mean the traits we deny, the urges we despise, the needs we see as weak.'

'I'm not weak.' He stalked away.

His troubles compounded as babies grew to toddlers, then children who raced freely through their Eden setting. He detested noise; particularly the shrieks and giggles of young ones at play. One couple had three noisy boys and privately Richard regretted the absence of canes. They required a strict father, the kind he'd had, to control them. They were the kind of mischievous brats who'd made his childhood a misery. He did not mind the little girl, Rowena, though her parents were an unsettled pair. The mother, an erratic and temperamental woman, had some incipient mental disorder. The father, Hugh, mild and obliging as he seemed, astonished the entire community by running off with Marie, then a girl considerably his junior. For weeks, little Rowena wandered disconsolately from door to door, asking where her daddy was. She took a liking to Richard and would bring her treasures to his door. Holding a bird's egg or a flower, she'd come trustingly to share her discoveries. He did not know how to behave towards her and awkwardly sent her on her way, but seeing how pale and listless she looked, he privately expressed concern to Honor.

'She needs a father figure, Richard,' Honor suggested.

'I did not come here to be a nanny. She must look elsewhere.' The sad child, a reflection of his own past, called up too many unpleasant memories for him to bear her near him.

'I think Richard has met his little mirror image,' Honor commented to Laurie; adding, 'I wonder if he'll look deeply enough to find healing.' But Richard did not stay around for her to conjecture further. He announced he intended to leave Pelican and, putting his goods into storage, he resumed his life of enterprise: travelling, buying, selling, and generally living the material life he decided a man should stick to. Apart from sporadic visits to the commune, he did not come back until he married Tuti. The exotic setting and isolation were ideal conditions in which to keep his wife safe for his own enjoyment. He saw her like that; as a work of art he had selected with great care and discrimination. He did not want to share his treasure with others who might come to covet her. He did not want Tuti deciding, when she came to know him well, that another man would suit her better than himself.

'Do you need to have a prescription made up?' he asked his wife when he went to collect her from the surgery in Trundle. She shook her head and at once changed the subject to Richard's own plans, asking whether he had seen his prospective business partner.

'Not yet. I thought we might go there together. You're sure you feel well?' For he thought she seemed flushed and distracted.

'Quite well! The check up was fine. I'd like to visit Mr Lal. Let's go now.'

Pleased, Richard drove to the end of Alexandra Avenue and considered the imposing edifice of brick and tile. Yes, the fellow had money; perhaps not for long, if he really expected to implement his strange ideas.

'Do you realise this Indian thinks he can import his culture to Trundle?' He laughed and rested a tolerant hand on Tuti's thigh. 'I hope you appreciate a sane husband. Imagine living with a man ruled by emotion!'

Together they passed through the high gates, skirted the barking dog, and came to the front door. An old woman answered, and scuttled away in search of Mr Lal. Tuti slipped off her sandals. Richard, ignoring the protocol of shoes lined up outside, walked in and stood sizing up the chandelier and marble entrance hall decorated with a hand-woven carpet. Their host descended the stairs, ushered them in to sit in buttoned leather armchairs and called for tea. As business talk ensued, Tuti sipped her cooling drink, surveyed her suave husband and tried to match up this image with the enraged man he would become when she could no longer keep her pregnancy a secret. She had perhaps a month or two. Already her body showed early changes. After that…Unable to imagine further she sank into reverie while the two men, oblivious to her conflict, examined options and alternatives for the next half-hour.

'Vimla,' said Mr Lal to his daughter over dinner that evening, 'I am going to Sydney on business in a few weeks. Could you get time off to accompany me?'

His decision followed on the unsatisfactory discussion with Van Rjien. Amicable though their talk had been, nothing had eventuated and, if the project was not to stagnate and die, it was clear that he had to act. The faith and energy that drives on a project was waning as time passed. Shanti's wishes felt less and less real and weeks had passed since he'd taken down her ashes. When he picked up her gilt-enclosed photograph, he could not infuse it with any sense of life. He'd thought of her as younger. Now he was sure the time had come to seek concrete advice on raising venture capital and, if his business trip could provide a diversion for his peaky daughter, all to the good.

'That could be difficult,' Vim said. 'Nick's taking time off.' She added, 'But I'd like to come with you. I'll ask.' Connections were sparking in her mind, for the less interest Nick showed in her, the more she embroidered her passion with the rich silks of imagination. Knowing his tenure at the paper was coming to an end added a desperate note to her resolve. Nothing could happen here, in Trundle. He'd implied that. With or without permission, she knew she would go to the city.

At work, she waited to choose her moment. Nick was preoccupied. Setting aside his dilemma over Ronnie, he had his mind on the coming court case and the many practical details of his Sydney trip. He had instructed his tenants to vacate and had to make his house ready for sale. At the same time he was preparing for Mac to take back the reins, and writing up his leaders for the coming weeks' issues. He'd gathered an interesting story at Pelican from the young couple in their tent. They claimed no one had told them they could not occupy the cheap land in which they'd invested all their savings. A few other buyers sounded similarly unhappy. It would be an interesting note of controversy with which to seal his brief editorship.

He called Vim to go over her assignments. They were the usual mundane reports but she had tried to write them succinctly and professionally, as he liked. He barely glanced at them as he took a phone call and stood up with a distracted gesture.

'Sorry, Vim. I clean forgot I made an appointment with the council. This copy looks ready to go.' He hurried away. Calmly she slid open the top drawer of his desk, noted the correspondence from his lawyer and copied down his home address from an old business card.

'Make our bookings for the last week in August,' she announced. Her father noted the return of colour to her cheeks and was pleased his suggestion was having the desired effect.

The city-bound train pulled out of Trundle station shortly after dawn. Veiled in drizzle and pressed upon by grey cloud, the waking landscape looked stunted and forlorn. Here and there, driven by man and dog, cattle lumbered towards the milking sheds. Paying no attention to the passing scene, Mr Lal opened up his briefcase and went through his business papers. His daughter closed her eyes, though not to sleep like her fellow passengers dozing amid their arrays of bags, umbrellas and knitting. She visualised Nick, begging her to leave Trundle. And she heard herself, agreeing, yes! She'd go without a backward glance. With each lurch and halt, at each drab station with its potted palms and naked garden beds, Vim rehearsed their meeting, her cheek pressed to the cold glass of the carriage window.

Steady rain greeted their arrival at the terminus. Vim let herself be swept along with the exodus as her father summoned a cab and had them driven to Kings Cross. It was a handy access point to town, less expensive than a central hotel, he said. While he went about his round of financial affairs, Vim could take the book of maps, visit the Art Gallery and The Rocks, or go shopping as she pleased. He treated her to lunch at the expensive dining room before leaving her for the afternoon.

As soon as he left, Vim showered, made up and dressed with care. The telephone book confirmed Nick's address in a street within walking distance of the hotel. Outside the hotel's calm opulence, she was surprised by the suburb's rough tone. Even in daylight, with shoppers carrying kit bags stuffed with celery and oranges, the disreputable air was marked. Neon signs flashed crude outlines of strippers; worn women and girls younger than she was solicited openly. Her high heels clicking, Vim strode out to find Nick Questro, passing drunks asleep in doorways and derelicts sprawled on park benches. Quite soon the seedy air gave way to old-time elegance sketched by the balustrades and iron lacework of restored apartments. Mature oak trees blessed the shelters of the well to do who could afford this elite pocket of inner-city living. The rush of traffic quietened as brass plates identified consultant architects' and doctors' offices.

She found Nick's street, its deserted air suggesting the residents were all away earning their right of occupation. His next-door neighbour, an old woman with rheumy watchdog eyes, peered through her greasy fringe as Vim tapped at his door.

'He's out.' She saw Vim's crestfallen look. 'Gone to court again. Jury's out today. I hope they lock that crazy driver up and throw away the key. Mrs Questro was a lovely kind soul. So young to die! You could see how much in love they were. You don't see much of that round here. Tarts and streetwalkers…They even have a Union. Can I give him any message, love?'

Vim shook her head. 'I'll call again.'

'Better come of an evening. Case has dragged on since Tuesday. Cut and dried, I say. Beats me!'

Disappointed, Vim walked away, piecing together the old woman's rambling words as she went. A cold steady rain began to fall, turning the asphalt gleaming wet. Soon her dress clung and her shoes were soaked but she thought of Nick and walked along, head high. Old people might say anything at all. She determined to return when he was home, regardless of her father's plans. Back at the hotel, she had a hot shower, lay down and fell into a deep sleep.

Mr Lal came back late in the afternoon. He seemed despondent as they shared an elegant dinner table. His broker had dwelt on negative growth, the downturn in the economy, a dearth of investors. 'It seems my only course is to sell up my assets,' he said.

Vim saw how his hair was greying and a lifetime's worry and hard work scored his face. Trying to understand why he would consider throwing his efforts away, she realised they shared a mute emotion; a need to prove they truly loved. Suffering, her months of pain and longing, had been her coin, while he was on the verge of squandering his entire life's savings on a monument no one would value.

'Do you still miss Mummy?' she asked quietly. Now she saw another parallel. Her father and Nick were both quite recent widowers, wounded in a way she could not share.

'Vimla, talking about these things is hard for me, you see. I never was that kind of man. Your mother's gone. I have adjusted. What else is one to do?'

His resignation frightened her. He seemed so passive, as though an adult had no control over life.

'But do you really think you should sell assets?'

'I don't know what to do. Is it all a fantasy? I was so sure your mother wanted it.'

'She was thrifty.'

'Very thrifty!' He smiled faintly. 'She was my wife.'

'She wouldn't expect you to take risks.'

His deep and heartfelt sigh came slowly. 'It's hard to let go. She's gone, Vijay's gone; who knows, soon even you? Only Bimbo will be left to keep me company.'

He was trying to make a small joke of his regretful words, but tears of sympathy filled her eyes. He mistook her feelings.

'My poor little girl. I suppose you miss your mother every bit as much as I do?'

She nodded, wishing for a way to be a child again. She wanted comfort. Like her father, she was on the verge of waking from a dream. The adult world seemed a cold and lonely place to her as father and daughter left the table and made their way back to their tenth-floor suite. In the elevator mirror, Vim saw the small dark man and the attractive girl like a pair of itinerants, uncertain of any true purpose or destination.

'An early night will do us both good,' Mr Lal announced and he went to shower. Within the hour he was snoring softly from the bedroom. Vim, who was using the divan bed in the main room, lay listening to the unaccustomed sounds of noisy traffic in the street below. The Cross came alive at night. She stood at the window, gazing down upon the wet street with its reflections of coloured neon and streaky lights. Pedestrians intent on finding food and pleasure surged past. She had come so close to reaching Nick, just a fifteen-minute walk from here, but he might as well be on the moon.

She could not let her chance to see him pass. Her love felt so strong, surely he must care too? It was a question she had to have answered, though she felt full of fear at making herself so vulnerable. Pulling on a pair of jeans and a parka and slipping on flat shoes, she went quietly to the lift, rode down to the foyer and walked out to join the curious, hungry or addicted passers-by who supported the Cross's dubious transactions. Too nervous and keyed-up to notice rowdy groups and soliciting drunks, Vim hurried back to Nick.

There were lights in his windows, and the drone of a vacuum cleaner inside. She knocked and waited, her heart beating furiously as she tried to compose herself. The droning died away. He opened the door, peering at her as though she was an unwelcome ghost. Struck dumb, her question faded. She stood still, not knowing what to say.

'Come in.' He looked anything but welcoming.

'I'm just in town with my father. I don't want anything, Nick.'

'Good. As long as you've got that straight.' Stern, he signalled her inside. The house had that forlorn air of occupants in transit. Buckets, brooms and mops stood about the empty rooms and boxes were stacked in the hall. 'Tenants didn't bother cleaning up. The house is going on the market so it's up to me.' He gave a yawn and rubbed his eyes. 'God, what a week! I'm exhausted.'

'Can I make coffee?'

He nodded wearily. 'I'll go on vacuuming. Kitchen's there.'

She was glad to feel useful, finding disposable cups and boiling up water in an old saucepan. There were no chairs. They drank the coffee sitting side by side on the stairs.

'What are you doing in Sydney?'

215

She could tell his mind was elsewhere and answered briefly. 'Daddy had business to do. We're staying up the road. Want a hand? I've got nothing else to do.'

Nick managed a small smile. 'The stove's filthy. There's rubber gloves, if you like.'

Vim, who had never scoured a greasy oven, spent the next hour on her knees, while Nick went on with the floors. Strangely, she felt soothed by the mechanical work, the changing of filthy water, the slow emerging of shiny enamel from the grease and grime. Nick came to inspect progress and nodded approvingly.

'I don't know why you're here, Vim, but it's decent of you to lend a hand.' He stretched. 'I've had enough though. Want to go for a walk?'

'Isn't it late?' She'd lost all sense of time.

'Sydney never sleeps.'

Outside, the street smelt fresh and rain-washed. Vim remembered walking home with him after the public meeting, several months before. He was taking a route away from the Cross, downhill towards the harbour. She had to step out to keep up with him.

'Where are we going?'

'You'll see.' He sounded much friendlier. Her daydreams had never envisaged an evening such as they were spending now yet she was enjoying herself, walking with him. He did not talk, and she knew he was lost in thoughts she could not broach.

Soon she saw the shining of pearly sails as they climbed the approach to the Opera House, which soared high above them on a night sea lit by harbour craft and arching bridge. She could hear the lapping of the tide and, she thought, a hint of music. Nick wandered over to read the advertising posters.

'Richard Strauss' *Tone Poems*. Glorious! *Don Juan* as a hero lost in the adventure of being alive. He was in search of immortal beauty and undying passion. Strauss captures it all: the ecstasy, the tenderness. You really don't know it?' As she shook her head his tone was affectionate. 'Vim, you have so much to look forward to. You told me you'd never been to a concert or opera. This is as far as I can bring you, so promise you'll come back one day?'

Moved by his words and by the night's shimmer of lights and music, a deep longing overwhelmed her and she shivered.

'Cold? Come on, let's get going.'

Obediently she followed him. This would be their last personal encounter. He would leave Trundle and her life forever. She would keep this memory fast; a few hours made keen with yearning, sharp with loss. She would never forget them.

He walked her back to the hotel.

'I suppose you've finished at the paper?' she asked forlornly.

'Providing Mac agrees. I do have some gear to collect from the flat, and there's a friend I want to see at Pelican.' With a brotherly squeeze to her shoulder, he waved and walked off with her dreams of love. Her father's rhythmic snores echoed as she crept in to bed. Curled up, she began to sob, her heart in upheaval as her hopes finally dissolved.

3

Nick's parting shot as editor had been to publish the allegations on the misrepresentation of land sales in Trundle. Mac Booth read the write-up on his first day back at work, then sat back, musing that a good story was always controversial, though his old friend Sam would be smarting. His attention returned to the pleasure of resuming his old role. He felt warm affection for the pens and pencils, the old bar radiator, the chipped coffee mugs and heaps of paper spilling everywhere. Culling the small news of a little town might not seem like much but he was glad to be back in harness.

Kitty Playfair read the paper as she sat at the breakfast table after seeing Sam off to work. With a pleasant sense of wrongdoing, for the minister condemned astrology, she scanned the horoscopes for the fate of Cancerians. Pluto was on a slow transit of her fourth house. Sewers, drains and plumbing could give trouble and domestic relationships were subject to breakdown. She started as though the evil eye was fixed on her as she flipped the page and read the leading article. Bold letters announced *Local Land Scam Scare.* Dismayed, she read how naïve young couples and migrants with poor command of English had thrown away their savings on land they couldn't build on.

She stared again at the headline which, through a haze, seemed to read *Local Land Sam Scare.* She recollected Sam saying something about selling land by the coast, just about the same time that he'd agreed to the purchase of new carpets. He certainly wouldn't have planned to cheat foreigners and innocent young people. He was a fair and honourable man, yet in kitchens and offices people were drinking in these lies. She felt quite ill as she prepared for work. Before she left, she phoned Sam's office. He wasn't in. She left a message for him to get hold of the newspaper and to contact her before lunch, feeling a consolidated public appearance was called for.

At morning teatime she put up her *Back In 10* sign and, concealing the newspaper as though it was a parcel bomb, went to show the article to her friend. Marie skimmed it, frowned and gave it back to Kitty.

'See why I don't buy the paper? People will print anything.'

'It's so unfair! Sam will be furious, and how will this affect the children?'

'I'll put the kettle on. You do sound upset!'

'Everything's going wrong, Marie. Holly won't go to church and she's picked up with that unemployed man from Railway Street and Leaza's been playing hooky from school and I keep finding sweets and chocolate in Joel's room and I'm afraid he's stealing money. Now this! We'll never be able to hold up our heads again.'

'People soon forget,' said Marie, who knew she'd survived scandal of a far more serious nature in Trundle terms.

'But Sam's work depends on his reputation.'

Kitty looked as confused and frightened as a child. Marie took her hand. 'It will blow over. Wait and see.'

'Can I use the phone? I need to talk to Sam.'

'Of course.' Leaving Kitty in privacy, Marie busied herself at the far end of the shop.

Sam listened while his wife read out the article and cursed himself for ever getting involved with Bryan O'Brian. He'd rather mow lawns or work in a hamburger joint than collude in another man's dishonesty. These accusations were of a more serious nature than the misrepresentations and half-truths that were part of the game. Of course every strategically placed rug hid a stain. Every property had some flaw. Vendor and agent alike weren't compelled to go into the details of smelly drains, leaky roofs or ghastly neighbours. Point out rust and rot and watch the buyers take cover! A go-between couldn't win. Sam had concluded long ago that, for a property owner with a mortgage to meet, the waters of compassion were at best a trickle. Some tenants, on the other hand, might have done well in the Secret Service, given their skills with forged references and sudden disappearance. While some paid the rent and cut the grass, others lived in a state of siege, their world so precarious they travelled light and moved fast.

'Are you still there, Sam?'

'I'm here.' He would have liked to be anywhere else. Once again, he'd let Kitty down. She cared so much about good opinion.

'I'm going to give that editor a piece of my mind.'

'Don't do that, Kitty.' The more breath you gave a spark, the more it flared.

'But what about your good name?'

He sighed. 'Whatever you think best.' He agreed they'd meet at the Club for lunch. Kitty seemed determined to make a moral stand.

The office was empty as he sat reflecting. Bryan was due back from Queensland. Sam decided to try and track him down. He was bearing the brunt of gossip when he'd done nothing, except ignore a hesitant inner voice. When a prospective homebuyer failed to keep her appointment, he hoped it was no more than coincidence.

Sam set out to pay a visit to Railway Street. Bryan's mother might know her son's whereabouts. While he was in the vicinity, he could try and get some rent out of the Halpins. They were way in arrears again. He'd known it would come to eviction. Once again, he'd have to do the dirty work. Unfortunately he couldn't toss a scatter rug over the Halpins. They'd have to go.

Turning in to the slum street, he met up with Holly, on her way to see Peter. Sam liked his daughter's boyfriend, despite Kitty's views about the unemployed. His wife did not understand how it was for young people in a country town. His step quickened as he observed Bryan's four-wheel drive parked outside Mrs O'Brian's place.

'The man I'm looking for!' He jogged ahead, leaving Holly to field Ernie Hood's rambling greeting. As usual the old sailor was on the watch, a figurehead in his nautical cap. There was something about the old fellow that she mistrusted and she hurried on, pulling her coat close. It might be the first day of spring, but Railway Street looked at its worst, the few wind-lashed trees scabrous, their leaf remnants despondent.

Looking after her, Ernie shrugged. Young women held no interest for him.

Sam was in the throes of an argument at the O'Brian's gate. Bryan, however, merely eyed Holly and smiled. 'Peter's girl? He's done all right for once.'

He swung aboard the high vehicle as though mounting his horse with a flash of spur and bold halloo. Winding down the passenger's window, he waved to Sam. 'Old boy, don't take life so seriously. It's all a game!'

His mother, making her way back along the cracked path, turned as the vehicle roared away. 'Fancy him paying a visit! Says he's taking Dixie on some cruise to Hong Kong. Waste of money. Plenty of foreign shows on telly.' She pulled a handful of notes out of her apron pocket. 'Look at this. Guilt money. Never mind, cash is cash.'

'Is Peter home?' asked Holly.

'Tinkering out the back, lovey. Some contraption for the regatta.' She turned to Sam. 'Coming in?'

But Sam had just spotted Nora as she pulled aside the curtain. Even from a distance she looked ravaged; hair frizzed up like a pie frill around her bruised face. The curtain fell and the house resumed its uninhabited air.

'Not what you'd call a happy home there,' suggested Mrs O'Brian.

Despite Sam's several knocks, Nora didn't answer the door. Trouble was on the way. She was sick of the fights; Tag roaring drunk, the kids cringing, broken furniture, holes punched in the walls, yet she didn't have the energy to hate Tag, couldn't pity him either, feelings dead somehow.

Misery pinched her guts. Once they'd been two of a kind: smoking, boozing, joking, telling the world where to go. Not fair, that kick in the head he'd collected playing footy. Now they all had to cop it. Oh, for years she'd hoped. Fresh starts, promises... It all came back to this. Money didn't fix things. She'd never had so much to call her own, what with tips and overtime. She'd bought a washing machine, put toys on lay-by, given Tag an electric razor to make him smarten up. Just made him nasty, crazy. Calling her rotten names. A few times he'd followed her, making out the pub was just a front for tarts to operate.

She gave it five minutes, then checked the door. Sam had gone. There was his business card, pushed into the hall. *Please call in to see me before next Friday or I will be obliged to instigate eviction proceedings.* She ripped the card into tiny pieces. She'd fix shitface! She had a few tricks up her sleeve. Maybe a sad story in the newspaper.

At the office, Sam looked up as Nora Halpin entered. Her bruised face suggested the purple and navy hues of a thundery sky. Sam chose to study the computer printout on her rent arrears.

'You'll have to bring this up to date,' he said.

'C'mon Sam, giz a break.' She reminded him they'd been at school together, life was tough, Tag was out of work, the kids were sick. The agent had a peculiar urge to ask her to sit in his ergonomically correct office chair and view the world as it appeared to him. Give her a turn at playing God. Let him see what it felt like to grizzle about his worries; perhaps display the festering wounds to his self-esteem which, while they might not have the spectacular impact of Nora's abuse, caused him suffering. They had little chance of healing while Kitty referred nightly to the slur she saw upon the whole family.

His wife was falling apart. She said their name was mud. The children were nothing but a worry. Leaza had been reported parked along the river road with a young man in a plumber's van. A packet of condoms turned up in the picnic basket. Holly said she no longer believed in Christianity. Whenever she took Joel with her to Railway Street he would return with lollies stuffed in his pockets, and wouldn't explain how he'd come by them. Kitty cried often and worried all the time.

Sam forced himself to establish eye contact with his client.

'Enough's enough. You haven't paid us a brass razoo for weeks.'

She tried half-hearted bluff. 'The dump's falling down, that's why. Holes in the walls. Door's off the stove. Drains stink.'

'The landlord attended to those repairs months ago. You haven't reported further problems.'

'I'm reporting them now. You fix the place up or I'll take my story to the newspaper.'

Sam laughed. 'Where's the money? Gone on booze?'

'Got any better ideas?' was all she answered.

He almost said, 'You're absolutely right.' The idea of leaving the office, strolling with her to the pub and getting blind drunk together had a certain quirkiness. Instead he issued an ultimatum to her to pay her rent. Of course she would ignore him, leaving him to play the role of villain, complete with bailiff, sorrowing mother and huddled children. Only the snow would be missing.

Nora stood uncertainly outside the land agency. She might get the money; at least enough to shut Sam up. Or they'd move on. Sometimes a fresh start set the old juices running. She liked the idea of leaving their troubles behind. No. Trouble chased you, wherever you went. As she walked along Main Road, she felt like a little green man from Mars, who stared at the folk on earth and wondered at the way they stood in bank queues, bought Lotto tickets, rummaged through the tomatoes to find the best ones. If this was what life was meant to be, why did she feel so out of it? She caught sight of herself in the plate glass; saw a tough, sad face, belonging to a woman she didn't know.

She came to Marie's shop. From its wicker seat in the display window, a big pouty doll, done up in lace and ribbons, held out its arms invitingly. She hesitated, then pushed open the door. At the sound of chimes, the shopkeeper glanced up and smiled. The old girl was the only person who'd done anything for her. The rest of the people took one look at her bruises and hurried past.

'G'day! Just passing. Thought I'd say hello.' She meant to sound cheery. Marie, advancing into the brighter light, paused and her hand moved protectively to her own face as though in sympathy with the sight she saw.

'My dear! You can't go on like this. There are places you can go to, refuges for battered women.'

Nora stared at her. She wasn't used to intervention.

'What sort of places?' She was thinking of a group of Asian women she'd seen on the telly. They were on a hunger strike because they said they'd rather die than be deported back to Laos. They were refugees. She'd never thought of herself as one.

'A house where you can take the children and be safe, while things are sorted out. I don't know much about it but I'm sure I could find out.'

'Sorted out how?'

'I don't know. Counselling. Alternative accommodation. A benefit.'

'Social workers?' Thanks to nosy neighbours, she'd had dealings with a few in the past and wasn't impressed with toffee noses who came round to tell her how to bring up her own kids. 'No thanks!'

'Nora, you have to think about the children. The effect this violence must be having on them.'

'Bugger them, it's me that's getting thumped!' She felt indignant. The old girl was sounding like the rest of them. She knew nothing and was full of useless advice.

'I'm worried for your safety. Would you like me to make enquiries on your behalf? Anonymously?'

Nora was about to respond to the note of urgency and kind concern when the door gave its musical tinkle and a dark-skinned man walked in. She'd heard her landlord was an Indian. She backed away. 'I'll let you know. See ya!'

And she made a hurried exit, the little bell tolling as she went.

Marie was finding Pelican anything but a place of peace and spiritual refreshment. For months, Rowena had grumbled to her stepmother about Ben's lack of direction and support. Now she had taken off, leaving Marie a cryptic note that simply said she had to get away on her own for a time. The note ended with the words, *Please look after Pippin.*

'And how am I to do that?' Marie was discussing the news with Kitty, who had stopped by to deliver Marie's deckle-edged invitation to Sam's birthday party. Pippin was playing happily enough at the back of the shop, but the prospect of an entire day with her among the antique dolls and valuables made Marie shudder.

Kitty handed her the envelope. 'Do you think Mr Lal would like to come?'

Marie hid her surprise. 'I expect so,' she said. 'Ask him and see.'

'I'd rather you did.' Kitty placed a second invitation on the counter, having decided an accountant could be an asset among the prominent citizens on the invitation list. 'I'm busy with the regatta.'

This annual event raised money for a community project. All over the town, in back yards, garages and workshops, marvels of flotation were taking shape as citizens looked forward to friendly rivalry. The rules were simple. Whatever was launched must float long enough to cross the finish line. Holly said her boyfriend was building a craft for Joel to enter in the race. Kitty had heard all about the design, involving bicycle handles, a sun umbrella and flags. Her attitude to Peter had softened; Sam was too preoccupied to spend time with Joel.

There was a crash from the back of the shop. Pippin began to cry as Marie hurried to pick up a shattered figurine.

'Never mind,' she said, obviously minding very much. Kitty was having a closer look at the little girl.

'Spots everywhere! Measles, I'd say.'

'Oh no! Are you sure?'

'Take her to the doctor. She ought to be in bed.'

'I suppose I'll have to close up.'

'It's hard to be a working mother.' Kitty sounded unsympathetic, perhaps because of the many years she'd served her time in that capacity without much help. Listing her duties involved with marquee hire, coloured lights and the loudspeaker system, she left Marie to shut up shop and take the fretful child out to Pelican. She hoped someone there could babysit, but when Victor confirmed the diagnosis she found that nobody wanted to help. Ronnie said she was working at the clinic, Ben couldn't be located, and Honor was nursing Laurie with a lung infection. As for Sandy and Tuti, both girls received the news of German measles as though it was the plague.

Victorian Gilt would have to close until the little girl was better. So much for Pelican's founding principles of community, peaceful coexistence and mutual sharing. The present residents were proving to be as humanly self-centred as anybody living a worldly life. Yet Marie reminded herself she'd been the same, with Hugh. As a girl, how wrapped up in her own wants she'd been! Now she'd be happy to resume the mundane life she'd led with her sister, but even Ronnie had changed. They hadn't heard the end of Nick Questro.

But this wasn't the time to speculate on romance; a sick child was enough of a challenge and Pippin was calling for attention.

4

Rosa had tied back her hair with a velvet bow. A gaunt figure, she wore a high-necked violet frock, opaque stockings and the white court shoes she kept for best. As Victor leaned out to pay the bridge toll and steered her old Vauxhall into the city lane, she gazed down at the harbour with its pleasure craft, a smile on her mauve lips. This journey reminded her of past adventures when, pursued by suitors, she'd lived for romance. Now she cast a glance at the handsome profile of her escort. Her admiring gaze moved to his hands, gripping the steering wheel. His gold wedding ring did not bother her. What sort of wife would let him cross the seas alone!

'May I direct you?' she offered. He was lost in the unfamiliar maze of traffic lanes and one-way streets. She led him to an area near Pyrmont, where he parked and leaned back, stretching wearily.

'Here we are.' The purpose of the trip was to buy equipment for the clinic. Her offer had led him to believe she was one of those wealthy women who liked to support good causes. As well, he hoped to divert money from the buying spree to enable him to speak long-distance with his wife. It was true they'd parted on an ambivalent note; he'd been so used to Elizabeth's resentment that he'd hardly taken any notice of her ultimatums. Now his mystification grew with every unanswered call.

'Well Rosa, are you ready to go shopping?' He would be glad to deal with the purchases, talk to his wife and head back to Pelican.

'You don't want me trailing along, Victor.'

'Of course I do!' He was thinking of her purse.

'I plan to rest a while.' She indicated an old hotel on the corner. 'You can meet me here.' She took out a chequebook and signed several blanks. 'Buy what you need.'

'You don't carry cash?'

She shook her head. 'Where are the medical suppliers based?'

He mentioned a suburb. She explained the western route and collected her small case from the boot.

'See you at the Sunburst.' Rosa watched until the car turned the corner, then walked in to the shabby two-storied building and booked a room. Stretched out on the double bed, she lay anticipating the night. Excitement ruled out her plan of rest. Instead she ran a bath and lay back in the rust-ringed tub of the communal bathroom. Her credit card might be at the limit and her cheque account empty. Her mind rearranged any doubts; the spirit of her gift was what mattered.

An aggressive thumping on the door interrupted her reverie. Drying herself, she regretted how time and illness had ravaged her once-beautiful body. She dressed, called a taxi and went to David Jones, where she selected a satin and *crêpe-de-chine* nightgown and a bottle of *My Sin*. She paid with her worthless cheques, feeling as young as the girl who'd run political gauntlets and satiated herself with lovers. In the coffee shop, by dint of prolonged sipping, she was able to make one gilt-topped percolator last an hour before spending her dwindling coins on a return trip to the hotel. The barman gave her a sour look and asked for cash when she went to buy whisky to offer Victor on his return.

She was waiting for him in the downstairs lounge when he arrived, late in the afternoon.

'I'm afraid I've taken advantage of your generosity.' The doctor launched into technical details of the various diagnostic monitors that would assist in his treatment options.

Rosa stuffed the receipts into her handbag. 'I took a room for the day. Perhaps you'll come up for a whisky before we dine?'

'Time's getting on.' He checked his watch. 'We've got a long drive ahead.'

'But we must eat! I'm sure you've had nothing. And I feel a little weak.'

He followed her upstairs and stood at the window, taking in the view of vacant workshops and commercial sites.

'Drink up!' She tipped whisky into the water glass and indicated the wooden chair; the only furniture apart from the bed and dressing table.

'Rosa, I have to drive.'

'One drink won't hurt. Why don't you have a shower? I'll just read my book.'

It seemed easier to go along with her suggestions, although he felt a stirring of alarm. Rosa wasn't the first female patient to develop a crush on her doctor, but he'd never been actively pursued in so determined a way. Hadn't Elizabeth warned him he didn't know how to deal with emotion? If only she were with him now! Leaving Rosa, he went downstairs alone to phone England, adding the charges to the room bill. It would be breakfast time at home. But an unknown woman took the call. Her news shocked him. She said she was the new owner; his family had moved out the previous week. Even the cultured accents of home sounded foreign as he wrote down a forwarding address in Sussex. It was evident that Elizabeth wasn't coming to Australia. He could forget renting the sisters' house. Apparently his wife had left him. All he wanted was to get back to Pelican and sort out some way to raise the airfare home and resolve the issue.

He was tired of Rosa and her delays. The sooner they had dinner the sooner he could leave. But in the dining room she ordered wine and picked at her food. Halfway through the main course she pressed a hand to her forehead.

'I feel so giddy. I must lie down.'

She was a cancer patient; his medical training forced him to set aside his irritation.

He helped her upstairs. 'There you are. Lie down for a bit.'

He spread the thin quilt over her corpse-like body. She closed her eyes and seemed to drift off to sleep. Victor sat on the hard chair, wondering if he would ever see his children again. An hour must have passed before the half-bottle of whisky on the dressing table was empty and Rosa stirred.

'I'm so cold.' She shivered. 'I'll take a shower.'

'Very well.' His patience was about to snap. 'Then we'll get going.'

She eyed the bottle. 'Victor, you mustn't drive tonight.'

Appalled, he knew she was right. When she came back from the bathroom, she was wearing the kind of nightwear he associated with a bride. The reek of cloying perfume reached him.

'Dearest!' She was gazing at him with patent love. Her bony hands were reaching for him. He stumbled to his feet.

'Oh Victor, don't be shy, let me love you.'

His impulse was to run for the door but his legs felt weak and his mind was spinning with feelings of loss and abandonment. He reached for the light switch. Thinking of Elizabeth, he collapsed on the bed, and Rosa lay down beside him in the darkness.

With Victor away, Ronnie was in the midst of crisis. Called to the Stedmans' chalet, she found Laurie with fever and chest pain. He had taken the antibiotics Victor had prescribed but Ronnie was alarmed when she checked the thermometer. The aged were vulnerable. Within the hour, they were on their way to hospital, where Laurie was admitted to the medical ward and sent for X-rays and tests. Staff greeted Ronnie warmly, asking when she would be coming back to work. She felt oddly ambivalent. True, she was ready to move on, yet the sameness of ward routine had a backward feel. Caring for others could be an escape. She drove Honor back to the commune, offering a reassurance she privately doubted. Honor herself was on the verge of collapse. Without makeup, her buttons awry, she looked ten years older. Before Ronnie left her at her chalet, she insisted Honor lie down, and covered her with a mohair rug.

Pelican was hardly a peaceful retreat today. As she passed the Van Rjiens' door, shouts suggested that violence was going on inside. She was standing there, deciding to intervene, when Tuti rushed outside and ran into the bush. Ronnie wandered on, unsettled by thoughts of Laurie, Tuti and her own future. She sat for a while on one of the rocks edging the pool where she and Nick had swum. No promises had been made, but she could not forget him. Even so, returning to nursing would be the sensible thing to do. Who could say they'd ever meet again?

She whiled away the afternoon, reading, then called in on Honor, who only agreed to eat dinner if she could go back into town and visit Laurie. Ronnie acquiesced. Maintaining the cheer that bolsters sickbed vigils was exhausting. By nightfall, Victor and Rosa hadn't returned, nor was there any message to explain their change of plan. Giving up on the day, Ronnie went to bed.

Victor was back when she looked in at the clinic in the morning. His manner, however, was so aloof and cold that she wished he'd stayed away. The only time he spoke in a civil way was when she told him about Laurie.

'I was afraid it would turn to pneumonia,' he said. 'I'll go and see him this morning.'

'What about Rosa? She's booked in for a check-up.'

'Cancel it.'

Shaken and weeping, Tuti went to Sandy for help. In her childhood she'd known of men who drank and beat their wives, but Richard had never before shown her anything but affection. The news that she was pregnant had enraged him. He'd ordered her to have an abortion. She refused. He'd swept her up in an angry grip, dropped her on the bed and seemed about to attack her. Screaming, she'd slithered from his clutches, knocking over a life-size wooden carving as she escaped. Now she believed she had no option except to somehow return to Indonesia.

'Can you help me, Sandy?' Hands protectively clasped over her abdomen, she glanced around. 'Richard is going to kill me.'

Tuti's words sounded like a clip from one of the agony columns Sandy liked to read. Now she felt the same sense of disbelief.

'Anyone can see he's mad about you, Tuti.'

'He is very mad! Before we married he made me promise no children. I'm pregnant! He'll force me to have an abortion.' Tears streamed down her cheeks. 'I must get money to go home. My family will send. You can post my letter. Now I have to hide.' She drew her index finger across her throat. 'If he finds me…'

Seeing Tuti's sweet face, so swollen and distorted with fear, Sandy was converted into a willing accomplice.

'There's a house in town,' she said, thinking of the sisters' vacant property next door to the Lals. 'Your husband won't think of looking for you there. When will you get the airfare?'

'They will send money straight away, when they know what he is like.'

Tuti was still looking around the room as though Richard might spring out from behind the curtains.

'There's no one here. Vijay's training again. He won't be back for ages.' Sandy's complicity suggested that even good-natured husbands could be problematic. 'You're quite safe. Let's pack some clothes and food. You can do the letter now. We'll sneak in to town and I'll show you the empty house.'

'How kind you are!'

Sandy was pleased to discover someone in a worse predicament than her own. Vijay's obsession with fitness had stretched her patience. She could have pointed out that, if she'd wanted a boyfriend with the body of a wrestler, she wouldn't have picked Vijay. Naturally contemplative, she found comfort in nature. She'd expected Pelican would bring them closer, for it was a beautiful setting, rich in native plants and bird life. But all he could talk about these days was his body. He seemed to have set aside all the things she'd liked about him: his musical flair, his talk of meditation and meaning. These, while unusual, had set him aside from men who boozed at the pub and took bets on race day. She didn't care about his lazy ways, his fondness for sweets. She'd been happy with him then. Now she felt she was waiting for him to grow up. He irritated her. She might be expecting his baby; a child who would need more from a father than an unpaid waste of energy. Not knowing how to put such thoughts to Vijay, she looked preoccupied and even stooped, perhaps hiding her pregnancy from the world.

How grateful she was to share her secret with Tuti! The girls discussed their physical changes and symptoms. Allies, they stole along the bush track to the main road, where they hitched into town. The letter posted, they walked to Alexandra Avenue. It was as Sandy thought. She proved to have a talent with old locks and it seemed that Tuti's escape was assured.

'I better head back.' Sandy was reluctant as she passed the Lals' front gate. Bimbo raced down to the fence, and she reached through the bars to give him a wistful pat.

Mr Lal, looking out to investigate the commotion, was puzzled to see her walk away. Surely his daughter-in-law-to-be could have called in to say hello?

Sandy, unaware that she'd been observed, set off to hitch a ride to Pelican.

5

'Did we ever run this story?'

Mac Booth was browsing through Vim's rejected article about Shah Jahan and Mumtaz Mahal. His cadet was low in spirits and he tried an encouraging smile.

'Your father's fantasy is a whimsical story. I like it. We've had enough critical journalism.'

He was keen to re-establish the paper as he'd left it. Trundle was too small a community to want hard-hitting social policy. He handed Vim the draft story.

'I'll feature this. Cast your eye over it first. Maybe dig up a photo of the Taj.'

Vim was pleased. But Mr Lal was less uplifted when his daughter passed on this news. His business affairs were at a standstill and his home felt like a mausoleum. He'd tried to fill this void with a vision. Now he didn't know. To be laughed at would be a deep humiliation. Perhaps you couldn't superimpose a model of one culture on another. Visitors might laugh at his Taj as if to say, *What have bazaars, saris and elephants to do with us?* Did even he care about those symbols now? He knew why he hadn't been back to India. He had no close living relatives left. He doubted he could converse fluently in his dialect. Too much would have changed. He had turned into an Australian without knowing it. To make that long journey without Shanti was pointless.

He was on the point of abandoning the whole idea. But Vim's apathy worried him. The flirtatious teenager he'd spent half his waking hours worrying about now went nowhere except to the office. Otherwise she stayed at home, staring at whatever show happened to be on television. The glamorous young woman who'd painted her nails and strutted in high heels now roamed the house in a dressing gown, her tangled hair unbrushed. He did not have the heart to ask her to withdraw the piece. He decided to go to Pelican and try negotiation one more time.

The commune members must surely have come to a resolution by now. But when he telephoned Richard, the Dutchman's mobile phone repeated the same monotonous information; the number could not be connected.

Mr Lal thought of Marie. She would know which way the vote had swung. He waded through knee-high grass to knock on the sisters' door, but no one answered. Yet he'd surely seen movements next door as he'd stood looking from his upstairs window.

Back at home, he found Vim on her way to bed.

'Vimla! Would you drive me out to Pelican tomorrow?'

She agreed at once. He recognised she must be bored with only the company of her father and elderly grandparents. He wished he could tell her she was beautiful, he loved her, he was worried about her state of mind. Such words were too hard to utter, though he did his best.

'I think you miss Vijay and Sandy? You should go out with your friends. Or ask them here?'

She managed a faint smile. 'Do you want a cup of tea before I go to bed?'

She was thoughtful towards him since their Sydney trip. He'd even seen her in the kitchen, struggling to cook *chapati* as her mother used to.

As they drove out first thing next morning, he passed conjecture about the delays and divisions slowing down the prospective sale of communal land.

'Mr Van Rjien blames community and Council, but I suspect it is his own manner that alienates people. He is a clever man, but with an aloof way of talking, even to his wife.' He sat reflecting on the difficulties of communication, wishing Vim would tell him the cause of whatever hurt she carried. 'Men of my generation were not encouraged to express feelings.'

'That hasn't changed,' was all Vim said. As usual, she seemed locked within her own thoughts and he felt rebuffed.

'Are women experts?' He spoke wryly. She did not answer. However, ten minutes out of town, she pulled off the road and parked near the river. 'Let's walk for a while. Australians don't get up at dawn!'

Together they strolled along the river path where willows brushed the water, their leafy reflections tinted pink by the morning sky. Although father and daughter had shared countless preoccupied hours in the everyday ways of eating and sleeping, their inner lives had been secretive and solitary. Together now, distracted by nothing more than the sound of their footsteps and the tremors of the leaves, each forgot past dreams and losses and felt grateful for the present affection connecting them.

They drove on to Pelican in amicable silence. No one seemed to be about. Vijay and Sandy were still in bed. In her pyjamas, Sandy went to make tea while Vijay asked his father what he was doing at Pelican so early in the morning. He shook his head when his father explained the purpose of his visit.

'You won't be able to see Richard,' he said. 'Tuti's gone.'

'Gone where?'

'Nobody knows. Richard's locked himself in his chalet. He won't speak to anyone.'

'Tuti's pregnant,' said Sandy. 'Richard won't let her have the baby. She came and talked to me.'

'Do you know where she is?'

'She does,' said Vijay. 'She won't tell anyone.'

Sandy wore her mysterious look. 'We're out of milk,' was all she said.

'Pregnant?' Mr Lal remembered the uncomfortable scene between the couple on the night of the dinner.

His son nodded. 'Richard should be proud to be a father.'

'Why do you say that?' Sandy spoke so urgently that the others looked surprised.

'I don't know. I would be.'

'Would you?' was all Sandy said, but she smiled with an air of relief as she handed him his cup of lemon and hot water.

Sounds from outside suggested that the commune was awake.

Mr Lal stood up. 'Now I will go and speak to the Dutchman.'

'Everyone's saying he's gone mad. They've all tried but he won't come out.'

'No harm to try.'

Leaving Vim with her brother and Sandy, he walked across to Richard's chalet. Business negotiations would have to wait. He knew firsthand the inertia that could descend if the emotional life collapsed.

Richard's chalet door was locked, and the curtains drawn. Mr Lal knocked several times, then sat down on the step. A window flew open behind him and an unshaven face peered out.

'Get off my property!'

'I intend to stay.'

'I've nothing to say to you.'

'I am sorry to hear about your wife.'

At once Richard slammed the window shut. The Indian took a calculator and notebook from his pocket. Hours passed. As the sun rose higher, he moved to the shade of a nearby casuarina tree. There he seated himself on the grass. His back against the trunk and his legs outstretched, he scraped up fallen needles and corralled frenetic ants.

At lunchtime, Vijay came looking for him. He carried a lunch tray.

'Sandy sent you this.'

'She's a good girl. I hope you appreciate her.'

'Of course. What are you doing?'

'Just waiting. Our friend is troubled. When are you coming home, Vijay? We miss you.'

A look of disbelief creased his son's face. 'I'm in training here.'

'What for?'

'Fitness.'

His father said nothing. Bodybuilding was a strange Western obsession. Affluent as he was, he had never expected to change his undernourished appearance.

'I know you're not interested. It isn't something Indians do.'

Mr Lal did not disagree. The labour so many of his countrymen had to bear to eke out a living precluded routines like jogging and going to the gym. His son's enthusiasms invariably confused him.

Wanting to mend their differences, he held out the plate. 'You have this.'

Vijay eyed the iced cake with disgust. 'Sugar's the white poison.'

There was a silence while Mr Lal stared at the cake. He began to eat it himself, meanwhile searching his mind for any common interest.

'A fine girl, Sandy.' He brushed a few crumbs from his lap.

Vijay's face lit up. 'She's just given me wonderful news. You may become a grandfather.'

Relieved this was a topic for which he could feel genuine happiness, Mr Lal beamed.

'You'd like a grandchild, wouldn't you? Only don't quiz Sandy yet. She says she isn't sure.'

'Let us hope. So you'll be getting married?'

His son's expression changed. 'What for?'

'It's the proper thing to do.' Life would resume its former course; his home might fill again with family. 'If Sandy is having a child, there must be a wedding.'

Vijay stood up. From the advantage of height, he spoke abruptly. 'I will decide that. Not you.'

They parted company under the casuarina tree.

Maintaining his vigil, the Indian remained at his post all day, only going into the bush twice to relieve himself. Late in the afternoon Richard slammed the window up again.

'Do you plan to roost there all night? What do you want?'

'Nothing.'

'Then go away!'

'I have come as a friend.'

'I don't want friends.'

'Your wife has left you. So has mine. We are men alone. Why not invite me in?'

Scowling, Richard opened the door. In his crumpled Hawaiian shirt, bedraggled and unshaven, he had the look of a man regretting a wild overnight beach party.

'Anything to get rid of you. I need nobody. Women are irrational. Men are better off without them. As for any partnership with me, forget it. I'm leaving Pelican.'

Although this was expected news, Mr Lal felt a stab of pain. His Taj with its guard of elephants crumbled, no poetic couplet came to mind, and he sat with bowed head, absorbing his loss.

'Where are you going?'

'Away. My wife betrayed our contract. So much for her!' He snapped his fingers.

'Marriage isn't a business deal,' Mr Lal pointed out.

'Is that so? Do share your wisdom.'

It was possible that, in such a bitter mood, he might toss an unwelcome visitor down the steps.

'There are difficult times in every marriage.' Mr Lal spoke with care. 'Men behave one way, women entirely another. They are sensitive, while we must seem strong...'

'People blame me. Am I a monster? Don't bother answering. I don't care. My wife replaces me in her affections with a parasitical egg sac and I'm expected to be pleased. She has a lot to learn!'

'Surely new life is a happy event? This is not good news?'

'We had a clear understanding. She tried every trick to change my mind, then organised her own pregnancy. Now she's run away. Why would I care?'

'I see you do,' suggested his visitor. 'Is it that you're not the father of the child?'

'Of course I'm the father! I offered to give her a palace. She said this simple home was all she wanted. She told me she was happy.' He was on the verge of breaking down.

'It's true. She seemed happy.' Mr Lal remembered all the nights he'd paced about, blaming fate for stealing his wife. Richard too was suffering, but his complaint seemed senseless. Now he indulged in a stream of self-pity.

'I should be used to it. At school they bullied me, my father beat me, now my gentle wife manipulates me. I can see her cringing as she confessed...'

'What happened?' Mr Lal was thinking back to Shanti, sharing similar news. They'd embraced and gone to offer thanks for the blessing on their marriage.

'She admitted what she'd done. She wasn't even guilty.'

'Guilty? What for? A baby is a gift; as a seal of love.'

'Love? You lot think birth's a miracle. Your country's so overpopulated thousands of your precious babies die from malnutrition. Who cares, so long as it's a son?'

'The problems of world population also concern me,' Mr Lal contradicted. 'I have only two children. Neither one has turned out as I expected. It's a hard lesson, trying to see life through their eyes. I've had to forget my preconceived ideas.' Surprised at his next words, he added, 'Yet my son and my daughter are among the real rewards of my life.'

'You must be cut out to be a father.'

'Actually no. Most of their childhood I wasn't available.' Mr Lal scratched his ankle, where a green ant had bitten him. 'They called to me outside my study door; I ordered their mother to stop their games. I was too busy. I thought to provide was right. Now my son rejects the material world as though it's a rival. When we talk, we're strangers.'

'Why bother trying?'

'A link of steel connects my heart to his. I love him. But I can't tell him that.'

A look of pain crossed his dark features.

'That's your affair.'

Sensing Richard's discomfort, Mr Lal continued in a low and serious voice. 'My friend, I've spent time with you and Tuti. The woman loves you! A child won't change that. On the contrary, she'll love you all the more.'

'You expect me to grovel?'

'You must find her. Apologise. Try to understand her needs. Ask her to come home. Take the risk, or you will be very unhappy.'

Richard stopped pacing. He shook his head. 'It's too late. I've lost her. When she told me, I was furious. I carried her in and threw her on the bed. She cried and pleaded.'

'You raped your pregnant wife?' Mr Lal could not hide his shock.

'Sex—why not? That's how she'd used me. But no, at the point, how could I? Then she ran off. I don't know where she is. She won't come back now.'

Mr Lal remembered the movements he had detected in the house next door, and Sandy's knowing silence. 'What if I have an idea where she is?'

A look of hope alerted Richard's red-rimmed eyes. 'Do you know? Are you lying? Tell me!'

'I can only say I might know where she is. Take the risk! Fatherhood is an honourable state. You might be better at it than you expect. You're not a bad fellow, really.' Mr Lal offered his hand in friendship for he sensed within Richard a sensitive, needy man with more capacity for love than he knew.

Touched by such genuine good will, the Dutchman reached out.

238

'Thank you. Of course you're right. I'm devastated. I know I'm a fool. As for our deal, I'm sorry it's off.'

'If you truly want your wife back, come to my house this afternoon. I have a fair idea where Tuti might be.' Why else would Sandy have been in Alexandra Avenue? Richard's about-face would cost him his armour, but that wasn't much of a price to pay for a wife's love. Mr Lal felt optimistic as he walked away.

PART 6

OTHER LIVES TO LEAD

PART 6

1

Blue-mauve jacaranda flowers petalled the grassy park where tents, stalls and the food marquee were being erected for the next day's regatta. Sam Playfair did not notice. Hands linked behind his back, he walked head down, his mind a maze of problems as he followed his paunch to Railway Street. The job he had to do there was unpleasant. He did not feel the sun or breeze, nor see the broad-beamed Labrador swaying along from scent to scent. He rehearsed his lines. He would hear out Nora's complaints, then issue the final rent demand. She was the type who'd run to the Tribunal with a sob story if he wasn't careful. He wanted this eviction to be quick and watertight.

Nora wasn't the worst of his problems. In orderly rotation he dwelt on the mishaps of the year: his edgy marriage, financial pressures, the bad publicity of the land deal. He could add his children to the list as Kitty worried over Joel and wept as her daughters battled for autonomy. She'd done Sam proud with his birthday this year, throwing a party that seemed to involve half of Trundle. But that, like the regatta committee, was only a temporary distraction. His wife tried so hard to manage life! He had an image of her as she'd sat in bed last night, rubbing on face cream, ticking off her list of stalls and entries for the weekend contest. Her sigh had been a sound of self-encouragement. His was the left side of the bed and, as he tied his pyjama cord into a bow and climbed in beside her, he'd wondered what she'd say if he suggested that they change places. As the hall clock struck ten, the time they always settled down to sleep, Kitty turned her back, murmured a goodnight, and switched off the bedside lamp.

The folk in Railway Street were out in force, tending their scraps of garden or basking in the sunshine. When the agent stopped at Nora's gate and walked up the crumbling concrete strip, Ernie Hood was watching from his porch. Sam stayed a few minutes, inspected a blocked drain and broken window and pointed out that wilful damage was the responsibility of the tenant. Ernie noted the visitor leave in a hurry, Nora shouting after him before she slammed the door so hard that he felt his own porch floor vibrate in sympathy. *A bit of action!* In Ernie's mind, others existed only in their capacity to provide pleasure or stir fear. He was like a species of bird, without a conscience, waiting for a titbit, wary, ready to take wing. Affection was an unlikely outcome of his wants; he had no experience of it. His forays were towards bright-eyed little boys who smelled of sunshine and grime; children whose ready hands would receive the lure of shiny coins and secrets.

Ernie sighed. Life was a rum deal and the sea a hard-hearted mistress who left you to lonely old age. Apart from the grubby urchins next door, he hadn't seen a kid for a week or more. The sweetly rounded child with the head of hair like white silk had vanished off the face of the earth. Ernie sat on at his watch, but all afternoon saw no one except Tag, blind drunk by the look of him as he staggered homewards. Before he hit the front door he was raging. The ruckus was well and truly on. Ernie stuck his fingers in his ears and went inside. He didn't hold with language like that in front of women. But he wasn't going to interfere. He'd met up with a few like Tag. You couldn't be sure when they'd go off, but when it happened you wouldn't want to be standing in the way.

Nora made a point of doing herself up before she went to work that evening. She'd had enough. Tag wasn't anything she could care about now. She'd seen that as she picked up the kitchen knife and realised she could run him through, easy as filleting a flounder. He'd stopped the assault, his arm mid-air, making a slow-motion connection even through the fug of alcohol and brain damage. Then he'd given her an evil look and walked away.

He was snoring now. Nora powdered her face, applied cheap scent and lippy, and pulled on new stockings with sparkles on the ankles. She lifted the red silk dress from its special hanger and slipped it over her head. Its softness caressed her and she thought of Marie. Soon she'd take the old girl's advice; grab the kids, go to the refuge, never mind her pride. You couldn't trust a man with a mad look in his eyes. Today in the kitchen she'd seen danger, fair and square.

She combed her hair and tied the headband. She didn't look bad, considering. It would be tough at first, striking out on her own. But better. She felt a kind of hope.

'Youse kids keep quiet,' she warned them. 'Play in the shed and don't wake him up or you'll get what for. I'm going to work. Come up the shop and get fish and chips, OK?'

They slipped away, conspirators. Nora paid for the order and let them have Mars bars for a treat. 'Don't wake him up, for Crissake!' she called back, her heels tapping on the pavement. She turned with a last wave, her mind full of plans. Tag was out to get her. But she'd survive. And she'd make good. She had her pride.

The morning of the regatta dawned clear and warm. By nine, groups were gathering and contestants arrived to unload a wondrous assortment of watercraft on the banks of Trundle's placid river. Beneath the trees, stall-owners arranged their displays: jam, pickles and preserves, knitted baby wear, crocheted coat hangers, pottery, toys, books and recycled clothing. Food vendors set out their signs. The air grew dense with the smell of hot oil and the tinkling music of colourful fairground rides. The regatta was always popular. Its history supposedly went back a century. Funds raised were donated to worthy local projects and this year the *Save Our Rail* committee had them earmarked. Socially the event marked the approach of holidays and the conclusion of a productive year.

The Lals arrived separately. Vim and Mac conferred on their respective reporting areas, while Mr Lal settled his in-laws comfortably on a picnic rug and went to shake hands with the Rotary Club president. Vijay and Sandy were roped in to help amuse the children. Vijay did his best to launch kites in the feeble breeze. Sandy was handing out clues for the treasure hunt when Joel Playfair faced her.

'What is the treasure?'

Sandy laughed. 'I don't know.'

'Then how will we know if we find it?'

'Won't looking be fun?'

She watched the little boy run off with his slip of paper. One day her own child would join in games and ask unanswerable questions. She could see Vijay, running fast, the dead kite dragging behind him like an unwilling pet. He wanted their baby!

Why are you pleased? She'd asked him that. He'd never said he liked children.

My life matters now. A queer answer! He'd looked as happy as if she'd bought him a jar of his favourite honey. Life was accidental; things slotting in anyhow and yet the patterns took on such shape and colour. Vijay, the river, the kite, the heartbeat of life she carried; all could belong and have a place.

Kitty bustled past the serene young woman standing there in the light. She was in her element as she masterminded the arrival of the dance troupe and directed the busload of geriatrics to the marquee. Mac Booth wanted to interview her, she had to welcome the mayor, she needed more ice for the meat raffle prizes...

The races were scheduled to start after lunch.

Over the course of the next few hours, anything that might float was dragged or carried to the launch point. Tension there was building as competitors assessed their adversaries. Coxes and oarsmen prudently loaded buckets, dippers and scoops. Peter's paddlewheel made an impressive splash as it submerged like a hippopotamus, then surfaced. Peter beckoned Joel and the little boy came aboard and grasped his bicycle handlebars, his face flushed with the importance of his duties.

The starter's gun sounded. A bizarre procession forged ahead: rowboats, rafts, punts, pontoons, barges, dinghies, wine barrels and an inflatable crocodile. Supporters and hecklers ran alongside, cheering and whistling. A crisis struck when an upturned table suddenly shipped water and sank, its occupants having to scramble up the muddy banks to accompanying hoots and assorted airborne missiles. Peter pedalled furiously, lights flashed, bells rang, the generator whirled and Joel swung the handlebars. The paddlewheel was making a splendid bid for victory when a sly canoe slipped past, creating a photo finish and bringing the cries of the crowd to fever pitch.

'Don't we get the prize?' Joel was upset. Peter had to promise him a hot-dog and remind him the junior event was yet to come. There was applause when the judges wisely declared a dead heat.

The race itself had taken only a few minutes, but the docking, unloading and re-launching of entries took up a great deal of time. The compère announced that, in the under-ten event, all children who completed the course would be eligible for a prize. It was a popular decision with parents, who urged along their offspring as though they were Olympic finalists. Afterwards the mayor gave his address. He was a man of Trundle, born and bred. Sincerely he spoke of the town's value, its citizens' good will, the solidarity created by such events. He awarded rosettes and ribbons, congratulated the hardworking organisers, and announced that the substantial monies gathered would go to the *Save Our Rail* fund. Kitty Playfair was thanked and presented with a bouquet. Sam bestowed a public kiss on her cheek, which gleamed with the heat and enterprise of the day.

Official events were now over and people began to gather up their campstools and drift away. The craft were loaded and tied down. Men and women chatted while the children, reluctant to go home, begged last rides on the merry-go-round or played hide and seek among the willows along the bank.

Joel was among that excited group whose leader, chasing in and out of the sheltering boughs, noticed something bright caught there at the river's edge. Curious, they crowded forward and discovered the body of a woman, her red dress drifting as currents washed around her. The wide-eyed children knew better than to touch her. They called their parents, who summoned police. As the fairground music was silenced and the food stalls closed, the day's happy mood was replaced by sombre, low-voiced analysis. The corpse was removed on a covered stretcher and a constable was posted to keep away the curious. Cordons sealed off the site where Nora died. Mac Booth had never had such a story with which to mark Regatta Day in Trundle.

When police came to Railway Street, Mr Lal's rental house was locked. Police broke in and removed the frightened children into care. The arrival of the Force was noted; by Mrs O'Brian curiously, by Ernie apprehensively. Those fights next door had conjured for him memories of evil-smelling alleyways and punch-drunk men hot on the scent of violence. He'd known trouble was on the way. Now it was here. Time he made a move.

2

Trundle was suddenly famous. National networks reported Nora's murder in the detached language that buffered the most horrible crimes. The victim, a forty-year-old barmaid, had gone to work as usual and had been last seen as she left the hotel at closing time. Walking home, she had been attacked and bludgeoned to death. Her body had been thrown in the river, where children had found it the following day. The dead woman was a mother of two. The police were interviewing a man in connection with the death.

The Trundle Times had its first scoop since 1965, when a bank robber had elected to hide out in the vicinity. Mac Booth handled the story himself, allowing Vim to watch and learn the ropes of major crime reporting. They attended a police briefing, visited the hospital where the post-mortem would proceed and continued on to Railway Street. The Halpin's place was locked and silent. Tag was in custody, his children taken into care by Social Welfare. The photographer, finding no blood stains or murder weapon, did his best to inject significance into the drab scene where violence had taken root and flourished. Litter stirred in the gutters. Yards were empty, front doors shut, curtains drawn against sightseers and the sun, which shone as indifferently as it had when Nora was alive.

Vim stood and watched. She tried to imagine her own life snuffed out like that. Everything about her, the way she dressed and moved and spoke, stamped her as an outsider here. She'd never been poor, alone, abused. A tender scolding was the worst reprimand her parents had ever issued. Waiting in the mean street where she'd first encountered the O'Brians, the Halpins and Ernie Hood, she wondered whether Nora could have had a different life. Once she must have dreamed of happiness and love. She must have felt like Vim on the day she'd walked down Railway Street with Nick and felt so full of hope. Vim still suffered over that lost love, even as she was learning that desire was misleading; the world of your imagination was unreal.

Methodically the police traced Nora's contacts on the afternoon before she died. The fish and chip shop owner had noticed that Nora had been dressed up fit to kill. The children were unable to tell of anything different. There'd been a big row. Mum often said to hide in the shed and not wake Dad. They'd eaten their tea there, played games until it was dark and gone to sleep on the old mattress they'd once dragged back from the dump.

A detective interviewed Marie. She described Nora's bruises and said she'd tried to persuade Nora to take her children and go to a refuge. Nora had refused. Asked how well she knew the victim, she described her as a poor unfortunate woman who sometimes called in, seeming to look for friendship and a chat. Marie had once provided her with clothing for a job interview. She could verify that a red silk dress came from her shop.

The man took notes and left. Marie however could not rid herself of the image of Nora's defiled body. Distressed and strangely guilt-stricken, she found no comfort in the refinement of her surroundings. Soon she locked up and walked along to Kitty's gift shop. It too was empty of customers. Kitty was grateful to see her friend.

'The police have just been talking to me,' Marie said. 'I *knew* something was going to happen to the poor woman. If only I'd been more assertive... I used to wish she'd keep away. I didn't want to see those dreadful scars.'

'Don't blame yourself. At least you tried.'

'Ronnie would have known what to do.'

'Nora didn't turn to Ronnie. She came to you.'

'I wish she hadn't! Where does such violence start?'

Kitty had no answer. Instead she said, 'The police want to interview Sam today. He saw Nora on Friday. The Halpins were being evicted. You can imagine how he feels now.'

'He was only doing his job.'

'We know that! He blames himself for putting pressure on them. He knew Nora in school. She was always in trouble.'

'Poor soul. Her troubles are over now.' Marie sighed and wiped her eyes. Kitty seemed on the verge of tears herself, as though Nora's face was pressed to the shop window, pleading for something they could not give.

Sam Playfair seldom noticed the police station or the hospital. Today, these edifices assumed an awesome significance as he gave his statement and stepped out into the sunshine. The single-storied station with its posters describing missing persons and its fusty smell of misdemeanour was suddenly empowered with all the arbitrary rights of the law. Waiting to be interviewed, Sam had been as frightened as a little boy who imagines dungeons, torture instruments, and the hangman's noose.

The statement took much longer than he expected. Each sentence was typed into a computer, read back to him and checked. He answered calmly and appended his signature in the indicated places but his heart was still pounding as he was thanked by the impassive officer and excused from further questioning. In a hurry to be anywhere but there on the steps of justice, he headed towards the hospital. Somewhere in its bowels lay Nora, or what remained of Nora once the coroner had completed his examination.

Sam felt light-headed and lost, like one of those characters in a video movie who wake up after a car crash to find they are wading knee-deep in clouds. He kept seeing Nora: the rough, tough look, the nasal twang, and the challenge in her manner. He imagined her floating in the river and laid out under knives in a room stinking of formaldehyde.

He'd gone to Railway Street to call her bluff and proceed with eviction. If the newspapers liked, they could have a field day with him. Until the recent adverse publicity, he'd thought of a land agent as an ordinary bloke; of selling and renting property as a mundane job. He'd considered he was a family man who'd never had the inclination or initiative to be otherwise. He'd never realised the double-dealing that might be read into normal commercial practice, nor felt tormented with self-doubt. The slurs on the characters of devious entrepreneurs and politicians might be true about him. He was implicated in Nora's death. He couldn't work out why. But he was.

He was passing the hospital when an ambulance pulled up. Two officers with the efficient movements of carriers shifting a piano unloaded an inert figure and delivered the stretcher through the emergency doors. Sam was a healthy man; he'd never had a day's serious illness. Apart from visiting his wife in the maternity wing, he'd never had to set foot in there. Nurses were those tough-minded girls on shows like *All Saints*. The elderly were dear old souls or deceased estates. His customers in real estate excluded the mentally ill, teenage paraplegics, children with terminal sicknesses. He didn't sell investment property to people crippled by wasting diseases. These folk existed, appeals came to the door and Kitty gave a donation, but where were they? Perhaps through those swing doors? Nora might not have placed herself among that disadvantaged group yet there she was, discreetly smuggled in through some back entrance.

Tragedy might tap Sam's shoulder as suddenly as Nora's. He felt an urgent desire to start life all over again. He'd become implicated in land scams, eviction procedures, an ugly murder. His family was falling apart, his kids were playing up, and Kitty was all at sea. If every job had its agenda, it would be wise to choose one's career with the utmost care. If you married with an attitude of sincerity, you'd better know a lifetime's duty might drag. If you had a family, you had to face those cute kids becoming independent. Your power failed. You might reap freedom in the process? He'd like that; not to calculate, judge, be bothered with the rights and wrongs of people's lives. His own was hard enough to figure.

Few shoppers were out and about. No doubt sensation-seekers were on the prowl, trying to view the cordoned area of the river or get a look at the Halpin's yard. The news broadcasts had turned Trundle into a town of notoriety. On impulse, Sam stopped by his wife's shop. Marie was there, seated at a table with Kitty. The two women had a shocked appearance. He must look the same for Kitty asked in a concerned way if he was all right. She bustled away to brew fresh tea and he sat down on the hard chair. They'd disagreed over the purchase of these particular wrought-iron sets. They were uncomfortable, he'd argued. She'd loved the design and had her way. They'd been cool towards each other for days. It seemed very trivial today. She came fussing with a tray and napkin; the little niceties he liked. He should tell her he appreciated them.

Marie judged it was time to leave. 'I've closed for the day. I'll drive out to Pelican. Ronnie's used to dealing with awful things.' She did not explore her instinct to draw close to family.

'Who's minding Pippin today?'

'Didn't I tell you? Rowena came back a few days ago.' Her relief at relinquishing the limelight of childcare was heartfelt. She waved and went. Kitty shut the door, hung the 'closed' sign and looked at Sam.

'I need to talk to you,' she said. She sounded so sad that he put down his cup and took her hand. 'This morning I found out what's been happening to Joel. He had a cache of lollies hidden in his music case. He's been getting them from some old man who lives in Railway Street.' She sat motionless, still pretty in her frilly apron. Suddenly she covered her face with her hands and began to cry. Sam's fingers caressed her wedding band.

'Got a hanky?'

He passed it to her. Purpose united them as they began to talk; partners who must uncover and deal with hard truths.

3

'I've brought you today's paper,' said Marie, walking in to Ronnie's chalet. The climb up to Pelican had taxed her; she sank onto the chair, kicked off her canvas shoes and fanned herself with *The Trundle Times*. Ronnie was grateful for the visit. Sometimes the life at the commune was monotonous, and she was no longer the fragile recluse who'd first come here. Her former drive was asserting itself, and the changes and departures going on within the group added to her restlessness.

She smiled at her sister. 'I'm glad you're here. I need to talk to you.'

Marie had her own need to talk about Nora's murder. She began a distressed account of her association with the dead woman. 'I knew her quite well. She used to come in to my shop, bruised black and blue. Ronnie, I ought to have done something! What was wrong with me? Why didn't I step in?'

'What could you have done.' Ronnie's flat statement was meant as a closure to the subject of Nora. Tragedies happened all the time. She had nothing useful to contribute. Only the barest facts had reached the Pelican community and in any case she was preoccupied with Nick's latest news. Her sister, however, was determined to go on and on as though Nora had been their personal friend.

'It was so obvious she was looking for help. I'll never forgive myself.'

In this self-reproachful mood, Marie would expound for an hour on her shortcomings. Ronnie interrupted. 'Can I ask your opinion? I've had a letter. Nick's going overseas.'

'Is that all you wanted to talk about?'

Marie sounded offended. She had never chosen to know the details of her sister's liaison; had even evaded Ronnie's confidences as though by ignoring them she could negate the situation. She must have reservations about Nick. Yet she knew nothing about him.

'He wants me to go with him. What do you think?'

'Why would it matter what I think?' Marie tossed the newspaper on the floor as if to say that Pelican's insularity had its callous side.

'Just because I'd like to know. You've met him. What do you think?'

'If you really want to know, Ronnie, my impression is he's not looking for a permanent relationship.'

'But I don't know if I am, either.'

'There, you see? You don't want my opinion at all. Just do what you want. Make up your own mind, Ronnie.'

'Why are you annoyed? I've always dreamed of Italy and France. This is my chance.'

'Then go.'

Ronnie knew that tone of voice. Marie could convey hurt feelings without ever saying a disapproving word. She had nothing else to say about Nick, and Ronnie had no wish to keep rehashing the story of Nora. To defuse tension she began to talk about changes at the commune.

'Tuti and Richard have made up. I still can't believe Tuti was hiding out in our house! Richard had to go and woo her to come home.'

'What about the pregnancy?'

'He's accepted it. I heard there was a huge scene. But Tuti stood her ground and he capitulated. He's taking her home to see her family.'

'Good for her.' Marie was proving hard to distract as Ronnie pressed on.

'Now the drama's Rosa and Victor. You heard they went to Sydney together? Whatever went on, he refuses to even treat her as a patient. I'm stuck as the go-between. Rosa went round Sydney bouncing cheques. Now we're dealing with nasty letters and orders to return the goods. Victor's ropable. It's almost a farce.'

But Marie did not smile. 'Can I have a cup of tea?' was all she said as she picked up the paper and silently began to re-read the news report.

'Of course. I'll make it.'

Nick Questro was on Ronnie's mind to an extent she couldn't ignore. As she boiled water and set out biscuits she relived their last encounter. They'd ended up in bed before he went back to the city to prepare for his court case. Afterwards, while he slept, she'd sat cross-legged on the rumpled bed, gazing at her sleeping lover and resisting an urge to tuck the blankets over him. She knew he wasn't a man to welcome mothering. Sexy, sensuous, but hardly devoted. Well, that suited her. Tenderly she'd stroked a scar on his shoulder. Old burn tissue, still livid. Healings were never complete.

He'd woken and pulled her close.

She curled up, liking his smell. 'This is nice. You're usually gone by morning.'

'*Gone by morning.* Sounds like a blues song. Ronnie Gale, do you want to sing a verse or two with me?'

She laughed and moved into his embrace. An hour passed before he went off to shower and dress. She lay in bed, drained and moist. Some barrier had toppled; he'd let go as though he trusted her. But love? It wasn't mentioned.

Since then the letter had arrived. She was on the brink of journeys and yet it wasn't physical distance that made her so uneasy. Her sister wasn't about to help with her conflict. Had she expected that Ronnie would settle down in Trundle with her forever? Yet it was Marie who'd pulled her out of her depression and sent her away to Pelican, the place she'd always seemed to love.

'Did you vote for the disbanding?' she asked, carrying in the mugs. For while the Indian's elaborate scheme was apparently abandoned, other buyers had expressed interest in the land. Offers were coming in at a time when almost everyone at Pelican was on the brink of major readjustment.

'No point in resisting change.' Her sister sounded listless. 'Richard and Honor were the main shareholders, and they both voted to sell.'

'Will you get anything out of it?'

'A little money. I only bought a small parcel; a gesture of support really.'

'Still, that was back in the '70s. You might be surprised. Perhaps you'll have a nest-egg.'

'I wish!'

The mood lightened as they planned a walk along the beach later in the afternoon. Meanwhile, light-hearted gossip and speculation about the other commune members and their quirks proved much easier than delving into the complexities of their own relationships.

Galleons of cumulus sailed the clear sky as Vijay jogged along the sand. Running relieved the frustration he felt whenever he thought about his father. They had nothing in common. True, grieving had softened his heart. He'd been delighted at the prospect of a grandchild and wanted the young couple to return to the family home, but Vijay hesitated. He'd won a little independence at Pelican. His mother had given up on life. He didn't want to imitate her, creeping home as though he was a casualty.

He saw the sisters strolling arm and arm, and Victor, striding down the dunes. It appeared he was in a hurry; breaking into a trot as the figure of Rosa pursued him to the water's edge. The sand anchor delayed him long enough for her to catch him up and climb into the boat as he pushed off from the tide line. The momentary scene conveyed a peculiar tension that stopped Vijay in his tracks. He stood with Marie and Ronnie; the little group's attention focused on the boat as Victor started rowing furiously hard, as though driven by anger or a longing to escape.

'What's going on?' said Marie.

'There's been trouble between them.'

The boat had drifted parallel to the shore. They could see the two silhouettes merge and separate; a shout reached them.

'Vijay! I think Victor's hurt.'

The women seemed helpless. Vijay remembered his fear of water. He could swim quite well now, though had never gone much distance. 'Get help,' was all he said, pulling off his shoes and outerwear before he plunged into the water. He hoped his months of training had prepared him. He only had his body to depend on. Under his rule it worked, obedient as a broken horse. He settled into the even rhythm of his stroke.

The sun's shaft was lower on the darkening water. The turbulent life of fishes and water creatures flowed beneath him. He rested, turning to float, and heard seabirds screech as though they shared his struggle. The little boat seemed far away. It bobbed there, a restless point between the headlands funnelling the bay's waters out to sea. He swam and rested; swam and rested. A runner found his rhythm beyond perceived limits. There was nowhere else to go but on.

He wanted to give up. Childhood surfaced and mocking jeers replayed in his memory. Hands grasped his legs and dragged him down.

Just six years old, he'd understood the fear of death that day. He thought of Sandy and their growing child. How fragile that little creature's existence! Yet it persevered, cells dividing, minute heart pumping like his own. He had to survive.

At last he was at his goal. The doctor, bloodstained and evidently disabled, used his one good arm to tug him aboard. Vijay, gasping and shivering, stared at Rosa who lay huddled in the bottom of the boat.

'Are you all right?'

'It's a stab wound to the shoulder. I can't manage to row. Can you?'

'Not much.' But Vijay took over the rower's seat and tested the oars. He felt that, if required, he could part the seas and they could walk on dry land to the shore.

Help waited on the beach. Victor stepped ashore first. He seemed to feel no resentment to his assailant, who remained unconscious.

'A brain haemorrhage, I'd say,' was his diagnosis. He hardly seemed to register Ronnie's attentions as she staunched his wound with a folded handkerchief.

'Be careful moving her,' was all he said as they prepared to make their slow way back to Pelican. Even then, refusing to rest, he travelled in to the hospital with the sick woman.

'Will you report this to the police?' Ronnie marvelled that he could sit in the back seat of her car, supporting with such care a woman who had attacked him.

'Poor soul. Secondaries in the brain. She's not responsible.' He sounded quite detached in his role of doctor.

4

Ripples spread from Nora's death, bringing officers of the law to rap on Ernie Hood's door. The sight of police cars in Railway Street shifted his mood to high alert as he undid the deadlock. He was asked if anything unusual had taken place on the day Nora died, and he described the drunken argument. By the time the detectives nodded and said they might need him for further questioning, Ernie had made up his mind to pack and climb aboard the next train. Where he was headed he didn't care, as long as it was well away from questions concerning violations of the law.

Mac Booth had asked his cadet to work late with him, researching back-up material for his sober editorial. Vim sat at her desk, examining a newspaper clipping. Sharp as proof shots snapped by memory were her images of that particular day when she and Nick Questro had walked down Railway Street. His article on small-town poverty left them linked in mysterious alliance with the dead woman. She put the cutting to one side. Mac might want a blow-up of that photograph of Nora, cocky and defiant as she stood with Tag beside a toppled gate. Vim's mind was back on her work, and she was determined to become a first class reporter. Her boss hadn't had to press home the importance of the assignment. She would stay as long as it took to get the work done.

Mac yawned and stretched, then walked over to her desk. His clothes hung loosely as he persevered with the new regime of daily walks and low-fat cooking but tonight he was tempted by the prospect of McDonald's; one didn't report on a murder every day of the week.

'Feel like take-away, Vim? We'll be here till all hours tonight.'

She nodded.

That week *The Trundle Times* sold out. In main centres Nora was allocated her day of fame before her story gave way to news of freak hailstorms and government policy reversals. The Party leader appeared on the *Today* show and spoke warmly to rural people, the backbone of our nation. He now deplored centralisation and promised country trains would run as long as he was at the ship's helm.

This news provided Mac with further editorial grist and a dilemma over the *Save Our Rail* Fund. The newspaper had a large sum of donations to hand, while the regatta proceeds were also earmarked for the fund. Mac called a meeting with the bank manager, lawyer and council members. It was felt that an alternative community project should be voted on. It was after this gathering that Bart Bexley went to Mr Lal's house to seek his collaboration in a new vision as bright as Mr Lal's own Taj Mahal. Bart regretted he had not been able to facilitate that dream. Now it was his turn to propose an alternative. The council was in favour of a children's fantasy park, paid for by public money. Its theme would reflect Indian life and culture; Mr Lal would be appointed as co-ordinator.

Bart reminded his host of the success of similar attractions. 'We build monuments everywhere. Aussies love them!'

Mr Lal considered the outsized merinos and oysters edging the highways of his adopted land. 'I see no connection.' He sounded offended.

'We've got the Big Banana, the Big Pineapple. What's wrong with the Big Elephant?'

He ignored the Indian's look of distaste. 'Think of the money it would bring in to Trundle. Drivers couldn't miss it.' He waved his plump hands as though conducting a symphony. 'Inside the elephant, your treasure house. The bazaar, the eating stands, the stalls...not to mention a video narrative, account of history of the Taj, admission fee. What a winner!'

'Really, I have abandoned my plan.' Mr Lal spoke with regret and Bart's pink face exuded beads of moisture.

'At least hear me out. I can see a wonderful playground for the kiddies. Life size replicas of those exotic animals we mustn't keep in zoos now. Leopards, tigers, surely you have them in India?' His host nodded, yet was not persuaded. 'So it's not exactly what you wanted. But unless you can fund your own plan independently...'

'I think not. My proposed partner has withdrawn.'

'Rotary will back this. We can try a submission to State government. The town's in the doldrums. We need jobs and tourists. The whole community will get behind this. Anything for children's a goer.' His spaniel-like eyes pleaded on behalf of all the little ones. 'A fifteen-metre elephant; what a traffic stopper!'

'It is too big an adjustment to my original concept.'

Bart leaned forward, cupping his hands as though offering his heart to the implacable Indian. 'There'd still be a Taj. A miniature one. For the children. Why, you will be a grandfather yourself, one day.'

Bart was unaware that Mr Lal already knew Vijay and Sandy were expecting. The Indian sat deep in thought. A small boy walked with him to visit his grandfather's world inside the famous elephant of Trundle. Bright eyes stared at the brass and sandalwood artefacts; little fingers stroked the textures of silk and carpets. Ganesh smiled and Kali glared as the child examined the illuminated replica of the Taj and Dadaji told the story of Shah Jahan and Mumtaz Mahal, and the monument to love and immortality.

'Miniatures can be an art form,' he conceded.

'Then you see my point?'

'I am thinking of the elephant.'

'The logistics of building the beast?'

'Not that. I am acquainted with an inventor and a clever architect. It can be done. My concern is with aesthetics. To build anything is to impose on nature. This could seem vulgar.'

Bart laughed. 'As a people, we're not refined. We have an iffy background on the whole. We like big things. Look at the landscape we grow up in. This park will be a goer, my friend.' Happy as one of his own successful loan applicants, the bank manager sat back.

Mr Lal reconsidered his hypothetical outing with Vijay's son. If the little boy grew bored, there would be refreshments at the food stall and a playground of tigers and rhinos. Why not wild boar, deer? Perhaps a chain of baby elephants, their trunks entwined? Inspiration could benefit from revision. He had already gained advantage. The town's leaders now saw him as an important man; and apparently they were prepared to pay the bills.

Later, hearing Bimbo's barking, he went to investigate activity next door and found Marie, weeding her herb garden. She smiled from under her tattered straw hat and struggled upright, brushing a trail of earth across her forehead.

'Leaving Pelican?' He missed seeing lights at his neighbour's windows. 'Vijay and Sandy are returning home. I will be happy about that too.'

It seemed both their solitary lives were about to change. Rowena and Pippin were planning to board with the sisters when they left the commune.

'So it is really closing?'

'Everybody's going. The land's up for sale. The founding members think Pelican has served its purpose. Laurie's dying, you know.'

'What will happen to Honor?' He felt concerned. Old age was the time when people turned to family, but she had nobody.

'She's going to live with her sister in England. Victor will take her home.'

'And Mr Van Rjein and his wife?' Mr Lal thought of the day he'd tried to appease the enraged Dutchman. He had thought his effort wasted but Marie laughed.

'Whatever you said to him, he's taken it to heart. He's accepted Tuti's pregnancy. They're going back to visit her family in Indonesia. What did you say to him, by the way?'

'No wisdom, I assure you. I am a practical man. Which brings me to a favour I wish to ask of you. My wife's anniversary has passed. It is time she went to rest.'

'Are you going back to India?'

'On reflection, it would be folly. To carry her like luggage is not right. I will devise a private ceremony here. Will you attend?'

'I'd be honoured. I'm sure your wife understands your feelings.'

Discussing Shanti with a woman friend made him uneasy. He changed the subject. 'And how is business?'

'Booming!'

Her answer surprised him; he did not think of her as businesslike. But thanks to a deal she said she'd made to supply a Sydney antique buyer, she was out of debt. 'And I owe that stroke of luck to you, Mr Lal. It came up when I was enquiring about a buyer for your miniature. But I've done no good with that. Perhaps if you approach the Art Gallery?'

'No hurry! It was no more than a possibility.' He told her about Bart Bexley's visit. 'Mysterious, how one idea transmutes into another.' His desire to help Marie financially had resolved in a different solution, and in a manner entirely appropriate to her own personality. For she seemed to enjoy her crises. Now she was back from the brink of foreclosure, mischievous concerning risks that would have turned his silver hair to white.

Honor had been called to the hospital at midday. Now it was evening and she was weary, with an impulse to rest her head down on the pillow beside Laurie. Her thoughts circled about their life together as she watched and waited for its close.

A home in this world…I never really found one. Laurie, do you remember me saying that to you? I never did conform. There were the other gals in that proper London scene, fiddling with watercolours while I hulked casts that turned my nails ragged and my hands to sandpaper. The cold cream I used, longing for femininity! But I always did turn my back on every avenue a woman of my time and background was steered towards. Angels and daemons hid in the weave, and I tried everything to tempt them out; chipped away at the stone, turned my back on love, became entangled with sages and charlatans, faced the brink of war, read, studied, trailed half way round the world to end up here, with you, at Pelican. After all my sojourns— Africa, Europe, India—and my mentors—Gurdjieff, Bennett, Swami—I really thought I'd come home at last. It has been our home. We've been happy, haven't we, in our retreat where spirit and body both found balance? So many came who had suffered and needed comfort. Not many of us escape, do you think, when you add up all the hurts we're subject to? We heard so many stories! I listened and advised. You wheeled in the tea trolley. Always a team, a pair.

And now that's over. Oh Laurie, can you hear me? You seem so far away. No longer with me here. Not yet there. They have warned me you could slip away at any time. Where are you going? Did either one of us ever settle that question? Though

I was the philosopher and you made the jam, are we any the wiser? I hope you know how much I love you and how happy you have made me. I think you do. What will I do, Laurie, when you've gone? What will I do? I know. You'd simply smile and pat my hand if you could.

I'm sorry you have to be here. A hospital is such a size! I fancy we like small spaces for our private moments. I'm grateful God gave us the night to whisper our words of love or cry when we feel lonely. Wherever you are going, Laurie, I'm beside you in my thoughts and you are in my heart. At least that will remain. How strange, how hard! Life isn't a gentle passage, is it? Is dying difficult? You make it look peaceful but that could be an act. You never did make a fuss. I'm the old woman sitting by your bedside, worrying away. Stop that, Honor! You could always read my mind. That strange link between us. We felt it from the beginning. It's there even now, as your breath labours in and out and alien processes break down your body.

Goodbye, my dearest Laurie. Forgive my tears. I know we must be brave about this but it breaks my heart to part.

5

Once again Mr Lal's lists grew long as he noted necessary tasks. As co-ordinator of Trundle's Big Elephant Theme Park, he could delegate certain areas to the bank manager, the editor, Council and the Rotary Club. However, he retained control and had decided Peter, the young inventor he'd met at the Playfair's party, would be an ideal consultant for the unusual project.

No longer a stranger among his neighbours, he strolled along Alexandra Avenue, noting the advent of Christmas. A holly wreath decorated the Playfair's front door; from the porch, Kitty waved. Next door, where a delivery van was disgorging crates of liquor, coloured lights starred the pine tree in the Bexley's yard.

Tinsel, sleighs and festive bells decorated shop fronts in town. In his childhood, Christmas had been a festival of little account. Its symbols did not stir wistful memories in Mr Lal, who hadn't encouraged his own family to expect spending sprees. As a concession to his children's pleading, he'd allocated extra money for a few presents and a good meal. Now he wished he had allowed Vim and Vijay to adopt the customs their school friends took for granted. Preserving one's own past was worthwhile but so was allowing an entrance for new ways. Each culture's symbols stood for common dreams. These kindly Santas who beamed on the young reminded him now of Ganesh who blessed hope and enterprise.

Past months had often set him thinking along regretful lines as he judged the man he'd been. It was too late to reconstruct his past. The children were grown; his wife was dead. He could not help his nature and conditioning but he did not feel comforted. Apologising for his defects was no use. Who cared if he now admitted he'd been harsh and unaware at times? His only audience was his own unsympathetic conscience.

He stopped to stare into the toyshop window, imagining the excitement of a little boy or girl. He'd never had such wonders. Perhaps that was why he couldn't conceive of parents spending with no apparent caution. Generosity and playfulness weren't natural impulses for him, whereas Vijay, like a child, lived in the present. When he had children, whatever security they might lack, they would enjoy the benefits of fun and horseplay. Their Christmases would be cornucopias. Mr Lal stared at computerised robots, space ships, precocious dolls equipped with fashion wardrobes. His grandchildren would teach him how to give. The prospect pleased him, for Sandy and Vijay had come home and his son was actively looking for work. Mr Lal had an idea that somewhere in the running of the theme park there might be a place for Vijay.

A rotund Santa inside the toyshop waved to him. The Indian raised his hand in return before walking on to Railway Street. There, life had resumed its everyday pattern. Big black bins along the kerbsides formed a guard of honour for the council rubbish truck. Clatters echoed from the dump, where the crushers were at work. Ernie's cottage was up for lease and the Halpin's place bore a *For Sale* sign.

Mrs O'Brian saw an Indian turn in at her gate and yelled for Peter to answer the front door. Let him deal with darkies. The goings-on in the street hadn't surprised her; those Halpins weren't the first troubled folk she'd lived beside. An unlucky house, that one. Amazing, the stories she'd collected up in her long life. She didn't need to travel around the world or read books and newspapers. Back-street abortion, fights, tarts, drinkers, she'd seen the lot, right on her own back doorstep. She yawned and hoisted up her pants. The elastic was saggy. She felt like taking out her teeth and having a darn good scratch. It looked like the visitor had some business with Peter. The two of them were out in the yard; Peter showing off his inventions like prize marrows and the visitor nodding all impressed. She'd better make a cup of tea for everyone. Hundreds, thousands of cups she'd brewed, marking the once-significant moments of engagements, weddings, births, and deaths. Now even the dramas of life seemed like shows to while away the time.

While she poured the tea and put out biscuits, she tried to follow the men's discussion. The darkie was friendly, but he must be away with the pixies, going on about tigers, cheetahs and Brahman cows built from

265

ferro-cement and chicken wire. Now they were on about a big elephant. What would Trundle folks want with an elephant? The world was going mad and Peter going along with all the jabber as though he had nothing better to do with his time. That boy would never get a proper job. Never mind. At least his heart was in the right place, not like Bryan's. He'd sell off his own mother pound by pound if the price was right.

The men shook hands and the Indian went off.

'What was all that about?' she said. Peter looked pleased enough.

'I've got a job, Mum. We're getting a theme park in town and I'm going to build the animals.'

'Good boy.' She reached over and picked a crumb from his beard. 'Will you get wages?'

'Of course I will.' He mentioned a sum of money that set her back on her heels. 'I've got something else to tell you, Mum.'

'Oh yes?'

'I'm going to marry Holly. We got engaged yesterday.'

'That's nice, son.'

'I'll be moving out. But we don't want you to be lonely. You can come and live with us.'

'We'll see.' She didn't want to hurt his feelings. Her love for her children had dimmed to a wry acceptance of their chalk and cheese contrasts. They were both queer fish. But what did it matter? Life squashed up and made room for everyone. She wouldn't budge from Railway Street. This was her home. As long as she could prise open her eyes to see one more day, as long as she could hear another train whiz past the fence, that was all she cared about.

Resuming nursing duties, Ronnie felt adrift. She made desultory trips to the supermarket and shrugged when Marie proposed they hire a permanent lawn man. Her free time was spent reading travel books, waiting for the postman and writing to Nick Questro. His own plans to go to Europe sounded definite. While she envied him, his invitation to join him as a travelling partner felt unreal. She hardly knew him, yet their interludes together had opened her heart to emotions she had set aside for ever.

Now they were a household of four people and the house had taken on a communal feel. Living with a small child eliminated any chance of order or routine. Marie was happy to sacrifice her herb bed for a sandpit. Spills and stains began to give the renovations that lived-in look, and any day a kitten or a puppy would arrive to join the frolic. Rowena was an interesting girl, but moody. Pippin's creative imagination and quaint sayings could be amusing, but Ronnie had never pretended to be the maternal kind.

Marie came in from the garden with roses. She arranged them in a glass bowl and set them beside her sister. '*Celeste.* First of the season. For you.'

Ronnie stared at the delicate petals as though they were lures. Her sister wasn't helping her decision. Marie shied away from news of Nick and suddenly had a lot to say about the advantages of superannuation and stable employment.

Now she eyed Ronnie's library book. '*Guide to Europe on a Shoestring?* A trip like that would cost a fortune.'

'I'm not insolvent! Half this house belongs to me. I could easily get a loan.'

'But think of all the interest.'

Ronnie recognised the issue filling Marie with practical concerns had little to do with money or the threat of unemployment. Better to change the subject. 'You know, I owe you a big thanks for introducing me to Pelican? I was always cynical about the place. In a funny way, it's changed my life. Does it have to disband?'

'That was the final decision. Sam Playfair's handling the sale. Tuti and Richard have gone to Indonesia and Honor's finalised her plans.'

'Which are?'

'She's going home to England.'

'Starting over at her age?' Honor's dream of sanctuary was gone. She was elderly, alone. Ronnie breathed in the perfume of the drooping blooms. While she vacillated over Nick, Honor could embark on a voyage half way around the world.

'It's a big step, but I've known Honor for a long time. She'll never be old, whatever fate befalls her body. Her spirit's too buoyant.'

'Sad about Laurie. They were proper lovebirds. How will she manage the trip?'

'Victor's escorting her. I'm driving them down to the airport next week.'

'Victor!' Ronnie remembered the embarrassment of recent weeks as she'd helped dismantle the clinic after Rosa's cheques had bounced, drawing formal demands for dishonour charges and return of equipment. 'He couldn't pay his rent, much less an air fare.'

'Honor put it to him that she needed a travelling companion. She has money. And I think she felt responsible for persuading him to come. He finally tracked down his wife, you know.'

'Will she have him back?'

Marie laughed. 'Do you think he'd discuss such personal issues with me?'

'I'll grant him this; he's a dedicated doctor. Spends hours with Rosa at the hospital. Even reads to her. She won't last long, poor soul.'

Ronnie's small revelation restored Marie's initial liking for Victor. It was good to set aside fantasy and resentment. Victor could be a friend sitting at a bedside, forgiving Rosa when medical science could not cure her.

They were washing dishes a few days later when Ronnie took a long-distance phone call. She moved off to talk on the extension. The conversation didn't take long. She came back to the kitchen and sank onto a chair, causing Marie to guess the nature of the call.

'Was that Nick?'

'When you go to Sydney, can I come?'

'I guess. We'll have to go in your car. What's the hurry?'

'Nick wants to book his flights. He needs my answer.'

' What are you going to do?'

'I don't know.'

They were kind and polite to each other over the remaining days.

Cheerfully urbane in his well-cut suit, Victor stowed the bags in the car boot and ushered Honor from the motel where they had stayed overnight. She walked with the cautious tread of an older person, but otherwise might have been a teenager heading to her first overseas holiday. She took the front passenger seat, and the car filled with the sharp scent of Tweed. Victor bent double, easing his tall frame to occupy the back seat next to Ronnie.

'You're absolutely sure you have the tickets, Victor?'

Honor's travels had preceded the Internet age. The doctor reassured her. His fruitless medical pilgrimage to Pelican had presented him with personal lessons, and he was happy to go back to England and his family, equipped with changed understandings.

Honor's rambling anecdotes occupied the first leg of the journey as she gave an account of the Van Rjien's farewell party, where Richard had undergone a change of heart and announced Tuti's pregnancy as though it was his purely personal achievement. Road noise blurred half her words and Ronnie's attention soon drifted. She felt she was on an isolated road, journeying to an unknown destination. Was it the thrill an explorer knew as he approached a final obstacle, or the fatalistic acceptance of a captured wild creature? There were elements of both as she stared at familiar place names unreeling like film of a former life. The back of Marie's head blocked her view of the road ahead. Her sister had said very little since Nick's last phone call. Her silence had felt poignant, suggesting she would not stand in Ronnie's way, yet making it plain how much she would be missed. To go, to stay… Small towns like Trundle might offer wide enough horizons for many people; perhaps even Ronnie. It was Nick, the man she hardly knew, who possessed a power to call her further.

Victor's words disturbed her reverie.

'I haven't thanked you for your help at the clinic.'

'Don't be silly!'

That interlude already seemed trivial and of the past.

'You shouldn't turn down honest appreciation.' It was so unlike him to make a personal remark that Ronnie became aware of a habit that was meant to deflect praise but which, she saw, could imply rejection. Easy to sound brusque, offhand. She knew Nick would not wait for her indefinitely.

Two hours along the freeway, Marie, announcing 'Pit stop!' pulled off into a Caltex station where they had refreshments and filled up with petrol. Ronnie would take over the driving as far as the city, before leaving the others to make their way out to the airport. Marie had paid for everyone's food—a typical Marie kind of thing to do. Her sister seemed very loveable. Ronnie called her aside, then stood silent, unable to find easy words to explain her choice.

'You're going with him?'

'I think I have to.'

'I know. Be happy, darling.'

I'm standing under this wide blue Australian sky, beside a petrol bowser, telling the one person I know I love that I'm leaving.

'Marie, am I mad?'

'No. It was the same with Hugh. The heart knows.'

'I'll have a lot to organise.'

'Never mind. I'll help you pack.'

The words were said. Stepping close, they shared a sisterly embrace.

*

Shanti had died a year ago. In the wake of that shock came sorrow; towering waves of sorrow, swamping him in desolation. Later, he tried to take control. Finding her in every small reminder of their lives together, he formulated a plan, his Taj, for her. Now he understood that all he'd done was for himself. Action was what people turned to, when mourning replaced pure grief. His Taj had helped him through. He'd found friends and earned a place in his community. Somehow (had Shanti guided them?) his daughter had matured and his son had become a man. Now it was at an end.

Mr Lal decided the time for the ceremony should be at sunset, and the place at Pelican. The river's flow was too sluggish. Shanti's remains deserved an ocean, there to enter the boundless depths. Now the time had come, he felt apprehensive. His power to throw his wife's ashes into the current and free himself from his past disturbed him. He told his family to allow him privacy and withdrew to his bedroom. There he took down the ashes. With tears in his eyes, he sat holding the package. Was he not like a faithless husband deserting a good woman? Yet it was Shanti who had committed the ultimate rejection when she died, taking from him not only herself but also every role he'd lived by. He'd been left to recreate himself alone. Now, if she could return, she would expect him to fit some old definition, in the way parents saw a grown man as still their child. She would view him as a man of ambition, with much to prove to strangers in a new land. She would think he cared for money, for intelligence, for thoughtful analysis of life's purpose.

He still did. A man was given his nature at birth. Its fullness, however, was only known at the end of life's experiences. Now he didn't need to work and worry, striving to make good. It was time to try other things. As he said his last goodbye he felt a deeply loving impulse. They had lived together a long time, building a family and a marriage, but she had travelled beyond his understanding. Their link was cut. He wept and felt free.

The trek to his chosen site would be too much for his in-laws. They joined in a private farewell at the house before Mr Lal and his children met up with Marie for the drive out to Pelican. It seemed the right place to pay final respects. Through the community and its dealings with himself and with his family, friendships had been forged as members became open to their fears and endured pain and parting. Now the group was disbanding. He'd said his goodbyes, thinking he too must allow the past to take its rightful place. He sat quietly, his gaze fixed on Shanti's package on his lap, as Marie's ancient car rocked along the track.

At Pelican, they walked across the marsh and stepped out onto the deserted strip of sand.

'There should be a sunset.' Marie studied the sky, wanting to present him with a memorable setting. He just smiled.

'What can we control in life? Never mind. We will borrow the boat.'

The four stepped aboard and managed to row out a little way, where Mr Lal began to strip the wrapping from his parcel. Marie wondered what form the ceremony might take: prayer, a eulogy, a recitation from Hindu scriptures. They'd never defined their personal religious attitudes. She did not know the exact title of his god, or her own, although they seemed to promote a cheerful faith in life.

Silently he prised open the package and tapped its gritty contents into the water. When no trace was left, he tossed the container overboard to bob away towards the open sea.

'Is that all?' said Vim.

'That is that.' He signalled Vijay to row them to the beach.

Beneath a grey sky, they walked back to the community. Vim and Vijay went ahead to farewell the last stragglers. Marie glanced at her companion. His face showed calm acceptance and he began to ask about Ronnie, as though Shanti was no longer his main focus.

'I thought my sister and I would simply settle down and go on as before,' she told him. She sounded forlorn, and he stopped walking.

'You have your doubts? Concerning this man, or the travel?'

'Oh, nothing like that. Life's unpredictable.'

'You fear loneliness?'

'Not exactly. I'll have my stepdaughter and little Pippin. It's just...' There was a break in her voice. 'She's my sister! I love her. When I was adrift she brought me home. I simply can't imagine life without her.'

He nodded. 'How well I understand! We need others. Have I thanked you for your help to me? One thing at least I hope; our friendship will endure?'

Marie smiled as she linked her arm through his. 'Of course it will.'

He looked satisfied. 'In that case, let us follow the children.'

With tact he slowed his pace as they began the climb up to the dimming outline of Pelican.

THE TRUNDLE TIMES

Editorial, December 10th 2002

THOREAU LEAVES TRUNDLE?

The Pelican community has announced its intention to disband. Trundle residents first heard of the group in the early '80s, when a group of alternative lifestylers acquired land on the outskirts of town. Those of us conditioned by memories of *Woodstock, Hair,* and the self-indulgent '70s wondered what to expect. The aims of the group, however, purported to be environmental rather than psychedelic. They said they desired a peaceful and co-operative lifestyle close to nature, and welcomed anyone seeking a similar way of life.

A casual visit to the centre recently confirms that much thought, energy and creative vision has gone into the development of Pelican. Gardens have replaced the wilderness. A healing clinic has operated in recent times. Visitors in need of rest, and the sick who seek recovery, have attended the peaceful retreat.

Yet residents now say the time has come to close the doors and move on. Mr Richard Van Rjien, a founding member, confirmed commercial growers are interested in establishing an olive tree plantation on the site. He and his wife have returned to Indonesia.

Another long-term member preparing to depart this week is Mrs Honor Stedman, whose husband passed away recently. 'I have been a traveller all my life,' she said. 'So Pelican always seemed like home to me and I never expected I'd be packing my bags again.' Mrs Stedman plans to return to Sussex where she will stay with her sister.

Mrs Marie Mortimer, a well-known resident of Trundle, has also had connections with the group since its inception. Mrs Mortimer, who owns and operates *Victorian Gilt,* the antique and old wares shop on Main Road, remembers Pelican in its early days. 'It was a very special place,' she recalls, 'a place of beauty and of peace, where you could get away from the hustle and bustle of daily life. I met some wonderful people there. In fact, that's where I first met my husband, twenty years ago.'

With all these references to peace and beauty, why then would the group be disbanding? Why leave this idyllic-sounding life? Mrs Mortimer smiled as she folded a lace tablecloth at her counter. 'Thoreau went off and lived by himself in the woods for years. People asked him the same question when he left. His answer—'For the same reason I went there. I had other lives to lead."

Mac Booth